"*Segu* is an overwhelming accomplishment. It injects into the density of history characters who are as alive as you and I. Passionate, lusty, greedy, they are in conflict with themselves as well as with God and Mammon. Maryse Condé has done us all a tremendous service by rendering history so compelling and exciting. *Segu* is a literary masterpiece I could not put down."
                    Louise Meriwether

"A stunning reaffirmation of Africa and its peoples as set down by others whose works have gone unnoticed. Ms. Condé not only backs them up, but provides new insights as well . . . *Segu* has its own dynamic. It's a starburst."
                    John A. Williams

"A novel of wide scope, depth and power. Condé proves herself a careful observer of human behavior as she helps the reader to understand and feel the turmoil of a confused continent. She captures a fascinating time in history with its earth spirituality, religious fervor and the violent nature of a people and their growing nation . . . Brims over with intelligence and wit."
                    Anniston (Alabama) *Star*

"*Segu*, a tale of love and intrigue, is fascinating, for the reader experiences the fervor of those tumultuous times."
                    Louise Rothe
                    Chattanooga News-Free Press

S·E·G·U

MARYSE CONDÉ

Translated from the French by Barbara Bray

BALLANTINE BOOKS
NEW YORK

Library of Congress Catalog Card Number: 87-91707

ISBN: 0-345-35306-4

This edition published by arrangement
with Viking Penguin Inc.

Cover design by James R. Harris
Cover painting by Donna Diamond
Designed by Ann Gold
Maps and Family Tree by Paul Pugliese
Manufactured in the United States of America

First Ballantine Books Edition: May 1988

10 9 8 7 6 5 4 3 2 1

For my Bambara ancestress

CONTENTS

PART FIVE
And The Gods Trembled
419

NOTES
491

Maps appear on pages x–xii.
Family tree appears on page xiii.

Acknowledgments

It would be impossible for me to name all those who have helped me with suggestions for reading or by making their records available to me.

But I should like to offer special thanks to my friends—historians and researchers in the human sciences—Amouzouvi Akakpo, Adame Ba Konare, Ibrahima Baba Kake, Lilyan Kesteloot, Elikia M'Bokolo, Madina Ly Tall, Olabiyi Yai, Robert Pageard and Oliveira dos Santos. Thanks to them this fiction does not take too many liberties with the facts.

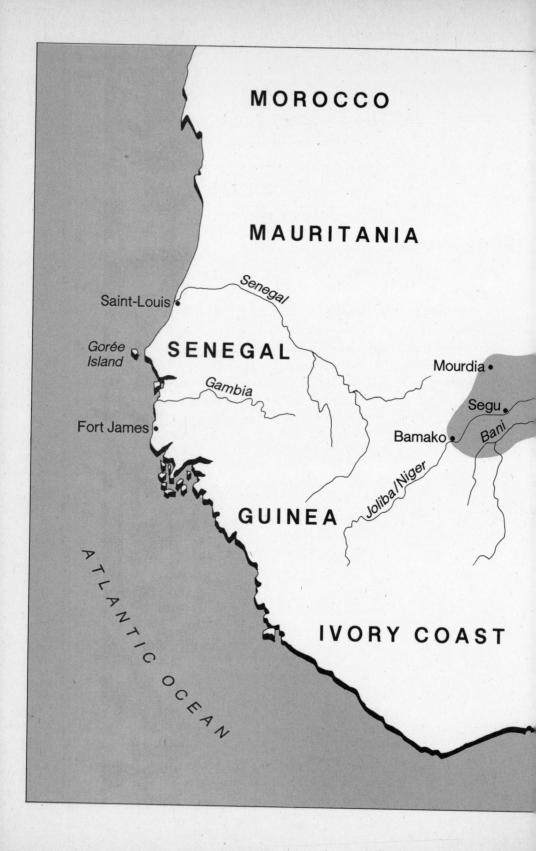

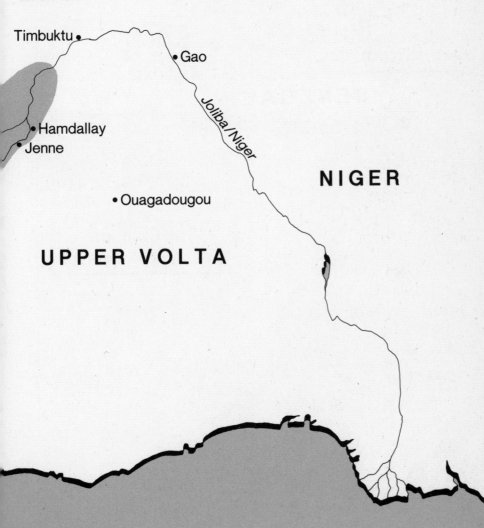

The Kingdom of Segu
(18th—19th c.)

ALGERIA

MALI

• Taoudenni

Timbuktu •

• Gao

Joliba / Niger

• Hamdallay
• Jenne

NIGER

• Ouagadougou

UPPER VOLTA

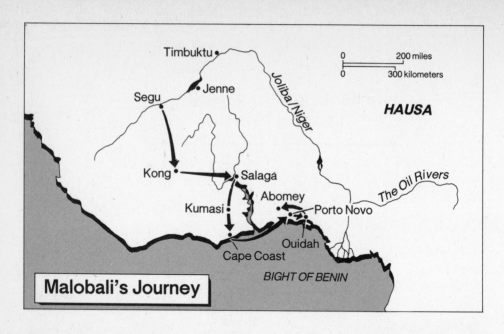

Malobali's Journey

Timbuktu

Jenne

Segu

Joliba / Niger

HAUSA

Kong

Salaga

The Oil Rivers

Kumasi

Abomey

Porto Novo

Cape Coast

Ouidah

BIGHT OF BENIN

0   200 miles

0   300 kilometers

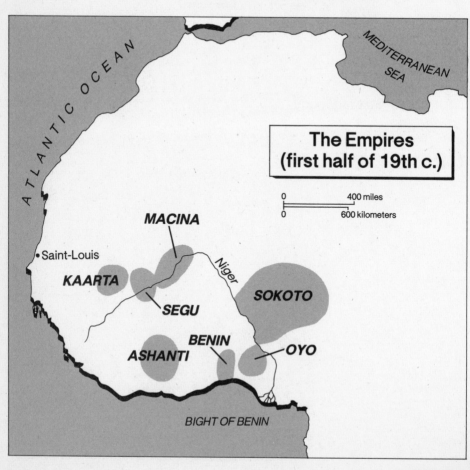

The Empires
(first half of 19th c.)

A T L A N T I C   O C E A N

MEDITERRANEAN SEA

MACINA

Saint-Louis

KAARTA

Niger

SEGU

SOKOTO

ASHANTI

BENIN

OYO

BIGHT OF BENIN

0   400 miles

0   600 kilometers

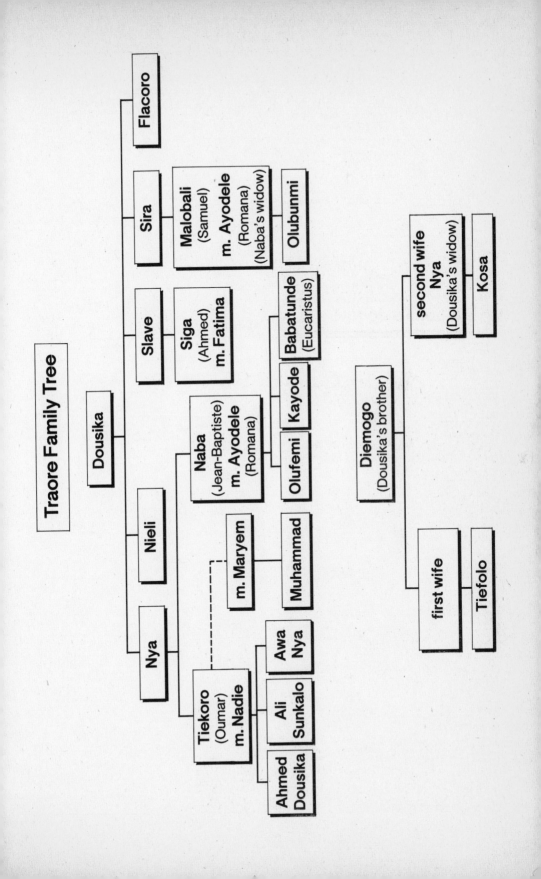

Traore Family Tree

Dousika

- **Flacoro**
- **Sira**
  - **Malobali** (Samuel) m. **Ayodele** (Romana) (Naba's widow)
  - **Olubunmi**
- **Slave**
  - **Siga** (Ahmed) m. **Fatima**
    - **Babatunde** (Eucaristus)
- **Nieli**
- **Naba** (Jean-Baptiste) m. **Ayodele** (Romana)
  - **Olufemi**
  - **Kayode**
  - m. **Maryem**
    - **Muhammad**
- **Nya**
  - **Tiekoro** (Oumar) m. **Nadie**
    - **Ahmed Dousika**
    - **Ali Sunkalo**
    - **Awa Nya**

Diemogo (Dousika's brother)

- **second wife Nya** (Dousika's widow)
  - **Kosa**
- **first wife**
  - **Tiefolo**

PART ONE

THE WORD THAT DESCENDS BY NIGHT

CHAPTER

1

Segu is a garden where cunning grows. Segu is built on treachery. Speak of Segu outside Segu, but do not speak of Segu in Segu.

Why couldn't Dousika get the song of the griots out of his head, the song he'd heard so often without paying any special attention? Why this fear, persistent as the sickness of a pregnant woman? Why this dread on the brink of day? Dousika went over his dreams for a sign, a clue to what might lie ahead. But there was nothing. He'd slept soundly and been visited by none of his ancestors. As he sat on a mat in the entrance to his hut, Dousika swallowed a mouthful of *degue*, the millet gruel mixed with curds and honey that was his favorite breakfast. It was too runny, and he shouted crossly for Nya, his first wife, to scold her about it. As he waited he inserted his tooth twig between his fine filed teeth: the sap from the wood, mixed with his saliva, would increase his physical strength and sexual potency.

As Nya didn't answer he rose, left the hut, and went into the first courtyard of the compound where his wives lived.

It was deserted. Deserted?

Only a few millet sieves and some little wooden stools lay there on the spotless sand.

Dousika was a nobleman or *yerewolo*, a member of the royal council, a personal friend of the king and the father of ten legitimate sons, ruling as *fa* or patriarch over five families, his own and those of his younger brothers. His compound reflected his standing in Segu society. Its tall facade overlooking the street was ornamented with sculptures as well as triangular patterns carved into the clay, and surmounted by turrets of varying height and pleasing effect. Within were a number of flat-roofed huts, also of mud, connected by a series of courtyards. The first contained a magnificent *dubale* tree whose foliage formed a dome of greenery, supported by some fifty columns, roots grown down from the main trunk.

The *dubale* might be called the witness and guardian of the life of the Traores. Beneath its powerful roots the placentas of many of their ancestors had been buried after a safe delivery. In its shade the women and children sat to tell stories, the men to make family decisions. In the dry season it gave protection from the sun. In the rainy season it provided firewood. At night the spirits of the ancestors hid in its branches and watched over the sleep of the living. When they were displeased they showed it by making faint sounds, at once mysterious and as clear as a code. Then those experienced enough to decipher them shook their heads and said: "Beware—tonight our fathers have spoken!"

Anyone who crossed the threshold of the Traore compound knew at once what sort of people they were, guessed that they owned plenty of good land planted with millet, cotton and fonio, worked by hundreds of slaves—house slaves and captives. There were storerooms crammed with bags full of cowrie shells and gold dust lavishly bestowed by the king, the Mansa. In a paddock behind the huts were Arab steeds, purchased from the Moors. Signs of wealth were everywhere.

And why was the outer courtyard empty now, which was usually swarming with people? With girls and boys, all naked, the first with a string of beads or cowrie shells around their waists, the second with only a cotton string. With women pounding or sieving millet, or spinning cotton as they listened to the jokes of a jester or the epics of a griot singing for a dish of gruel. With men chatting together as they sharpened arrows for hunting or whetted farming implements. Dousika, getting more and more vexed, went on into the second courtyard, overlooked by the huts of his three wives and of Sira, his concubine.

He found the latter lying prostrate on a mat, her beautiful face gleaming with sweat and distorted with suffering.

"Where is everyone?" he barked.

She made an effort to sit up, and said in her imperfect Bambara, "By the river, *koke*."

"By the river?" he almost yelled. "What are they all doing there?"

"A white man!" she managed to murmur. "There's a white man on the bank of the Joliba!"*

A white man? Was the woman delirious? Dousika looked down at her belly, which was enormous under the loosely tied *pagne*,† then up, apprehensively, at the clay walls of the hut. Alone with a woman about to give birth!

"What's the matter with you?" he asked roughly, to hide his fear.

"I think my time has come," she stammered apologetically.

For several months, out of regard for the life she bore within her, Dousika hadn't been near Sira, now pregnant for the second time. Similarly he was supposed, throughout the birth, to stay away from her, and only put in an appearance after the delivery, with the fetish priest, when she was already holding the baby in her arms. Might it not vex the ancestors if he were there while she was in labor? He was just hesitating about retreating and leaving her alone when Nya appeared, with one child on her back and two more clinging to her indigo cotton skirts.

"Where were you?" he exploded. "I can understand everyone else here losing their heads. But not you!"

Without a word of explanation, still less one of apology, Nya moved past him and bent over Sira.

"Have you had the pains for long?"

"No," whispered the other. "They started just now."

From anyone else but Nya, Dousika wouldn't have put up with such offhandedness, verging on impertinence. But she was his first wife, his *bara muso*, to whom he had delegated part of his authority and who could therefore address him as an equal.

---

* Bambara name for the Niger.
† Length of cotton cloth draped over the shoulder or head and wound around the body to form a sort of toga.—TRANS.

Moreover she'd been born a Kulibaly, related to the ancient ruling family of Segu, and noble though he himself was, Dousika couldn't boast of such distinguished origins. It was Nya's ancestors who had founded this city on the banks of the Joliba, which soon became the heart of a vast empire. It was the brothers of her ancestors who ruled over Kaarta. So the love Dousika bore her contained a large element of respect, almost fear. He withdrew, and in the outer courtyard ran into a messenger from the palace. The man threw himself down in the dust as a sign of respect, and from there saluted him.

"You and the light!"

Then came the motto of the Traores: "Traore, Traore, Traore—the long-named man need not pay to cross the river."

Finally he delivered his message. "Traore, the Mansa wants you to come to the palace as quickly as possible!"

Dousika was surprised.

"The palace? But it's not the day for the council!"

The man looked up.

"It's not for the council. There's a white man by the river, asking to see the Mansa . . ."

"A white man?"

So Sira wasn't delirious! And Dousika had already heard of this white man. Some horsemen coming from Kaarta had said they'd met him riding a horse as exhausted as himself. But Dousika had thought it must be one of the stories women amuse children with in the evening, and had taken no notice. Now, putting on his conical hat, for the sun was beginning to rise in the sky, Dousika left his compound.

In 1797, Segu, the city with 1444 sacred balanza trees, each an earthly avatar of Pemba, god of creation—Segu, capital of the Bambara kingdom of the same name, was a vast place made up of four residential quarters built along the banks of the Joliba, which at this point was a good three hundred yards wide. The quarter known as Segu Korro contained the tomb of Biton Kulibaly, the founding father, while Segu See Korro could boast the palace of Mansa Monzon Diarra. A livelier place was not to be found within a radius of several days' march. The main market was held in a big square surrounded with mud-roofed sheds divided by partitions of wood or woven matting. Here, women sold everything that could be sold: millet, onions, rice, sweet potatoes, smoked fish, fresh fish, peppers, shea butter and chickens, while craftsmen hung the products of their trade on strings: strips of woven cotton, sandals, saddles and finely decorated gourds. To the left was the slave market, where prisoners of war were crammed together, attached to one another by means of branches torn from saplings. Dousika disregarded this all-too-familiar sight. At the risk of lowering his dignity he hurried along, waving away the griots always lurking in the streets ready to sing the praises of well-born men.

Segu was at the height of its glory. Its power stretched as far as the outskirts of Jenne, the great trading center on the banks of the Bani, and it was feared as far away as Timbuktu on the edge of the desert. The Fulani of Macina were Segu's vassals and paid a heavy yearly tribute of cattle and gold. Admittedly, things had not always been like this. A hundred or a hundred and fifty years earlier, Segu was not numbered among the cities of the Sudan.* It was only a village where Ngolo Kulibaly took refuge, while his brother Barangolo settled further north. Then Biton, his son, made friends with the god Faro, master of water and knowledge, and with his protection transformed a collection of daub huts into a proud city at whose name the Somono, Bozo, Dogon, Tuareg, Fulani and Sarakole people all trembled. Segu made war on them all, thus acquiring slaves who were either sold in its markets or made to work in its fields. War was the essence of Segu's power and glory.

If Dousika was hurrying it was because the Mansa's summons reassured him, made him think he hadn't fallen from favor as he'd feared. There were plenty of people at court who were envious of his closeness to Monzon Diarra and of the special relationship of jesting, friendship and mutual aid that existed between them. These people had taken advantage of Dousika's attitude to war to whisper in Monzon's ear, "Dousika Traore is the only one who opposes your glory. He says the Bambara have

* Sudan here refers to the various states (including Ghana, Kanem, Songhay and Hausa) which together made up a civilization that flourished in west and central Africa from the fourth century onward, to be distinguished altogether from the Nilotic region south of Egypt, the modern Republic of the Sudan.— TRANS.

had enough of fighting. And it's because, deep down, he's jealous of you and your success. Don't forget that his wife is a Kulibaly!"

And gradually Dousika had seen mistrust dawn in Monzon's eyes. Every time they looked at him they seemed to be asking, "Is he my friend or my enemy?"

Dousika entered the palace courtyard. The palace was a magnificent building, the work of masons from Jenne, surrounded by a mud-brick wall as thick as the walls of a town. The wall had just one gate, watched over by a permanent guard armed with guns brought from the coast by the slave traders. Dousika passed through seven antechambers full of *tondyons** to the council chamber, outside of which fetish priests were predicting the future by means of kola nuts and cowrie shells, while courtiers had to wait to be allowed into the Mansa's presence.

Monzon Diarra lay on an oxhide spread upon a dais, his left elbow propped on a goatskin pillow decorated with arabesques. He looked worried. With one hand he was stroking one of the two long braids that started on the top of his head and crossed under his chin. With the other he was toying with the ring in his left ear. Three slaves were fanning him. Two more crouched nearby, preparing snuff in little mortars and offering it to him in golden boxes.

The council members were all present, and Dousika was furious to think he was the last arrival. Following the customary procedure he beat his breast and bowed low, then moved on his knees to his place beside his mortal enemy, Samake.

Monzon Diarra had inherited the beauty of his mother Makoro, whose memory the griots still celebrated. His entire being inspired respect and terror, as if the kingship which his father Ngolo had usurped from Biton Kulibaly's descendants had become legitimate in him. He wore a white cotton tunic woven on Segu's finest looms, and white trousers held in at the waist with a wide belt. There was a strip of cotton around his head. His muscular arms were adorned not only with animal horns and teeth, supposedly for protection, but also with amulets confected by priests—finely worked little leather pouches containing verses from the Koran. He looked down at Dousika.

---

* Members of an army founded by Biton Kulibaly, founder of the city.

"Well, Dousika," he laughed, "which of your wives has been keeping you?"

All the fawning courtiers burst out laughing, while Dousika, restraining his anger, made his apology.

"Master of energies," he said, "it is not long since your messenger reached me. See—I've come so fast I'm still perspiring . . ."

After this interruption Tietiguiba Dante, the head griot, who conveyed the Mansa's words to the assembly, rose and said: "The master of gods and men, he who sits on the royal hide, the great Mansa Monzon, has brought you here for a reason. There is a white man, white, with two red ears like embers, on the other bank of the river, asking to be received in audience. What does he want?"

Then Tietiguiba sat down, and in accordance with the usual ceremony another griot rose. Everyone was in awe of Tietiguiba because of his intimacy with the king. His appearance was imposing. He wore a white and indigo cotton tunic, and on his head a crest trimmed with fur and cowrie shells. As he also acted as a spy, he let his eyes rest on each member of the council in turn, as if to appraise and then report on them. When the second griot had finished speaking, he stood up again.

"The white man says he is not like a Moor. He does not want to buy or sell. He says he has come to look at the Joliba . . ."

There was a shout of laughter. Were there no rivers in the white man's country? And isn't one river like another? No, it must be a trap—the white man didn't want to reveal the true object of his visit.

Dousika asked leave to speak.

"Have the *buguridalas* and the *moris** been questioned?" he said.

"We didn't wait for *you* to do that . . ." murmured Samake.

Once again Dousika got the better of his wrath and repeated his question. Tietiguiba answered.

"They haven't given any answer."

They'd given no answer? That showed how serious the situation was!

"They say," Tietiguiba went on, "that whatever we do with

* Muslim holy men.

this white man, others like him will come and multiply amongst us."

The members of the council stared at one another in amazement. White men come and live in Segu among the Bambara? It seemed impossible, whether they were friends or enemies! Dousika leaned forward and spoke to his friend Kone, sitting a little way off.

"Have you seen this white man?"

Unfortunately, in the silence, everyone could hear this rather childish question. The Mansa sat up.

"If you want to see him," he said ironically, "he's on the other side of the Joliba. With the women and children and outcasts."

Once again the assembly burst into obsequious laughter, and again Dousika was the object of jokes and sarcastic remarks. But what did they really have against him? He was accused of speaking with a forked tongue. Of professing to hate war while taking his share of the booty; of getting rich without effort, since he seldom took part in any campaigns; of letting his familiarity with the Mansa and his wife's royal origins go to his head, and looking down on everyone else; in short, of growing arrogant and vain. Some said he took after his father Fale, the haughtiest *yerewolo* who'd ever trod the streets of Segu, and who was punished by the gods with an ignominious death. His horse had thrown him in the middle of a swamp, where he'd struggled for hours before drowning.

No one went so far as to wish such a fate on Dousika. But everyone at court thought a good lesson wouldn't do him any harm.

Meanwhile, Nya had been tending Sira.

The two women were no longer alone. Because so many people had wanted to see the white man, the dugout canoes crossing the river had been crowded out, and many slaves, after hours of waiting, had been obliged to return disappointed to their tasks in the compound.

Nya had sent in haste for Souka the midwife, who had delivered all Dousika's wives and with her skillful hands revived more than one infant reluctant to enter the visible world. As she waited for Souka to arrive, Nya gave orders for certain plants to be burned to drive away evil spirits and help the milk to come. Then she returned to Sira, who was squatting in order to facilitate the birth.

Sira occupied a special position in the compound. She was a Fulani, not a Bambara. Mansa Monzon, during an expedition against his Fulani vassals in Macina whose *ardo** were always slow to pay their taxes, had, by way of reprisal, taken captive a dozen or so boys and girls selected from among the best families in the capital, Tenenkou. It was his intention to give them back as soon as the money was paid. But one day Dousika, crossing the palace courtyards on the way to a meeting of the council, had caught a glimpse of Sira and wanted her as his concubine. Because of the bonds between them, Monzon, though unwilling, had not been able to refuse. In due course the tax was paid and Sira's family sent a delegation to get her back. But Dousika refused to let her go. Besides, it was too late: Sira was already pregnant. As she was both foreign and a captive, Dousika hadn't been able to marry her, but it was plain that he preferred her to his legitimate partners, those who had the same language and the same gods as he.

At first Nya had hated Sira. Admittedly it wasn't the first time Dousika had had a concubine: it was impossible to count the number of slaves who had taken their turn in his hut at night. But never before had one meant so much to him. There was no doubt about it: Nya could detect his passion from a thousand signs invisible to others. Then somehow her hatred and jealousy had given way to feelings of pity, solidarity and affection. Sira's fate might well have been her own. The violence of men, the whim of one of them, might easily have snatched her too from her father's house and her mother's arms, and made her into an object of barter. So to everyone's surprise she began to take her former rival under her wing.

Despite her self-restraint, Sira uttered a groan. Nya, who didn't want it to be said that her co-wife had been lacking in courage at the moment of supreme trial, clapped her hand over Sira's mouth. As she did so she thought how, once Souka had come, she would go and make another offering in the altar hut

* Fulani war chiefs, belonging to the Diallo clan.

in the innermost hut of the compound. She had already been there once soon after she awoke that morning, but as Sira had already had a stillborn child the previous rainy season, extra precautions were needed. Nya had a white cock put by in case of emergency: its color would be pleasing to the god Faro, who watched over the smooth running of the universe night and day.

Souka entered. She was already an old woman, the wife of a fetish priest, herself in communication with the tutelary powers and possessing an air of great authority. Around her neck she wore a necklace of animal horns full of healing salves and powders. A glance at Sira told her she still had hours of waiting ahead, and she started pounding up roots and leaves in a mortar, muttering prayers known only to herself. Reassured by Souka's presence, Nya went out to fetch some goat's milk to give to the baby before he drank his mother's.

The courtyards were full of life again. Everyone seemed to be back from the river. Nieli, the second wife, was sitting at her door greedily devouring some *n'gomi*, millet fritters prepared for her by one of her slave girls. Nya reproached herself for her feelings toward Nieli, who ought to have been like a younger sister. But how could anyone put up with her laziness, her whims and fancies, her constant whining? For Nieli could never forget how she had come to be here in the compound. Years ago, Fale, Dousika's father, had gone with Mansa Ngolo Diarra to Niamina, where, spending one evening at the house of a Bambara nobleman and noticing that his host's wife was pregnant, he had, in accordance with the custom, asked to have the child for his son if it turned out to be a girl.

Dousika was a dutiful son and had always dealt justly with this wife who was not of his choosing, but he had never loved her. And since Sira's arrival this difference of feeling, obvious in countless details, had been torture to Nieli.

She stopped chewing her *n'gomi* to ask, "Has the stranger had her baby yet?"

That was how she always referred to Sira. Nya took no notice.

"No," she said. "The little newcomer isn't yet among us. May the ancestors give him an easy journey!"

Nieli was obliged to mutter the customary prayer. Nya went on toward the little hut that sheltered the altars. It was a secret place accessible only to the fetish priests attached to the family, the heads of the various family units, and a few women who like herself were invested with a certain amount of authority. In the second courtyard she came upon Dousika, back from the palace and clearly looking for her.

"Monzon has humiliated me again," he began, "and—"

She interrupted.

"Undo your belt. Sira is in labor."

Would she never overcome her bitterness? She no longer resented Sira's presence, but what galled her was the way time had lessened his feelings for her: the death of his desire. Their relationship had become one of mere routine. During the nights she spent now in his hut they slept together without touching. They never talked to one another about anything but the children, the managing of the property, the worries of public life. Oh, it's sad, growing old!

"Listen!" he said imploringly. "Monzon made fun of me twice right in the middle of the council, I tell you! . . . Send for Koumare . . ."

Nya stared at the ground: sand, mixed with finely ground pebbles.

"When do you want to see him?" she asked.

"As soon as possible, of course!"

Koumare was a fetish priest, the high priest of the Komo.* For years he'd been interpreting the signs of the visible and the invisible for Dousika, trying to ward off undesirable events. He'd have to be called in soon anyway, to surround Sira's child with protection as soon as it was born. Nya started to go on. But just as she was about to enter the third courtyard she felt sorry for Dousika, standing there wondering whether to go with her or return to his hut. She turned around and said kindly: "Wait for me. I'll be back in a moment."

He watched her go, torn between the grief he felt at her indifference and the desire to clutch at her skirt like a little child. How old was she? He didn't know her age, any more than he knew his own. They had been married sixteen dry seasons ago. So she must be thirty-two! She'd lost her figure. Her breasts

* Influential secret society run by priests.

drooped, and the wrinkles of responsibility already emphasized her features, which were lofty and fine like those of all the Kulibaly, said to be the handsomest among the Bambara. In repose she looked severe, but when she smiled a light beamed from her long, slanting eyes. Nya!—he needed her strength! Why did she refuse it?

The altar hut that Nya entered contained a block of wood called a *pembele*, a representation of the god Pemba, who by whirling around had created the earth while the god Faro took care of the sky and the waters. Around the *pembele* were red stones representing the family's ancestors, together with *boli* or fetishes made of every kind of material: hyenas' and scorpions' tails, bark, tree roots, all regularly sprinkled with animal blood and acting as concentrated symbols of the powers of the universe, designed to bring the family happiness, prosperity and fertility.

Nya took up a little broom made of vegetable fiber and carefully swept the floor. Everything was as it should be, except that the blood on the *boli* was dry. She'd come back soon and see to it: they must be thirsty.

CHAPTER

2

Sira was alone with her fear and her pain.

Fear, because the previous year she'd had a stillborn child. Nine months of anxiety just to bring forth a little lump of flesh into which the gods hadn't deigned to breathe life. Why? Were they angry at the unnatural alliance between a Fulani woman and a Bambara man?

Fulani, keep your flock.
Black, keep your spade, your wearisome spade.

That was what the herdsmen's poem said. No link was possible between the two peoples. Yet the gods knew very well she hadn't wanted it herself, she'd been a mere victim. So why had they punished her? And were they going to punish her again? Condemn her to this fruitless waiting? To another funeral, when she'd been hoping to exult in the glory of a name-giving ceremony? She looked at the mound in her hut where the little creature had been buried, snatched away immediately from her love, and her eyes filled with tears. Oh, that the gods would grant life to this child, even if it was only the child of a Bambara, of a man she ought to have hated.

She groaned in spite of herself, and Souka came over and adjusted her squatting position, helped her to clasp her hands at the nape of her neck, then, singing softly, gently massaged her belly. Her nostrils filled with the smell of burning *wolo*, a plant beloved of the god Faro and favorable to childbirth. She sneezed, triggering such a wave of pain she thought she would die. She remembered the precepts of her mother, of Nya, and of all the women who had passed through that ordeal before her. Don't flinch. Master your pain. But it was impossible. Impossible! She gritted her teeth, bit her lips, was conscious of the insipid taste of blood, then opened her eyes on Souka's finely braided hair, bristling with gris-gris, bending over her abdomen.

When she was a child she had ventured with one of her brothers into Dia creek, where he took the cows to graze in the dry season. But this time it was the rainy season and the waters were high, and they'd lost their footing and found themselves being swept away helpless amid the weeds that covered the surface. They were just thinking they would never see their mother or their father's house again when suddenly a rice field appeared, offering them the help of its as yet fragile stems. It was the same terror that she was experiencing now, the same distress, and suddenly, unexpectedly, the same peace.

Incredulous, she heard a cry, or rather a wail.

"What is it?" she stammered.

Souka rose, and carried over to the calabash of warm water a little bundle of bloody flesh, which she started to wash with astonishing care and gentleness.

"One more *bilakoro*,"* she said.

Then the slaves rushed in with Nya, some bringing soup made of dried fish and pepper, some bringing powdered vines with which to massage her stomach.

"Is he alive—really alive?" she murmured, turning to Nya.

Nya pretended not to hear this unfortunate question, which might make the gods angry.

Souka was looking at the child. She had received so many of them in her ample and powerful hands! Cut so many umbilical cords, buried so many placentas! So she only had to look at the shape of a mouth or an eyelid to tell which child would be its parents' pride, and which would drag itself about for years on legs

---

* Uncircumcised male child.

too weak for its body. And she knew that the little boy she held in her lap now would be a bold one, doomed to a singular fate. It would be a good thing if Nya offered up to the family *boli* an egg laid by a black hen without a single white feather, and some antelopes' hearts. And Dousika must be lavish with the red cockerels whose blood he would spill to anoint the baby's penis. The precautions were needed to ensure a good life. Souka rubbed the warm, shapeless little body with shea butter, wrapped it in a fine white cloth, and handed it to its mother, giving silent answer to the question in Nya's eyes: "Yes, of course—a fine boy! And the gods will lend him life . . . "

Sira held her son to her at last. Traditionally he would not be given a name until the eighth day, but she knew that as he came after an elder son who was stillborn he'd be called Malobali. She pressed the fragile little mouth against her own, amazed that so light a flesh could already have such weight in her own life. Her son was there, really and truly alive. No matter what the circumstances of his birth, he avenged her for her humiliation, her sufferings, her disgrace as the daughter of a Fulani *ardo*, master of hundreds of head of cattle, becoming the concubine of a farmer.

Sira could scarcely believe it had ever happened, when she thought of her former existence. In Macina life was ordered in accordance with the seasons, as the flocks came and went from the Dia to the Mourdia pastures. The women milked the cows and made butter which the slaves bartered for millet at the neighboring markets. The men loved their livestock better than their wives, and sang of their beauty at night around the wood fires. Other peoples made fun of them:

> *Your father died, you didn't weep.*
> *Your mother died, you didn't weep.*
> *Some cow or other dies and you howl!—*
> *Boo-hoo, the house is destroyed!*

But did other peoples matter? Sira's only had anything to do with them in the dry season, to make arrangements about pastures and water for the cattle.

Then one day the Bambara *tondyons* had appeared in their

twin-peaked caps and short yellow tunics, all covered with animal horns and teeth and amulets bought from the Muslims. With
the smell of gunpowder still in her nostrils, Sira found herself in
Segu, in the Mansa's palace. There, despite the grief she felt at
her captivity, she couldn't help admiring her new surroundings.
Behind walls that challenged the sky, slaves sat beneath awnings
weaving on looms made from four vertical posts set in the ground,
joined together with four horizontal shafts. She never tired of
watching, fascinated, as the long white snake of material
emerged. Masons worked at repairing and replastering the fronts
of the houses. Everywhere merchants offered for sale carpets from
Barbary, perfumes and silks. Jesters, in their loose patchwork cos-
tumes of hide studded with cowrie shells, cut capers to entertain
the royal children. Sira was intrigued by all this: her own people,
the Fulani, did not build; they made do with their round huts
made of plaited straw or branches.

Was it to punish her for her involuntary, almost unconscious
admiration for her conquerors that the gods had delivered her
into Dousika's hands?

No, she mustn't think about Dousika or her present happiness would be spoiled. Yet how could one separate a child from
its father?

At that moment Dousika entered, accompanied by Koumare,
who'd been sent for in haste to perform the first sacrifices. She
turned her head away so as not to meet Dousika's eyes and share
his joy. As she did so, she rebuked herself for her hypocrisy. What
was to stop her leaving him, leaving Segu? She'd told herself she
was waiting for her own gods or her own people to execute some
staggering revenge, better than anything she herself could do. But
was it true?

A few weeks ago a Fulani woodworker had come into the
compound selling pestles, mortars and handles for tools. They
had recognized each other through their language, the sweet
sounding Fulfulde tongue, and he'd given her news from home.
The Fulani had had enough of Segu's domination and of the Bambaras' raids and exactions. They'd turned away from Ya Gallo,
the war chief of the Dialloube* clan, and now pinned all their

---

* Name derived from "Diallo," patronymic of the ruling dynasty.

hopes on a young man of the Barri clan, Amadou Hammadi Boubou, a fervent Muslim who'd sworn to unite them all in one
sovereign state that would acknowledge no master but Allah. At
that, people began to whisper a prediction made several centuries
ago to Askia or King Muhammad, of the Songhay kingdom of
Gao. He'd been told a Fulani would deal the Bambara kingdom
a mortal blow and found a huge empire. And that Fulani might
be Amadou Hammadi Boubou!

Was it possible?

Sira, gently stroking her baby's head, imagined the forked
tongue of the fire serpent licking at the Mansa's palace, the compounds and the clumps of mahogany trees, then halting at the
edge of the Joliba River after consuming the Somonos' fleets of
canoes. Ah, nothing less would be enough to avenge her! She
shut her eyes.

Souka was listing all the physical details that would enable
Koumare to say of which ancestor the baby was a reincarnation.
Then Sira heard the flapping of wings and the brief squawk of a
cockerel as the fetish priest slit its throat. Then all was silent,
and she was alone with her son.

Naba tugged at Tiekoro's tunic.

"Let's go home now," he wailed. "I'm hungry. And tired."

But Tiekoro couldn't bring himself to go back: he longed with
all his heart to see the white man. He stopped a man coming
toward them, his naked body covered with sweat.

"Did you see him?" he asked. "What's he like?"

The man grimaced.

"Like a Moor, except that he's got two red ears and hair the
color of grass in the dry season."

Tiekoro had an inspiration.

"The trees! We must climb a tree!"

But when he looked up he saw that too was impossible. The
branches of the shea and silk cotton trees were all covered with
human beings, like fruit.

"Come on then!" he said crossly.

At fifteen Tiekoro, Dousika's first born, son of Nya, was almost as tall as a man. The griots who came and sang the family's

praises in the compound compared him to a palmyra growing in the desert and foretold a marvelous future for him. He was a silent, thoughtful youth: everyone thought he was arrogant. He'd been circumcised a few months ago but had not yet been initiated into the Komo.

The fact was that Tiekoro had a secret, a secret that tormented him.

It all began when, out of curiosity, he went into a mosque. He'd heard the call of the muezzin the day before, and something inexpressible had awakened within him. It was to him that sublime voice was speaking, he was sure of it. But he couldn't overcome his shyness, and hadn't gone into the mosque right away with the Muslim Somonos. It wasn't until the next day that he found the courage, after spending all night summoning up his resolution.

A man the same age as his father was sitting on a mat in a courtyard. He was wearing a loose dark blue robe over dark blue trousers, pale yellow heel-less slippers, and a little dark red cap on his closely shaven head. So far there was nothing unusual. It wasn't the first time Tiekoro had seen men dressed like that, even in the Mansa's palace, where he sometimes went with his father. But what intrigued Tiekoro was what the man was doing. In his right hand he was holding a thin piece of wood with a pointed end. He dipped it into a small pot and then drew some tiny patterns on a white surface. Tiekoro crouched down beside him.

"What are you doing?" he asked.

The man smiled.

"You can see what I'm doing! Writing!"

Tiekoro hadn't heard this word before, and he turned it over in his head. Then he seemed to see a light. He remembered the amulets some people wore.

"Oh," he said. "You're practicing magic."

The man laughed.

"You're a Bambara, aren't you?" he said.

Tiekoro, aware of the contempt in his voice, answered proudly: "Yes. I'm the son of Dousika Traore, court councillor."

"I'm not surprised you don't know about writing, then."

Tiekoro was furious. He tried to think of a stinging answer, but couldn't. Anyway, what can a child do against a grown-up? But the following day he went to the mosque again, and from then on he went every day.

Now Naba was complaining.

"You're going too fast!"

Tiekoro slowed down.

"What would you do if I went away?"

The child looked at him in surprise.

"To the war? With the Mansa?" he asked.

Tiekoro shook his head vigorously.

"No, no—I'd never fight in that sort of war!"

Killing, raping, looting! All that spilling of blood! Segu's whole history was bloody and violent!

From its very foundation to its expansion under Biton and right up to the present day, there had been nothing but murders and massacres. Young men walled up alive, virgins immolated on thresholds, emperors strangled by their slaves with strips of cotton. And, as a constant thread running through it all, sacrifices. Sacrifices to the *boli* of the town, the kingdom, the ancestors, the family. Tiekoro shuddered every time he passed the hut that held the *boli* of the Traores. One day he'd plucked up the courage to go in, and had wondered in terror where the blood drying on those obscene shapes had come from.

O for another religion, that would talk of love! That would forbid those sinister sacrifices! That would free man from fear! Fear of the invisible, and even of the visible!

As they went past the Somonos' mosque Tiekoro walked faster, lest anyone should recognize him, and Naba find out his secret. Then he was ashamed of his cowardice. Shouldn't a believer be ready to die for his faith? And he was a believer, wasn't he?

"There is no god but God, and Muhammad is His Prophet!"

The words intoxicated him. He had but one desire—to leave Segu and go to Jenne, or better still to Timbuktu and enter Sankore University.

The two boys started to run at top speed through the winding streets, jumping over sheep and goats, just missing the Fulani women who at that time of day came selling their gourds full of milk. The *tondyons*, drinking their *dolo* or millet beer, shouted jokes at the boys from the taverns.

When they arrived, bathed in sweat, at the compound, all the people rushed up to them and plied them with questions.

"Did you see him? Did you see him?"

"Have you seen the white man?"

They had to admit they hadn't. Flacoro, Dousika's third wife, hardly any older than Tiekoro, made a face.

"Not really worth spending all day by the river then . . ."

Then she added, "Sira's had a son."

A son? And living? Tiekoro's heart filled with joy.

His friendship with Sira had begun at the same time as his interest in Islam. He'd heard that many Fulani practiced that religion. But when he summoned up the courage to ask Sira about it, she hadn't been able to tell him anything. One of her uncles had been converted, but she didn't know anything abut him. Islam was new to the region, brought there by the Arab caravans like some exotic merchandise!

Tiekoro went to Sira's hut, though he knew no one would be allowed in for a week. He saw his father come out with Koumare the fetish priest. Hiding his fear of the latter, he greeted the two men politely and was about to run off when his father signaled him to follow. Trembling, he obeyed.

A few years before, Tiekoro had looked up to his father as a god. He had admired him much more than the Mansa. When had he started to think of him as a barbarian and an ignorant drinker of *dolo*? It was when the achievements of the Muslims had begun to acquire importance in his life. But the fact that he'd stopped admiring his father didn't mean he didn't love him any more. So Tiekoro suffered from a conflict between his heart and his head, between instinctive feelings and intellectual reasoning.

He sat down silently in a corner of the entry and, conscious of the honor being given him, took a pinch of snuff from the box that was offered. He dared not look in Koumare's direction, for he believed the priest could decipher his thoughts and discover what he'd been hiding from everyone. And indeed Koumare was staring at him with his red-flecked eyes. As soon as he could do so without disrespect, Tiekoro rose and went outside. Apprehension and effort combined to make his stomach contract, and he vomited painfully against the wall of one of the huts, bringing up a brown liquid streaked with mucus. Then he stood still, his head burning. How much longer could he keep his secret?

Meanwhile Koumare, left alone with Dousika, was thoughtful. He still gazed at the low door through which Tiekoro had left. Something was troubling that boy. What?

He took a set of a dozen divining cowries out of a little bag and spread them on the ground. He was so surprised by what he saw that he picked them up, meaning to try again later. Dousika had noticed his astonishment.

"What can you see, Koumare?" he asked eagerly. "What can you see?"

He was really thinking only of himself and how he had been made fun of in the council. Koumare decided not to disabuse him.

"I can't say. It's not clear. I shall work all night—then I'll be able to talk to you."

It certainly wasn't clear! One son was arriving, another going away! The father was rising, then falling! Veritable chaos was invading a hitherto orderly compound. Why?

Koumare belonged to one of the three great families of blacksmiths whose ancestors, from the underground village of Gwonna, had discovered the secret of metals. One day when they were warming themselves at a big fire they'd seen one of the stones in the hearth melt. When they examined it later they found it was so hard they couldn't break it: it was the first piece of copper. Afterward they discovered the secrets of gold and iron, and made weapons, knives, arrows and tips for various implements. Thanks to them the Bambara were able to abandon their old silex tools. And as the blacksmiths were under the protection of the god Faro and his aides, the spirits of wind and air, they were also the masters of the art of divination.

The unseen held no secrets for Koumare.

CHAPTER

3

"An evil word is like a stench. It attacks a man's strength, going from the nose to the throat, the liver and the sex."

So thought Monzon Diarra as he looked at Samake. He interrupted him sharply.

"What is there to prove that what you say is true? How do you know all this?"

Samake managed to meet his glance, which the griots compared to that of a jackal.

"Master," he answered, "I know it through my first wife Sanaba, who as you know is in the same age group as Nya, Dousika's first wife. They belong to the same sisterhood, too. And you know how women talk. The day before yesterday Dousika received a delegation from Dessekoro, whom you defeated at Guemou, and who fell back on Dioka with his court. He wants to reconcile the two Kulibaly clans—the one in Kaarta and the one in Segu. And with just one object: to overthrow you and unite the two kingdoms under the same family."

Monzon shook his head.

"I don't believe you," he said.

The Kulibaly of Kaarta and the Kulibaly of Segu hated one another. Reconciliation between them was unthinkable! Tietiguiba Dante, who'd arranged this secret interview and was in league with Samake and the rest of those who wanted to destroy Dousika, intervened.

"Master of energies, make no mistake. The Kulibaly have never resigned themselves to losing the throne of Segu to your father. They'll stop at nothing to get back into power. Dousika, as you know, is greedy for wealth, though he hasn't got the energy to fight for it. They'll have promised him gold . . ."

Monzon looked pained.

"Dousika is my blood brother," he said in a low voice. "We were circumcised on the same day. Why? Why? What can he get from betraying me that I can't give him?"

Samake and Tietiguiba exchanged looks, surprised at the sincerity of Monzon's grief. Then the Mansa jumped up and began to pace about the room. The slaves scattered in fear, afraid the royal wrath might descend on them. Then Monzon regained his self-control, and came and sat down on his oxhide again.

"I'll question him in the council tomorrow," he said. "He'll have to confess, with the knife at his throat."

Tietiguiba shook his head.

"You're as impetuous and hotheaded as your father!" he said. "No, master, that's not what you should do. Catch him by guile . . ."

He drew nearer the king, though remaining at a respectful distance so that his breath should not reach him.

"Dishonor him. Accuse him of having cheated on his taxes. Banish him from court for it. Take away his seat on the council and in the law court. Then put him under surveillance. You'll soon see how he behaves then."

Monzon said nothing, and remained deep in thought. He was not as cruel as some of his predecessors. As Dekoro, for example, the son of Biton who, angry at the defeat of his troops at Kirango and Doroni, got his priest to mark out a square, placed sixty of his men on each side of it, and then had them all built up alive into a rampart, crying, "I'll live in the middle, and my slaves shall serve me whether they like it or not!"

Monzon exercised his royal powers with justice and tolerance. Dousika's treachery wounded him. What had Dousika to gain by changing masters? Could a new mansa treat him any more generously? Was it true he was influenced by Nya, his first wife? If so, anything was possible. Who knew how far a woman could lead a man once she made herself mistress of his soul or of his body?

At that moment a slave came to tell him Mori Zoumana was asking to see him. Mori Zoumana was one of Segu's most powerful soothsayers. He worked with the four great *boli*, but had also learned the magic of the Arabs and spoke their language perfectly. He was dressed in the Muslim manner, in a white caftan and trousers, with an Arab cloak over his head. To show his independence he did not prostrate himself before the Mansa, but crouched down on his haunches.

"Master of energies," he said, "the spirit of your father himself has come to tell me what ought to be done. Tomorrow morning, send a messenger to the white man. Tell him you wish to help him, a stranger so far from his own country, so you're sending him a sack of five thousand cowries to buy food with. Say he can use your messenger as a guide to Jenne, if that's where he's going. But do not allow him to enter Segu."

Monzon gave a sign of assent.

"Where is the white man now?" he asked.

"A woman has given him shelter."

The four men looked at one another and began to laugh. Monzon, despite his depression at the news of Dousika's treachery, permitted himself a joke.

"Well, in that case he'll get to be an expert on both Segu's river and Segu's women."

Samake, Tietiguiba Dante and Mori Zoumana withdrew. Monzon, to take his mind off things, sent for Macalou, one of his favorite griots, who came with his *tamani* drum under his arm. Seeing the mood his master was in, Macalou asked gently, "What would you like me to sing? The story of the founding of Segu? Or the story of your father?"

Monzon indicated that he left the choice to Macalou, and the griot, who knew his master's preferences, began to sing the story of Ngolo Diarra.

"Ngolo's father having died, Menkoro, one of his uncles, had to go to King Biton to pay the dues, and he took the child with him to Segu. As usual, Menkoro lodged with Dante Balo, wife of one of the smiths at court. As usual he spent all his time in the taverns, filling his belly with *dolo*, so that next day he realized he had squandered all the funds that were meant to pay the dues. So he went to his hostess and told her that the *tondyons* had robbed him during the night, and lamented what would be his fate at the hands of Biton. The good woman was taken in by his show of despair, and agreed to plead with Biton and ask him to take the child as a pledge . . ."

Monzon listened to the familiar tale, of Biton, charmed by Ngolo's intelligence and telling him all his secrets, then suspicious and trying to get rid of him. In vain. After Biton's death and years of anarchy, Ngolo seized power. Then he went back to his native village and had all his relatives put to death to punish them for having delivered him into slavery.

Through the familiar words and pleasing music, Monzon's thoughts still dwelt on Dousika and on the white man at the gates of his kingdom. Were the two things connected, his friend's betrayal and the presence of the stranger, perhaps spewed up from some terrifying other world? Were they two deceptively distinct signs sent him by the gods? What were they trying to warn him against?

He had thought himself invincible, and his kingdom too. And now, perhaps, hidden dangers were threatening them both. He shivered.

Around him the room was growing dark: the wicks in the lamps had drunk up all the shea butter, and as it was very late the slaves, who were half asleep anyway, hadn't liked to replace them.

Macalou's song was ending.

"Ngolo Diarra reigned for sixteen years, and before he died he consulted his fetish priest about how to make his name immortal. They told him to give one of his daughters to Allah, which he did at once, entrusting her to the marabout Markake Darbo from the village of Kalabougou. Then the fetish priests told him to put earrings into the ears of a hundred and twenty crocodiles. 'Thus,' they said, 'your name will never die as long as there are crocodiles in the river.'"

As long as there are crocodiles in the river! The gods have a way of mocking men by such cryptic phrases, open to all kinds of interpretation! Did it mean that in a thousand years, ten thousand, posterity really would remember Ngolo? And what would remain of him, Monzon? The memory of a just and strong mansa? Strong, when the Fulani, whom he'd never completely subjugated, were beginning to be restless? Now they'd found a new excuse—religion. Islam. Monzon, even though he made use of the services of Muslim marabouts, had feelings of the greatest repugnance against Islam, which castrated men, reduced the number of wives they might have, and forbade *dolo*. Could a man live without *dolo*? Without it, where was he to find the strength to face each succeeding day?

As if to prove him right, Tietiguiba Dante and Samake, in another room in the palace, were emptying gourd after gourd of *dolo* with Fatoma, the war chief who was also involved in the plot against Dousika, and other *tondyons*.

"Soon," bellowed the war chief, "I'll be putting on my yellow robes, my war dress, and going off to battle. Segu wasn't meant for peace. Segu loves the smell of gunpowder and the taste of blood."

They all agreed.

But Samake had things to do, so he left the drinkers to get more drunk. Every time he went through the royal palace at night, with its series of antechambers either dimly lit or else quite dark, Samake was more frightened than he'd ever been in battle. The fact was, men are not to be feared, only spirits, and Samake was always expecting them to rise up out of the bulging earthen jars full of the offerings which were meant to appease them but which had not succeeded in doing so.

Fane, his fetish priest, was waiting for him, and emerged from the darkness of the third antechamber.

"Well?" said Samake.

"She's had a son."

"Alive?"

"Yes."

"Is that what I pay you for?" cried Samake angrily.

Fane walked along beside him, explaining.

"Dousika Traore is a very rich man, and he's not mean. He gave Koumare twice what you gave me, so I couldn't undo his work. The child lived. But believe me, he won't have a good life. His parents will not see all the harvest of his sowing, and he

won't be at their bedside when they leave this world. He'll be a
poisoned arrow in his mother's heart. He'll meet with a bad end."

Samake was the center of the plot against Dousika. He was
also a nobleman, a *yerewolo*. But his relatives, who came from
the Pogo region, had long been enemies of Segu, and he was the
first of his family to be in favor there. Even so, Monzon subtly
treated him like a conquered vassal. After military expeditions
in which he distinguished himself regularly by his rash bravery,
his share of the booty was always smaller than that of Dousika,
who took as little part as possible in the fighting. And twice
Dousika had humiliated him, luring women away from him by
better presents than Samake could afford to offer. For all these
reasons he had decided to destroy Dousika.

When the moon refused to rise over the Joliba in Segu, it was
like being shrouded in a thick veil, darker than the darkest indigo.
The only lights were those of the taverns where people were
drinking *dolo*. *Dolo* was no ordinary drink, just fit for warming
the stomach. In the days of Biton Kulibaly, the trade in it had
been to all intents and purposes a royal monopoly. While the
monopoly was now a thing of the past, Monzon Diarra did still
keep a strict watch over the taverns where it was drunk. His spies
were in league with the women who kept the places, and mingled
with the drinkers slumped for hours on end in front of the
seething kettles. People peddled everything there. Traders from
Kangaba or Boure offered gold at a price lower than that fixed
by the Mansa. There was sweet kola from Goutougou. Amulets
bought from Muslim Moors. Plotting too. Fane and Samake
hurried along, for they were both afraid of being swallowed up
by the darkness. Fane was going home to the smiths' quarter
backing on the river. Samake was going to Batanemba's tavern,
where his friends were awaiting the outcome of his interview
with the Mansa.

"She's thrown herself down the well! She's thrown herself
down the well!"

Twenty heads crowded around over the gaping shaft. Whiffs
of chill air rose from it; in its depths, water glittered. Using a
complicated system of ropes and vines they'd drawn up the fragile

corpse, its breasts pointed like those of a scarcely nubile girl, its belly curved like a little mound. They'd laid her on the earth she'd so greatly offended by daring to take her own life. A woman had had pity on her and taken off one of her own skirts to cover her nakedness.

Who would touch the corpse now? The corpse of a suicide? The corpse of a criminal?

At that point Siga awoke from his dream.

Night. Like a ponderous presence. He was afraid. Of the dark, or of his dream? He didn't know if that was how it had been. He'd been too young, only two or three, and afterwards no one had ever talked to him about his mother. All he knew was that she'd thrown herself down the well.

Siga was Dousika's son, born the same day as Tiekoro, with only a few hours in between. But Siga's mother was only a captive whom Dousika must have lain with one day, aroused by the tightness of her skirt over her buttocks. So while on the eighth day the blood of white rams had flowed in honor of Tiekoro, amid the clamor of trumpets, xylophones and drums of all shapes and sizes, for him, Siga, only a couple of cockerels had been dispatched to the gods and the ancestors, so that they might not be totally against him. Similarly when it came to circumcision: Siga and Tiekoro had both been equally brave under the priest's knife, and when finally they were men, soon to be allowed to wear trousers, they had danced side by side amid the women's acclamations, the pistol shots, and the griots' shouts announcing the new and bloody birth. But Dousika and the family had eyes only for Tiekoro in his ochre tunic and his tall cap with earflaps and long strings. So the ceremony that should have filled Siga with pride had left him only with a sense of frustration, dust and ashes.

Alas, the hazards of birth! If he'd been born of this womb rather than that, his life would have been quite different. He was just as handsome as Tiekoro, just as tall. They were often mistaken for one another, with their dark black skin like their father's, their large bright eyes, their full bluish lips, and on their cheeks the ritual scarifications of noblemen's sons. And yet everything else was different.

It was not surprising that Siga's whole existence had reduced itself to a battle, not to rival the favorite, for that was unthinkable, but to force Tiekoro to look at him if not as an equal at least as another human being. But Tiekoro did not even see Siga. He adored his younger brother Naba, who trailed faithfully after him wherever he went. He didn't despise Siga—he ignored him.

For some time Siga too had had a secret. One that tormented him.

Siga's secret was Tiekoro's.

Siga knew there were Muslims in Segu. They were Moors, Somonos, Sarakoles—in any case, strangers and strange folk who wore long loose garments and whose daughters did not go bare-breasted. They could be seen flocking like sheep to their mosques, which were curiously topped with crescent moons; or else just flopping down in the dust in the streets or squares or markets. He felt the same contempt for them as any good Bambara would have done.

And now hadn't he with his own eyes seen Tiekoro go into a mosque? Flattened against the wall of the mosque, hadn't he seen his brother take off his cowhide sandals and bow down with the rest? Another time he'd seen him making cabalistic signs on a board, instructed by an old man. Had he gone mad? Siga's first impulse had been to run to Nya and tell her all about it. Then he'd been afraid. The sin was so great. Might he not meet with the usual fate of the bearer of bad news, and be beaten, punished, disgraced forever? So he'd said nothing; but the silence that made him an accomplice was torture. He was wasting away, unable to eat or sleep, and people whispered that his mother, weary of roaming from branch to branch like an evil spirit unable to find rein-carnation, wanted his company and was drinking his blood. Nya became worried and took him to see Koumare, but the latter wasn't going to put himself out for the son of a slave, and just prescribed baths of water mixed with roots and powdered palmyra.

Like Tiekoro and Naba and all the children of the family, Siga adored and respected Nya. It was she who had brought him up. After his mother's suicide she had collected him from the banco*pit near which he'd been crawling, and taken him into her own hut. She'd fed him with her own milk after Tiekoro had

---

* Clay mixed with water, sand, dung and straw to form a building material.

had his fill. She'd given him the food Tiekoro left or refused. She'd been fair. She'd been kind. But, people must know their place: the son of a slave is not the son of a princess.

Siga rose and stepped over two or three naked bodies lying around him. He wasn't old enough yet to have a hut of his own, and slept with ten or so boys of his own age: sons of Dousika or of the latter's four younger brothers, Diemogo, Bo, Da and Mama. The boys called them all father, and were growing up under their joint authority.

Siga went and crouched by the door, staring at the ebony rectangle beyond.

Night over Segu.

Not a star in the sky. Above the flat roofs of the houses, crowded together like frightened animals, rose the tufted tops of the mahoganies, the baobabs, and the slenderer palmyras. The smell of oysters and river mud was mitigated by a cool night breeze, though the day had been like an oven. It was one of the charms of the town, this respite the dark afforded to weary bodies. Siga could hear a chorus of snores that made him feel more unable to sleep than ever. Somewhere a cock crowed. But the stupid bird had made a mistake—the night was still young and strong, full of spirits taking revenge for the neglect of the living and trying to communicate with them through dreams.

Were there countries where there was no night?

The country of the white men, perhaps? Like all the other inhabitants of Segu, Siga had hurried to the riverbank to see the strange visitor. But he'd seen nothing except a great scuffle, with canoes besieged and the more venturesome splashing about in the water. Where was the white man now? Had he found a roof to shelter him? Siga was gripped by superstitious terror. Perhaps after all it wasn't a man, but an evil spirit. If so the Mansa had been right not to let him enter the town. Siga felt a fleeting sense of gratitude toward the ruler. Then he went back to his mat and curled himself up to sleep.

"She's thrown herself down the well! She's thrown herself down the well!"

The crowd drew closer. The frail body. The pointed breasts. The little curve of the belly. The pitying gesture of the woman.

Siga realized he'd fallen asleep for a few moments and returned to the obsession that haunted his nights. Which of his two obsessions did he prefer? The one that haunted his days! Siga came to a decision. He knew Nya was the first to wake in the morning. After sprinkling her hut with water and fumigating it to drive away any spirits lingering on into daylight, she went to the women's bathing hut, where she washed herself at great length with senna soap. Then, dispensing with the help of her slaves, for she liked to do everything herself, she put some bread to bake in the *banco* oven, and prepared the *degue* for the younger children.

There was no use trying to talk to her during all that. Siga crouched down to the left of the door, waiting for the time when, after having been greeted by all, she allowed herself to sit down and drink some of the senna tea she took for her migraine. Siga buried his head in his hands, praying the gods to forgive him for the pain he was going to inflict.

CHAPTER

4

The king's heralds stopped at every street corner and announced to all the dismissal of Dousika Traore, member of the king's council and judge in the royal courts. Such a thing had never happened as far back as the inhabitants of Segu, the Segukaw could remember! A nobleman publicly denounced as a thief! The news spread from the capital to the villages of the warriors, where Dousika did not lack friends. Everyone smelled a rat, a plot. What was this luxury tax, the equivalent of a fortieth of his wealth in gold and cowries, that Dousika was supposed not to have paid? Hadn't he been given his wealth by the Mansa himself? That being so, why should he have to pay taxes on it? But some people said the Mansa, who evidently wanted to undermine Dousika's position, was letting him off lightly. He'd been guilty of plotting with the hereditary enemy from Kaarta, and for that he could be put to death.

But this theory was generally considered unconvincing.

The causes of the quarrel between Segu and the Bambara of Kaarta were lost in the mists of time: they went back to the differences between the two brothers Niangolo and Barangolo. The quarrel had deepened from year to year, especially since the Diarra had overthrown the Kulibaly clan. What would Dousika have had to gain from getting involved? Those who remembered that his wife was a Kulibaly forgot the hatred between the Kulibaly of Segu and those of Kaarta.

Amid all this confusion, it would have been a good thing if Dousika had defended himself like a man. But he did nothing of the kind.

As soon as the decree banishing him from court was made public, he was no longer to be seen in the streets of Segu, listening to a griot on some street corner, ordering sandals from his favorite shoemaker, emptying a calabash of *dolo* with the men of his age group, or going to a tavern to talk and laugh and play *wori** with them. An atmosphere of mourning had alighted on his compound. Those who lurked around its walls out of curiosity reported that they could hear nothing. Not even a child crying, or women quarreling.

And it was true that, for Dousika, night had fallen over the world. Forever. In the darkness of his hut, his eyes closed, he lay prostrate on his mat, always a prey to the same crowding questions. When had he neglected his gods or his ancestors? When had he failed to offer them a share of his harvest? When had he forgotten to sprinkle the *boli* with blood? When had he put food to his lips without first satisfying our mother earth? Rage seized him. He had nothing to reproach himself with. It was all because of his eldest son, Tiekoro, the very one who ought to have been his pride. He remembered the boy's cool audacity as he stood before him: "*Fa*, I assure you—there is no god but Allah, and Muhammad is His Prophet!"

Dangerous words, which had brought down upon Dousika, the fury of the gods and the ancestors, which in turn brought down the wrath of the Mansa! What, a Traore a Muslim? A Traore turning his back on the protectors of his clan?

Oh, it was not Samake and his disciples who were the causes of his ruin. They were only the instruments of a higher anger aroused by his own son. Dousika groaned, and tossed feverishly from side to side. Then he heard Nya's footsteps in the entrance to the hut. He would have liked her to pity him, to console him as if he were a child. But although she tended and watched over him without ceasing, her voice and her looks had in them shades of coolness and contempt, as if she blamed him for giving way

---

* Game resembling checkers.

to discouragement. She stood for a while in a corner of the room, then said, "Koumare is here to see you."

Apart from Nya, Koumare was the only person who had crossed Dousika's threshold since his dismissal. When he entered, Dousika tried to read signs as to his own future in the other's dark and inscrutable countenance. Koumare began by scattering pinches of snuff in the four corners of the room. Then he crouched down and stayed still for a long while, as if listening. Finally he approached the mat where Dousika sat feverishly watching his every movement.

"It's been difficult, Traore, but at last your father and grandfather have come and spoken to me. And this is what they have said: 'Dousika, let Tiekoro go wherever he wants.'"

Stunned and incredulous, Dousika just managed to answer: "Is that all they said?"

"That is all," said Koumare, nodding. "So let him go to Timbuktu and rub his face in the dust. But I must say I'd like to know why the ancestors have spoken like that. I shall keep on questioning them. So I shall withdraw for a week. Don't let your son leave Segu until I come back."

Thereupon he rose. The kola nut and the various plants he was always chewing to help with his predictions made the inside of his mouth red so that his lower lip looked bloody, like the whites of his eyes, which seemed to be alive with the flames of his forge. He spat a blackish liquid carefully to the side of the mat and left. Near the *dubale* tree he came on Nya, who had tactfully retired during his conversation with Dousika.

"What is going to happen to my son?" she asked him humbly, almost apologizing for her temerity.

"Don't worry," Koumare deigned to reply. "He's going away! Our gods are not taking back his life."

Nya could not speak for sudden joy.

Dousika too was happy, or at least reassured that his father and grandfather had consented to leave the unseen to tell Koumare of their wishes. If they were prepared to talk it meant forgiveness was possible. For the first time in a fortnight Dousika felt strong enough to get up and leave his hut.

Noon was not far off. The sky, in this dry season, was like a new indigo *pagne*, with the golden pattern of the sun in the middle. Life went on.

Dousika thought of his last-born, Malobali. Because of Dousika's illness it was Diemogo, his next eldest brother, who had presided over the naming ceremony, performed the sacrifices with Koumare, and entertained relatives and other visitors. Dousika felt slightly guilty toward the child, and directed his steps toward Sira's hut.

Her ritual seclusion was over and she was standing in the door of her hut, holding the baby in her arms. At the sight of her figure, slim again now, her plump shoulders, her light and glowing skin, so typical of the Fulani women, Dousika felt an upsurge of desire. Trying not to show it, he examined his son. All the infant's silky baby hair had been shaved off except for a strip running from his forehead to the nape of his neck. His slanting eyes, the lids blackened with antimony, were as bright as his mother's and there was something about his high cheekbones which recalled his Fulani origins beyond any doubt.

"Too beautiful!" thought Dousika. "Only a woman has a right to be as good-looking as that!"

He took the little body, then held it up by the feet to check the flexibility of its muscles. Sira protested gently: "He's just been fed, *koke* . . ."

But Malobali didn't throw up and didn't cry. His sparkling eyes glanced from right to left as if to try to make out what had suddenly turned his universe upside down. He would be a fine fellow, with a lively curiosity about people and things. Dousika handed him back to his mother.

One son comes, another goes. Life is like a strip of cotton on a loom: the grave and resurrection, bridal chamber and womb, all in one.

Dousika hadn't seen Sira since her confinement and would have liked to hear what she had to say about the terrible events that had afflicted him. But she said nothing, turning her head away slightly so as not to meet his eye.

"What do you think of what has been happening to our family?" he asked.

She turned to face him.

"It's not my family," she said.

"It's your son's . . ."

She didn't waver.

"It isn't mine."

It was true. Dousika was ashamed of himself, standing there begging for love from a captive. Who in this whole compound cared about him? No one. Neither Nya nor Sira set any store by him, and the other women didn't count. He went sadly back to his hut.

Nya had meanwhile gone straight to the courtyard where the boys of the family lived. Tiekoro who, far from trying to pass unnoticed, now flaunted his religious beliefs, was sitting in the doorway of one of the huts inscribing signs on a piece of wood, surrounded by a group of onlookers.

Nya shuddered: her son had become some peculiar kind of magician! How had this transformation come about without her knowledge? A sort of holy terror reinforced the blind love she felt for Tiekoro, her firstborn son.

Tiekoro pointed to the marks he had been making.

"Do you know what I've been writing?" he asked.

Nya did not answer, and with reason.

"It's the divine name of Allah," he said.

Nya hung her head, overcome by her own ignorance and unworthiness. But Tiekoro was not trying to humiliate his mother. He was only expressing the overflowing happiness he felt at no longer having to conceal his faith, at seeing the four sacred letters—alif, lam, lam, ha—explode like a burst of stars.

Tiekoro could remember how uncertain his hand had once been, and the way his teacher had mocked him. El-Hadj Ibrahima hadn't beaten him as he did the little Moors and Somonos in his school, whom he also burned sometimes with sticks taken from the fire when their recitations from the Koran really displeased him. No, with Tiekoro he just used mockery, saying, "Go on, Bambara—you'll never be anything but a wretched fetish worshipper!" or "Be off and sacrifice your chickens!"

Then Tiekoro would grit his teeth and curse his clumsy fingers and poor memory. "Word of God, you will flow in me and make a temple of my body." But when he had recited a passage without making any mistakes, El-Hadj Ibrahima would smile, and he'd take that smile back with him to the compound, where it lit up his evenings and nights and gave him the strength to go on learning.

Now Nya laid her hand on his.

"Tiekoro," she said, "Koumare has just told me you are going away to Timbuktu. The ancestors have unbarred the way for you."

Mother and son looked at each other. Tiekoro loved his mother, had always thought of her as part of himself, the foundation of his being. He knew that his conversion to Islam might separate them, and it pained him. He tried to think it wasn't so, but the fact remained he was indeed going to leave her, going to live far away, and for how many years? And so the news which should have filled him with joy made his eyes fill with tears. He wanted to ask her forgiveness. Yet at the same time he felt an enormous exhilaration.

He jumped up and ran to tell his teacher.

Koumare got into a little straw boat and rowed toward a small island in the middle of the river.

It was nightfall, for he needed darkness and secrecy for what he had to do. As they saw him embark, the last of the Somono fishermen taking home their catch prudently averted their gaze, for they recognized the redoubtable fetish priest and knew that what was about to happen was outside the ken of ordinary mortals. As Koumare plied his oars, the walls of Segu vanished in the gathering dusk. Hordes of vultures sat motionless on the walls, indistinguishable from the tall stakes protruding at intervals. There were vague shapes on the rocky beach below. Koumare drew closer around his shoulders the goatskin he wore against variations in the temperature, for the air was growing cooler. He took a pinch of snuff from an antelope horn and put it up his nostrils. Then he took up the oars again.

He was soon at his destination. Hiding his boat among the reeds, he went over to a little hillock on which there stood a straw shelter like those of the Fulani herdsmen. But everyone knew that this one was a temple where strange conversations were held with the unseen.

For the last three days Koumare had abstained from all sexual intercourse with his wives: he did not want to dissipate his strength by spilling his seed. He was also chewing *daga* for second sight. He lost no time before starting to search among the plants growing around the hut for those he needed in his work.

It was a hard task that lay before him. An indeterminate mass of troubles and bereavements seemed to be in store for Dousika's family. Why? Because of the eldest son's conversion to Islam? In that case, why had the gods and the ancestors agreed to his going to Timbuktu? Was it a trick? An even more deadly way of destroying Dousika? What other storms did they intend to unleash on him?

Koumare put some fresh mahogany bark into a little gourd, together with some warthog hairs, and on top of these some drops of menstrual blood from a woman who'd miscarried seven times. To this he added some dried lion's heart in powdered form, muttering as he did so the ritual words:

> *Ke korte*, father, ancestor,
> There in the region below,
> You see I am quite blind.
> *Ke korte*, lend me your eyes . . .

The paste that resulted from his mixture he put carefully on a baobab leaf, which he folded in four and began to chew. Then he lay down on the bare earth and seemed to go to sleep.

In fact he was going into a trance. His spirit, leaving its human body behind, was traveling in the region below.

The journey lasted seven days and seven nights, but human time and the time of the region below are not measured in the same way. In human time, Koumare's journey lasted only three days and three nights.

And during those three days and three nights, Segu's life as a capital city went on as usual. The fleets of civilian and military canoes going up and down the river laden with passengers, merchandise and horses raced against shoals of migrating fish. The asses used for transporting the merchandise trotted meekly between the various markets. There was no more talk of the white man. People had other worries, other subjects of conversation. Islam!

Now it had struck at one of the best families in the kingdom! It appeared that Dousika Traore's eldest son had been converted by the imam of the Somono mosque. Until now, by a kind of tacit agreement, the Muslims hadn't tried to make converts among the Bambara. But now that they were breaking that rule, the Mansa ought to intervene and strike a decisive blow: shut all the mosques, persecute any who dared make the obscene profession of faith, "There is no god but Allah, and Muhammad is His Prophet!"

Instead of doing that, the Mansa was temporizing.

He was temporizing because he knew the kingdom of Segu was becoming every day more like an island; an island surrounded by other countries won over to Islam. Yet the new religion had advantages as well as disadvantages. To begin with, its cabalistic signs were as effective as many sacrifices. For generations the mansas of Segu had availed themselves of the *mori* of the Somono families—the Kane, Dyire and Tyere—and they had resolved the kings' problems just as satisfactorily as the priests. Furthermore, these signs made it possible to maintain and strengthen alliances with other peoples far away, and created a kind of moral community to which it was a good thing to belong. On the other hand, Islam was dangerous: it undermined the power of kings, according sovereignty to one supreme god who was completely alien to the Bambara universe. How could one fail to be suspicious of this Allah whose city was somewhere in the east?

At the end of his journey through the region below, Koumare awoke, his ears still ringing with the tumult that prevailed there: the groans of spirits neglected by their descendants who omitted the necessary sacrifices and libations; the lamentations of spirits trying in vain to be reincarnated in the bodies of male infants; the angry cries of spirits outraged by the dreadful crimes that human beings ceaselessly commit. Koumare went and fetched the roots he had left in a gourd. Powdered and chewed they would bring him back to the world of men.

At last he could read the Traores' future. The leniency of the gods and the ancestors toward Tiekoro was merely apparent. In reality the combined efforts of Dousika's many enemies had made them deaf to all prayers and unmoved by any sacrifice.

Things were going very badly for Dousika, and Koumare's hard work had been able to do no more than limit the damage.

Four sons—Tiekoro, Siga, Naba and Malobali, the lastborn—had to be regarded as hostages or scapegoats, to be wantonly ill used by fate so that the family as a whole might not perish. Four sons—Tiekoro, Siga, Naba and Malobali—out of twenty or so children in all. Dousika was getting off quite lightly, really.

But Koumare was troubled. The spirits of the gods and of the ancestors hadn't concealed from him the fact that this new god, this Allah who'd adopted young Tiekoro, was invincible. He would be like a sword. In his name the earth would run with blood, fire would crackle through the fields. Peaceful nations would take up arms, son would turn away from father, brother from brother. A new aristocracy would be born, and new relationships between human beings.

Day was breaking. Wreaths of gray mist were vanishing from all over the sky, replaced by the proud silhouette of the palmyras. Men and beasts were waking up and throwing off the fears of night. The men examined their dreams; the animals' terror would linger on for hours. Koumare made his way thoughtfully to the river and into the cold water. It made him shiver, but he dived in, into the water of the Joliba, favorite home of the god Faro. Water—the essential element. In it a child takes on life and shape in its mother's womb. Every time he reenters it a man is regenerated. Koumare swam for a long while, following the current. Crocodiles and other aquatic animals, sensing his power, made way for him. Then he returned to the bank and set off again in his boat back to Segu.

Perhaps Allah and the gods of the Bambara would manage to come to some arrangement? One by which the Bambara deities would let the proud newcomer occupy the forefront of the stage, while they themselves worked on unseen, for it was impossible that they should be entirely defeated. If Makungoba, Nangoloko, Kontara and Bagala, great fetishes honored every year in brilliant ceremonies, were ever scorned or forgotten, Segu would no longer be Segu, but only a concubine, a captive, subject to a conqueror.

On the gray bank of the Joliba, dotted with the shells of giant oysters, women were drawing water in great gourds. Slaves were being driven along in single file by an overseer. Everyone carefully avoided looking at the priest, for it was never wise to get in the way of a master of Komo. You never knew when he might be angry and unleash the forces that brought barrenness, violent death or epidemics. So Koumare met only with lowered eyelids, closed eyes, attitudes of furtiveness and fear.

Soon he was within sight of Dousika's compound. He could hardly wait to convey to him the orders from the other world, "Yes, your son Tiekoro must go. But his brother Siga must go with him. Siga and Tiekoro are two contrasting breaths of the same spirit; doubles. One has no identity without the other. Their fates are complementary. The threads of their lives are as closely interwoven as those in a strip of cotton coming off the loom."

As Koumare was entering the first courtyard, still deserted at this early hour, Tiekoro emerged from among the huts. He must be on his way to the first prayer, for the voice of the muezzin could be heard somewhere in the distance above the flat roofs. He stood rooted to the spot, obviously frightened. Koumare had never paid any special attention to the boy; for him he was just like all the others in the compound. It was Koumare's own knife that had removed Tiekoro's foreskin, but at the time he hadn't struck him as any braver than the rest; they all gritted their teeth so as not to cry out. But now, suddenly, he discerned in the still-childish features evidence of boldness and intelligence, together with signs of an extraordinary inner rigor. What strength had set this youth on the path to Islam? Where had he found the courage to turn away from the time-honored practices of his family and his people? It was impossible to imagine his solitary struggle.

Tiekoro gazed at Koumare, and gradually his fear vanished. Instead of some terrifying form, all he saw before him was a middle-aged man, almost old, with a bristly unkempt beard, his body hung with the heads of birds, deer's horns wrapped in red cloth, cows' tails and a grayish goatskin. A regular scarecrow.

Calmly, condescendingly, Tiekoro greeted him, "*As salam aleykum. . . .*" Peace be upon you.

CHAPTER

5

When you leave Segu you are on the edge of the desert.

The earth is the color of ochre and burning hot. The grass, when it manages to grow at all, is yellow. But usually there is nothing but a desolate stony crust from which only the baobab can derive nourishment, together with the acacia and the shea tree, symbols of the whole region.

Sometimes from the bare flatness of the surrounding plain a steep cliff arises like a rampart, shutting out the horizon—a mountain and a citadel for the Dogon people. Everything bends before the harmattan when it blows, driving the Fulani and their herds ever further toward the water holes. Then stone disappears, vanquished by sands pierced here and there by grasses with needle-sharp seeds. As far as the eye can see, vast yellowish-white plains stretch away under a pale red sky. No song of bird is heard, no snarl of wild beast. It is as if there were no life apart from an occasional glimpse of the river, like a mirage born of loneliness and fear.

Yet, to their own surprise, Siga and Tiekoro fell in love with these arid landscapes, so indifferent to all that was human. When Tiekoro, with the Moors in the caravan, prostrated himself toward Mecca, he felt himself filled with God, invaded by His presence as by a searing wind. Even Siga had a feeling of peace he had never known before, as if the ghost of his mother was willing to rest at last in its shroud. The two brothers suddenly found themselves close to one another, like travelers on a raft.

Timbuktu, when they got there, was no more than a captive remembering past splendor. Centuries ago Timbuktu and Gao had been the jewels in the crown of the Songhay empire, still called the empire of gold and salt. The Songhay empire had destroyed the empire of Mali, annexing its northern provinces so as to obtain control of the gold of Bambouk and Galam. The prosperity of the Songhay empire had been based on trade: not only, as in Segu, trade in slaves destined for north Africa, but also trade in kola, gold, ivory and salt. Caravans armed against raids by the Moors and the Tuareg used to set off for the "Saharan sea," whence finally came first danger and then ruin. In the sixteenth century the Moroccans under Sultan Mulay Ahmed, who was after the gold mines and salt deposits, completely destroyed the Songhay empire and handed it over to their descendants, the sons born to them by the wives they had taken from among the Arma, the local aristocracy. Since the Moroccan conquest Timbuktu, once praised by scholars and travelers as they might have praised a woman or a Fulani his cattle, was no more than a body without a soul. Yet Siga and Tiekoro did not find it entirely without charm.

The two young men and their guides entered the city through Albaradiou, an outlying district which served as a caravanserai for travelers, especially those from north Africa. Then Siga and Tiekoro parted from the Moors with whom they'd made the journey, for the Moors' intention was just to rest, then sell their merchandise, load up with other goods and start out on the return trip. The boys soon reached the Madougou, the palace built by Mansa Musa on his return from Mecca. They knew nothing about the history of the city and dared not approach passersby with questions, for those they met were chiefly Tuaregs, terrifying in their heavy indigo robes, with their turbans, veils, two-edged swords with cross-shaped hilts, and daggers ready for use in wide leather wristbands. They went through the meat market, a gruesome sight with its whole quarters of beef and mutton covered in flies. Men recognizable as Muslims by their clothes and their shaven skulls were roasting legs of mutton on wooden tripods.

Of the two boys, Tiekoro was the more disappointed, for El-

Hadj Ibrahima, his teacher in Segu, had told him so much about Timbuktu, "the abode of saints and pious men, whose soil had never been sullied by idol worship," that he had been expecting some kind of paradise. In fact, Timbuktu was no more attractive than Segu. But more than anything Tiekoro was suffering from the anonymity that had engulfed him ever since the walls of his birthplace vanished in the distance. For all those around him he was just a Bambara, one of a people who were powerful perhaps, but regarded as bloodthirsty and idolatrous. Whenever he told anyone he was going to study theology at the university of Sankore they would laugh and say, "Since when have the Bambara taken up study and Islam?"

Or else they made fun of his poor knowledge of Arabic, for El-Hadj Ibrahima had been able to teach him no more than the rudiments.

Tiekoro turned to Siga, who stood rooted to the sand, terrified by two Tuaregs who were not taking the slightest notice of him. How many different peoples the two brothers had met with on their journey! First the Bozo and Somono, whom they knew already, fishermen who practically lived on the bed of the river and who called themselves "the masters of the water." Then the Sarakole, "masters of the earth," great farmers whose fields of cotton, tobacco and indigo were dotted with little scarecrows on tall forked sticks; the Dogon, at once shy and fierce, emerging in groups from their houses perched among or hollowed out of the cliffs; and the Malinke, merchant aristocrats still living on the memory of the great empire of Mali founded by their ancestors and refusing to admit its decline into a mere vassal of Segu. And everywhere the Fulani, some of them Muslims, some of them still fetishists, but all supremely contemptuous of other races; and the Arabs, leading interminable caravans of camels.

El-Hadj Ibrahima had given Tiekoro a letter to his friend El-Hadj Baba Abou, a great Muslim scholar in Timbuktu, asking him to help this boy from a fetishist family who all by himself had found the way to the true God.

After wandering about for some time, Tiekoro and Siga arrived in the Kisimo Banku quarter in the southern part of the city. El-Hadj Baba Abou lived in a fine mud house built like the houses in Segu, except that instead of being covered with a red-

dish plaster mixed with shea butter it was daubed with kaolin.
Also, instead of presenting to the street an unbroken facade with
just one door, it was surrounded by a wall so low that you could
see what was going on inside. The first floor ended in a flat roof
on which reclined a group of girls, who burst out laughing as they
saw the strangers approach. And the boys were certainly not
much to look at after nights spent in primitive halts, skimpily
washing out their mouths with water from a goatskin and thinking themselves lucky when they were near enough to the river
for a bath. No one would think they were well-born youths whose
lineage was lauded by the griots!

Tiekoro knocked at the door, using the handsome copper
knocker shaped like a closed fist. After a moment the door was
opened by an arrogant-looking slim young man in a spotless
white caftan, whose cold tone and expression contradicted his
words, *"As salam aleykum!"*

Tiekoro explained himself as best he could, then took out
from the depths of his robe the precious letter that he had kept
for months against his skin. The young man received it with some
disgust.

"El-Hadj Baba's asleep," he said. "Wait, please."

And he shut the door. Tiekoro and Siga sat down on the wide
mud seat built along the front of the house.

"A guest is a gift of God"—Tiekoro kept thinking of this
saying of El-Hadj Ibrahima's as he sat there waiting in the sun
with his brother, stared at by all the passersby. He remembered
too how his father treated strangers; how Nya would take them
to the rest hut, send them hot water to bathe in and then provide
them with a lavish meal. If they had to stay the night they were
offered a woman so that they might satisfy their desires. How
far away such courtesy was now!

After an endless interval El-Hadj Baba Abou finished his siesta
and appeared in the street. He was a very tall man, with an ascetic
countenance and a light skin indicating Arab blood. His skull
was closely shaven, and around his neck he wore a scarf of fine
white silk. He was dressed in a long robe unlike anything Tiekoro
or Siga had ever seen before. After a rapid exchange of greetings
he said, "There are two of you. The letter mentions one student
only."

"The student is me," stammered Tiekoro. "This is my brother."

El-Hadj made a peremptory gesture. "If he's not a student, and above all if he isn't a Muslim, I can't accept him as my guest. *You* can come with me."

What was to be done? As El-Hadj opened the door Tiekoro, overwhelmed, could only obey. And Siga found himself alone in a narrow street in a foreign town. Above his head he heard again the girls' laughter. What were they laughing at? His braids? The gris-gris he wore on his arms and around his neck? The ring in his ear?

All through their journey the Moors with whom the brothers traveled, though friendly on the whole, had made fun of their clothes, their filed teeth, and above all the color of their skin. If Siga hadn't reacted as violently as Tiekoro to these pleasantries it was only because he didn't understand them. Wasn't it an excellent thing to be black, with a fine, shining skin fitting neatly over the joints and well oiled with shea butter?

The mockery of the strange girls filled him with fury, adding to his sense of loneliness and despair. What was going to become of him in this town where he didn't know anyone?

What had he come for? To keep Tiekoro company. And why? Why had they made him a servant, almost a slave, to his brother? And how little that brother had bothered about him, hurrying after his host without a word of protest! Couldn't he have said, "No, I can't—he's my brother"? But no, he'd done nothing!

What would the family say when they knew? Yes, but who was going to tell them? Siga could see himself lost, dead perhaps, many days' march from his people. Then he pulled himself together and decided to find the Moors who'd brought them there; to go back to the caravanserai.

Since the Albaradiou quarter was north of the city as you came from Kisimo Banku it was a long way away, and when Siga reached the caravanserai it was almost nightfall. The torrid heat that had prevailed all day, as if some fire were setting sand and stone ablaze, had abated. But though he looked everywhere, Siga could find no trace of the three Moors. He asked other caravaneers, lying by their tents engaged in the interminable ceremony of drinking green tea, but could get no information about them.

No one had seen them, no one knew in which direction they'd gone nor what they had done with their camels. They seemed to have vanished into thin air! Siga pondered over their disappearance. Were the three Moors spirits, obeying the ancestors' commands to bring Dousika's sons safely to their destination? Hadn't the way Dousika had found them in the market at Segu been just as mysterious as their vanishing now? Siga tried to remember some detail that might help to prove that they were supernatural, but in vain. They had eaten and drunk and laughed like human beings. But then didn't spirits have the gift of deluding men?

What was he to do? Go back to Segu? But how? Siga sat down in the sand. As he crouched there with his head in his hands a boy of his own age came up.

"Do you speak Arabic?" he asked.

Siga indicated his limitations.

"Do you speak Dyula?"*

"That's practically my own language."

"Where's the boy who was with you this morning?"

Siga shrugged. He didn't want to go into it. The young stranger sat down beside him and put a friendly hand on his shoulder.

"I see," he said. "He's left you in the lurch and you're on your own here. I'd better give you a few tips."

Siga shook off his hand roughly.

"What's your name, first?"

"Call me Ismael," said the boy, smiling mysteriously. "And listen—you won't get anywhere here if you're not a Muslim. You can't imagine what the people are like—if you don't pray five times a day and go to the mosque on Friday, you're less than a dog to them. They wouldn't give you food even if you were starving."

"I don't want to become a Muslim," growled Siga.

"Who said you have to become one?" laughed the other. "All you have to do is look like one. Cut off those braids, get rid of those baubles."

Get rid of the objects that brought him protection? Some had been given him at birth, others after he was circumcised, not to

* Dyula, Bambara and Malinka are all Mande or Mali languages.

mention those Koumare had bestowed on him before he left Segu to keep him safe in this foreign land.

Ismael laughed.

"Hide them then. Do what everyone else does. If you knew what those great scholars hide under their caftans! Call yourself Ahmed, don't drink in public, and there you are!"

Siga looked at him doubtfully.

"And how would that help me?"

"If you do as I say I could get you a job tomorrow morning. I'm a donkey boy—I'll introduce you to the *ara-koy*.* It's a good job, and after a couple of months you'll have enough money to go back home. Or somewhere else, if you prefer."

Siga shook his head firmly. He had no wish to be a donkey boy and have to look after stupid, dirty animals. He stood up and was just walking off when Ismael's mocking voice stopped him.

"You don't even know where you're going to sleep tonight. Don't you know the *hakim*† round up all the people they find sleeping out of doors, especially when they're rigged out like you?"

El-Hadj Baba Abou belonged to the family of the eminent jurist Ahmed Baba, whose fame had spread across north Africa as far as Bougie and Algiers. He himself was a scholar, author of a treatise on astrology and a book on the castes of western Sudan. For all these reasons there had been several attempts to draw him into political intrigues, but he had refused. He made a very good living from the Koranic school in which he prepared a hundred and twenty pupils for entry into the city's three universities. During his student days in Marrakesh he had married a Moroccan as his first wife, then back in Timbuktu he had taken as his second wife a Songhay woman who was descended from slaves, to demonstrate that, like his ancestor Ahmed Baba he condemned "the calamity of the age," slavery. He was a supercilious, short-tempered man, whose lofty principles and preoccupation with God did not make him any the more tolerant of human weakness.

* Songhay for head donkey man.
† Songhay for policemen.

He handed Tiekoro over to his secretary, Ahmed Ali, with words that were far from charitable, "See that he takes a bath. He stinks."

Tiekoro really only smelled of the shea butter with which, like all the other inhabitants of Segu, he lavishly anointed his body.

El-Hadj Baba Abou was not very pleased at the arrival of such an ignorant bumpkin. At the same time he couldn't offend his friend El-Hadj Ibrahima, who stressed the importance of recruiting some pupils from among the fetishist families so that they might eventually convert their own relatives. El-Hadj Baba Abou disagreed on this point: the Islam of such converts was so impure, so mixed with magical practices that it was offensive to God.

Tiekoro, waiting in a corner of the courtyard, was thinking of Siga. What was happening to him, alone, without friends or relatives, without gold or cowries? But he was too worried by his own position to fret about his brother, here in a house where every object and every face subtly indicated that the only person he should be pitying was himself. At one point half a dozen youths burst into the courtyard dressed in identical dark brown caftans, and half a dozen pairs of eyes stared at Tiekoro. With veiled irony Ahmed Ali performed the introductions.

"Your new fellow student, Tiekoro Traore . . ."

"Tiekoro?" said one of the youths, raising his eyebrows.

"He comes from Segu," explained Ahmed Ali, smiling.

Fortunately at this point the servants brought in water and a large dish of millet couscous and mutton. Everyone sat down, and for a while the only activity was the movement of hands between food and mouths. Tiekoro, despite his hunger, could scarcely bring himself to eat. What did they have against him? His ethnic origins? Was this the face of Islam? Didn't it say that all men were equal, like teeth in a comb?

As soon as the meal was over the others started a learned conversation about a manuscript by Ahmed Baba written in 1589, a year before the Moroccan conquest of the Songhay empire. Tiekoro was sure this display of knowledge was put on to impress him, and his idea was confirmed when one of the youths addressed him.

"What's your opinion of this text? Do you agree it has nothing to do with the politics of its day?"

Tiekoro found the courage to stand up and say quite simply: "I think I'll go to bed. Last night I slept in the open."

The room he'd been allocated was small but with a very high ceiling and was decorated with a thick wool rug. The bed consisted of an oxhide stretched between four posts stuck in the ground and covered with a rough camel's hair blanket. It all seemed very comfortable to Tiekoro, and despite his unhappiness and humiliation he fell asleep at once.

If he'd heard the jokes that were made as soon as his back was turned his slumbers would no doubt have been less peaceful. El-Hadj Baba Abou's boarders came from the princely families in Gao and the most important families in Timbuktu. For generations their fathers, the councillors and companions of the Askias, had shaved their heads and bowed to Allah. Their libraries held hundreds of Arabic manuscripts written by scholars who were their kinsmen, on such subjects as jurisprudence, Koranic exegesis and the sources of the law. In looking down on Tiekoro they were despising not only what they called "fetishism" or "polytheism" but also an unwritten culture which they considered inferior to their own, and the smell of the earth, which their forefathers had never cultivated. Only one boy came to Tiekoro's defense. This was Mulay Abdallah, whose father was a *cadi* or judge. He was deeply religious, with a touch of mysticism, and his companions' arrogance pained him. He decided to take Tiekoro under his wing, to help him with his studies so that he wouldn't lose heart. Was not this a way to join Allah in His holy house? All night the thought of this task filled him with excitement, and in the morning, when Tiekoro had performed his ablutions and his first prayer, he found Mulay Abdallah waiting for him in the courtyard.

"Our master wants to see you," he said, smiling kindly. "I haven't any lessons this morning, and if you like I'll show you around the city afterwards."

Tiekoro accepted eagerly, and went inside the house. He was overwhelmed by what he saw. In Segu the huts were empty but for mats, stools, and *canaris*, earthenware jars to hold drinking water. Here the floors were entirely covered with carpets. But what struck Tiekoro most of all were the hangings on the walls. One was embroidered alternately with silk and gold, with an elegant floral pattern in between. Another had flowery stars against a turquoise blue silk background. El-Hadj Baba Abou himself was sitting on a low divan covered with a thick white rug; his caftan and his heelless slippers were also white. He held a book in his fine ivory-colored hands, which were slightly paler than his face with its silky, parted beard. He signaled to Tiekoro to sit down in front of him.

"There are certain things we didn't discuss yesterday," he said. "It's clear your knowledge of Arabic and theology is not sufficient for you to enter the university right away. So you will attend my Koranic school, and Mulay Abdallah, one of your fellow pupils, has offered to help you privately. By the way, how do you propose to pay your fees?"

"I've got fifty gold *mithkal* . . . ," stammered Tiekoro.

El-Hadj Baba looked astonished.

"Where is it?" he said.

Tiekoro dived into his robe and brought out a little goatskin pouch.

"My father gave me this before I left. He was afraid—they say these things happen—that some Moors might carry my brother and me off into slavery in Barbary. If that had happened we could have purchased our freedom."

For the first time a smile lit up the teacher's austere countenance, and he seized the pouch. At that moment a girl came into the room. Her complexion was even paler than El-Hadj Baba's; she had long black hair worn in braids and half hidden beneath a red scarf; around her neck hung numerous necklaces of old silver; she had square earrings, and in her left nostril a little ring. To Tiekoro she seemed a supernatural apparation. El-Hadj Baba seemed annoyed by the intrusion, and above all by Tiekoro's frank looks of admiration. He told the girl roughly to go away, then, feeling he had been discourteous, muttered, as she paused in the doorway: "My daughter Ayisha . . . Oumar, a new pupil . . ."

Oumar? Tiekoro didn't protest, and as the interview was over he stood up. El-Hadj Baba was definitely more kindly disposed now.

"Get someone to take you to my tailor and my shoemaker," he said. "You're dressed like a heathen."

At fifteen and a half, Tiekoro was not much more than a child, and a good night's sleep, a new friend and the prospect of new clothes were enough to make him happy. When they were in the street, Mulay Abdallah took his arm and began to talk to him in the slightly affected manner that seemed customary here.

"Now I'll tell you about the city where you're going to spend some years," he said. "The people of Timbuktu are as chauvinistic as anyone can be. They hate everybody. The Tuareg to begin with—they call them a race deserted by God; the Moroccans; the Bambara; the Fulani—especially the Fulani. Did you know that Muhammad Aq-it, the ancestor of the Aq-it clan, left Macina because he was afraid his children might mix with the Fulani and some of his descendants might be sullied with their blood?"

Although some of these remarks irritated his Bambara pride, Tiekoro paid little attention to them. He was mainly taken by the way his companion expressed himself. One day he too would speak with such assurance, elegance and ease.

"You know the story of the city, don't you?" The other went on: "A Tuareg camp was left in charge of a woman called 'Tomboutou,' which means 'mother with the big navel.' Gradually the place became a caravan halt, and it grew and grew inside its wall of matting made from the leaves of desert palms. It was conquered by Kankan Musa after his pilgrimage to Mecca. Then recaptured by the Tuareg. Then Sonni Ali Ber of Songhay took it from them. Then came the Moroccans. This city's like a woman, fought over by men but belonging to no one. And look how beautiful it is!"

Tiekoro looked but he was forced to conclude that Segu was both more beautiful and more lively. When they came to the great mosque of Jinguereber he saw the first building that had impressed him so far. Made of *banco* bricks and gray as the earth in the desert, its countless balconies gave a first impression of confusion and disorder, though in fact they formed a harmonious whole. They were all supported on pillars and looked out over a square courtyard in which a number of old men were saying their prayers. Tiekoro admired the truncated pyramids that were the minaret towers, and their triangular decoration. The work that must have gone into this building to the glory of God! Tiekoro kept walking around it, then went in under the high vaulting to the wooden platform, in a niche, where the marabout read out verses from the Koran. Mulay Abdallah had to drag him away.

Timbuktu was not surrounded by walls, so the eye could see the outlying area where the slaves and the transient population lived in straw huts. What a contrast there was between these wretched dwellings and those of the Arma, current masters of the city, or the residences of the merchants!

The boys went into a market where a multitude of goods were for sale: strips of cotton, hides dyed red and yellow, pestles and mortars, cushions, carpets, matting, and everywhere boots of fine red leather decorated with yellow embroidery. Yes, the Bambara capital was boisterous and merry, like a child who thinks the best part of his life is still to come. But Timbuktu was seductive, like a woman of much and dubious experience.

In the shop of El-Hadj Baba Abou's tailor nine workmen plied their needles on blue and white stuff being made up into caftans, while some old men intoned verses from the Koran. Tiekoro was fascinated by the fineness of the embroidery they were producing; there was nothing like it in Segu. The way of life now being revealed to him had an elegance which derived partly from distant peoples which Tiekoro's own nation had never encountered, in countries like Morocco, Egypt and Spain.

After they had ordered a pair of trousers and two caftans the boys resumed their tour, this time making for the port. But their way was barred by a string of heavily laden donkeys, whacked along by four boys with cudgels who seemed to be enjoying themselves immensely. Tiekoro's eyes met those of one of the boys, and in a silence that gripped his whole being, so that he could count his every heartbeat, he recognized Siga. Siga had shaved his head but he still wore the ring in his left ear, and this lent him a rather swashbuckling air that was completely new. The wide V-shaped opening of his tunic showed his neck, straight and smooth as the trunk of a young tree. Perhaps for the first time, Tiekoro noticed how much he resembled his father. It was as if Dousika, twenty years younger, were gazing at him and silently asking, "What have you done with your brother?"

Siga stood still and speechless, as if waiting for a gesture or a sign. But Mulay Abdallah had taken Tiekoro's arm again. Could he free himself and rush over and declare his relationship to someone in so humiliating a position? Could he expose himself to what this time would be justifiable mockery? At that moment one of the donkey boys called out, not angrily, but on the contrary with good humor: "What's the matter, Ahmed? Seen a djinn?"

Siga turned and ran after the other boy, waving his cudgel over his head as if in farewell to his brother. Oumar? Ahmed? Tiekoro's eyes filled with tears; he had to choke back sobs. Meanwhile Mulay Abdallah was saying, as he led him along: "Did you see the lovely Ayisha when you went in to see our teacher this morning? I bet she only came to have a good look at you. But watch out for her! She's made us all fall in love with her one after the other, but in the end she only makes fun of us."

C H A P T E R

6

Nya's sorrow after her eldest son's departure was painful to see. In order to be with him in spirit and avert the dangers he might encounter in the unknown heathen country he had gone to, she invited numerous fetish priests to the compound. Some of these only sacrificed chickens to appease the family *boli*, especially that of Tiekoro himself, which Nya kept in the entrance to her hut, surrounded by corn cobs and gourds full of milk. Others threw cowries and kola nuts into the air from morn till night, noting the patterns they made when they fell.

But people were secretly critical of Nya. After all, she had nine children, five of them sons. Why should she lose her head just because one of them had gone away? What would she have done if it had been death that had taken him away—if, like an unripe fruit falling before a fruit that is ripe, he had departed this life before her? Didn't she still have a hut full of laughter, little round heads and affectionate squabbles?

Nya knew perfectly well what those about her were thinking, and that her behavior might seem unreasonable. But others didn't understand what Tiekoro meant to her. He wasn't merely her firstborn—he was a sign, a reminder of the love that had once been between her and Dousika. She had conceived him on her wedding night.

Her family lived in Farako, on the other side of the river.

When the Diarra usurped the throne it was no longer safe for the Kulibaly to remain within the walls of Segu, so her grandfather and his brothers had gathered together their wives, children, slaves and captives and gone to settle on other lands belonging to their clan which, after lying fallow for years, were now covered with *tiekala*, plants that showed the earth was ready for sowing again. It was there that Bouba Kale, Dousika's father's griot, came to see Nya's father. At first the latter hesitated, because of the special links between the Diarra and the Traore. Then, thinking of all that land, all that gold, and all those slaves, he had allowed himself to be persuaded. In accordance with tradition, Nya never saw Dousika until the marriage, not even until she was actually taken into his hut. It was at night. Her mother had told her the fetish priests were sure it would be a good and fruitful marriage, but still she was afraid. Afraid of the stranger who would suddenly have power of life and death over her, who would own her as he owned his fields of millet. Then Dousika had come in. She'd heard his footsteps as he hesitated in the entrance, then there he was beside her, lighting his way with a burning branch. All she could see was his face, but that wore a shy, embarrassed smile that emphasized the gentleness of his expression. Nya instinctively gave thanks to the gods for his being handsome and not a swaggerer.

He sat down beside her. She turned her head away. For a few moments they couldn't think of anything to say to each other, then suddenly the almost-burned-out branch scorched his fingers and he gave a little yell of pain. Afterwards she tried in vain to remember the instructions given her by her mother's sisters: no crying out, no unseemly moans. Pleasure, like pain, should be suffered in silence. Had she obeyed instructions?

The next morning the priestesses responsible for seeing that the marriage was properly consummated and the bride a virgin had displayed the cotton *pagne* stained with fresh blood. Nine months later to the day, Tiekoro was born. And so, every time he stood before her, she relived that night—that flood of emotion, of unknown and uncontrollable sensations, the dizziness, the peace, the pain. Yes, she had conceived nine times, given birth nine times, but that first experience was all that mattered!

Forgetting that it was Tiekoro himself who had asked to go,

Nya held Dousika responsible, and this added to her resentment. Not only did he humiliate her by flaunting his love for a concubine, he also had separated her from her favorite son. She was glad his quarrel with the Mansa had made him old, gloomy, silent, as if mortally stunned. Every so often her love for him would get the upper hand, but then she would see him looking at Sira as he had once looked at herself, and her grudge would reawaken.

Yet Nya's sorrow over Tiekoro's departure was not as great as Naba's. He had grown up in his elder brother's shadow, learning to walk by holding on to his legs, learning to fight by thumping his chest, learning to dance by watching him perform in the evening amid a circle of admiring girls. Tiekoro's absence made Naba a kind of orphan; he had the sense of injustice people feel when someone dear to them dies. To fill the gap left by Tiekoro, Naba made friends with Tiefolo, the eldest son of Diemogo, Dousika's younger brother.

Despite his youth Tiefolo was one of the best known hunters in Segu and the surrounding region. People had heard of him as far away as Banankoro in the north and Sidabugu in the south. When he was ten years old he had disappeared into the bush. His parents gave him up for dead, and his mother was already mourning him when he reappeared with a lion skin slung over his shoulders. Then Kemenani, the great Gow* master hunter, took the boy under his wing, and not only taught him the secret of the poisonous plants which paralyze wild animals and prevent their escape, but also shared with him his own personal *boli*, which he fed antelope hearts. He revealed to Tiefolo the prayers, incantations and sacrifices that make a man emerge victorious from all his encounters with animals. At first Naba felt some repugnance about hunting, for Tiekoro had passed on to him a horror of bloodshed. Then he got caught up in it, though even now, whenever his quarry fell to its knees before its final collapse, giving its tormentor a look of utter incomprehension, a chill still went down his spine. Then he rushed toward the animal and passionately whispered into its ear the ritual phrases designed to win him forgiveness.

He found Tiefolo busy preparing a poison, cooking over a low

* An ethnic group of hunters, holding sway over the uncultivated bush.

fire a mixture of poisonous *ouabaine*, snakes' heads, scorpions' tails, menstrual blood and a substance he obtained from the sap of the palmyra. Naba took care not to disturb him, for the incantations he was muttering made the brew more deadly. Like all hunters, Tiefolo went nearly naked, his body covered with gris-gris, his only garment a loincloth made from the skins of the animals he had killed. He had fashioned the mane of the lion he killed when he was ten into a kind of belt, fastened over the hips. His preparations complete, he began carefully smearing his arrows with the poison, and beckoned Naba over.

"Some lions have eaten part of the herd belonging to the Fulani near Masala," he said. "We'll have to go and teach them a lesson—the Fulani themselves haven't been able to do anything."

Naba thought he must have misunderstood, then the truth dawned on him.

"Do you mean you're going to take me with you?" he asked incredulously.

Tiefolo merely smiled by way of reply. He'd often taken Naba with him hunting antelope, warthogs and wild buffalo. But lion hunting, the pursuit of the prince of the bare savannah, whose coat was as tawny, whose eyes as burning as the plain itself, that was something only for the Gow masters and their pupils the *karamoko*. No place here for the fainthearted! It took endurance to follow the lion, sometimes for days on end; it took cunning to outwit him: and what valor to refrain from flight in disorder when his roars thundered into your very depths! The earth trembled, then, and clouds of dust rose up! The terrified villagers barricaded themselves in their huts as best they could. And the lion cried out, "Beware—the prince is hungry!"

Naba couldn't contain his impatience.

"When do we leave?" he stammered.

"Not just yet, little brother," said Tiefolo. "We must get ready first. Come, we'll go and see Kemenani, the master hunter."

Tiefolo was handsome, Tiefolo was brave, and to walk beside him through the streets of Segu was to taste the pleasure of conquerors: the *tondyons*, back with their booty after sacking a city, enjoyed no greater respect. The women came to their doors, the men called out greetings, and the griots beat their drums and sang his praises, recalling especially the famous exploit of his childhood, when he slew a lion with a bow.

> *The yellow lion with tawny glints,*
> *The lion forsakes the flocks of men*
> *And feeds on that which lives in liberty.*
> *Face to face with him, Tiefolo of Segu*
> *At the height of the hunt was still a boy.*
> *Tiefolo Traore . . .*

All this adulation went to Naba's head. Now it was meant for another, but soon it would be for him. He too would come back victorious from the bush with a lion over his shoulders. He'd be called a *karamoko*, and throw down his lion in the main court-yard of the Mansa's palace to remind the man who humiliated his father of Dousika's progeny. He dreamed of the day when he would go with Tiefolo and present himself to the grand masters of the hunters' brotherhood with ten red kola nuts, two cockerels, a hen and some *dolo* as offerings to Sanene and Kontoro, the spirits of the hunt. Yes, one day the people of Segu would talk about him.

Kemenani was a direct descendant of Kourouyore, ancestor of the Gows. In the courtyards of his compound all the master hunters from every corner of the kingdom were gathered together, for attacks by lions were getting more and more frequent; some-times the beasts were bold enough to tear a herdsman to pieces. Slaves served the hunters with bowls of millet porridge as they waited for the results of the sacrifices. Kemenani had spent the night conferring with the chief priests, especially Koumare, who'd said the hunt would not be successful. The spirits of the bush were angry and might show their wrath by striking someone down. So everyone was waiting. Tiefolo shrugged. The hunt would not be successful—what did that mean?

He sat down sulkily in a corner with Naba and a few other young equally impatient hunters. Some of them were *karamoko* like himself, who'd already killed fur as well as feather. One of them, Masakoulou, was Samake's eldest son.

"Koumare, always Koumare," he said angrily. "If you listen to only one voice you hear only one opinion. Why don't they ask another fetish priest?"

"I agree," said Tiefolo with a sigh. "Unfortunately no one ever asks us what we think."

This was a feeling the young men rarely expressed, accustomed as they were to absolute obedience. But a breath of rebellion was wafting over them, surprising even themselves.

"What about Fane?" Masakoulou went on. "He's a master of the Komo, too."

There was a silence. Then all the youths looked at each other as if Masakoulou's words had produced the same effect upon them all. It was Tiefolo who spoke first.

"Can you take us to him?" he asked.

The middle of the day is the time when the bush lives most intensely. One would think that after having borne so much of the heat of the sun it would begin to be drowsy. Instead, every blade of grass, every insect that it hides, every shrub, every animal calls to the others, and the seemingly still air throbs with a multitude of cries. That is why, for man, this is the time for mirages and hallucinations, the most difficult time of the day.

The group of young men, led by Tiefolo and Masakoulou, had been walking since morning, for Tiefolo, who had automatically become head of the expedition, thought they should reach Sorotomo that night so as to be in the Masala region early the next day. They followed the course of the river, almost walking along its bed. Here the vegetation was dense, with enormous grasses, silk cotton trees, bastard mahoganies, and of course balanzas and shea trees. There was no one to be seen, not a woman crouching at the water's edge, not a Somono fisherman in his boat, nor a Bozo hut made out of a mosaic of woven mats. The heat was like a hot bandage clamped over one's mouth. Masakoulou suddenly halted.

"I'm hungry," he said. "Shall we have something to eat?"

Without waiting for an answer he sat down and took some provisions out of a goatskin bag. All the others followed his lead, Naba among the first.

Tiefolo was vexed.

"Let's press on to Konodimini," he said. "We can get some

food there—it'll be better to keep our own stuff until tomorrow, which is going to be difficult."

Masakoulou took a bite of dried fish.

"Don't think you can give us all orders, Tiefolo," he said, "just because you once killed a sick lion. Admit it now—it was sick, wasn't it? Lame?"

Everyone laughed, even Naba. It was the sort of joke youths of the same age always exchange, but Tiefolo thought he saw a gleam in Masakoulou's expression that reflected a real desire to hurt. What irritated him even more was that Masakoulou seemed to be taking Naba under his wing, showing him a familiarity that was bound to go to the boy's head. What was his game? Tiefolo was annoyed with himself for disregarding the hatred that existed between the Samakes and the Traore family. It had occurred to him, but he'd set it aside: must sons always perpetuate the quarrels of their fathers? Now he tried to calm down, walking away, taking off the cord around his waist, and going toward the water. As he did so, Masakoulou's mocking voice was heard again.

"I've seen bigger!"

Hoots of laughter. It was too much. Tiefolo retraced his steps and in one bound he was on Masakoulou. With one hand he seized him by the throat, while with the other he punched him in the face, over and over again.

It was a terrible fight. At first the other boys merely gathered around, urging the combatants on in the usual way. But when they saw the turn things were taking and the vicious blows each was receiving they decided to intervene. They had some difficulty in separating the two.

"Just as my father told me!" yelled Masakoulou, his face all bloody. "Wherever there's a Traore there's no peace or friendship. They always have to lord it over everyone else!"

The other boys were inclined to agree. Why had Tiefolo reacted so violently to a harmless joke? Did he think his penis was as big as an elephant's, or as that of a buffalo in the river Bagoe? But all that mattered now was to reconcile the two adversaries so that the expedition wasn't spoiled. The boys whispered among themselves.

"Let's make them make a blood pact!"

"They never will!"

The group somehow resumed its journey. Their path now lay away from the river and over a hard surface seamed here and there with fissures through which a hot vapor arose burning their ankles. They thought they saw the straw huts and shelters of some Fulani nomads, but it was only the effect of the heat. Great black birds swooped low on invisible prey. Three snakes slithered right in front of the boy who was leading the way—Tiefolo now lagged behind to demonstrate his aloofness. Suddenly a herd of oxen appeared, accompanied by some herdsmen in leather aprons and funnel hats, who looked very frightened. Yes, they had heard about the lions, but they had also heard about some men who burned villages, raped and killed the women and took away the men.

Where?

The Fulani herdsmen didn't know. The young hunters looked at one another in confusion. They were all thinking the same thing, though no one dared to utter it. Should they go on? Or should they go back to Segu? In such hours of indecision every group needs a leader. Tiefolo was standing aside, chewing some straws, apparently deep in contemplation of the hides of the oxen. All eyes turned anxiously toward him. For a moment he bore their gaze with a kind of arrogance, then without a word walked around the others and resumed the lead. In the end they reached Sorotomo.

What matchless music there was in the sound of the pestles and mortars, in the voices of girls urging one another on in their work, in the laughter of the children waiting for the moon to rise before they went to sleep! Sorotomo seemed to welcome them, with its peaceful herd of huts gathered around the balanza in its midst. The men there were just holding a council. The chief greeted the young hunters courteously, but he was visibly gripped by fear. Yes, he had heard of the lions eating the cattle. But it wasn't because of them that he was preparing to send a delegation to the Mansa. There were men who were attacking the villages, setting fire to the huts, killing the women and children and carrying off the men. Men? What race did they belong to? Where did they come from? Did they know what sort of people they would have to deal with? Segu had reduced all its enemies, and controlled the whole region. It crushed all attempts at revolt among the Fulani in Macina. It terrified the Bambara in Kaarta. Who could these strangers be? The villagers didn't know. The dead hadn't been able to say, nor had the captives. But the bowls of *to* served with a sauce made from baobab and sibala leaves appeased the travelers' hunger and, for a while, their anxiety. In the rest hut put at their disposal by the chief, they all went to sleep. All except Tiefolo.

When he went over the events of the last few days in his mind it seemed to him that someone else had been inside his skin and head, acting and speaking in his stead. Never before in his life had he disobeyed someone older than himself. And what had he done now but cast doubt on the opinions of Kemenani, a great master hunter, and of Koumare, a great master of Komo? His audacity terrified him. What spirit could have possessed him, and why? And he'd dragged someone younger than himself with him! There was only one thing to do: go back to Segu. He got up, stepped carefully over the sleeping forms of his companions, and went over to where Masakoulou slept on a mat by the door.

"Masakoulou, wake up!" he whispered.

The two boys went out of the hut. The only sounds were the breathing of the spirits, moving freely at last in the world whose loss they still mourned, and the silky flapping of the bats. Tiefolo tried to stifle his fears.

"Listen," he breathed. "We must go back to Segu. We'll have to persuade the others . . ."

Masakoulou fell back a step. In the darkness he looked huge, with a face as distorted as if it wore a mask, and haunted by some unknown spirit. When he spoke, even his voice was different: cold, dry, brittle as sticks in a fire.

"Do you know my name?" he asked. "Do you know what Samake means? It means elephant man, child and son of the elephant. And you come and talk to me about retreat? It's true— you're a son of a bastard."

It was so great an insult that Masakoulou couldn't have uttered it unless he, like Tiefolo, was not himself. Someone else was in his skin, thinking, acting and speaking in his stead. Tiefolo reflected. Had one of them performed the sexual act before they set off? Or offended the ancestors who protected hunters by doing something even worse? No, some spirit was playing with them.

But why? Tiefolo tried to recall some ritual phrase to undo the spell, but was too disturbed to think of anything.

Misfortune is like a child in its mother's womb: nothing can stop it being born. It grows invisibly stronger and stronger; its network of veins and arteries develops. Then one day it appears, in a deluge of uncleanness, water and blood.

CHAPTER

7

In Segu, no one noticed the disappearance of the young hunters at first. Then, the next day, their families realized, one after another, that they hadn't slept in their huts. It was as if a storm of amazement and grief had broken over the city. Young people disobeying their elders! Men defying the warnings of spirits! No Segukaw alive could remember such a thing. It paralleled the audacity of Tiekoro Traore, deliberately turning his back on the gods of his ancestors and embracing Islam.

In all the public places, markets and compounds, even in the Mansa's palace, people discussed it. Did it mean that all the younger generation was dangerous? Every father looked his son in the eye, every mother scrutinized her daughter. Were these lithe, graceful creatures, hitherto ready to bend the knee, lower their eyes, obey and be silent, henceforward going to be sources of contradiction and peril? When the family fetish priests were consulted on the subject they said that indeed this was about to happen.

At daybreak Fane left his compound in the quarter of the fetish priests, though it was not wise to walk the streets of Segu before sunrise. The walls of clay remembered the fears of the night: they were dark, slimy, and exuded an unhealthy damp. There was no living creature about: the spirits were returning to the lower world, and the humans were waiting for the sun to appear. But Fane liked this time of day, when it was possible to mold men's minds. He entered Samake's compound, crouched down beside his hut, and then, sticking a millet stalk into the ground, silently called him. Samake appeared at once, his face drawn, for he had lain awake all night worrying about his son Masakoulou.

"Fane," he muttered angrily, "I pay you all that gold and all those cowries, and then you let a misfortune like this happen to me!"

Fane shrugged. How little trust men have!

"Nothing will happen to your son—he'll come back safe and sound, and so will all the others. All except Dousika's son. That's what I came to tell you."

"Are you sure?" breathed Samake.

Fane scorned to reply to this.

"The day before yesterday," he went on, "the young men came and consulted me, but they won't remember anything about it, because I sowed forgetfulness in their minds. And now you must lead an expedition and go in search of them. You will find them in the Kangaba region, and the tracks of the gazelle will lead you there."

Samake hurried off, reassured and yet uneasy still. He went to Dousika's compound, which despite the early hour was full of sympathizers. Neighbors, friends and distant relations had all rallied around to support the stricken family. First Dousika's downfall, then Tiekoro's conversion, and now the disappearance of Naba and Tiefolo! At the same time, despite the shock occasioned by all these misfortunes, people were beginning to wonder whether they weren't deserved. For there isn't such a thing as an innocent victim. Some whispered that it was all because of Sira: Dousika ought not to have brought a Fulani into his house.

When Samake entered, everyone fell silent. Then, obedient to the laws of courtesy, Dousika came forward to greet his enemy. Samake took him by the shoulders.

"Brother," he said, "misfortune brings us together. I am going to lead an expedition to find our children. Are you coming with us?"

Diemogo, Dousika's younger brother and Tiefolo's father, intervened.

"Don't you take any risks," he said. "I'll go."

And, as Dousika, not Diemogo was the *fa*, and responsible for the smooth running of the whole compound, all the rest of the family begged the elder brother to accept his offer.

Already some forty horsemen were gathered outside the Mansa's palace, among them Prince Bin, the Mansa's own son. For once some *tondyons* had joined the peaceful expedition, and this array of horses and riders, hunters and fetish priests, delighted the children, all unconscious of the situation's tragic undertones. They nipped in and out among the horses' hooves and dung, stroking their black or brown coats. Samake took his place at the head of the line, and the whole cavalcade galloped off to the northern gate of the city.

When they had disappeared and the clouds of dust settled down again behind them, Dousika was overcome by a sense of complete helplessness. If only he'd been able to jump on a horse and go and snatch his son from the bush! But no—too many responsibilities kept him tied to the compound. What would become of his three wives, his concubine and his twenty or so children if he should die?

Nya, so strong, the center of his own life.

Seeing her brokenhearted and weeping, he had felt the foundations of that life crumbling. What was the use of making every possible sacrifice if the ancestors remained unmoved? If the gods carried off his legitimate sons one after the other? Dousika took fright at the thought of these rebellious feelings within him, and started to make his way home. Then at a street corner he came upon Sira leading Malobali, who had already learned to walk, by the hand.

He stopped her and asked where she was going.

"To the market," she said. "I heard some Hausa merchants had brought some amber necklaces."

He stared at her, appalled.

"You can think of amber necklaces at a time like this?" he asked.

Instead of answering she detached the little boy, who had been clinging to his father's legs, and turned away. Dousika held her back. Never in his life had he ill treated a woman, not even by so much as a slap delivered in anger. But this was too much. The whole family was afflicted and lamenting Naba's disappearance, and all she cared about was finery. As she stared at him with a kind of insolence, he lost patience and hit her. She stood there without flinching. The shock had made her bite her lip, which began to stream with blood. Dousika was suddenly ashamed, and walked away.

Sira had left the compound precisely to try to maintain her attitude as a captive who remained untamed, indifferent, almost hostile, throwing off her fortuitous surroundings like an old rag. For what affected those around her affected her too. Especially Nya's grief. Was transplanting someone by force enough to make her forget her real home? Did human beings put down roots more easily than plants? Sira wiped her mouth with a corner of her *pagne.* Then she hoisted Malobali onto her back and went on along the path beside the river. Beyond its deceptively peaceful bluish waters, beyond the savannah, lay Macina, her own country. But the phrase meant nothing. Segu was her country now.

There were plenty of Fulani in the city, especially those who looked after the royal livestock. But Sira had always despised them, as people who enjoyed their own subjugation. But was she really any different from them?

Sira sometimes thought of running away. After all, her family would not reject her. But what should she do with Malobali? Take him with her? How would he be treated, as partial offspring of a race both feared and scorned? Might he not be an outcast? On the other hand, if he was made welcome and turned into a Fulani, wouldn't he spontaneously turn back to his father, Segu, and the fascinating, barbaric Bambara builders? So what if she left him behind? She knew Nya would immediately take him to her own breast, but Sira couldn't bear the thought of that. Malobali was such a fine child you couldn't look at him without uttering the ritual phrases designed to avert envy and jealousy. At this moment he was walking in front of her, tottering, tumbling, and picking himself up again determinedly and without tears, as if practicing to conquer the universe. Through her love for him, Sira could understand Nya's grief. To lose two children, one after the other!

But after all, neither Tiekoro nor Naba was really lost. The first would come home full of the prestige of his new religion. The second would be found and temporarily excluded from the hunters' brotherhood as a punishment for his incredible diso-bedience. Then everything would return to normal.

Meanwhile Samake and his companions were going as fast as they could to Masala. Astonished villagers scarcely had time to emerge from their huts to watch them ride by. The warriors wondered if war had broken out again, and almost began to re-joice. But the captives trembled. Were they going to be sold again in exchange for arms? If so, into whose hands would they fall? They had finally grown accustomed to the villages where they'd been sent to live.

Demba, another of the Mansa's sons, lived in Masala, and he received the newcomers with princely courtesy and complaints about the young hunters' behavior toward himself. Instead of presenting themselves before him as they ought, they had made a detour around his village and consorted instead with the "public Fulani" who kept Demba's huge herds. No doubt they had been afraid that Demba, who was familiar with Segu society, would be surprised that neither Kemenani nor any of the other great Gow master hunters was with them, and then press them with questions, discover what they were up to, and hold them back by force.

Demba provided the riders with fresh and mettlesome horses, and the expedition went on its way toward the region of Kiranga. Some peasants had set fire to the bush, and the earth was scarred with great black patches. Buffalo wallowing in a muddy pool turned hostile eyes toward the travelers beneath the heavy hel-met of their horns. Herdsmen tried to collect their charges to-gether after they'd been frightened by the horses. At last the riders came to a parting of the ways. Which path should they take? Samake, remembering what Fane had said, dismounted and began to inspect the ground, and on a bank he found some little round holes full of water, as if it had rained the previous day. Yet it was the middle of the dry season. "The tracks of the gazelle."

The tracks remained visible for several hours and the riders thought they would never finish galloping through the bush. As they went ever further south they realized they must be getting nearer and nearer to the frontiers of the empire. All at once they came to the banks of a river. What was it? The Bani, a tributary of the Joliba? Crowned cranes were pacing up and down the pebble strand, looking simultaneously haughty and vexed. At the sight of these holy birds, the sources of language, everyone dismounted, and the griots recited some verses.

> Hail, crowned crane,
> Mighty crowned crane,
> Bird of the word,
> Bird of beauty,
> Speech is your part in creation.

Then suddenly a herd of gazelles leapt out of a thicket, swerved in front of the horses as if in defiance, then all flew off in a new direction. Again the men mounted and flew after them. Again the pursuit lasted for hours. The sun began to go down and the riders, Samake included, began to wonder whether, despite Fane's assurances, the gods were not playing one of their tricks on them. At last they saw the straw roofs of a village.

But how silent it was!

The horses' hooves echoed like war drums on the dry sand. It was a village inhabited by captives, to judge from all the carefully cultivated fields of cotton and millet surrounding it. But where were all the people? A herd of wild boar ran snorting and snuffling across the path.

It was in the last of the huts that they found the young hunters, seemingly fast asleep, but thin, emaciated. They were all there except Naba. For the rest of his life Diemogo was to reproach himself for the selfish joy that flooded through him as he recognized his own son. Like all the other boys, Tiefolo was almost unrecognizable, like someone who has suffered a long illness, with yellow pus in the corners of his eyes. But he was alive. After a moment, thanks to the fetish priests, the boys opened their eyes and were able to hear the older men's questions. But they could not answer them. It was as if they had been stricken with a kind of amnesia. What had happened since they left Segu nearly a week ago? Where had they been? What had they said? What had become of Naba?

The older men inwardly accepted fate's decree. The young hunters had sinned, and the gods had chosen a victim to expiate the wrong. There was nothing anyone could do about it. It was just a matter of form that they decided to scour the bush in search of the missing boy. As night had fallen they lit dry branches, which made the frightened horses whinny and gallop off in all directions. Some of the men would have preferred to wait till dawn, for night belongs to the spirits and it is unwise for human beings to disturb their councils with shouts and cries and the sound of horses' hooves. But Samake and Diemogo insisted.

It is impossible to describe Tiefolo's state of mind when he became fully conscious again and realized Naba had disappeared. At first he was just stunned, then he was overwhelmed with guilt. Then he got up and had to be prevented, first from leaping onto a horse, then from dashing his head against a tree. But he hadn't the strength, and one of the priests hastily prepared a potion to make him sleep. Toward the middle of the night Samake, Diemogo and the rest of the expedition returned. Empty-handed. They decided to rest a little and resume the search at sunrise.

As a matter of fact it wasn't unusual for some disaster to happen in the course of a hunting expedition. It was a "bloody trade" that demanded victims. Sometimes the most celebrated *karamoko* were conquered by an animal's spirit and killed as they tried to kill it. But there was something strange and supernatural about Naba's disappearance, and the fetish priests who had accompanied the party read on their divining boards the signs of an irrevocable fate which they could not understand. Could some Traore have killed a black monkey, a dog-faced baboon or a crowned crane, thus breaking his totemic taboo? No, that was impossible! Then why had the gods been so angry?

Just before dawn the inhabitants of the village reappeared. They were indeed royal captives, as could be seen from their shaven heads and the three slashes they bore on either temple. They had been hiding in the bush, having heard of groups of Markas raiding for slaves in the area. Was that a sign of the fate which had befallen Naba? Samake and Diemogo sent men from their escorts off to inspect the markets in the trading cities of Nyamina, Sinsanin, Busen and Nyaro. No stone was left unturned.

Strangely enough, now that Samake, who out of envy and meanness had been the chief cause of Dousika's downfall, could see his vengeance taking its ultimate toll, instead of enjoying the situation he was appalled by it. Like many criminals contemplating their crime, he could hardly prevent himself from crying out: "Oh, no—this is not what I meant!"

He found himself asking a sacrilegious question. Were the gods and the ancestors sadistic? Cruel? By more than fulfilling wishes expressed in moments of jealousy or anger, did they amuse themselves by mortifying both the persecutor and the victim? Did they take pleasure in reversing the roles, mixing them up, causing sorrow, unease, anguish and despair on both sides? None of the others could understand Samake's grief or the desperation with which he searched for Naba. Wasn't he Dousika's enemy? As they refreshed themselves with to supplied by the village women, the rest of the expedition murmured among themselves.

"Shouldn't we go back to Segu now? Dousika's very rich— he can pay some tondyons to look for his son and some priests to tell him where he is. There's nothing more we can do. Samake's tiring us out for nothing."

Finally Prince Bin who, young as he was, enjoyed great authority as the Mansa's son, spoke for all the rest, and they started back to Segu.

Meanwhile Naba was not far off—scarcely a few hours' march away.

A dozen or so "mad dogs in the bush"—kidnappers—had taken him captive when he'd strayed from his companions. The "mad dogs" were not Markas, as the villagers had suggested, but Bambara tondyons from Dakala, forced to make a living in this manner by the relative peace reigning now in this part of the country. Usually they preferred to snatch children, as they were easily frightened and could without difficulty be hidden in a large sack, to be carried to a slave market and sold for a small fortune. Naba, at nearly sixteen, was already too big for such methods.

But he was there, and defenseless, having put down his bow

and arrows. He was just approaching the age much prized by the slave traders, and clearly well fed and groomed. The temptation was too much for them.

And now they were riding to the village of a Marka go-between. They had to put themselves out of reach of the Mansa's justice, for such crimes against any of his subjects were punishable by death. They had knocked Naba out, bound him firmly hand and foot, wrapped him in a blanket, and slung him across one of their mounts.

When he regained consciousness he found himself in a hut where the doorway was blocked with tree trunks. He could tell from the color of the light filtering in between them that it would soon be day. Sleeping on the ground beside him were three children between six and eight years old, bound as he was.

Until lately Dousika's compound had been for Naba, as for the other children in the family, a comfortable universe deaf to all rumors from the outside world, rumors of war, captivity and the slave trade. Sometimes a grown-up would refer to such things, but the children paid much more attention to the adventures of Souroukou the hyena, Badeni the camel and Diarra the lion told around the fire in the evening. The first breach in this wall of happiness had been made by Tiekoro's conversion to Islam, and by his going away. And now, suddenly, Naba was face to face with fear, horror, blind evil. He had often seen captives in the courtyards of his father's compound or in the Mansa's palace, but he had never paid any attention. He had never pitied them, because they belonged to a vanquished race and one that was not his own. Was he now going to meet the same fate? Was he too going to be stripped of his identity, and given over into the power of a master, to farm his land and be universally despised? He tried to sit up but his bonds prevented him. Then he began to cry, like the child he still was.

Then a young boy came in carrying a large bowl of porridge. Naba turned toward him as best he could.

"Help me to get out of here," he called. "My father's very rich. He'll give you anything you like if you take me back to him."

The boy sat on the ground. He was a puny, unhealthy-looking little fellow, his body covered with the marks of blows.

"If your father owned all the gold in Bambuk I couldn't help you," he said. "I myself was captured when I was no bigger than these children here. My name's Allahina."

"Are you a Muslim?"

"My master is. He's very rich. He sells slaves in several markets, and supplies the white men's representatives directly. I've heard him say he's going to sell you to them because you're so good-looking."

Naba thought he would faint. Allahina, with a sort of kindness, thrust a spoonful of gruel between his lips.

"Come on, eat something," he said. "If you try to starve yourself to death they'll beat you unmercifully."

The other children were now waking up and calling for their mothers in the various languages. In their villages they had heard of the child-snatchers who took their little victims far away, and they were starting to wonder if they would ever see their homes again.

Allahina got up and fed them as gently as he had Naba.

"What will they do with them?" asked Naba.

"They're the best catch of all," said Allahina sardonically. "They soon forget where they come from, they get fond of their master's family, and so they never revolt."

When he heard this, Naba wept more bitterly still, overwhelmed by the wickedness of a practice he had never thought about before. What reason could there be for parting children from their mothers, men and women from their homes and fellow countrymen? What did those who did it get in return? Material wealth? Was that enough to purchase human souls?

At this point four men set aside the tree trunks blocking the door and entered the hut. Two of them were Bambara, the other two foreigners with very little knowledge of that language. It was the latter pair who came over to Naba, crouched down beside him and examined him as if he were a horse or a heifer for sale in a market. One even went so far as to weigh his penis in his hand, laughing and exchanging incomprehensible words with his companion. Then he spoke to Naba. "The white men like that," he said. "Big *foro** . . . they play with it themselves."

---

* Bambara word for male sexual organ.

And all four roared with laughter. Then the two foreigners pulled Naba roughly to his feet, put a sort of cowl over his head and took him out of the hut. The air was still cool and smelled of wood smoke. Naba could hear the sound of women's voices as they set about their first tasks of the day, the laughter and weeping of children, the braying of an ass. All harmless, familiar sounds, as if his life had not just been turned upside down, as if he were not shipwrecked there alone. No helping hand was stretched out to him; no one protested. Bambara men had sold him, men who believed in the same gods as he, who perhaps bore the same *diamou* or patronymic, or shared the same totemic taboos—the black monkey, the dog-faced baboon, the crowned crane and the panther.

No one had asked, "Who are you? A Kulibaly from Segu? A Massasi Kulibaly from Kaarta? A Diarra, a Traore, a Dembele, a Samake, a Louyate, an Ouane, an Ouarate? We found you out hunting. So are you a Gow, a descendant of Kourouyore, the ancestor from the sky who had intercourse with a female spirit and begat Moti? Who are you? What womb bore you and what penis planted you?"

No, nothing like that. They had merely weighed his flesh, counted his teeth, measured his penis and tested his biceps. He no longer counted as a human being.

Meanwhile the two Markas had decided to go further south to sell Naba, to Kankan in the Malinke country, so as to put as much distance as possible between themselves and Segu. Kankan had become one of the main trading centers. Dyula merchants went down to the coast with slaves and returned with guns, gunpowder, cotton goods and brandy that they got from the agents of the French and English chartered companies. A personable slave was worth twenty-five or thirty guns, with one or two long Dutch pipes thrown in. Naba was the sort of catch that was haggled over for a long while, a real "Indies specimen," as male slaves of about eighteen were called. The two Markas were already gloating over the yards of Pondicherry chintz they would be able to sell in the Songhay country: the fashionable ladies of Timbuktu and Gao doted on it.

When Naba was captured about a hundred kilometers away from home, the slave trade was at its height. For centuries European merchants had built forts on the coast—the Grain Coast, the Ivory Coast, the Gold Coast and the Slave Coast—from Arguin Island to the Bight of Benin. At first they dealt mainly in gold, ivory and wax, but with the discovery of the New World and the expansion of the sugar plantations and the slave traffic, "hunting for men" became the only really profitable trade. There was fierce and unscrupulous competition between the French and the English. But though they hated each other, they were at one in distrusting the African slave traders, whom they regarded as "sly, cunning, and skilled in false weights and measures and every other kind of double dealing."

CHAPTER

8

"Ahmed—there's someone to see you."

At first Siga, who couldn't get used to his new name, did not move, then, realizing the words were addressed to him, he jumped up, washed his hands in the basin by the door and went out into the courtyard of the cheap eating house where he took his meals.

A young man stood waiting for him. It was Tiekoro.

The two brothers had not met since the day after their arrival in Timbuktu six months ago. Siga, as he led his string of donkeys through the streets of the city to the port at Kabara, had kept looking for his brother, hoping to see him among the groups of students in white caftans and skullcaps who strolled about discussing some hadith* in a manner at once devout and swaggering. But when his search proved vain, Siga began to feel a growing resentment that was as bitter as hatred itself, and imagined what he would do if he suddenly met Tiekoro at some street corner. Perhaps he would spit in his face and call him a bastard. Sometimes he found himself going toward El-Hadj Baba Abou's house with the idea of going into the courtyard and insulting him to his heart's content. Probably everyone would be on his side: blood is thicker than water. Then he would remember the icy expres-

---

* An item in the great body of oral tradition preserving the sayings and deeds of the Prophet (still the subject of dispute).—TRANS.

sion of Tiekoro's teacher, and realize that for this light-skinned Muslim a black Bambara idol worshipper didn't exist. He'd have his servants chase him away like a stinking hyena. The arrogance of these Arabs and their half-castes, their contempt for the blacks! Siga had had plenty of opportunity to observe it.

But gradually his resentment had abated, for he was a good-natured fellow. He even came to make excuses for Tiekoro. He'd thought only of himself and his own future, but could he be blamed for that? His university studies meant so much to him. What would have been the point of the Timbuktu escapade at all if in the end he'd been unable to make his dream come true?

Tiekoro's thoughts had taken exactly the opposite course. At first he'd invented hundreds of excuses for his own behavior, but then these ceased to convince him and instead he was overcome by such remorse and guilt that he woke in the night and wept. But the resolutions he made in the darkness faded by daylight, and he did not rush to Kabara, where he knew he would be sure to find Siga. So with every day that passed he became more convinced of his own cowardice.

Once in Siga's presence he was unable to speak a word in his own defense. "Siga," he mumbled, looking at the ground, "I've had news from home. Bad news. Naba has disappeared."

"Disappeared?" stammered Siga, not understanding. "What do you mean—disappeared?"

"He was out hunting, and they think some Markas caught him, to sell him."

The news was so terrible that the words died on Siga's lips, and he could only burst into tears.

He had never been really close to Naba, the younger brother whom Tiekoro had taken over, but he could picture the grief of the family and especially of Nya. Then he thought of his brother's horrible fate. During his and Tiekoro's journey to Timbuktu they had met with long lines of slaves, their necks clamped between two pieces of wood tied together with string, being cudgeled on their way by the men taking them to the local markets. Naba would lose his name and identity and become just an animal toiling in the fields.

"But what can we do?" he cried.

Tiekoro gave a shrug of despair.

"What do you think? Nothing!"

Then he seemed to repent of this, and hurriedly corrected himself. "We must pray to God!"

Silence fell between the two brothers, then Tiekoro blurted out awkwardly: "Do you need anything?"

Siga turned on his heel without a word. Tiekoro caught hold of his arm. "Forgive me . . ." he murmured.

Given Tiekoro's usual arrogance, this was extraordinary enough, and Siga thought he must have misheard. He swung around to see his brother standing there hanging his head, embarrassed and ashamed in his fine silk caftan. Siga took pity on him, tried to make him feel better.

"Don't worry about me," he said. "I'm all right. You were even lucky to find me, because this is my last day here. A merchant is taking me on as his assistant."

"Do you mean to say you're going into trade?" Tiekoro exclaimed in horror. As a Bambara nobleman he despised trade and considered agriculture the only occupation worthy of him.

Siga laughed. "Would you prefer me to stay a donkey boy? Anyway, you're going to be a priest!"

Tiekoro said nothing for a moment, then asked: "Where can I find you if I want you?"

"You'll manage," said Siga, shrugging.

Then he turned and went back into the eating house, from which his companions had been watching the scene with interest.

Siga was now like the poor wretches he lived among—muscular, neglected, even dirty. He wore a short jacket made of strips of cotton dyed blue, and baggy trousers coming down to just above the ankle. His feet, now rough and broad, walked unshod through the dust. The two brothers no longer had anything in common. Even the family tragedy which had temporarily brought them together couldn't bridge the gap between them.

Tiekoro walked slowly toward the river. He felt he was responsible for Naba's disappearance, for if he hadn't left him to go and study, would his younger brother have attached himself to Tiefolo? Would he have become a hunter, would he have embarked on that hopeless expedition? What should he do now,

Tiekoro wondered. Go back to Segu to dry their mother's tears? Would that bring Naba back to her?

Kabara, which had served Timbuktu as a port ever since the river Issa-Ber had altered its course, was seething with life, and full of goods packed up ready to be loaded onto boats. There was millet, rice, corn, watermelons, together with tobacco and gum arabic, which was collected in large quantities around Goundam and Lake Faguibine. Traders from Fittouga brought clay pots, dried fish and ivory in their dugout canoes. One of their boats had a cargo of slaves, a dozen or so haggard and emaciated men tied together with ropes made from tree roots. A few weeks ago Tiekoro would have paid no attention to so familiar a sight, but now everything was different. He went over to two men who were wielding cudgels to make the slaves disembark.

"What are you going to do with them?" he asked.

One of the men muttered in poor Arabic that they were Mossi captives, due to be delivered to a Moor.

Tiekoro raised his voice.

"Don't you realize they are men, like you?"

Then he realized he was being ridiculous. What could he do against so ancient a practice? Black slaves had worked in the cane fields of Morocco since the sixteenth century, and there were royal slaves scattered all over the empire. He turned back to Timbuktu.

When he arrived in the university courtyard adjoining the mosque a crowd of students was already in the arcades, waiting for the library to open. Although many of its manuscripts had been lost as a result of the Moroccan invasion, and almost all Ahmed Baba's works were missing, many scholars had made gifts to the library from their own family treasures. Tiekoro had soon made such progress in his studies that he won his teachers' admiration, and from being almost an object of derision he became one of their most brilliant students in Arabic linguistics and theology. He was already teaching in one of Timbuktu's hundred and forty-five Koranic schools, and no one could rival him in interpreting the words and deeds of the Prophet. And yet Tiekoro wasn't happy. He wasn't happy because he was desperately in love, as desperately as young men of his age often are, and he wasn't sure his love was requited.

The object of his affections was Ayisha, fifth daughter of his host El-Hadj Baba Abou's first wife. Sometimes Ayisha's fine slanting eyes told him she was quite aware of his feelings; sometimes they expressed only the coldest disdain. She affected never to address him directly, using her younger brother Abi Zayd, an unruly lad of nine, as her intermediary.

"Ayisha would like an amber necklace."

"Ayisha would like a silver bracelet."

"Ayisha would like some *takoula* and honey."

And Tiekoro hastened to satisfy all these requests, though he knew very well that to carry on like this with El-Hadj Baba Abou's daughter was a crime which if discovered would bring down his teacher's wrath upon him.

Moreover, as Tiekoro had been used to making love to his father's young slaves ever since he was twelve years old, the purity and chastity laid upon him by his chosen religion was a torture. He couldn't prevent himself from staring at every woman as if she were a forbidden paradise, and the convulsive stirrings of his loins beneath his caftan terrified him. Sometimes his vision clouded, so torn was he by desire for a warm, consenting body. He would wake to find his thighs covered with sperm, and as he washed himself he implored God to forgive him. To crown all, his confidant and mentor Mulay Abdallah, having completed his study of Islamic law, had gone back to Gao to take over his father's post as *cadi*, and Tiekoro was terribly lonely.

To take his mind off things when his lessons were over, Tiekoro had gotten into the habit of going to a little bar kept by some Moors, where the customers drank green tea, ate little ginger biscuits and played a game from the white men's country in which you pushed little wooden discs about on a wooden board. There was something in the lazy, good-natured atmosphere that reminded Tiekoro of his father's compound.

He was coming out of the privy, a little straw-thatched hut at the back of the sandy courtyard, when he saw a girl, entirely naked except for a loincloth made of plant fiber around her waist. The setting sun glinted on her black skin. The sight of a naked virgin or bare breasts was common enough in the streets of Segu, but in Timbuktu, where customs were influenced by Islam, it had been disapproved of since the days of Askia Muhammad. Here women and even girls covered themselves in garments made of materials from Europe. At the sight of those breasts and hips, Tiekoro's head swam. The girl was fanning a fire of camel dung, for wood was scarce. Tiekoro walked past her without a word, went back inside the bar and, going over to Al-Hassan, the owner, asked who the girl was.

"A slave," the man replied indifferently. "Some Markas offered her to some Moroccans for the harems. But she isn't pretty enough, so I got her for next to nothing."

Tiekoro went outside again. The courtyard was empty. The girl had finished kindling her fire and was standing with her hands hanging idle and her long wiry legs slightly apart, showing the inside of the thighs. Tiekoro flung himself on her and dragged her into the privy. He did not know what possessed him. It was as if some savage beast lurking in his belly were trying to tear its way out. He entered her and she gave a little cry like a child, but didn't try to defend herself. He took her several times, avenging himself for the long months of solitude, for his abstinence, and also for the disappearance of his younger brother.

At last he pulled away. He was aware now of the terrible stench of excrement and urine, and wished he could die on the spot. He went out into the courtyard. The girl followed. He would have liked her to fight him, to cry out. But she just stood there behind him, silent.

"What's your name?" he finally managed to ask, in Arabic.

"Nadie," she said.

He shuddered, turned, and looked at her for the first time.

"Nadie? You're a Bambara, then?" he said.

She nodded.

"From Beledougou,* *fama*,"† she said.

A Bambara! How was it he hadn't recognized her by the tattooing on her lower lip and scarification on her temples? He'd raped a girl belonging to his own people, a girl he ought to have protected. He'd added to her humiliation. He was no better than

---

* A small Bambara kingdom independent of Segu.
† Bambara for "my lord."

the slave traders he'd rebuked the day before. Nadie put a hand on his shoulder, and he started as if he'd been touched by some unclean animal—or perhaps because he could feel his desire reawakening. Rushing into the street, he ran all the way back to El-Hadj Baba Abou's house. Old men reclining on mats at their doors, children, sellers of kola nuts, all stared as he went by, wondering who this man pursued by djinns could be.

In the courtyard he came upon his host and a stout, magnificently dressed man with a turban and the complexion of a Moor. He greeted them briefly and was just going into his room when Abi Zayd sprang up in front of him and told him, without waiting to be asked: "Abbas Ibrahim is a scholar from Marrakesh who teaches at the university. He's written several books about metaphysics. It's a great honor, his coming to see us and asking to marry my sister."

Tiekoro broke out in a cold sweat, for El-Hadj Baba Abou's four elder daughters were married already.

"Which one?" he asked.

Abi Zayd hopped from one foot to the other.

"Ayisha," he said mockingly.

How swift was God's punishment! thought Tiekoro. He was guilty of fornication, he had made himself unworthy of the one he loved, and at once she had been taken from him. And yet he couldn't resign himself and accept it all meekly. In Segu the rules concerning marriage were at once simple and complicated. It was a matter conducted between families of equal rank, from the exchange of presents, kola nuts and cowrie shells to the payment of the dowry in cattle and gold and the final ceremony. If he had stayed at home, Dousika would have sent for him one day and told him it was time for him to take a wife, and his father would have suggested who that wife should be. But Tiekoro didn't know anything about marriage procedures in Timbuktu. He realized that in El-Hadj Baba Abou's eyes he, a foreigner, was no possible match for his daughter despite his birth. But he would have faced him if he'd known something of Ayisha's feelings. But how was he to find out? How could he get near her and speak to her in private?

At that point a servant came in with hot water for the bath.

"Your caftan's covered in mud!" he said.

Tiekoro was transported back to that horrible scene. The privy, with its wooden plank with a round hole in it over an earthenware jar. Himself wallowing in the mire. And yet at the same time he wanted to see the girl again and plunge once more into the waters of her belly. Was God bent on driving him mad? What was the explanation of this contrast between the longings of his heart and the desires of his flesh?

> *The fire of Allah, the burning fire,*
> *That rises up over the courts of the damned!*
> *Like a canopy above them,*
> *Resting on lofty columns!*

Suddenly Tiekoro had a flash of inspiration. Mulay Abdallah! He'd ask him to come to Timbuktu. He was the only one who could advise him: he knew the local customs and could tell him how to act. He sat down at once and wrote to him.

Three groups made up distinguished society in Timbuktu: the Arma, who exercised military and political power; the lawyers; and the merchants. The latter were the main bastion of the social order, and their caravans, boats and shops were the first targets in time of trouble. Siga's employer, Abdallah, belonged to the eminent Arma family, the Mubarak al-Dari. But his quiet temperament wasn't suited to soldiering, and one day he renounced the attributes of his class—the wearing of the sword, the white robes with red, yellow, green or black shawls according to rank—and went into trade. And he chose well, for he was now one of the richest men in the city. His house near the port of Kabara, built of round bricks, contained a multitude of servants and slaves. He traded, mainly in bars of salt but also in cloth, senna and sesame, with merchants in Fez, Marrakesh, Algiers, Tripoli and Tunis. Some ten years ago he had lost his two wives and five children in the great epidemic of plague. He did not marry again but satisfied his fleshly desires, if he had any, with one of his maids.

He was, as may be imagined, a gloomy, taciturn man, who could spend whole days without saying a word. But he had grown

fond of Siga. He liked the reliable way he conveyed his merchandise to the port, he liked his modesty, and he was sure this
young Bambara was more honest than all the other boys of his
age engaged in the same work. So he offered to take him into his
own service: he would be given bed and board and respectable
clothes, and would be able to learn all the mysteries of commerce.
Siga, tired of his hard life as a donkey boy, accepted with alacrity.
As a matter of fact he had by then been sleeping for two years
among a dozen or so malodorous bodies in a tiny hut in the Albaradiou district, rising before daybreak, carrying considerable
weights on his own head or shoulders, looked down on by everyone. Sometimes, when he thought of Segu and his parents, he
was seized with a violent resentment. If Tiekoro took it into his
head to be converted and become a student, why did they have
to send him, Siga, along too? Was he his brother's slave? And so,
when he thought of going home, he saw himself as proud, triumphant, followed by a caravan of twelve camels laden with things
never seen before in Segu. Everyone would run out into the street.

"Look," they'd say. "Isn't that the son of the woman who
threw herself down the well?"

The griots, scenting gold, would hover around him, and Dousika would be sorry he hadn't treated him properly.

Abdallah's voice broke into his dreams of glory.

"I've left some clothes in your room," he said. "They belong
to me, but I make you a present of them. You're so big and tall
they'll fit you. Then go to the pasha with the Pondicherry
chintzes. I ordered them for his wives."

While Siga was discovering how delightful it was to walk the
streets as a young man exercising an honorable trade, followed
by two slaves, Tiekoro was still fretting. If El-Hadj Baba Abou
was contemplating giving his daughter to a man from Marrakesh,
it meant he had nothing against foreigners. True, the man in
question was a Moroccan, and Tiekoro was aware of the special
relationship between the people of Morocco and those of Timbuktu and the neighboring region. Anyway, his love and desire
for Ayisha were such that he felt equal to facing her father. But
first he needed to know whether she would back him up. Should
he wait for Mulay Abdallah to act as a go-between? His letter,

which was going by boat, would take at least four weeks to reach Gao.

The Koranic school where Tiekoro taught imparted only rudimentary knowledge: a little calligraphy, the *fatiha*, and the first suras of the Koran. As every pupil paid seven cowries a week, and he had some twenty pupils, he was quite comfortably off. He sent the children home, and instead of going to the university decided to go back to El-Hadj Baba Abou's house.

Tiekoro's feelings about Timbuktu had changed with time. Almost two years had passed. During the early months, he had hoped to be able to become part of the famous city, to make friends and connections there. But he gradually came to see that this was impossible. The pride and arrogance of the scholars he came in contact with ruled it out. A man had to be "well born," with ulemas among his ancestors. So he began to hate Timbuktu, to wish the Tuareg would destroy it again as they had so often before, and leave nothing but a heap of ashes and bleached bones. He found himself watching for signs that might herald the city's decline—a wall that was cracked or crumbling, for example, the holes stopped up with matting or tufts of straw. How happy he would be when he saw the high walls of Segu again, and the banks of the Joliba covered with bare-breasted women doing their washing and drawing water in calabashes!

He walked along swiftly, not seeing the people he passed: Moorish women in indigo robes, Tuaregs gripping their sabers, Armas, crowds of water carriers coming back from the wells in the northwest, slaves carrying bars of salt tied together. The sight would have intrigued him in days gone by. Now it left him cold.

How could he find out what Ayisha felt about him? Get Abi Zayd to give her a letter? But what if it fell into the hands of El-Hadj Baba Abou?

Then, pushing open the gate, he found himself face to face with Ayisha in the courtyard, where she was waiting for the slave who was supposed to chaperone her.

It was very unusual for them to be alone together. Ayisha was always accompanied by a slave, a younger sister, a friend or a relative. Moreover, El-Hadj Baba Abou's huge house was divided into two parts, one devoted to his school and his passing or permanent guests, the other his own private residence. The latter was itself subdivided into reception rooms furnished in the Moroccan manner, a study, a library with shelves of valuable manuscripts, and the women's and children's apartments. This meant that the women and children were never seen. In two years Tiekoro hadn't met his host's wives—the Moroccan wife and the Songhay former slave—more than three times.

Ayisha was standing in the middle of the courtyard, a charming little creature nearing sixteen. The Moroccan blood she got from her mother and the mixed blood she inherited from her father made her a perfect *mwallidun*, a mulatto, with a light, glowing complexion and long curly hair braided with gold thread that hung down to her waist. Her lips were curled in a little grimace, perhaps mocking, perhaps friendly.

"In the name of Allah, Ayisha," breathed Tiekoro, "I must speak to you."

She seemed to hesitate, turned toward the slave now hurrying to join her, and murmured: "I'll send Zubeida, my favorite slave, to fetch you in your room during siesta."

At first Tiekoro thought he must be dreaming. It was only a dream that Ayisha was looking on him kindly and, more incredible still, smiling. In everyday reality she was completely indifferent. He stood rooted to the spot, going alternately hot and cold, as Ayisha and Zubeida vanished into the house. Then panic swept over him. Was it a trap? He remembered the warnings of his friend Mulay Abdallah: "She's a coquette. She's made us all fall in love with her, but in the end she only makes fun of us."

But why should she make fun of him? No, she must share his love, his desire. He imagined holding her in his arms and nearly fainted with emotion. Ayisha. Three incomparable syllables! The time had never passed so slowly.

At last there was a light tap at his door. Zubeida held out a caftan.

"Here, wear this and they'll think you're a Hausa merchant selling perfumes," she said.

Tiekoro followed her into the house. On the first floor lived El-Hadj Baba Abou's two wives and their youngest children. A spiral stair led to the second floor where the older children had their quarters, girls on one side and boys on the other, in large rooms with doum palm rafters painted white. Little girls and boys rushed noisily to and fro, playing. Ayisha was alone in her room. The white-painted mud floor was strewn with garments of silk and fine cotton. Baggy trousers, wide belts, shawls, short embroidered tunics—all had been flung down pell-mell by their owner's impatient hand. Earthenware bowls were full of carnelian rings, amber neckaces, chased silver bangles, and cross-shaped pendants on gold filigree chains. A tiny pair of heelless mules ornamented with gold thread seemed to be waiting for Ayisha to slip them on again.

Tiekoro gazed at all this, entranced.

He had never been in a woman's bedroom before, and if he had done so in Segu he would have seen only the most rudimentary furnishings—a mat on the floor and a few gourds in a corner; perhaps a stool. And the slaves with whom he slaked his desires used to go bare-bosomed, their *pagnes* drawn tight over their hips. Now he was finding that open nudity was less disturbing than this body covered with fabrics and so near he could smell its perfume. He tried to make out her figure—the pointed breasts, the belly . . .

Ayisha cut short this inspection.

"What do you want with me?" she said brusquely. "You've been goggling at me for months. What do you want?"

This wasn't what he'd expected.

"It's awful living in a foreign country," he stammered, taken by surprise. "No one knows your family or rank. At home I'm a nobleman. My father used to be an important court official and he's one of the richest—"

"Is he an idol worshipper?" interrupted Ayisha.

Tiekoro had foreseen this objection.

"He practices the religion of his fathers," he said calmly. "They believe the world was created by two complementary principles, Pemba and Faro, both offspring of the spirit . . ."

"Stupid blasphemies!" she cried.

Tiekoro could feel the anger rising in him, but he went on.

"I myself have broken with idolatry. Isn't that what matters?"

Ayisha turned her lovely, inscrutable light brown eyes on him.

"In your country, I'm told, you eat out of gourds instead of earthenware bowls. You sleep on straw mats instead of oxhide beds. The girls go naked," she said.

Tiekoro tried to think of a reply. But the worst was still to come. Ayisha started to twist one of her braids around her fingers.

"They say you make human sacrifices to your gods," she said.

Tiekoro felt as if he were on fire.

"A long time ago!" he cried. "A long time ago! And then only for important matters of state!"

Ayisha smiled, revealing a row of dazzling little white teeth, then threw herself back among her bed cushions. As she did so, her tunic rode up, showing the silky white skin of her belly. It was more than Tiekoro could endure. He was overcome by a surge of desire combined with a determination both to get back at her for the humiliating interrogation he'd just been put through and to demonstrate Bambara virility. What pleasure he would give her! Would she be able to hide it? With a bound he was upon her, thrusting a hand between her breasts, gripping her with his knees. As he roughly brought his face close to hers, she spat on him.

"Hands off, you dirty nigger!" she hissed.

Tiekoro drew back. Ayisha's eyes were green with anger. Hatred took all prettiness from her face.

"Hands off! You're black, you stink—and do you really think I'd marry you? Hands off, I say! Zubeida!"

Siga had gone to bed early. He was tired. All day he'd been out in the sun, supervising the unloading of a caravan of kola nuts from the empire of Ashanti which had come by way of Bon-doukou and Boan. The nuts arrived in big wicker baskets, and first the baskets had to be counted, then their contents examined. Then the traders who'd brought them had to be paid, and they were always ready to cheat the buyer out of a few cowries. As Siga was young and a newcomer to Abdallah's business, everyone was out to take advantage of him. His new job was certainly no sinecure!

He was deep in the pleasant drowsiness that precedes sleep, when all the senses are dimmed. It seemed to him he was back in Segu with Nya, the only person who'd ever loved him. How was she bearing up under Naba's disappearance? That meant three of the sons she'd brought up, three of her children, were gone away. But Siga would be back. He'd come back and lay all the gold he'd amassed at her feet. He'd say:

> Mother dear
> Who freely gives all she has
> Who never deserts our home
> Mother, I greet you
> The weeping child calls for his mother
> Mother dear, here I am!

At that moment there was a sharp knock at the door. Siga twitched with annoyance. Who was this disturbing him? His friend, Ismael the donkey boy? But he'd seen him at the midday meal. He got up and opened the heavy mahogany door, and there in the shadows stood Tiekoro.

"You again!" he said in astonishment. "You spring up behind every grain of sand!"

"Let me in!" said Tiekoro hoarsely. "You can joke later on!"

Siga was tenderhearted. He had suffered too much as a child not to recognize sorrow when he saw it. He could tell at once that something terrible must have happened to his brother, something that was to him even more terrible than Naba's disappearance.

"What is it?" he asked. "What's the matter?"

Tiekoro's only answer was to burst into tears. The arrogant Tiekoro weeping, clutching his head in his hands like a child or a woman—it was incredible! Siga knelt down beside him.

"Come on, tell me," he whispered.

After a moment Tiekoro managed to control himself. In short, broken phrases he told his story. The rendezvous with Ayisha had really been a trap. Zubeida had told Ayisha's mother, who was resting on the first floor, and she had filled the house with her hysterical shrieks. As soon as El-Hadj Baba Abou came home from a meal with a friend in the chiefs' quarter, not far from the pasha's residence, his wife told him what had happened and he had Tiekoro thrown out into the street. And Tiekoro was sure the matter wouldn't end there. El-Hadj Baba Abou would have

him expelled from the university. And then what would become
of him?

Siga tried to reassure him.

"Why should he do such a thing? So long as you're not in his
house any more, hanging around his daughter. Since he doesn't
want you to marry her . . ."

Tiekoro shook his head passionately.

"No," he said, "you don't know how arrogant these *mwallidun* are. They hate and despise us. But why? Why? We're as
rich as they are. And as well born."

The fact was that Tiekoro did not think of himself as a
"black" or a "Negro." The words meant nothing to him. He was
a Bambara, a subject of a powerful kingdom feared by all the
peoples in the region, and it was incomprehensible to him that
anyone should reproach him for the color of his skin. True, he'd
been attracted by the color of Ayisha's skin, but only because he
hadn't seen many like it. He knew, moreover, that many of the
people in Segu, who were afraid of albinos, would regard Ayisha
as one and would have to be persuaded otherwise. But why should
she wish to destroy him? If she didn't share his feelings, why not
simply tell him so? He started to pace to and fro, debating various
courses of action.

"What if I went and threw myself on El-Hadj Baba Abou's
mercy? No, he wouldn't see me. What if I went to the imam of
the university mosque? But that would be dangerous—El-Hadj
might not have told him anything. What am I to do?"

Suddenly he stopped in his tracks.

"Have you got pen and paper?"

"Pen and paper?"

Siga didn't even know how to write!

"I must write a letter to my friend Mulay Abdallah. He's a
cadi in Gao, like his father before him, so he's got plenty of
connections among the ulemas. He's the only person who can
get me out of this terrible mess."

Siga, good-natured though he was, couldn't help deriving
some satisfaction from seeing his formerly haughty brother down
on his luck. But blood was thicker than water, and he was ready
to take him in and help him as long as necessary. He unrolled a

mat he kept in a corner for the girls who sometimes spent the night with him.

"Make yourself at home. I don't need to tell you that what's mine is yours," he said.

Tiekoro lay down. What else could he do? But he couldn't sleep. He kept remembering the words of one of his teachers at the university. There were three degrees in the faith. The first relates to the masses, who are guided by the prescriptions of the law. The second belongs to men who have overcome their faults and set out on the path that leads to truth. The third is that of an elite, and those who attain it worship God in truth and pure, colorless light. The divine Truth blooms in the fields of Love and Charity. That was the degree of faith which Tiekoro aspired to. But would his body, his stupid, greedy, despicable body, let him reach it?

CHAPTER
9

As she lay on a mat on the balcony of her house on Gorée Island, Anne Pépin felt bored. She had been bored for ten years, ever since her lover, the Chevalier de Boufflers, who had been governor of the island, went back to France. He had amassed enough money to marry his fair friend the Comtesse de Sabran; Anne still lay awake at night thinking about his ingratitude. She couldn't forget that for a few months she had ridden high—given parties, masked balls and theatrical entertainments like those at the court of the king of France. But now it was all over and here she was, abandoned on this chunk of basalt dumped in the sea off Cape Verde, the only French settlement in Africa apart from Saint-Louis at the mouth of the Senegal River.

Things had been going from bad to worse for years. No one could make out what was happening in France. There had been the Revolution in 1789, and then the Republic, after which one contradictory order had followed another: abolition of the slave trade, reintroduction of the slave trade, plus attacks by the English, commercial rivals of the French.

Fortunately this did not interfere with business. Ships of all nationalities, on the pretext of taking on water or of urgent repairs, continued to put in at Gorée and exchange their cargoes for slaves.

Anne Pépin was thirty-five but admitted to twenty-five, as if

she wanted to bring her life to a halt at the departure of the
Chevalier de Boufflers. She had been, and still was, extremely
beautiful. An officer who was also a bit of a poet, and who had
wooed her in vain, said she combined the subtle distinction of
Europe with the impetuous sensuality of Africa, for while her
father was Jean Pépin, a surgeon attached to the fort at Gorée,
her mother was a Wolof Negress he had fallen in love with.
Anne's skin was quite dark but she had long silky brown hair
with tawny tints, which when it was loose fell right down her
back. Her most extraordinary feature, however, was her eyes: it
was impossible to say whether they were blue or gray or green—
they varied according to the time of day and the color of the light.
She dressed like the other *signares* or half-caste women of Gorée,
the offspring of love affairs between African women and officers
from the fort or officers in the various trading companies. These
companies had tried to make fortunes by dealing in cloth, alcohol,
arms, iron bars and above all slaves, but they had rarely succeeded
because of the depredations of their own employees. Anne wore
a full skirt of blue and mauve silk check overlaid with white; a
tunic of patterned lace; a huge sulfur-yellow shawl; and a match-
ing head scarf tied so as to give a provocative glimpse of the curls
at the nape of her neck.

Anne Pépin was not the only one in Gorée who was bored.
Nothing ever happened there. Life was punctuated only by the
coming and going of ships taking on slaves. Once or twice a
month the men would distract themselves by hunting game in
the forests of Rufisque on the mainland, by playing cards or by
drinking brandy. But the women—if they were not religious and
didn't spend their time saying their prayers—what was there for
them to do? There were lovers, of course; but you can't be making
love all day! Anne sighed, rose, and went across the balcony to
tell a slave to bring her a cold drink.

It was Jean-Baptiste who reluctantly looked up when she
called.

A year earlier Anne's brother Nicolas Pépin had brought Jean-
Baptiste back from a visit to his friend the governor of the fort
at Saint-Louis, a kind of barge anchored in the Senegal River. The
governor had paid a high price for Jean-Baptiste because he was
so good-looking; he had intended to employ the lad as a footman.

But unfortunately Jean-Baptiste had turned out to be afflicted with a kind of lethargy, from which he emerged only to try to commit suicide. Nicolas, who had watched his father at work, had become very interested in the boy's illness. He brought him back to the hospital in Gorée, and managed more or less to cure him. He even wrote a short paper on *Suicidal tendencies among Negroes on the Lesser Coast*, which earned him some celebrity. But once Jean-Baptiste began to get better, Nicolas lost interest in him and gave him to his sister. She lived on a more lavish scale than he did; her compound contained sixty-eight slaves.

If Jean-Baptiste looked up reluctantly it was because he hated the name, which had been given him during a semblance of baptism in the chapel of the fort. His real name was Naba. Moreover, the summons interrupted his favorite occupation, gardening. Without undue haste he went over to the bougainvillea-covered patio and told two slaves who were gossiping there that their mistress wanted them. One of them gathered up her full, flounced, lacy skirts and ran off.

The African population of Gorée consisted of two groups. The first and smaller group included the domestic slaves who worked for the officers in the fort, the *signares*, or the various officials working on the island. The second group consisted of the human cattle huddled into the slave houses. There was no connection between the two groups. The first were baptized and given Christian names and were in no danger of being sold. The second formed a nameless, suffering mass, waiting to be sent to the Americas. But the domestic slaves couldn't forget the presence of the others, whose fate revolted some, moved others to pity, but left none indifferent.

The domestic slaves kept one another informed about the sailings of the slave ships and the size of their cargoes, and would hurry along the road to Castel beach to try to see them set out. Yet of this they did their best to give no sign, continuing to perform their duties with eyes downcast, saying meekly, "Yes, master!" and "Yes, mistress!"

In the patio Naba picked up the gourd he'd come for and went back into the garden.

Anne Pépin had a huge garden. The soil, as on the rest of the island, was dry and sandy, but fortunately there was a well of slightly brackish water between the garden and the sea, and Naba had invented his own irrigation system. His skill produced specimens of all the foreign plants good to eat or look at that had been introduced to this part of the world by seafarers—melons, eggplants, oranges and lemons, cabbages. Naba used to talk to his plants. As soon as the first puckered shoot appeared with its two or three shy pale green buds, he would water it, seeing all his life in Segu rise up again before him, remembering the words his mother used to sing to him when he was a baby.

Nya would hold him in her arms and croon:

> Come, my little one
> Come, my little one
> Who frightened you?
> The hyena did!
> Quick, quick, carry him off to Koulikoro
> In Koulikoro there are two huts
> And the third is a kitchen.

Then she lifted him up three times toward the east and toward the west. Nya! His eyes filled with tears as he thought of her. What sorrow he'd caused her with his disobedience! Had she survived his disappearance? He remembered her face when he came out of the sacred wood after the circumcision ceremonies, and how she chanted proudly with the other women:

> A new thing has happened!
> Let everyone throw away the old things
> And take that which is new.

Sometimes, too, Naba thought of Tiekoro, his beloved elder brother whom he had lost so long ago. Almost two years had gone by. Had he become a scholar, as he'd dreamed of doing? Was he still in Timbuktu, or had he gone back to Segu? Was he married? Did he have sons?

Naba put his tomatoes carefully into a large gourd. What a strange fruit it was, the tomato! The god Faro used it to make women pregnant. It contained the germ of the embryo, for its seeds were multiples of seven, the figure linked to the twinning which lay at the origins of the human race. In Segu, beside her hut, Nya had a little bed of tomatoes which was dedicated to Faro; she used to crush the fruit and offer them up to the god in the altar hut. And so whenever he picked his own tomatoes Naba felt himself back near his mother, back in her smell and warmth.

He stood up now and took the bowl of tomatoes into the kitchen, where the slaves had resumed their gossiping. Now he had to go to the public garden which had been founded some years before by Dancourt, a director of the trading company. Anne Pépin allowed Naba to hire his services out for a small sum— enough to buy a few leaves of tobacco and a drop of brandy.

Gorée had developed considerably over the years. When the French captured it from the Dutch, who had taken it from the Portuguese, there were only two forts, mere stone redoubts some forty-five yards square with seven or eight cannon and surrounded by crenellated ramparts of stone and mud. They contained a hundred or so soldiers, a couple of dozen clerks and skilled workers, and a catechist to hold prayers and "console the sick." Then the French turned Gorée into the headquarters of the Senegal Company, which succeeded the West India Company and gave priority to the slave trade. The latter, though it did not enrich the companies themselves, did enrich the individuals in them who falsified accounts, made fake customs declarations and employed false weights and measures. Gradually Gorée attracted a whole population from the mainland. French officials of the companies were not allowed to have their wives with them, so they entered into relations with African women, producing a class of half-breeds who in turn made money through trade and employed many domestic slaves. Fine tall stone houses were built. Others were thatched or had flat roofs made of boards. There was also a big hospital, and a church where the *signares* vied with each other in elegance every Sunday.

In order to get from his mistress's house to the public garden Naba had to pass the main slave house, which had been built by the Dutch. It was a solid stone edifice designed to discourage any attempt at escape, surrounded by a wall several inches thick and opening onto the sea through a low barred gate. This was the way to the slave ships, come to fill their holds with a cargo of men. Naba was fascinated by the place. So much despair in so small a compass!

No visitors were allowed there, but the people of Gorée regarded Naba as mad, and the warders, freed slaves armed with guns and cat-o'-nine tails, let him move about freely among the inmates. He had become a familiar figure with the big bag of fruit he handed around among the women and children, and anyone else too sunk in despair. He now ran swiftly up the stone steps leading to the entrance. The slave house had been empty for some days, but the previous night a ship had unloaded its cargo. One of the warders was swaggering up and down the veranda, very pleased with himself because he had a gun and was smoking a Dutch pipe.

"You again!" he growled when he saw Naba.

Then he mopped his brow with a brand-new handkerchief from Pondicherry, bought from the European traders and thus a sure symbol of his social status.

Naba went on into the sinister building without taking any notice.

"I'm not joking, my dear! You must get it into your head that the slave trade is going to be abolished for good and all!"

Anne shrugged.

"Officially, perhaps. According to the law. But in actual fact it will be a different matter. People will always need slaves."

Anne and her brother Nicolas had inherited a respectable income from their father, but like all the other inhabitants of Gorée they derived their real wealth from the slave trade, together with dealings in wax and hides from the mainland.

Isidore Duchâtel pressed his point. "No, but you really ought to think of some other source of income. Listen—there's talk in Paris of developing Cape Verde and planting Egyptian cotton there. Also indigo, potatoes, olives and so on."

Anne laughed derisively. "It will turn out the way it did in Guiana—a fiasco!"

"Not at all!" said Isidore, shaking his head. "Guiana was on the other side of the world. Cape Verde is only a stone's throw away."

He went over to the window and pointed to the garden with its fruit trees and many-colored flower beds.

"Remember, Anne, this island, where so many things grow now, was once uninhabited and as bald as an egg. France plans to send experts to Cape Verde to start an experimental garden for plants from all over the world. It's a very ambitious project."

Anne Pépin shrugged again. Gorée without slaves, Gorée without trade—it was as unlikely as the sky without sun or stars! She glanced impatiently at Isidore, her latest lover, one of the few men who had managed to amuse her a little since the Chevalier's departure. But she suspected him of being unfaithful to her with Negresses, domestic slaves who looked after his house. She hadn't seen him for several days. Why? And instead of offering explanations, here he was droning on about farfetched theories.

"Is that all you have to say to me?" she asked crossly.

But Isidore was clearly uninterested in gallantry today.

"Sell me Jean-Baptiste," he said.

"Jean-Baptiste? My gardener?" she repeated, offended.

Isidore Duchâtel was a senior officer but he lived in a house that had once belonged to François Le Juge, a former director of the Senegal Company. This was because he didn't like living in the fort. Unlike most of the other officers he was intelligent, ambitious and rather witty, and garrison life irked him. So despite the fact that government regulations strictly forbade it he beguiled his idleness by engaging in trade, just like everyone else, acquiring goods imported into the island and reselling them at a profit. He managed to obtain the finest "India pieces" from slavers of his acquaintance. He was much intrigued by the idea of settling on the Cape Verde peninsula and setting up a plantation for himself on the model of those in the West Indies. Apparently people were making fortunes out there with sugarcane, coffee and tobacco! It was because of this that Naba's talents as a gardener had attracted his attention. What could one not do with the help of a slave like him! And he would be able to get his fellows to help in agricultural experiments far better than any white master could. Isidore could already see himself walking though his own fields when Anne Pépin brought him back to earth.

"I'll never sell you Jean-Baptiste," she said. "He's been baptized—have you forgotten?"

"All right then," answered Isidore, with some vexation. "Marry me, and all our property will belong to us both."

He referred, of course, to one of the sham marriages Frenchmen contracted with *signares* but which had no legal value and didn't stop the husbands from going back to France alone when their term of duty was over. The children were usually sent to France to be educated, especially the boys. And sometimes the fathers left some money and other property behind for their mothers.

Anne Pépin made no answer to this proposal. She was sulking. Isidore decided to leave. He bent over and kissed the hand negligently held out to him and took the straw hat a slave girl brought him.

The finest residence in Gorée was undoubtedly that of Caty Louet, who'd died the year before and had had three children by Monsieur Aussenac, the governor of Galam. But Anne's house was probably more remarkable. Its flat facade, as well as having a triangular pediment like a temple, also boasted a wooden balcony with a low veranda that made it resemble a loggia. Thanks to the efforts of Jean-Baptiste there were flowers everywhere; their perfume wafted as far as the street. There were a dozen or more rooms with inlaid floors, perfect imitations of an Italian technique carried out by slaves trained in cabinetwork. The house was also full of fine furniture, including portly commodes and tables and chairs with legs carved like sculptures. Some of these were local reproductions made so skillfully that they too were indistinguishable from originals imported from France. Admittedly these were found only in the public rooms. The bedrooms contained only straw mats, heaps of full gowns, gauze and tulle scarves and checked kerchiefs from the Indies, together with calabashes overflowing with gold and silver jewelery, pearls, and glass bead necklaces.

Anne was thoughtful. Isidore's words had not left her entirely unmoved. The land on the Cape Verde peninsula belonged to a people called the Lebus. The Chevalier de Boufflers, too, had wanted to see meadows and flowers of every kind flourish there; then he had given up the idea. Moreover, in recent years the Lebus had rebelled against the damel or king of Cayor* to whom they

---

* Kingdom situated in present-day Senegal.

paid tribute, and had more or less turned their settlements into forts. How was anyone to negotiate with them for the granting of land? And without their cooperation any attempt at colonization was doomed to failure. But despite all the difficulties it was still a tempting prospect.

Anne rose heavily to her feet: too much idleness and too much food were making her put on weight. Was it true Gorée had no future? That one day the slave trade would end? What would take its place? Admittedly there was gum arabic, the produce of a little thorny shrub, a kind of acacia; but that trade was entirely in the hands of the Moors, and in any case had never been able to rival the traffic in slaves.

Anne went down the stone stairs to the wide patio adjoining the garden, which in turn looked out over the sea. Some girls, bare-breasted, were pounding millet, others were washing linen and steeping it in blue water to make it whiter. One of the slaves was putting wheat-flour bread into a clay oven, while a crowd of children squabbled over the remains of a meal. When they saw their mistress, everyone tried to keep quiet: she was known to be quarrelsome and easily provoked. But, for a change, Anne made no comment and went straight on into the garden to have a look at the plants Naba conjured out of the ground. Until now she hadn't taken much notice of his work, but now she suddenly realized that here she might have the means of adding to her wealth.

There were melons, watermelons with fluffy red flesh, carrots and fat cabbages. Rows of orange trees, their branches weighed down with fruit. Above all tomatoes, for which Naba had a special affection.

The soil on Gorée was like the soil on the Cape Verde peninsula. What grew here would also bring in a yield on the mainland. Perhaps Isidore was right. Might not the future lie in the production of fruit and plants for sale, as in the West Indies? But who would cultivate them? Of course there would always be a demand for slaves!

Anyhow, Anne decided that if it was necessary to acquire land on the peninsula she would certainly do so. Her mother's family lived in the Rufisque area. She never saw them now, but one could always revive relationships if need be.

"She's like a flower!"

That was the thought that struck Naba; then he realized how absurd it was. With all his skill, and despite his bold experiments in crossbreeding, he'd never produced any black flowers. It was as if the color wasn't right; as if Nature didn't want anything to do with it.

And yet she did make him think of a flower. Fragile. Drooping. As the women were not chained, she was sitting, with infinite grace, on the filthy floor. The inside of the slave house was disgusting. As soon as you entered you were assailed by the stench—the stench of suffering, agony and death. Many men and women managed to do away with themselves by refusing the terrible food, and their corpses would remain there among the living until some warder noticed. Then everyone would be flogged for not denouncing the culprits. The big room was vaulted, with a paved floor covered in heaps of straw; the only light came from narrow windows with heavy iron bars. The men were chained to the walls by the ankle; those suspected of being stubborn also had their arms bound behind their backs. They were only untied for meals—sticky millet gruel served twice a day and so badly cooked it often caused sickness and diarrhea. So vomit and excrement mixed with the rotten straw already crawling with insects. Whenever a slave ship was in port the men and women were all made to stand up and were hastily sluiced free of vermin with buckets of cold water. Then the men's heads were shaved and they were taken into the next room, which served as a slave market. The traders in human flesh, come ashore for the purpose, then made their choices.

Naba made his way through bodies in every possible posture of despair, stopping beside a woman who had just given birth to a child; the slavers who brought her to Gorée hadn't noticed she was pregnant when they took her on board. Naba looked at the little bundle of flesh doomed to so horrible a fate, and held out some fruit to its mother. Then he came to the newcomer.

"Do you speak Dyula?" he whispered, kneeling in front of her.

A movement of the shoulders showed her incomprehension.

Where did she come from, then? From Sine, Saloum, or Cayor,
like most of the slaves who came through Gorée? Or from the
countries of the south—Allada or Ouidah? Naba squatted on his
heels, facing the girl. Tears drew little shining ribbons down her
black cheeks. She couldn't be more than fifteen to judge by her
slender figure and her scarcely swelling breasts, like the buds of
a rare and delicate plant. A plant! A strong wave of tenderness
swept through Naba's heart, and from the oxhide pouch he carried
over his shoulder he took one of the first oranges from his garden.
He peeled it, put one segment in his mouth, and signed to the
girl to do the same. She shook her head, but he was not discouraged. Tapping himself on the chest several times, he said,
"Naba!"

For a moment she remained still and distant, then her lips
rounded and she whispered, "Ayodele."*

Naba's eyes filled with tears. Despite their wretched situation, despite everything that separated them, they had built a
bridge. They had named themselves, taken their place in the long
line of humanity. He rummaged in his pouch again and brought
out a piece of wheat bread, a few lumps of sugar and some scraps
of chicken. He held them out to her, and again she refused to
touch them. Naba remembered the first days of his own captivity,
when he too had refused to eat. Oh, but she must live! Even if
life was only humiliation and imprisonment. But how could he
persuade her when they didn't speak the same language? Then
he remembered the song that Nya used to sing to him and that
he sang to his plants so that they might be watered with affection.

> Come, my little one
> Who frightened you?
> The hyena did!
> Quick, quick, carry him off to Koulikoro . . .

She stared at him wide-eyed, following the shape of his lips in
astonishment, and he knew that in the universe into which she
had been plunged there had been no place for pity, sharing, human
feeling. So he clasped her to him.

* Yoruba name meaning "Joy has entered my house."

Naba had had dealings with women before. When he was a hunter, with Tiefolo, he had made love to slaves. Then had come his own capture, captivity and illness, and he'd lost interest in everything. Except his plants. Suddenly, forgotten feelings and sensations reawoke in him. It was the hand of some ancestor who had brought them together in this house of slaves. To hold back death.

A warder carrying a cat-o'-nine-tails came up to him.

"Be off with you now, Jean-Baptiste!" he said, not too unkindly. "If the commandant sees you you'll get us all punished. You know no one's allowed around here."

Instead of doing as he was told, Naba asked, "Does she belong to anyone?"

"Not that I know of," said the other, shrugging. "But as she's so young I expect she's intended for Brazil or Cuba."

Naba shuddered as he imagined the martyrdom awaiting her. Once she was chosen by a merchant and passed as satisfactory, she'd be branded on the shoulder with a red-hot iron. Then one night, unexpectedly, to avoid any revolt, the slave ship would put to sea.

Men crammed in the hold. Whipped to force them to dance for exercise on the deck. Women raped by the sailors. Sick and dying thrown overboard. Groans of pain. Cries of rebellion and anguish. Then one day a land of exile and sorrow on the horizon.

Naba took the crumpled little hand, with its nails gray as the oyster shells in Joliba bay. If they'd met in the kingdom of Segu his father would have sent gold dust, cowrie shells and cattle to her father. They would have shared kola nuts. The griots would have sung, mockingly: "They say it's wrong to beat women. But to make iron grow straight in the fire, you have to beat it! You have to beat it!"

But the gods and the ancestors had decreed otherwise.

Instead of a compound with walls freshly daubed with kaolin to symbolize renewal, the stinking atmosphere of a prison. Instead of the generous beat of the *dounoumba*, the drum of rejoicing, the rebellious murmurs of slaves. Instead of the happy impatience for union, the wait for departure to a terrible unknown.

Never mind. They would make this hell their paradise.

At any other time Anne Pépin wouldn't have worried too much about Jean-Baptiste's disappearance. Everyone regarded him as odd but harmless, and he'd come back in the end. But Isidore's words had directed Anne's attention toward the young man's exceptional value. Were the orange and lemon and banana trees behind her house the harbingers of a fortune? To strengthen her own conviction she had questioned her brother Nicolas. He was just back from a visit to Paris, and he too had amazed her with what he said. Yes, it was true: since the 1789 Revolution and the Republic, people in Paris had been concerned about the blacks. They literally came to blows about them. On the one hand there were the planters in the West Indies, and especially those from an island called Santo Domingo, who opposed the abolition of slavery. On the other hand, the Society of Friends of the Blacks were in favor of it, and a certain number of politicians also invoked the Rights of Man. To this should be added pressure on the part of England, which had become overnight a nation of Negro-lovers! Yes, all this had to be squarely faced, and a way of making money other than selling slaves had to be found. Agricultural colonization really was in the cards.

Anne wasn't the only one who was worried. All these rumors were making the little world of the *signares* very anxious. Although trade was the monopoly of the various companies who had followed one another on Gorée, that had never stopped anyone from trafficking in every kind of merchandise, including some which should never have left the royal warehouses. If they were no longer able to sell Negroes, what would they do? The *signares* prepared for battle. They were used to it. They had had to fight to claim the property that had belonged to their fathers. They still remembered the struggles of the *signare* and children of Monsieur Delacombe, a former governor; they had all been turned into the street and scattered after his departure for France. Should they give everything up and look to the mainland? The only links they still had were with half-caste families in the region of Joal.

Anne sent a male slave to the little village in the southern part of the island where Jean-Baptiste, like the other domestic slaves, had a hut. He hadn't been seen for a week. Where could he be? There was a ship permanently berthed in the harbor, guarding the bay. Every evening the guards made their rounds, accompanied by assistants who'd been taught to use a gun. He couldn't have escaped. And why should he have done so? Wasn't he well treated? Practically free?

There were suggestions that he might have fallen ill again and thrown himself into the sea, providing a feast for the sharks. Anne finally came around to this theory.

One intriguing detail was that Jean-Baptiste's disappearance precipitated the break between Anne Pépin and Isidore Duchâtel.

Isidore had inquired into the work of the naturalist Michel Adanson, who had practiced botany in the village of Hann on the Cape Verde peninsula and studied the agricultural possibilities of the region. Thereupon Isidore, together with a friend of his called Baudin, decided to obtain a concession there and grow fruit trees from the West Indies and vegetables from Europe. As Jean-Baptiste was one of the key elements in this plan his disappearance caused Isidore much annoyance, and he vented his anger on Anne. Soon afterwards he left Gorée and returned to Bordeaux, his hometown. Baudin, left to his own devices, persevered with the project and made contact with the chief of a group of Lebus.

CHAPTER
10

Perhaps we ought to prepare ourselves in childhood for the destruction of our ambitions. Perhaps we should keep telling ourselves that life will never come up to our dreams. So reflected Tiekoro, faced with what he thought were the ruins of his young life. El-Hadj Baba Abou's vengeance had not been slow, and Tiekoro was expelled from the university. The imam had sent for him to tell him so. But what pained him even more than that was the contempt he'd been shown, a contempt that he felt went beyond himself to his people and his culture, and that up to now had been more or less hidden. They were punishing not an act of folly, but a Bambara who had dared to try to enter a closed and aristocratic world. He had been waiting for weeks to hear whether Mulay Abdallah's father had been successful in his efforts to get him into one of the universities in Jenne to finish his studies.

So the days passed slowly in Siga's modest room. Siga! Tiekoro was discovering the extreme kindness of the brother he had always unconsciously looked down on, and whom he had abandoned in such an ugly manner. There was never a word of reproach. Not even a joke. Siga shared everything—the millet porridge in the morning, the plate of couscous at noon, the mat at night. Tiekoro tried to think only of God, to accept these humiliations, to stifle his wild desire to rebel against fate. What had he done to be so cruelly punished? What was he expiating, and for whom?

After much thought he found an explanation for the tricks of fate. Nadie. He had raped a girl belonging to his own people. For that's what it was—rape. If it had happened in Segu he would have been severely punished by the family tribunal and made to pay compensation to his victim's parents. And here, what had he done? He had run away.

The thought of the young slave haunted him more every day. In the end he went back to the bar kept by the Moors; he hadn't been there for months. It hadn't changed. A clean floor, with mats; the smell of green tea and a fire of dried camel dung; men playing at checkers with passionate expressions. Al-Hassan looked at Tiekoro quizzically, as if he guessed the object of his visit. But Tiekoro plucked up the courage to speak.

"Al-Hassan," he said, "have you got a Bambara slave?"

"Who do you mean?" said the other, taking his church-warden pipe from his lips. "Nadie? The poor girl's ill."

"Ill?" cried Tiekoro, worried. "So have you sent her away?"

"That is not how Allah would have us treat those who serve us," replied Al-Hassan gravely. "My wife has taken her and is looking after her."

"Listen," said Tiekoro, giving up all pretense and with some admiration for his own humility, "I have done the girl a serious injury, and I must make amends."

Like many of the Moors, Al-Hassan hid his material prosperity beneath a semblance of poverty. There were cracks stuffed with straw in the walls of his compound, and its main courtyard was littered with tools, a heap of dirty linen, refuse, and children with ringworm. Tiekoro made his way to a big untidy room, its floor half covered with frayed matting, and soon a fat Moorish woman, with very white skin beneath her blue veils, appeared. Tiekoro came straight to the point. He was looking for a young Bambara slave girl who had worked in Al-Hassan's bar. He was a Bambara himself. . . . The Moorish woman interrupted him, looking him keenly in the eye.

"Are you the father of her child?" she demanded.

Tiekoro nearly fainted.

"What?" he breathed.

The woman went on looking at him with the same mixture of severity and scorn.

"The poor creature's three months gone," she said, "but however hard I try she won't tell me who's her lover. She only begs me to adopt the child so that it doesn't become a slave too."

For a moment Tiekoro was silent. His brain was in a whirl. To tell the truth, he couldn't have said quite clearly why he'd sought Nadie out, nor what he'd meant to do if he found her. In lucid moments he admitted to himself that at first he'd only wanted to lie with her again. Then righteousness would get the better of him and he'd tell himself he wanted to make some amends for the wrong he'd done her. And now yet again fate was making a cruel mockery of him. In the mud of the privy, amid the frightful reek of excrement, he had given life to a human being. A human being toward whom he had obligations, who would have the right to turn to him as he himself used to turn to Dousika. Who would have the right to judge him. To despise him. To hate him.

He looked up. The woman was chewing a kola nut.

"Can I see her?" he stammered.

The woman called out to someone and a little girl came into the room, casting curious glances at the stranger. Then she vanished, and after what seemed an interminable interval Nadie came in. She was shrouded, like her mistress, in an indigo veil, and Tiekoro noticed that she was very young and not very pretty, with slightly prominent teeth. But this did not seem a defect: it made her look as if she were smiling. She was also very shy.

"Forgive me," murmured Tiekoro, his eyes filling with tears.

"You've come back, *fama*," she said, with an air of complete submissiveness. "That's all that matters."

"But what do you mean to do now?" broke in the woman, roughly.

"Take her away with me," said Tiekoro simply.

As he spoke he remembered that he no longer had a roof over his head, any means of support, or any future. He wanted to die. Two years ago he had left Segu in search of glory. And what was he going to take back? A woman whose rank and family were unknown, who had been brought low by circumstance. When he thought of all the responsibilities and all the ceremony surrounding marriage in his own country, he knew Dousika would never forgive him if he married Nadie. Should he keep her with him as a concubine?

Reassured now as to his honorable intentions, the woman offered him green tea and chattered away freely. What was he studying at the university? Wasn't he from Segu? And was he a Muslim? She herself was from Fez, and found the people of Timbuktu very standoffish. What did he think?

Tiekoro didn't try to answer this meaningless babble. He was going over his life and couldn't understand why everything conspired against him. His faith was too strong for him to believe it could be the ancestors taking revenge on him for his conversion. And yet the fear was there, lurking in his mind. If he could, he would have consulted a fetish priest capable of understanding and interpreting the will of the unseen. But he didn't know any priest in Timbuktu. Nadie came back carrying a small bundle on her head. Without a word she followed Tiekoro outside.

They walked along without speaking, he hurrying ahead and she following in his footsteps as if this path had been marked out for her since time began. Thus they came to the port at Kabara and the house of Abdallah the merchant.

If Siga was surprised at Nadie's entry into his brother's life he showed no sign of it, merely taking his few possessions and going to stay with a friend. The couple then found themselves alone amid the crowd of relatives, passing guests, servants and hangers-on who filled Abdallah's house. No one took any notice of them or asked them questions, and for a few weeks Tiekoro lived in an illusion of happiness and peace. It was not surprising that Nadie had been destined for the harem of some Arab prince, for her body was exceptionally beautiful. As he mounted her, Tiekoro thought of a mare that the Mansa had given his father after the sacking of Guemou and which Dousika kept in a paddock behind the huts in his compound: like the horse Nadie was black, highly strung, thoroughbred, and yet docile. He made love to her whenever he felt like it, shrugging away her feeble protests.

"But it's daylight, *koke*," she'd say.*

Deep down, however, he knew these carnal excesses were really only a way of avenging for his disgrace. He would never be a doctor of theology and Arab linguistics, surrounded by an admiring group of students, corresponding with his peers in Marrakesh, Tunis and Egypt and writing learned commentaries on the hadiths. And yet, was paradise more delightful than this? Had the gods, meaning to mock him, really given him the best gift of all, in the body of a woman?

Curiously enough, he never tried to find out who Nadie really was, what family she came from, what sort of a life she had led before the fateful day he had seen her by the privy. The fact was, he was afraid of finding that she was not his inferior. He needed to despise her in order to despise himself; he wanted to turn her into a symbol of the destruction of his hopes. So he was vexed by the friendship that had grown between her and Siga. Of course it was only natural, as a bride enjoyed the greatest possible freedom in her relationships with her brothers-in-law, chatting, joking and laughing with them. But Nadie wasn't his wife, and by treating her as if she were, Siga seemed to be telling him indirectly what he ought to do. Tiekoro was too proud to put up with this, and one day, after the evening meal, he could bear it no longer. Nadie was in the courtyard, making an infusion of bitter quinqueliba leaves.

"Well, what are you trying to tell me?" he asked Siga.

Siga carefully cleaned his teeth with a twig.

"I?" he said. "Souroukou can tell a village that's lived in from a village in ruins."†

This impertinence made Tiekoro angrier still.

"Just because I'm temporarily dependent on you, does that mean you have the right to interfere in my life?"

* Tradition forbade lovemaking in daylight. It was punished by the birth of an albino child, thought to be a force of evil.
  † Proverb meaning "Everyone knows what he's doing."

Siga looked him in the eye, and once again his extraordinary likeness to Dousika made it seem to Tiekoro that he was confronting their father.

"She's from Goumene," Siga said. "It was the *tondyons* of Segu who destroyed her village, shared the loot, then divided up and sold her people."

Then he went out into the courtyard.

Tiekoro was rooted to the spot. He knew all about Segu's warlike history, its struggles against the Bambara of Kaarta, against the Soninke, against the Fulani. Was he to be held responsible? Did he have to make reparation for Segu's crimes?

At that moment Nadie entered. Her abdomen was beginning to stand out under her *pagne*, and for the first time Tiekoro thought clearly about the child that was to be born. A child is always a joy, yet there was no happy anticipation in Tiekoro's heart. Even more than its mother, the child would be a blatant sign of his own failure. A firstborn should be honored by the blood of bulls, the acclamations of the griots, and women dancing. But this child, instead, would be born in a stranger's house in a foreign town, with no faces to bend over him and predict his future strength and vigor. What a crime it was to give life without love! Tiekoro suddenly felt a pity akin to affection.

"What do you want to do?" he asked her. "Go and have the baby among my people? With my mother?"

She hung her head.

"I'll do whatever you like," she murmured. "But . . ."

"But what?" he said impatiently. "Speak up!"

Her voice became almost inaudible. "But I'd rather stay with you," she said.

Then, growing bolder, she looked him in the face. This was rare. "My mother taught me how to do lots of things, at home in Goumene. I can spin the finest and the whitest yarn."

"Spin!" cried Tiekoro. "But that's slave's work!"

She smiled faintly. "Didn't I become a slave?"

Then, leaving him no time to object, she went on.

"Almost all the yarn in Timbuktu comes from Jenne, and that makes it dearer. If I came to an arrangement with some weavers I could earn many cowries for my work. That would help Siga—he can't earn much himself."

Once again Tiekoro was ashamed. He'd often thought about working. But what was he to do? Apart from teaching in a Koranic school or becoming a government official, all employment struck him as degrading.

He was a nobleman! If he had remained in Segu, the only work appropriate to his position would have been on the land, and as he would have owned slaves he would have lived in idleness.

In her own way, Nadie was giving him a lesson in courage. He did not speak, and she, apparently taking his silence as acquiescence, continued. "I know how to dye material too. When I was little I used to watch my mother's slaves make the indigo—pounding the leaves and adding the ashes of wild baobab wood. Then they dug holes in the ground and filled them with water . . ."

At that point there was a noise in the courtyard. Someone was dismounting and calling for a servant to take care of his horse. Tiekoro recognized his voice. Mulay Abdallah, at last!

He rushed from the room. Mulay Abdallah, holding his horse by the bridle, stood there, his cape covered in dust from the desert, looking tired but happy.

"Allah is with us, *cellé*,"* he cried. "My father's managed to persuade a friend of his—Baba Iaro, a marabout from Kobassa in Pondori, who's very influential in Jenne and therabouts—and they've accepted you at the university there."

Tiekoro fell on his knees in the middle of the courtyard. His sinful heart had doubted the Creator's great goodness, and now here he was, overwhelmed by it! He didn't listen to what Mulay Abdallah was saying.

"Be careful when you're there. Jenne's even more dangerous than Timbuktu. Remember what Es Saadi wrote: 'The people of Jenne are by nature inclined to be jealous. If anyone else wins some favor or advantage they all unite against him and hate him.'"

Tiekoro went on praying.

"Lord, cure my troubled heart! Make me as faithful as him I call a dog. Give me strength, like him, to be in control of my

* Songhay for half brother.

own life when the time comes for me to do your will and follow you."

When the *podo* is flooded, shoals of fish sweep over the land and devour the young and tender grasses, devastating the rice fields, taking refuge from the crocodiles and big carnivorous fish among the labyrinthine stems of the *bourgou* weed. It was the Bozo fishermen, the earliest inhabitants of the region, who gave the name *podo* to the middle delta of the Joliba River, of which Jenne occupies the southernmost point. Sometimes the area is a huge steppe of *bourgou*, invaded by the Fulani and their herds; at other times it is a vast expanse of water, dotted with sandbanks.

When Tiekoro and Nadie arrived in Jenne the *podo* was submerged. It was the rainy season, and they shivered as much from the cold and damp as from apprehension. Tiekoro kept telling himself there were large colonies of Bambara living in Jenne and he and Nadie would not be alone, but he still felt vaguely afraid. They had come by dugout canoe from Timbuktu, embarking at Kabara and following the course of the river. They could have gotten onto one of the big boats that went up and down the Joliba and carried a couple of hundred passengers at a time, but these were unsafe and often sank at an ill-fated spot called the Mimsikayna-yendi. So Siga had spent a fortune—more than two thousand cowries—having a first-rate watertight canoe made for them. The journey had taken weeks.

The boatman and his undersized assistant had rigged up a sort of tent made of oxhide at the back of the canoe, and beneath it Tiekoro and Nadie ate, slept and made love. All about them lay the shining waters of the river, with its population of egrets and melancholy waders. In the distance the banks closed in to form a narrow corridor at the outlet of Lake Debo, full of crocodiles, fish and black-and-white-striped snakes. Tiekoro would have liked the journey to last forever. In the morning he never tired of watching the birds flying to the fields along the banks, and in the evening he waited for the rising of the moon, scarlet at first, then gradually shrouding itself in a veil of blue. On light nights he would sit in the bow with the boatman and fish with a harpoon. When it was dark, the two men would light a fire and watch the carp, thread fins and bitter-fleshed hyena fish swarming round the muck in the water. Sometimes the mane of a horsefish would cleave its way through the current.

They stopped at villages to exchange the fruits of the water for the fruits of the land, and Tiekoro kept thinking this was an ideal life. All his ambitions suddenly seemed absurd; time itself no longer existed. What was he going to Jenne for? Why not build himself a straw hut by the river, like a Bozo fisherman? Nadie would split open his catch, clean the fish and lay them out to dry on the ground. She would bear him children.

They spent two nights at Komoguel, a kind of islet at the confluence of the Bani and the Joliba. The canoe had been leaking, and the caulking needed reinforcing with hemp steeped in a paste made of baobab fruit and shea butter. Then they resumed their journey. Now the banks of the river were covered with Fulani encampments, recognizable by their semispherical straw huts grouped around that of the *dyoro*, their camp leader. Mulay Abdallah had told Tiekoro what a menace the Fulani were in the region about Jenne. Some obscure marabout called Amadou Hammadi Boubou, from Fittouga, was beginning to create a stir, greatly annoying the new ruler, the *ardo*, of Macina. Though he hadn't yet actually taken up arms, he was already talking about starting a jihad and destroying all the fetish priests. Tiekoro was not entirely against the idea of a jihad, but he did wonder whether the ostensible religious aims didn't hide others that were less laudable, such as a desire for worldly power, greed for material riches, ambitions of all kinds. For while Tiekoro had learned of the arrogance and intransigence of Islam, he hadn't yet found out all its benefits.

He tried not to think of Ayisha. He knew that if he thought of her he would be tempted once again to despair. And what crime is worse than despair, before Allah? His only refuge was Nadie's body.

He got to know her better than in Timbuktu, there in the cramped space of the canoe. She was gentle without being passive. Indeed she was active, and competent without ever trying to attract attention. She managed to fix up a sort of little kitchen where she cooked *degue* and fried the fish from the river in cow's butter. When they berthed at the side of the river she would mingle with the other women and wash the linen with great energy. Then she would find a quiet spot, perhaps a little back-water sheltered by *solo* trees, and bathe. To the shocked amaze-ment of the other women, Tiekoro used to go with her. He en-joyed trickling the water over her shoulder blades and soaping her hair, which, as a "married" woman, she now wore "in six braids." One day he could not resist making love to her when they came out of the water. They were just going away again afterwards when the person who owned the land, and who had been told of what they had done, demanded reparations for the sin they had just committed. As they had nothing to give him they hurried back to the canoe, pursued by his imprecations. After this incident Nadie was thoughtful for several days. Tiekoro only laughed, but deep down he kept asking himself one question: what was he to do with this woman, who had become as nec-essary to his body as the blood flowing through his veins? Mulay Abdallah, full of the prejudices of his class, had been quite definite.

"*Cellé*," he said, "you can't marry her. Make her your con-cubine and servant."

But was that fair? Tiekoro never stopped thinking about it.

When they reached Jenne the town towered like an island above the *podo*.

With copses of mahogany nestling under its walls, it seemed to be surrounded by a double belt of foliage and water. While Timbuktu was beginning to decline, Jenne was still at the height of its glory. It was gayer and more lively than Timbuktu, the "queen of the desert," and its busy streets reminded Tiekoro of Segu. He was about to go straight to the main mosque of which he had heard so much, when he remembered Nadie's condition. She was getting tired, so Tiekoro decided to go instead to the house of Baba Iaro, the friend of Mulay Abdallah's father. He stopped a passerby and after the usual greetings asked in Arabic: "Can you tell me where to find the house of moqaddem* Baba Iaro?"

"Aren't you a Bambara?" exclaimed the other.

---

* Religious teacher giving instruction to beginners.

It warmed Tiekoro's heart to be recognized and addressed in his own language, but what his interlocutor had to tell him was disturbing. The Bambara were hated in Jenne, even though the Mansa of Segu had a house in the southern part of the *podo*. This was because of Islam, now spreading like a forest fire. The whole area was falling into the hands of the Fulani! The bumpkins who used to live in huts thatched with leaves and trail around after their cattle had now transformed themselves into the warriors of Allah! Tiekoro was incredulous. He would have questioned the man further, but Nadie had had a slight fever since the previous evening and they had to find somewhere to sleep.

Baba Iaro lived quite near the great mosque, whose minaret towers could be seen from where they now stood. It was a typical Jenne house, square-built in a style introduced some centuries before by the Moors when they occupied both Jenne and Timbuktu and reduced them to vassalage. It was one storey high, its flat facade broken by a single door surrounded with quadrilateral decorations, and by three iron-barred windows. The door had iron fittings, and as he took hold of the ring which served as a knocker Tiekoro remembered the welcome that had met him two years before at El-Hadj Baba Abou's, and almost fled. Only the people of Segu know how to welcome a guest and treat him like a brother! But where else could he go, with this woman already weary and soon to be confined? He grasped the knocker firmly.

So Siga was alone again in Timbuktu.

His feelings about the place were quite different from his brother's. He had immediately taken his place among its floating population of slaves, foreigners and poor, and taken advantage of the network of solidarity that always exists among people going through hard times. So, while he hadn't been happy, neither had he ever been lonely. He had a dozen friends among the Kabara donkey boys, and a similar number among the employees of the big merchants. As for women, he wasn't hard to please, and made do either with the common prostitutes in the taverns or with the Moorish or Tuareg women who opened their warm thighs to him in their jealous husbands' absence. But Nadie had given him a taste for a permanent feminine presence. He longed to find the

room swept and the meal prepared; not to have to await the pleasure of Abdallah's maids, to pay them for their services, and to
have to endure their fits of impertinence or idleness.

He threw himself into his work. Abdallah had recently put
him in charge of his dealings in salt. Twice a month he went to
Teghaza or Taoudenni with a caravan to be laden with bars of
salt, seeing to it that they were properly bound together so that
they didn't suffer damage in transit. At those times he ruled over
a whole company of slaves, who carried the bars to and fro and
marked them with black lines or diamonds to indicate to whom
they belonged. Then he brought the bars back to Timbuktu and
sold them to merchants from Morocco, or even from the Middle
East and North Africa. It was hard work, but he liked it. As he
supervised the slaves and bargained with the merchants he had
a feeling of usefulness, if not of power. He was part of a great
system, a great network of trade and communication reaching
right across the world. But despite his everyday contacts he remained determinedly aloof from any Muslim influence. Although there were agents of the Kountas* among his business
acquaintances, their relationship never went any further than a
jest or a bowl of green tea together. A fetish worshipper he was,
and a fetish worshipper he meant to remain, whether those who
called him Ahmed liked it or not!

One day when he had just returned from Taoudenni, Abdallah
sent a maid to fetch him.

"Sit down," he said, "sit down! You work very hard, Ahmed!"

Siga gave a smile that might have meant anything and took
a little earthenware bowl of tea from a female slave.

After a pause Abdallah went on. "As you know, I have relatives in Fez with whom I do business. And I have reason to believe
they're cheating me. I'm owed a lot of money. I get no reply to
my letters. I've decided to send you to see what's going on."

"Me!" cried Siga.

Abdallah nodded.

"Yes, you! I've been watching you, Ahmed, and I have great
plans for you. You know that Allah has taken my own children

---

* Influential family of religious men and merchants, of Arab origin, which
produced a religious brotherhood known as the *Kounti*.

from me, may his will be done, and so he has left me free to choose the children of my spirit. Go to Fez, collect my debts, and when that's done, await my instructions."

What youth of eighteen would not be full of exultation at the prospect of a journey? Who hasn't imagined himself entering some unknown city in triumph, winning riches and loving women? Siga was no different from the rest. But at the same time he was afraid. True, he was better equipped for such a venture than he had been two years ago when he left Segu. He had mixed with people. He now spoke two languages—Arabic as well as his own. But wasn't he still rather inexperienced? However, not for a moment did he dream of refusing his employer's offer. It was another challenge to the son of a slave, the son of she who threw herself down the well. He looked up at Abdallah.

"How shall I get there?" he asked.

Abdallah took a sip of tea. "Everything's arranged," he said. "We'll soon perform the *debiha*,* and you'll be under the protection of my friend Mulay Ismael's men. You'll go first to Taoudenni, then to Teghaza, then to Touat in Morocco. That's where the worlds of north and south meet. The country there is rich in barley and has plenty of watering holes. You'll see gazelles and ostriches! What an experience for a young man of your age!"

* Ceremony to provide protection.

CHAPTER
11

The *Lusitania*, with some three hundred slaves on board, was making for Pernambuco. She wasn't following the usual route. Times were bad. She hadn't been able to take on a full cargo at São João de Ajuda* and had had to go as far afield as Gorée, which added still more to the costs. With all these English, Danish, French and Dutch traders cruising around the African coasts and wooing the local kings with barrels of brandy, guns and gunpowder, the competition was becoming terrible. The English and the Danes offered prices no ordinary trader could afford to rival. At this rate it would soon be impossible to buy Negroes, and the *Lusitania*, which could have carried six hundred men and women, already had its hold only half full.

But on the whole Captain Fereira was not dissatisfied with his cargo. There wasn't one slave over twenty years old, and there were even a few children. Soon it would be time to have them all on deck for a wash in seawater. Unlike those swine the French and English, Fereira and the other Portuguese traders didn't chain their slaves up and saw that they slept on clean matting. What was the point of paying such a high price for men and women and then having them die on the voyage?

Fereira had been sailing the seas for twenty years and knew

* Fort near Ouidah in present-day Benin.

all the forts from Arguin on: Saint-Louis, James Island, Cacheu, Assinie, Dixcove, Elmina, Anomabu. . . . After all those years he was hardened to his sinister trade. He'd ended up by not even hearing the terrible groan, part sorrow and part rebellion, that came from the slaves as the ship sailed away forever from the coasts of Africa. Fereira filled his pipe and looked about him. The sharp line of the jungle was still visible, so dark green as to be almost black. The sun, though just risen, was already as fierce as the eye of a Cyclops mad with drink and lust. Fereira opened his prayer book, for he was religious. Ashore—though he wasn't often ashore—he went to communion every Sunday, and he never took on slaves without having a missionary come aboard to baptize them.

As he was finishing his prayers he saw a couple emerge from the fore hatch. He recognized the man straight away: he was the lunatic stowaway. But "lunatic" wasn't the right word: he was a strapping young man of sixteen or seventeen, with a handsome, sensitive face. He was said to be a Bambara. But Fereira was familiar only with the Congolese, Gabindas and Angolans he was in the habit of taking on at the fort of São Tomé,* and, more recently, the Minas and Ardras he embarked at São João de Ajuda. Why had the youth come on board? The low door, known as "the door to death," which led from the main slave house in Gorée to the slave ships, was guarded day and night by soldiers and armed sailors. The only ones allowed through were those who had already been branded to show whom they belonged to, and carefully fettered. So the youth must have had accomplices. But that wasn't the real problem. The real problem was, how could a man offer himself up as a victim of the slave trade? How could he deliberately confront the terrible crossing? Was he mad?

When the sailors had found him and brought him to the captain the latter's first impulse had been to throw him overboard. He was probably an agitator, come to foment one of the slave mutinies of which all captains went in terror. But the man, with extraordinary dignity, had shown him a cross. Had he been baptized? A child of God couldn't be put to death, so Fereira was

---

* Island off equatorial Guinea, used by the slave trade as a staging port between Angola and Brazil.

trapped and had to put up with him. At first he had tried to stop him going near the part of the lower decks reserved for women, for he didn't want any promiscuity on board. But that had proved impossible. With the same calm authority as before, the man kept coming to protect a young Nago* woman whom Fereira had had the good fortune to get hold of at Gorée. Fereira laughed: when they got to Pernambuco they'd know what they were in for! The planters weren't given to such refinements. One of them would buy the man and send him into the hell of the sugar or coffee plantations. As for the girl, with her pretty little face and her youth she'd soon become a "house wife" with a string of half-caste bastards. Fereira himself had two or three, with a Mina woman.

Meanwhile the couple gazed at the sea. As long as the sea exists, man cannot be entirely unhappy or abandoned. O immense blue ornament on the body of the earth, your waters are bitter but the fruits of your womb are sweet! You are so strong that even man, greedy for gold, cowries, coffee, cotton and ivory, has not been able to tame you. He gallops across you on his wooden steeds, but when you are angry and hurl your waves he becomes a frightened child again.

* Synonymous with Yoruba, an ethnic group of present-day Nigeria.

PART TWO

THE WIND
SCATTERS
THE GRAINS
OF MILLET

CHAPTER

1

When Malobali was about ten and had just thrashed one of his playmates and knocked him down, the other child stood up and insulted him.

"Filthy Fulani!" he yelled.

Malobali came running into Nya's hut.

"Ba!" he cried. "A boy just called me a Fulani! Why?"

Nya looked at him gravely.

"You're dirty, you're sweating," she said. "Go and have a bath, and then come back."

Malobali went off to the children's bath hut, bawling to a slave woman to bring gourds of very hot water. He was a violent, quarrelsome little boy, completely spoiled because of his extreme good looks. He was used to being complimented and to being singled out from among all the other children. His mother worshipped him. Everything gave way before him.

He had his bath, anointed his body with shea butter, put on the loose drawers he'd worn ever since he'd been circumcised, and went back to Nya's hut. She had lit her lamp, fueled with butter, and shadows were playing over the walls. She signaled to him to sit down on the mat. But he threw himself into her arms.

"You're not a Fulani," she said gently. "But your mother was."

"My mother?" he repeated in astonishment. "Aren't you my mother?"

Nya clasped him more tightly to her. She had always dreaded this, but she knew it had to be faced up to. "I am your mother," she said, "because I'm your father's wife, and because I love you. But it wasn't I who carried you in my womb . . ."

And, very gently, she told him about Sira. About her captivity. About her being Dousika's concubine.

"One evening she came into my hut. She was holding you by the hand, and on her back she carried the little girl she had after you. She said, 'I'm going, but I'm going to entrust my son to you.'"

Malobali started.

"Why didn't she take me with her?"

Nya kissed him on the forehead. "Because boys belong to their father. You belong to the Traore clan."

Malobali dissolved into tears. "Why did she go away? Why?"

Nya gave a sigh. Would the child understand? She tried to find a simple explanation. "Well, you see, for a long time the Fulani lived alongside us and we didn't pay any attention to them. Sometimes we even looked down on them because they didn't build or farm, but just went here and there with their herds. Then one day everything changed. They all got together and declared war on us. All because of Islam. You see, Islam is a sword that divides. It took my firstborn son from me . . ."

But Malobali, who didn't care at all about the ravages of Islam, interrupted. "Have you ever heard what became of my mother?" he asked.

Nya nodded.

"Yes," she said. "A few years ago she sent to tell me she'd married again and was living in Tenenkou."

Malobali started to yell. "I hate her! I hate her!"

Nya quickly put her hand over his mouth. If only the ancestors hadn't heard him say that! Then she smothered him with kisses.

"It cost her a lot to leave you. Believe me—I saw it. But she had to go back to her own people. And your father hasn't been the same man since she went away: he has no interest in anything any more. He's suffered too many blows. First his estrangement from the Mansa, then Tiekoro's conversion and Naba's disappearance. . . . It's too much!"

Ashamed, Nya blinked back some tears of self-pity and tried to think only of the little boy's sorrow.

It was true, though, that life in Dousika's compound was no longer what it used to be.

The year before, Mansa Monzon had died of incurable diarrhea, and his death had been a final blow to Dousika. Now he was only an old man, endlessly puzzling over the reasons for the plot that had ousted him from court. If only he'd been able to make his peace with Monzon before he was snatched away by death! But no, it was only the funeral sound of the great ceremonial drum, the *tabala*, which had told him, like all the other inhabitants of the kingdom, that he was now an orphan. Then he went with the crowd to pay his last homage in the outer vestibule of the palace, where the late king's body lay in state. And when he saw the mortal remains of Monzon, anointed with guinea sorrel and shea butter, lying on a shroud with the tail of a freshly killed ox in his right hand, it seemed to Dousika that he was looking at his own corpse.

Nya hugged Malobali. "When you're grown up there'll be nothing to stop you from going to see your mother! She loved you so much I sometimes wonder how she lives without you."

Naturally Malobali didn't believe her. Wiping his tears away with his knuckles, he got up and left. Young as he was, he realized that from now on nothing around him would be the same. The night would be full of fear and anguish and all sorts of questions. His mother, the woman who'd carried him for nine months in her womb, had turned her back on him! She'd made a choice between her two children, choosing the one to take with her and the one to leave. What a horrible decision! And after that she'd been able to let herself be courted by another man, to give him her body, to give him sons and daughters? Cruel, unnatural mother! No insult was bad enough for her!

As Malobali went by the hut where he slept with a dozen or so half brothers and cousins, he saw Diemogo, who hastily beat a retreat. Diemogo didn't really know anything about Sira—he'd only repeated a word he'd heard coupled with Malobali's name in grown-up conversation. Malobali went on without stopping to Dousika's hut, determined, despite his youth, to question him.

But fate had decreed that father and son should not argue the matter that evening. Dousika had been complaining of pains for some days, and his condition had grown suddenly worse. His wives, with the exception of Nya, bustled around him, one bringing "hippopotamus leaf" fumigations to ease his stiffness, another making *nete* infusions to bring down his temperature and preparing a potion of *nyama* bark to stop his diarrhea. The whole hut smelled of senility and the odor that precedes the stench of death itself.

Dousika's younger brother Diemogo, who for two or three years had been acting as *fa* in the compound, was at the bedside.

"I'm dying," Dousika quavered. "That doesn't scare me, of course. But I'd like to see my sons again. At least those who are left—I'll never see Naba again in this world. I'd especially like to see Siga. I was obeying the ancestors when I sent him to Timbuktu with Tiekoro, but I wonder now whether I wasn't being a bit harsh, whether it wasn't unfair . . ."

Diemogo wondered whether his brother's approaching end wasn't making him delirious. Fancy casting doubt on the wisdom of a decision that was dictated by the ancestors! But he kept his thoughts to himself.

"*Koro,*"* he murmured, "where would we look for them? All we know is that Tiekoro's in Jenne. The last we ever heard about Siga was from some caravaneers who'd seen him in Touat."

Dousika closed his eyes. "I must see them," he said. "If I don't my spirit will never find peace. It will haunt you all, moaning."

"In that case, I'll do all I can," said Diemogo.

Malobali looked at all this through the eyes of a child. His father's condition didn't grieve him, but like all young creatures he found illness and physical decay repulsive. The tearstained faces of the women, the movements of the two or three healers squatting in the shadows, his father's moans, his shining face and fetid breath—all made up a picture he would not soon forget. Was death hiding in the dark corners of the room, biding its time? Without knowing why, when Malobali imagined death he thought of the bald old woman, her eyes all white, at once pathetic and fierce, whom he sometimes saw in the next compound.

---

* Bambara for elder brother.

One day she had dropped her *pagne* and he'd glimpsed her wrinkled buttocks, covered with excrement.

Suddenly Nieli, Dousika's second wife, who hated Malobali as she had hated his mother before him, caught sight of him and chased him out with hysterical shrieks.

Very serious things were happening in the kingdom of Segu.

Da Monzon had succeeded his father amid a tumult of *tabala* and *dounoumba*. He had sat on his ox hide facing the east to receive all the insignia of kingship: the bows, the arrows, the lance, the executioner's knife. Then the sages had crowned him with the cap decorated with dangling gold rings, while the chief griot cried at the top of his voice: "You no longer have a family, Da Monzon! All the children in Segu are your children! Always hold your hand out, not to receive, but to give!"

It was a day of huge rejoicing!

But alas, hardly had he been enthroned than Da Monzon had gone astray. For most of the Segukaw the Fulani were foreigners whom their mansas held in submission, raiding their cattle when the fancy took them. And now Da Monzon started to distinguish between Islamized Fulani and fetishist Fulani, allying himself with the second against the first. Was that wise? It was as if an outsider were to interfere in a family quarrel. Afterwards all the parties are reconciled, at his expense!

When the *ardo* of Macina, Gouori Dialli, told him that the marabout Amadou Hammadi Boubou was troubling him, Da Monzon sent some *tondyons* to help the *ardo* subdue him.

But the *tondyons* got themselves beaten at Noukouma. The *tondyons*, beaten! And by whom? Who was this Amadou Hammadi Boubou? No one in Segu knew for certain. All they knew was that he was a Fulani.

Da Monzon realized that Segu's power was beginning to crumble. He sent for Alfa Seydou Konate, the famous marabout from Sansanding.

"A Fulani has arisen," said the marabout, "who will check the power of Segu. And as regards you yourself, you will not be succeeded by your son Tiekoura but by one of your brothers.

Which, I cannot yet say. As for the ill that afflicts you, it will never be cured."

Silence fell after these terrible words. All the slaves had been sent away for the secret interview with the great fetish priest, and there was no one in the room but the king, the marabout, and Tietigui Banintieni, the chief griot. Seeing the Mansa's visible distress the griot directed a mocking smile at him, as if suggesting he should take the priest's predictions with a pinch of salt. Had he forgotten that there were fetish priests in Segu who could counter all the machinations of fate? But Da Monzon was not reassured. He started to walk about the room, his movements as halting as his thoughts: stopping suddenly, then going on, then retracing his steps. If the Fulani, now Islamized to the point of fanaticism, were becoming so dangerous, wasn't it urgent to make peace with his brothers and rivals in Kaarta and forge a common front? But on what pretext?

Alfa Seydou Konate rose.

"With your permission, master, I should like to withdraw. The way is long from Segu to Sansanding."

When Da Monzon indicated that he gave permission, Alfa Seydou Konate left the room with the typical proud bearing of the Muslims, who claimed never to prostrate themselves to anybody but God.

Da Monzon had made many changes to the inside of the palace since his accession. He had had a kind of private drawing room built, with European armchairs and low settees covered with Moroccan blankets. He had also bought some big shiny metal chandeliers with candles. So there was no such thing as night any more, and the king had been given a new title. To those he had already—master of battle, the long snake that protects Segu, source of vitality, and so on—was added "master of night suns."

Da Monzon paced to and fro in the artificial light of the candles, his face streaming with sweat. Then suddenly he sat down, regal once more.

"Tietigui," he said, "what if we asked Ntin Koro, the Mansa of Kaarta, for a wife?"

The chief griot stared at the Mansa in bewilderment. "A wife?" he gasped.

The king waved his hand impatiently, not deigning to explain himself further.

"Make inquiries!" he said. "Find out if Ntin Koro has any marriageable daughters and come back and tell me."

Da Monzon was not as good a strategist as his father. He was also vain, capable of putting to death anyone said to be more handsome than he. He spent fortunes on pretty faces. But in an emergency he could act. If the Fulani were a threat to the "fetishists," then the fetishists must forget their own differences and combine against them! Da Monzon couldn't understand how anyone could make war in the name of religion. Was not every people free to worship whomever they liked? Though Segu ruled over many foreign cities it had never tried to force its own gods or ancestors upon them. On the contrary, it had taken over its subjects' gods and ancestors, the better to control the subjects and to expand Segu's own pantheon.

There were many gods, not just one. Why should Allah claim to reign all alone and exclude the others?

So the old rivalry between the ruling families—Kulibaly of Kaarta on the one hand and Diarra of Segu on the other—ought to be forgotten. He would send a delegation to the Massasi and seal the new alliance with a wife. Then their armies would combine, and people would soon see if they couldn't send those herdsmen back to their cattle!

After this Da Monzon felt comparatively reassured. Looking around, he saw he was alone in the large room with its Moroccanstyle hangings. He clapped his hands loudly. The crowd of slaves and griots waiting in the other room came forward, sizing up the Mansa's somber mood as they did so. The griots vied with each other to please him.

"What would you like us to sing to you, master of the suns of night?"

Da Monzon hesitated. "What do you know about that Fulani who's beginning to bother me like a gadfly on a cow's tail?"

A young griot called Kela struck his *tamani* and began: "A cowherd of Fittouga who'd been converted to Islam met a cow girl in the mud of the *podo* not far from Jenne. They married, and soon the cow girl's belly swelled up like a pumpkin. After six months there emerged a son, puny like all his race: Amadou

Hammadi Boubou. The day he was circumcised he began to cry: 'Father, take away the knife! Why wound me so? Take away the knife!' The mother was ashamed of her son, and said, 'Be off, I don't want to see you again.' Then Amadou Hammadi Boubou went to Rounde Sirou, rubbed his forehead in the dust, and cried: 'Come, I am the messenger of Allah! *Bissimillahi*, Allah have mercy!'

"The Moroccans in Jenne were up in arms: 'Who is this cowherd who calls himself the messenger of Allah?' they asked, and sent him back to the mud of the marshes of Dia and his cattle."

Da Monzon listened without a smile to this satirical song, intended to amuse him. Cowherd or not, Amadou Hammadi Boubou had already beaten one of his columns, and while Alfa Seydou Konate might regard that as a minor incident, other encounters were bound to follow that might be fatal. Da Monzon suddenly wondered whether it might not be better to provoke such encounters and count on surprise to turn them into victory. But to be sure of success he needed to be strong. Very strong.

"'Who is this cowherd who says he's the messenger of Allah?' And they sent him back to the mud of the marshes of Dia," Kela went on. "Then the children came running and said, 'Since you are the messenger of Allah, you don't need your blanket.' And they snatched it away from him . . .''

Da Monzon signaled impatiently to Kela to stop. A singer at once took over, accompanying himself on a guitar, soon backed up by a *bala*; and these were the only sounds to be heard in the room.

Da Monzon went over in his mind the conquests made by his father, and the way he had extended the borders of the empire. And was he, Da Monzon, going to preside over its downfall? Would that be how the griots would remember him? No, tomorrow he would summon the chiefs of all the towns and villages in Segu and suggest a reconciliation with Kaarta. After coming to this decision he was just getting ready to return to his latest favorite when the griot Tietigui Banintieni reappeared.

"Master of waters and energies," he said, "I have just learned that Dousika Traore is at death's door. His brothers have asked the caravaneers to take messages to those of his sons who are far away."

Da Monzon shrugged. What life does not end in death?

But Tietigui came closer.

"Remember why your father banished him from court. Wasn't it because he was having dealings with the Kulibaly of Kaarta? If you mean to be reconciled with them yourself, wouldn't it be wise to seem to reinstate Dousika before he dies? He'll leave twenty or so children. Send presents to his wives, especially his *bara muso*. You might even go and see him before it's too late. All that will make a favorable impression on the Massasi and soften them up for what you're going to ask. For I think I know what you have in mind."

The two men looked at one another. A king had no more intimate councillor, no closer friend, no more useful tool than his chief griot. He undertook nothing without confiding in him, and could count on his devotion. When Da Monzon was still only a prince, Tietigui had already done all his dirty work and intrigued and flattered on his behalf. It was partly thanks to him that Da Monzon had gotten the better of the twelve brothers who had also been old enough to succeed on his father's death—especially his elder brother. Once again he admired Tietigui's shrewdness. Births, marriages and deaths—they were all events to be made use of by anyone who wanted to rule the world! He nodded.

"Send my personal healer to Dousika," he said, "and tell him to make plenty of fuss. I'll go and see him myself tomorrow."

Meanwhile, unnoticed, Dousika's soul had left his body. Every soul, airy and invisible to human eyes, enjoyed a few brief moments of liberty before being recovered by the fetish priests and assigned to its new home in the body of a newborn child. During that interval it floated above rivers, soared over hills, breathed in without a tremor the thick mist that rose from the marshes, and alighted in the most secret corners of compounds. Distance meant nothing to it. For it, the great checkerboard of the fields was but a dot in measureless space. It steered itself by the stars.

So Dousika's soul flew over the *podo*. The shallows were

covered with big mauve water lilies, for the first rains had fallen and the Fulani's cattle stood up to their knees in the rich earth. Then, leaving Jenne behind, Dousika's soul crossed over the Moura marsh to Tenenkou, the capital of Macina.

It must not be thought that all the Fulani were supporters of Amadou Hammadi Boubou's religious revolution. Admittedly none of them was sorry to see the warlike farmers who for so long had raided their cattle taught a lesson. But that didn't mean they were going to shave their heads, give up fermented liquor and prostrate themselves on the ground five times a day! Moreover, words never heard of before were beginning to circulate.

"Faith is like a red-hot iron," proclaimed Amadou Hammadi Boubou. "As it gets cold it shrinks and becomes hard to shape. So it must be heated in the furnace of Love and Charity. Our souls must be steeped in the life-giving waters of Love, we must keep the doors of our souls ever open to Charity. And then our thoughts will turn toward meditation."

What did it all mean?

Sira's husband was one of those who knew. Amadou Tassirou had been a pupil of Sheikh Ahmed Tijani, founder of a Muslim sect known as the Tijaniya, and though he himself did not bear the esteemed title of sheikh, but merely that of *modibo*, learned man, he was nevertheless a saint. He had a library of his own containing several books on theology, scholastic philosophy and law, including Sheikh Ahmed Tijani's celebrated *Jawahira el-Maani* or *Pearl of Meanings*. He had married Sira when no other man of his rank would, after she had been the concubine of a Bambara for so long. When she got back to Tenenkou she had at first gone to live with her mother, feeding her little girl on the proceeds from the food she cooked and sold in the market. So Amadou Tassirou thought that in marrying her he was acquiring a servant, overwhelmed with gratitude. But after a few months he had to admit he had been wrong. Sira was arrogant and devoid of any kind of feminine modesty; her critical, sardonic attitude drove him crazy. To humble her he married a second wife, a girl scarcely arrived at the age of puberty. She died in childbirth, and he realized God had inflicted Sira on him for a special reason. But what?

He tried to draw her to him. She stiffened.

"What's the matter with you?" she said impatiently. "The child has quickened."

So he was obliged to let her go. Otherwise she would just look at him derisively. What pious man who never forgot any of his prayers would try to make love to his pregnant wife after the permitted period?

In fact Sira was lying, and only wanted to mortify Amadou Tassirou. Every day her thoughts went back to Segu. The children she had borne Amadou Tassirou and the child she was now carrying could not make up to her for Malobali. What was he like now? A young palm of the desert, with braided hair, sparkling whites to his eyes, rather high cheekbones, a light complexion. Had Nya told him anything about her? If so, he must hate her. But if Nya had said nothing, wouldn't his ignorance be even more painful than hatred? He would be coming and going, running about, eating and sleeping without knowing that, a few days' distance away, his mother was always thinking of him. But at this particular moment, Sira wasn't only worried about Malobali. Some strange anguish had come over her, and in her mind's eye she saw again her life with Dousika. How long it had taken her to leave him! Every rainy season she had decided to go, only to put it off to the next dry season. It wasn't the clash of arms between the Bambara and the Fulani that had finally brought her to make up her mind. Nor was it any attachment to Islam, which the Bambara fiercely rejected. No—it was a desire to mortify herself. A slave ought not to love her master, otherwise she loses her self-respect. She must go. But she found her own people had become curiously alien. Tenenkou had changed. It was no longer a sprawling encampment of straw huts put up hastily around wickerwork frames. There were now a number of mud houses, some of them as elegant as the houses in Jenne. A real port had been built at Pinga on Dia creek, to which traders came from all the towns along the river. Masons from Jenne had built a mosque, without a minaret or any architectural ornament, around which there flourished about a hundred Koranic schools. But Sira couldn't forget Segu—the cheerful freedom of its streets, the singing that rose from the compounds, the women coming and going with water from the river, the whinnying of horses led by half-naked grooms. It seemed to her that Islam made life austere and gray. Children with wooden writing tablets under their arms went through the streets to the prison of school. Every morning shivering little schoolboys went around the town chanting: "Know that, as God Himself has said, the key to the knowledge of God is knowledge of the soul. The Prophet has said: 'He who knows his own soul knows his Lord.'"

And the women, shrouded in their shapeless garments, seemed not to care any more about their looks, which distracted men from thoughts of God.

Sira tossed and turned on her mat as if she could feel someone looking at her. She propped herself up on her elbow and peered into the darkness. Who was hiding in the shadows? Beside her, Amadou Tassirou had fallen asleep. She remembered the nights with Dousika. Sometimes the outline of the window would whiten before they fell asleep. Afterwards she would avoid the piercing glances of Nya and Nieli as she went back to her own hut, and there she would hate herself for the pleasure given and received. It was on a morning like that that she had decided to leave.

Sira finally sat up. She was sure there was something there, near the large gourds used for keeping clothes in. But when she hastily lit the shea butter lamp there was nothing to be seen but some mice, which swiftly disappeared.

Dousika?

It was he. He needed her.

Some merchants who had been to Segu had told her he was in failing health. His hair was going gray like the bush in the dry season; he was getting fat. But now, she could feel it, he was at death's door, and his soul was softly calling her. Perhaps it wanted to enter into the child she was carrying, so as to be near her! Sira was afraid, and put her hands over her stomach as if to protect herself. At that moment the ceiling—wooden laths covered with reeds—creaked, and she thought she recognized a familiar voice, lamenting.

Dousika! Yes, it was he!

The walls of the hut fell away. The waters of the *podo* rolled back and the damp air changed into a dry, scorching heat. Segu. In the courtyards of the Mansa's palace, slaves were spinning and weaving, or washing out cloth that had been steeped in mud. A man walked through the crowd. Their eyes met. Those were the happiest years of her life.

A slave ought not to love her master, otherwise she loses her self-respect. Sira put the lamp back in its niche in the wall, blew it out, and lay down again.

"What's the matter?" mumbled Amadou Tassirou.

Then he turned over and took her in his arms. After all, he had the right; he was her husband. She had been damaged goods, but he hadn't hesitated to give ten head of cattle for her, ten cattle with shining coats and tapering horns. He treated M'Pene, the daughter she had with Dousika, as his own child, for he was a man of God. What did she have against him?

Meanwhile Dousika's soul leaned back against the window, which was blocked by a scrap of pottery. Unable to bear the sight of Sira in Amadou Tassirou's arms, the soul was thinking up the worst kinds of revenge: entering Sira's womb, there to get into and kill her child; hunting down all her subsequent children and leading them one by one into the grave; occupying her womb completely and making her barren. Or seizing her body when it was abandoned in sleep and begetting monsters upon it.

Under this terrible gaze Sira huddled up on the mat, groaned, half woke, and then lapsed back again into unconsciousness.

CHAPTER

2

The royal griots were already arriving at Dousika's compound, followed by musicians, singers and dancers, when Da Monzon, surrounded by slaves fanning him with ostrich feathers, was just setting foot outside his palace. As he rarely appeared in public except on warlike expeditions, all the town was out to see and acclaim him. The children perched on the branches of the mahogany and shea trees, while the women shamelessly pushed and shoved to get near. Da Monzon was very simply clad in loose white drawers and a red *boubou* or long tunic. He had adopted this Muslim form of dress. The only insignia of royalty he bore were a long leather-bound stick and a broad saber. But he hadn't been able to resist the pleasure of wearing yellow leather boots embroidered in red, brought by slave traders from the coast.

Those who hadn't seen him since his enthronement exclaimed that he was even more handsome than his father, with the three royal scars on his temples, the same open copper ring in his ear and the two long braids crossed under his chin. But it was his walk that was most admired, the long, swinging stride that showed off his slimness. It was easy to understand why so many women went into raptures over him, and why his harem contained no fewer than eight hundred of his devotees.

But when the griot Kela entered the compound, one of Dousika's brothers told him in a whisper that Dousika hadn't waited for the Mansa and had just passed away. Kela ran back along the procession telling the musicians to mute their instruments, then threw himself in the dust at Da Monzon's feet.

"Forgive him, master of the waters and energies," he pleaded. "He's gone."

But Da Monzon didn't turn back.

Now the wailing of the women drowned out the sound of the music, and in accordance with a recently introduced custom they were firing off guns in the dead man's compound, guns he had gotten from the traders on the coast. This brought out other women, shrieking, from the neighboring compounds. They ran toward the house of mourning, some of them rolling in the dust of the streets. Crowds of griots appeared like a swarm of locusts descending on a field and began to proclaim Dousika's exploits and lineage. Da Monzon signaled discreetly to Kela, and he too started to sing. That was a supreme honor—to be praised by the Mansa's griot, in his presence!

But in Dousika's hut, silence reigned, contrasting with the tumult outside. Diemogo's wives were washing the corpse with warm water scented with basil, while Flacoro, Dousika's last wife, unfolded pieces of white cotton cloth made by the best weavers and carefully kept for this occasion. Nya and Nieli had lain a coarsely woven mat on the floor, covered with a soft, fine one made of *iphene* leaves. When Dousika's body had been laid on this, all the wives would sit down on little stools around the *bara muso* and receive condolences in silence. Nya didn't know whether she was sad or not.

To begin with she was relieved, for the Dousika soon to be buried was not the Dousika she had so loved. He was a man grown old before his time, forever going back over all his blighted hopes, as if every life wasn't in the end one long, bitter, mean affliction. Every morning, going into his hut, she had wondered who it was she was dealing with. Now death and the rites of purification were giving her back a companion worthy of her love and respect.

Diemogo was standing in the entrance to his brother's hut. He could hear the Mansa's procession approaching, but this belated rehabilitation gave him no pleasure. He knew the honors bestowed by kings were all hypocrisy, and he wondered what plots were being hatched around Dousika's body before it was even cold.

Then, even as he thanked the neighbors, friends and relations who were already bringing the poultry and sheep destined to provide the ritual meal of meat, he thought sadly that his brother's last wish had not been granted: he hadn't been able to see either Siga or Tiekoro again.

An ox must be killed, for Dousika was a man of importance and all the poor of Segu would come to eat at his expense one last time. Gourd upon gourd of *dolo* must be made, gourd upon gourd of *to*, gourd upon gourd of stew . . .

Da Monzon stood framed in the one door into the compound, then crossed the main courtyard full of awed and admiring children and approached the entrance to the hut. Diemogo threw himself down in the dust.

"Forgive him for not having waited for you, master of energies," he said.

As the Mansa signaled to him to get up, Tietigui Banintieni began to circle around him, crying:

> *Koro*, your only staff is broken
> You must learn to walk alone
> When you needed help
> You called your brother
> But when you need help now
> To whom will you turn?

Da Monzon didn't enter the hut, for the laying out was not yet finished. He signaled to his slaves to give the family the bags of cowries they had been carrying, and presented his condolences to Diemogo and his younger brothers. Koumare and the other fetish priests squatted around in the sand nearby, sounding out the will of the ancestors. Would Diemogo be a good *fa*? Would he be able to manage the family's vast possessions, protect all the women and children, prevent the slaves from quarreling? In Segu the slaves and their children often joined together and ruled the households they belonged to. Who would Dousika's wives go to? Would they be shared out among the brothers in order of age, or would they all be given to Diemogo, who already had four wives? All these questions had to be answered, and the fetish priests stared at the divining board. Koumare was especially intent, for he had to accompany Dousika's soul on its journey to the home of the ancestors. All the powers unleashed by those who had hated him in his lifetime lay in wait to lure him into the dark and torrid region where peace could never be found, so that he might never be reincarnated in the body of a male infant.

Koumare, after chewing a kola nut vigorously, spat the resulting pieces and brown juice at the walls of Dousika's hut, then went to cut the throats of the animals that would be cooked together to provide the funeral feast. Meanwhile another priest made a clay model of the departed, to be placed in the little hut which already contained the *boli* representing the rest of the family ancestors.

All these preparations reminded Da Monzon of those which had been made at the death of his own father a year earlier, though of course the presents had been on a different scale. When Monzon died no fewer than seven rooms in the palace had been needed to hold all the gold and cowries that flowed in from every corner of the kingdom. Horses and cattle were crammed into the courtyards. All the gifts had been distributed among the poor and passing travelers in accordance with the wishes of the departed, thus benefiting hundreds of people. But apart from the differences due to status, the atmosphere was the same: a mixture of compulsory rejoicing and private grief, necessary ostentation and real hospitality, and above all the sudden terror of the unknown that lay behind the jesting, singing and dancing.

Da Monzon couldn't help thinking of his own death, of the moment when he would be lowered into the grave and his sons would moisten the earth over him with the ritual words: "See this water and do not be angry. Forgive us and give us rain and an abundant harvest. Give us long life, many descendants, and wives and riches."

He shuddered and thought he would go back to the palace, but then saw that his griot Tietigui was deep in conversation with a handsome stranger. Judging by his height, his scarifications and his clothes he looked like someone from Kaarta. Tietigui never forgot the interests of the kingdom, thought Da Monzon.

Inside the hut Dousika's corpse swelled and decomposed rapidly, giving off a sickly odor. Koumare and the other fetish priests knew this was because of the humors provoked by the worry and disappointments of Dousika's last few years, and they advised the gravediggers to bury him as soon as possible. The gravediggers told the family, but Diemogo objected, saying the dead man's sons must be given a chance to get their father's terrible message and return to Segu. Most of those present thought this unwise: it would be enough if the sons were back for the fortieth-day ceremonies. And they jumped to the conclusion that Diemogo would not make a good *fa*: he was too timid and had too much respect for custom.

Now that Da Monzon had gone back to the palace the atmosphere was more relaxed, and under the influence of the *dolo* people were beginning to forget the dead man and to gossip, joke and look at the women. Above all they wondered what would happen between Diemogo and Nya. They knew they hated each other. When Dousika had started to fail, Nya had thought she would take over control of the household in the name of her son Tiekoro. But Diemogo had promptly convened the family council, which had dismissed her claim. If Nya now refused to marry Diemogo as tradition prescribed, she would have to go back to her own family. Then who would defend her children's interests? Tiefolo, Diemogo's eldest son, already seemed to enjoy an excessive preeminence over everyone else. People recalled that it was when he had taken Naba, Dousika's second son, hunting, that Naba had disappeared. It didn't take long for many to conclude that the whole thing was premeditated.

Diemogo finally had to take the fetish priests' advice and tell the gravediggers to put up the awning under which Dousika would briefly lie in state. Meanwhile work was begun on digging the grave behind his hut where he was to be buried. The singing and dancing redoubled, and everyone started to look at Tiefolo, thinking that he was behaving as if he were really the firstborn son and heir.

In fact, Tiefolo had never forgiven himself for the fateful hunting expedition, and ever since then his whole life had been a vain attempt to forget it. His aloof and taciturn manner, which people put down to pride, was really only a mask for his remorse. But now he had had an idea of how he might redeem himself. Had he once caused the destruction of a son belonging to the clan? Well, now he would bring another one back! Taking advantage of a moment when Diemogo was alone, he went up to him and whispered: "*Fa*, let me take a horse and ride to Jenne. I'm sure I can bring Tiekoro back before the fortieth day."

Diemogo didn't know what to say. It was undoubtedly a good idea: the slaves he had sent would never be as diligent as a child of the family itself. But given all that was going on in the region— Fulani ambushes, slaving raids from the coast—was it wise to let a young man take the risks involved in the journey? He made the only possible decision: "We'll consult Koumare."

At that moment a breath of air brought the pestilential odor that was now beginning to emanate from Dousika, and he realized that the funeral could not be put off any longer. He sent for Koumare, who was with the gravediggers, facing south and reciting the ritual prayers. When he came Diemogo took him away into a quiet corner. Koumare did not hesitate. Scarcely had he dipped his fingers in the sand than he looked up and said: "Your son may go, Diemogo."

"Will he bring Tiekoro back?" Diemogo insisted on knowing.

The other grimaced, making his face more terrifying than ever, and said: "The fisherman's net may catch other fish than the thread fin!"

Thereupon a slave led in a superb Macina horse with a gleaming coat, pure white except for one hoof. Its headstall was covered with gris-gris, amulets and little animal horns full of every kind of powder to protect both horse and rider. Then two bags were tied to the saddle containing provisions, cowries and an enormous quiver full of arrows. Tiefolo, after prostrating himself before his father, took his horse by the bridle, and all the children in the compound ran after him, shouting and clapping their hands. For them it was the culmination of an extraordinary day which had begun with the Mansa's visit and continued with an orgy of feasting and tamarind cider. The more sensible among them were content just to watch Tiefolo jump on the horse's back, but others ran after him through the sweltering streets as far as the Mansa's palace. The boldest of all went on beyond the walls of Segu to the banks of the Joliba, to see Tiefolo and his horse embark in a big dugout canoe. The horse was frightened, and whinnied and reared, but Tiefolo stroked and soothed it. Soon the boat was out in the middle of the river, where the currents were running high.

By the time most of the children got back to the compound, Dousika's corpse, wrapped in the two mats, was lying under an awning outside his hut, and each one had to master his fears, slink along in the wake of a grown-up and beg the departed's forgiveness. Those who could talk tried to join in the chorus: "Forgive! We loved you, we respect you, be happy and protect us . . ."

The shrill voices of the gravediggers, the faces of the fetish priests and their formidable array of gris-gris terrified the children: not the least attraction of this extraordinary day was its mixture of fear and pleasure, gaiety and grief, celebration and sorrow.

Then the gravediggers hoisted the body onto their shoulders and began to walk around the compound, after which they came back to the gaping red grave where all Dousika's sons were assembled. Diemogo stood holding his brother's sandals, his water jar and a little white chicken, all of which were to be buried with him. Diemogo's face streamed with tears, for he had loved his brother dearly. But the others didn't approve of this sign of weakness. Only women ought to sob and shriek. And yet Dousika's wives, who were still in his hut, sat there calmly on their little stools, shrouded in cotton robes. For them the long seclusion of mourning was about to begin: except in circumstances of absolute necessity, they would not venture out until the day of ritual purification.

CHAPTER

3

Tiekoro clapped his hands and his pupils dispersed, their wooden writing tablets under their arms. He didn't have many pupils, only fifteen or so from neighboring houses in this poor quarter, whose parents were often unable to pay him. Deep down, Tiekoro hated being paid for imparting the knowledge necessary for a spiritual and religious life. He had a profound horror of "marabout beggars," the holy men who lived on the charity of the faithful, but he couldn't let Nadie be responsible for the upkeep of the family. When his pupils couldn't bring him the cowries they owed him, he would accept millet, rice or poultry instead.

Were all his studies only for this? This small sandy courtyard with an awning in one corner for his pupils to sit under? This house furnished with the bare minimum of equipment? Tiekoro had applied for a job at the university but had been refused. Nor did he seem qualified to be an imam, *cadi* or muezzin. All he'd been granted was freedom to open a school, but he received no official subsidy and had to make do with private fees. But he was a doctor of Arabic theology and linguistics—so why this distrust, this ostracism? The simple answer was that he was a Bambara. In Jenne the Moroccans, the Fulani and the Songhay all hated the Bambara. They were as plainly branded with the opprobrium of "fetishism" as an orthodox worshipper was with the mark made on his brow by his prostrations. But sometimes it seemed to Tiekoro that something else was involved besides religion; that this scorn and hatred were directed at something different. But what?

He put his prayer beads in his pocket, stood up, brushed the pieces of straw from his tunic and set off home. The masons' guild in Jenne, the *bari*, were famous from Gao to Segu, across all Tekrour and even as far as North Africa. They were said to have learned the art of building from one Malam Idriss, who came from Morocco years before and constructed palaces for the Askia and the Mansa and mansions for the heads of leading families. Using soil from the *podo*, sometimes mixed with powdered oyster shells, the *bari* made bricks that were at once light and yet strong enough to withstand the worst extremes of the weather. But alas, Tiekoro didn't live in one of their houses. His was a little two-roomed place in the Joboro quarter, furnished with a few blankets, mats and stools and reached through a yard cluttered with chickens, goats and kitchen utensils. It was squashed between two other houses of the same kind in a narrow, uneven street. Every time Tiekoro approached it he felt a pang. So why didn't he go back to Segu?

The fact was that Tiekoro was very strict with himself. He knew that if he returned to Segu he would, whether he liked it or not, enjoy considerable prestige because of his travels abroad, his knowledge of foreign languages and even his conversion to the magical religion of Islam. He would easily be able to pass himself off as a figure of importance. But he couldn't conceal from himself that he was a failure, and he was no more willing to deceive others than he was to deceive himself. In a way he took pleasure in his poverty and solitude. As he entered his house, Ahmed Dousika and Ali Sunkalo both came running toward their father on their still uncertain little legs. Nadie quickly left what she was doing to come and meet her lord and master.

What would have become of him without her?

Scarcely had they arrived in Jenne than she had learned to make the biscuits of rice flour mixed with honey and pimento that were favorites both with the local people and with the traders from Timbuktu and Gao. She also learned to make *kolo*, little bean flour rolls cooked with butter, and many other tidbits. She started to sell them in the market, and before long had acquired quite a reputation. As Tiekoro became more bitter, anxious and

frantic, Nadie grew more serene. Her very white, slightly protruding teeth gave her a smiling expression that was contradicted
by the gravity in her deep-set eyes. Though not at all coquettish
by nature, she had adopted the Fulani women's custom of dec-
orating her hair with amber beads and cowrie shells. She was
beautiful, with a beauty that took you by surprise, like the perfume of certain flowers, which at first seems insignificant but
turns out to be unforgettable.

She set a gourd full of rice down on the mat in front of Tiekoro, together with a smaller one containing fish sauce. He made
a face.

"Haven't you got anything else?" he said. "All I feel like eating is some gruel."

"You must eat, *koke*," she answered firmly. "Remember how
ill you were last rainy season. You're still not strong."

Tiekoro shrugged but obeyed. She was about to withdraw
respectfully as he ate, but he called her back.

"Stay with me. . . . Tell me what they were saying in the
market this morning," he said.

She picked up Ali Sunkalo, who was trying to dip his fingers
into his father's food.

"They say there's soon going to be a war between Segu and
the Fulani of Macina. Amadou Hammadi Boubou has obtained
protection from another Muslim, Ousman dan Fodio, who's ordered him to overthrow all the fetishes."

Tiekoro pretended to be indifferent. "Well," he said, "we
don't live either in Segu or in Macina, so what does it matter to
us?"

There was a short silence.

"Amadou Hammadi Boubou means to make Jenne submit
too," said Nadie. "He says Islam is corrupt here, and the mosques
are sinks of iniquity."

Tiekoro sighed.

"Even though I think he's a fanatic and a menace," he said,
"I must say he's right about that."

He pushed away the dishes and washed his hands in a bowl
of clean water.

"How strange that the name of God should divide people,"
he said, "when God is Love and Power. The creation of all liv-

ing creatures comes from His love, and not from any other power . . ."

He checked himself, for he realized he was starting to lecture as he might have done beneath the arcades of a university. He stood up, and Nadie silently removed the remains of the meal. If there was one thing that grieved Tiekoro it was her attitude toward Islam. With mute obstinacy she rejected it, and he couldn't stop her from surrounding their children with the same protective measures he had been familiar with in Segu. Their bodies were covered with gris-gris, and if Tiekoro arrived home unexpectedly he might find some toothless old Bambara fetish priest there. Though furious with himself for his own weakness, he didn't like to turn the old fellow out. Several times he had destroyed the *boli* that Nadie hid in a corner of the yard, but as she always stubbornly replaced them he eventually stopped objecting.

Even after all these years of living together, Tiekoro had still not solved the problem of Nadie's status. She was still his concubine, and he had made no attempt to find out which family in Beledougou she belonged to and what had become of it. He felt guilty about this, but tried to absolve himself with the thought that she seemed happy. Happy to serve him; happy to give him children. She had found a place for herself in Jenne among a group of active, industrious Bambara women who were practically immune to the customs of the society around them.

Tiekoro went into the other room, which was dark as well as small because it had no window or door. Awa Nya, his little daughter, was sleeping there, wrapped in a bundle of rags. Tiekoro picked up the baby. Nadie had added yet another gris-gris to those the child already wore around her neck and wrists! Tiekoro was tempted to wrench the despicable things off. Hadn't the Prophet said, "Whoever wears an amulet on his body is impious"?

But he stopped himself. If the gris-gris might protect Awa Nya he mustn't interfere. He adored her. While his sons, he thought, would judge him in the future, he seemed to find only love, indulgence and protection in his daughter. As he did in Nadie. He put the child down beside him on his mat. Suddenly he heard rain drumming down on the roof; there was no end to this season. Tiekoro fell tranquilly asleep.

At the first drops of rain Nadie brought the little boys indoors, though they would have preferred to run about in it naked. Then she stacked the washing, the bowls and her stores of cow dung under the rudimentary awning beside the kitchen. Knowing Tiekoro, she had minimized the seriousness of the rumors circulating in the town. All the Bambara were preparing to go back to Segu or to the villages their families came from. It wasn't the first time the Bambara had had to leave Jenne. Askia Daoud had ordered them to be driven out of the city centuries ago. But despite official orders, large colonies of Bambara had prospered, especially in the southern part of the *podo*, in the Femay and Derari regions around Jenne, between the Joliba and the Bani. But now the situation was becoming more disturbing. Supporters of Amadou Hammadi Boubou were going through the town preaching at street corners and saying, "If you tell me you know yourself, I'll reply that you know the substance of your body, which is made up of your hands, your head, and the rest. But you know nothing of your soul."

They spoke of hurling unbelievers and bad Muslims into eternal fire after their leader had conquered the town. Moreover, Nadie had heard that the Muslims themselves were divided according to the brotherhoods they belonged to. Who was this god of division and disorder? Nadie kept asking herself. Tiekoro thought he was protected by his conversion to Islam, but Nadie didn't believe it: whether he remained a fetishist or not, a Bambara was always a Bambara in the eyes of those who resented Segu's power and greatness. Should they flee from Jenne, then? But Nadie was afraid of the unknown family that would take Tiekoro back, remind him that she was only a concubine with an embarrassing past, and force him to marry a wife of his own rank. She clasped her sons to her.

Tiekoro was a nobleman, whose family tree went back to time immemorial. When he got back home to his father's compound he would resume his former rank, prestige and greatness. And she—what would she be in the eyes first of his family and then of his legitimate wives? No more than a piece of cow or camel dung, fit to make a fire, but smelly and despised. Never. Never. She would rather die.

—

Meanwhile Tiefolo had arrived at the gates of Jenne.

People stared at the young man on his superb horse, recognizing him as a Bambara by his scarifications, his little braids and all the gris-gris on his arms. And they either hated or despised him.

Tiefolo, unaware of all this, entered the town. He was disappointed. Was this really Jenne? There were fewer people than in Segu, there was less trade going on. He galloped into a huge square with an enormous building in the middle of it. Was this a mosque? Tiefolo had never seen such a vast edifice. He rode his horse around it.

It stood on a kind of esplanade, and its rich *podo* clay bricks looked brown in the damp air, with glints of blue. Its main frontage consisted of a series of towers crowned with truncated pyramids, below which were triangular festoons. The side walls were made up of rectangles, some sunk and some in relief, producing the effect of tree trunks in a forest.

A group of men began to climb the steps leading up to the esplanade, then carefully piled their sandals in a corner. Tiefolo was intrigued. He decided to find out what it was all about, and whipped his horse up onto the esplanade. As the men were going toward a doorway high enough for a horse and rider to pass through, he followed them, and found himself in an inner courtyard bounded by slender columns. It was then that the men he had been following turned and began to yell at him. A tall old man in a loose robe emerged from behind a column and added his voice to the rest. Tiefolo, who was a polite young man, was about to dismount and try to calm him down when more white-robed men came running up, this time from inside the building. In less time than it takes to tell, Tiefolo was dragged from his horse amid a hail of insults and blows. At first, seeing his assailants were older than he, Tiefolo made no attempt to defend himself. Then, as the blows intensified, he began to lose patience. Soon some hotheads appeared armed with sticks, while others spat in his face. Now Tiefolo did start to defend himself, and to some effect, for he was a young hunter with a strong body, in good training. Using his feet, his fists and even his teeth, he soon put his adversaries to flight. After a moment, two of them who had disappeared suddenly returned, each carrying a large stone in his hand. Tiefolo yelled a protest—did they want to kill him? Too late. He'd already been struck on the forehead.

When he regained consciousness he was in a small room with a low ceiling, feebly illuminated by a little window. He was lying on a heap of straw so evil smelling that despite being half unconscious still, he couldn't stand it and tried to move away. Then it was as if a thousand ox horns pierced his skull, and his face ran with blood. He fainted again.

When he next came to he could see from the color of the sky through the window that a long time must have elapsed. In the tiny indigo rectangle a star was smiling mockingly. Tiefolo tried to feel his head and see how serious his wound was, but he couldn't move his arms. They were tied behind his back with a strong cord made of *da*. His ankles were similarly bound. Tiefolo wept like a child. Yet at the same time, despite his weakness and the fact that he hurt all over, he didn't lose hope. He knew all these ordeals were only temporary. Koumare had been quite definite: he would carry out his mission in the end. Then perhaps he fell asleep. Or perhaps he fainted again.

The indigo square went a darker blue still, then black, then began to lighten, passing through every shade of gray until it at last turned light blue speckled with white. Tiefolo had never in his life been shut up or deprived of freedom to move. On the contrary, he had always been master of the bush and its wide-open spaces. But he didn't lose heart.

Suddenly the door turned on its wooden hinges and a man appeared, carrying a bowl of gruel and a little hollowed-out gourd. He came and knelt by Tiefolo, examining him, to his surprise, with an expression of admiration on his face.

"Where do you come from?" he asked. "What is your country?"

"I'm a Bambara. I come from Segu," Tiefolo managed to reply.

The man laughed.

"I guessed as much," he said. "What a fellow! Do you know you half strangled the imam, and broke two of the muezzin's teeth? I'm a Bozo—that's why I can understand your language."

He undid Tiefolo's bonds, helped him sit up and fed him some of the gruel.

"They're going to bring you before the *cadi*," he said as he did so. "Take my advice: if you don't want to end up under the executioner's knife, agree to be converted to Islam."

Tiefolo shoved the man's hand away.

"Never!" he spat the words out.

The man tried to calm him.

"Agree!" he said. "They'll shave your head and call you Ahmed. What do you care?"

Tiefolo leaned back.

"Why did they all attack me?" he asked. "What did I do?"

"You rode into their mosque, and it seems your horse forgot himself and scattered urine and dung over the sand!"

He laughed, and Tiefolo might have done the same if he hadn't been in such pain. As he painfully swallowed another mouthful of gruel, three men with guns entered the room. They began by kicking him, making him cry out despite himself, then forced him upright. They wore short black jackets, wide leather belts fastened tightly around their waists and loose drawers reaching to halfway down their calves. Their faces were fierce. Tiefolo limped after them, expecting to faint at every step, the blood still streaming from his head. They went through a maze of corridors, reached a courtyard, then entered a rectangular room, its ceiling supported by pillars made of palmyra trunks. Seven men sat there on mats. They wore white robes and turbans. The same hatred and fierce determination could be read in all their eyes. A young boy, also wearing a turban, sat cross-legged in a corner, making marks on a big roll that was half unfolded.

Tiefolo realized he was appearing before a tribunal. The Bozo had been right. The building was a mosque, and these fanatics were going to punish him for having entered it.

"*As salam aleykum. Bissimillahi.*"

Tiefolo guessed that these were Muslim salutations, and to show that he meant to preserve his own identity he returned their greeting in Bambara. The seven men consulted together, then signaled to one of the soldiers, who came forward and acted thereafter as interpreter.

"Tell us who you are."

Tiefolo did so.

"What are you doing here in Jenne?"

"I've come to tell my brother that our father has passed on and that the family expects him for the fortieth-day ceremonies."

"What's your brother's name?"

"Tiekoro Traore. But apparently you call him Oumar."

The insolence of this answer was unmistakable, and the judges reacted angrily. But the interrogation continued.

"It was Da Monzon who sent you to provoke us in our place of worship, wasn't it? Confess, and your life will be spared."

Tiefolo almost laughed.

"Your place of worship? I didn't even know it was a mosque! In Segu—naturally—they're not nearly so big . . ."

"Why did you ride in on horseback? Why did you let your horse soil the floor?"

"In answer to the first question: I didn't know it was forbidden. If anyone had told me I'd have apologized and made amends. In answer to the second question: Am I responsible for my horse's innards?"

The judges consulted again among themselves. Tiefolo wondered if he were dreaming. Yes, his body must be lying on a mat somewhere while his spirit roamed encountering horrible experiences! These old men in white robes holding prayer beads in their hands. These soldiers. These absurd accusations. In Segu the only place one wasn't allowed to ride into was the Mansa's palace, and even there an exception was made for certain dignitaries.

"Do you know that you are liable to be put to death?"

Tiefolo shrugged.

"Is not death the door through which we shall all pass?" he answered calmly.

There was another silence. Then one of the judges rose. He was bent with age, but his eyes were still bright.

"I know a man called Oumar Traore, who stayed with me once. We'll send for him," he said. "Allah grant you have not lied to us!"

The soldiers then took Tiefolo back to prison. The sun was shining brightly, and as he went through the courtyards Tiefolo could see tufts of palmyra above the high *banco* walls. The prison occupied the western part of a compound built around a courtyard containing jars of water for use in ritual ablutions. In one corner a group of men sat sewing strips of cotton cloth into a sort of garment with a hood at one end.

Tiefolo shuddered at the thought they could be shrouds.

Whether it was an encouraging sign or not he couldn't tell, but instead of taking him back to the horrible cell where he had spent the night the soldiers led him to a cleaner and more airy room where the matting on the floor was fairly new. Soon afterwards the Bozo reappeared.

"Let me put a dressing of tamarind leaves on your wound," he said. "And I'll bring you an infusion of sukola—that will make the fever go down."

Tiefolo let the Bozo look after him, realizing he was the incarnation of a spirit sent by Koumare. He no longer had any doubt as to the outcome of his adventure: he would find Tiekoro and carry out his mission successfully. Meanwhile the Bozo chattered on, some of what he said incomprehensible because of his Jenne accent.

"You couldn't have come to a worse place," he said. "This is a real nest of pythons. Here it's fetishist Fulani against Muslim Fulani, Quadriya brotherhood against Tijaniya brotherhood against Kounti brotherhood. Songhay against Fulani, Moroccan against Fulani, and everyone against the Bambara. The place will soon run with blood—fine fresh bright red blood like yours. But I shall have gone—I shall be drinking the mead of the ancestors."

Tiefolo fell asleep.

A few days later, just as he was finishing his morning bowl of gruel, the soldiers came for him, and again he followed them through the maze of courtyards to the room where the tribunal sat. This time, as well as the judges, the scribe and the guards, there was also present a young man whose height and haughty expression were those of the people of Segu. He wore long loose robes and had a little brown skullcap on his closely shaven head. Tiefolo was thrilled to recognize Tiekoro, whom he'd never seen dressed like that. The two brothers* threw themselves in one another's arms, and the tears that had been gathering like the waters of the *podo* behind dams of earth and reeds now coursed

---

* In some parts of Africa, sons of brothers are themselves regarded not as cousins but as brothers.

down Tiefolo's sunken cheeks. He had come to this strange city and been treated like a criminal! What were these people made of, and why did their god teach them only to hate and to fight?

Tiekoro had to pay a heavy fine, of two thousand cowries, three hundred measures of grain, and a half bar of Teghaza salt.

What is a town? It isn't a collection of mud or straw houses; markets where people sell rice, millet, gourds, fish and manufactured goods; mosques where people prostrate themselves; temples where they spill the blood of victims. It is a collection of private memories, different for every individual, so that no town is like any other or has any real identity.

For Tiekoro, Jenne was a place where he had been profoundly humiliated and lonely. Like Timbuktu it was a paradise he never reached, a nugget of gold that had turned into a stone in his hand. Yet when it came time to leave he felt some regret for the great freedom he had enjoyed there and the anonymity he would lose as soon as he was back within the walls of Segu, where all his ancestors would resume their power. For Nadie, Jenne was a place where she had been happy in the unrivaled possession of the man she loved and in helping him to make a living. It was where her children had been born; the place where, though they had lived in utter poverty, she had had her heart's desire. She knew that what lay before her now was only humiliation and having to share. And for Tiefolo, Jenne was the place where he had been cruelly plunged into the experience of men's harshness and intransigence. So each of the three had a different view of the rows of houses with niches in their facades for shea butter lamps, and on their doors enormous iron nails imported from Timbuktu.

In the little booths near the mosque, leather workers made sandals consisting of a sole and a couple of thongs, together with boots, sheaths for sabers and deep saddles for camels. Although it was raining, all this activity went on as usual, with men and women splashing through the puddles and children making balls of wet sand and throwing them at each other amid peals of laughter. Yes, for each of them the scene had its own special associations. A week before, Nadie had still set up her stall in the corner of this square among the other women, and called to the turbaned

Tuareg, to the Moroccan merchants with fat paunches under their caftans, and to Songhay from Timbuktu and Gao, who spoke the language with a more guttural accent than the people of Jenne. She had her own special customers, and on market days, when the square was full of women from all over the region with their bundles of cotton and dried fish, their dark red pottery and their bowls of fruit juice, she didn't know where to put all the cowries she earned. As for Tiekoro, he used to climb the steps up to the mosque for the great Friday prayer, the only one in the week that had to be performed collectively. With his brow in the dust he recited to himself, "God reward those who walk in the path of righteousness," and tried to silence the bitterness in his heart. Yet among all these men pronouncing the same words and wearing the same clothes as himself, he felt at peace.

But now huge crowds were pressing around the gates of the town. The great exodus of the Bambara had begun, on donkeys, mules, horses and camels, and also on foot. The women carried enormous burdens on their heads and their children trotted after them, sheltered from the rain in little hoods made of jute. The men looked after the animals. All the Bambara were heading for Segu, Kaarta, Beledougou, Dodougou, Fanbougouri and beyond. They had more to fear from the Fulani than had the Marka, Bozo or Somono. They knew that if the Fulani were burying their differences it was to join together against an empire that had subjugated them for too long. They also knew that if, after showing so much hostility toward Amadou Hammadi Boubou, the Songhay and Moroccans in Jenne made peace with him, it would be at the Bambaras' expense. So the only thing to do was leave for their hometowns and villages, taking with them whatever they could and leaving behind the memories that are sometimes more precious than wealth.

Tiekoro had never realized how serious the situation was. He was too absorbed in his own personal troubles to sense the growing terror of his people. The most alarming rumors were circulating. Amadou Hammadi Boubou's Fulani had erected a barrier on the Gomitogo road out of Jenne and, armed with axes, were stopping everyone who went by, asking: "Are you against the Islamic religion? Or, worse still, are you a hypocrite?"

If they didn't like the answer, *pssst,* they cut the man's throat, and there was a sinister line of bloody heads all along the road. Moreover, the *tondyons* had been defeated, and starving, tattered fugitives were rounded up in villages and ordered to be converted. Da Monzon, who like his father before him had defeated Basi of Samaniana, Fombana, Toto, and Douga of Kore, was little more than a child when faced with Amadou Hammadi Boubou.

People were scrambling to get into the canoes on the landing stage by the Bani when suddenly a sort of gray drizzle started to fall and the waters of the heavens seemed to merge with the waters of the river. People ran in all directions, threw themselves into the Bani, swam, sank.

"It's true!" the women shrieked. "Allah has undone our gods. They have been routed!"

For the first time Tiekoro felt he had betrayed his own people. Had he not taken up with a religion in whose name they were being hunted down and murdered? He was like a man who'd married a wife from a family hostile to his own. He put out his hand to help an old man into the canoe he had hired.

"They'll never get me to stick my head in the dust like an ass!" the old man mumbled. On saying this, the old man looked at Tiekoro and realized he had been speaking to a Muslim, and with a yell he jumped over the side of the boat and back into the river.

Meanwhile Tiefolo had reached the riverbank, riding the horse which fortunately the *cadi* hadn't kept as reparation for the outrages he had committed. He leaped to the ground and offered his mount to a man with white hair.

"You take it, *fa*," he said. "You need it more than I do."

"No," replied the other. "You must save your strength—if we're attacked, we shall need it."

But he did agree to let Tiefolo's horse carry part of his baggage, and they struck up a conversation in which both cursed the Koranic schools and the "blackeners of boards," with their reed pens and their sheepskins. Tiefolo didn't dare reveal that his own brother was a convert.

Once they had crossed the Bani and the walls of Jenne were no longer in sight, a feeling of relief swept through the crowd, and the great assembly started to turn into a kind of celebration. They were crossing a landscape that was as flat as a pancake, with a few acacias and thorn bushes scattered here and there. As it was the rainy season the bush was green. People sat down on the banks and started to unpack their provisions. Women lit fires and stuck their mortars into the ground while they pounded their millet. Little boys went off to look for *fini* seeds or the *bayri* berries that made your lips red. Men passed around gourds full of *dolo*, and quack fetish priests, always ready to seize an opportunity, sold little gris-gris as protection against the Fulani. Tiekoro rebuked Nadie severely for buying three, but Tiefolo came to her defense.

Because of the reserve that usually exists between an elder and a younger brother, Tiefolo hadn't asked Tiekoro any questions about Nadie, but merely treated her with the greatest possible courtesy. Was she not the mother of three children belonging to the clan? But Tiekoro knew his people's ways well enough to know what lay behind this. What would be the attitude of Nya's co-wives, all daughters of important families? Tiekoro watched Nadie busying herself with the children, and noticed the dark rings around her eyes and the nervousness of her movements. She was suffering; she was afraid. If she wavered, what would become of him? He would have liked to take her in his arms there in the middle of the crowd, as he had once before, when they were coming down the Joliba, and murmur: "Don't be frightened. I'll never leave you. Never. And I'll never allow you to become a servant again. You're the dearest thing I have in the world, now that my dreams and ambitions are gone."

But how could you say such things to a woman?

Then suddenly a group of strangers rode up on some wretched nags. They were half naked, their genitals almost bare. Who could they be? All the crowd leapt up, ready to fly into a panic once more. Some men with rifles rushed up and aimed their weapons at the newcomers.

These were in fact *tondyons* who had been beaten at Noukouma. Too ashamed to return to Segu, they traveled about in bands and lived off what they could steal. But the sight of the formerly redoubtable *tondyons* reduced to such a state was enough to complete the crowd's demoralization. They plied the newcomers with questions. Was it true that the "red monkeys," the Fulani, spared your life if you repeated after them, "Allah Akbar"?

In such moments of great popular confusion, one man and his message is enough to sway the general opinion. Soumaoro Bagayoko was an eminent fetish priest who had settled in Femay, a region slightly to the north of Jenne, and made his fortune there. He was going back to Segu with a caravan of possessions, four wives, and thirty or so children.

He leapt up onto a bank and stretched out a hand for silence. "These red monkeys you're so much afraid of," he said, "will soon be defeated to the last man by other Muslims from Futa Toro. Nothing will be left of the capital they are going to build on the right bank of the Bani, which in their arrogance they will call Hamdallay, in praise of their god. They will go back to being stockbreeders, as before. Meanwhile, believe me, Segu is immortal. Its name will go down through the centuries, and after you the children of your children will speak it."

This calmed the people's fears. The women gave the men and children something to eat, and they all set off once more. Once they were in Seladougou they would be all right. It was a Bambara region under the control of Segu. And they needed to get there before nightfall. For at night it wasn't humans one had to fear, but the spirits who unleashed human wickedness, sickness, suffering and madness.

CHAPTER
4

Malobali looked at his elder brother and was almost amazed that he should hate him so much. Because of Tiekoro his whole life seemed to be disintegrating. Nya appeared to forget him, so absorbed was she by the three little brats: Ahmed Dousika, Ali Sunkalo and Awa Nya. She danced them on her knee, sang them songs he had thought were for him alone, bathed them, gave them their meals. One night when as usual he had escaped from the boys' hut to come to see her, he had found her with Ali Sunkalo in her arms and she had sent him away, rebuking him for being a baby.

As for the rest of the family! At night there were no more stories about Souroukou, Badeni, Diarra and their exploits. No! Tiekoro, the center of admiration, would tell the story of his life abroad. Everyone plied him with questions.

"Is Segu better than Timbuktu?"

"Is Segu better than Jenne?"

"Are the Moors white?"

"Are the Moroccans Moors?"

"Do the people of Jenne eat dogs?"

And Tiekoro would smugly hold forth, while Malobali's mouth would fill and almost overflow with bitter saliva. If only he could shut him up—shove his words back down his throat!

Even worse was the ostentation with which he fingered his prayer beads, sitting on a mat outside his hut, and then groveled five times a day in the dust. Once a week he went to the Somonos' mosque, taking with him his own two sons and dozens of other little boys. Had he forgotten the Muslims were making war against his own people? In Malobali's eyes Tiekoro was nothing but a traitor! He would have liked the men of the family to tell him so, but instead everyone gaped openmouthed.

"Have you seen Tiekoro reading his books?"

"Have you seen Tiekoro writing?"

Even the old men came out of the neighboring compounds to hear him sermonizing.

"The word is a fruit whose husk is called gossip, whose flesh is eloquence, and whose kernel is common sense. Once anyone is gifted with the word, no matter if he is highly educated or not, he is one of the privileged."

The worst of it was that the Mansa himself was affected by this craze. Soon after Tiekoro arrived he had summoned him to the palace. Only the gods and the ancestors knew what Tiekoro, schemer that he was, had told him. At any rate, the Mansa had entrusted to him the education of two of his sons, that they might know the secrets of Islam, and had made Tiekoro his adviser on Muslim affairs. So Tiekoro was now a member of the council, and gave his opinion on what relationships should be maintained or entered into with the Fulani of Futa Jallon, Katsina or Macina. There was talk of sending him on a mission to Ousmane dan Fodio in Sokoto, to counter the latter's treaties of alliance with Amadou Hammadi Boubou. In short, Tiekoro had become a leading figure and had restored his family's influence at court to such an extent that he overshadowed *fa* Diemogo himself, who was twice his age but did not hesitate to consult him about everything.

Something had been brewing for several days. The idea was to provide Tiekoro with a wife worthy of his rank. Griots had come and gone, presents had circulated. Malobali had heard that the lady in question was a princess related to the Mansa and living in the palace; he didn't know any more. But Malobali adored Nadie. His affection for her had begun by chance. One day when Tiekoro had spoken to him harshly, saying, "You're not a *bila-koro* any more—behave like a man!" he had met Nadie's eyes, and she had seemed to be saying, "Take no notice!"

Then, as he crept away shamefacedly to hide his tears, she had gone after him and offered him a *dyimita*, one of those incomparable dainties she had learned to cook in Jenne. And gradually he had gotten into the habit of going to her hut. Weren't they both victims? She deprived of her children and her mate, and he of Nya's affection?

Until now Malobali had never thought about the position of women. In his view, if Dousika hadn't married his mother it was because she was a foreigner, one who, in fact, when the occasion presented itself, had chosen to go back to her own people. But Nadie was a Bambara. What did they have against her? That she wasn't of noble birth? Was she responsible for the family misfortunes that had led her to be sold into slavery? Was that to be regarded as an indelible crime? Wasn't it enough that she should have contributed three children to the clan? That she was good-tempered and industrious? Who better than she could season a chicken, roast mutton, or brown a succulent couscous? Who was a finer weaver? In Jenne she had learned new dyeing techniques which she had passed on here to all the women in the family. But alas, all these virtues were held against her, for they were those of a slave, and only served to justify the attitude adopted toward her. At first Tiekoro had defended her and protected her against the petty humiliations that everyone inflicted on her daily. But then he seemed to have tired, as if he too saw her as a humble creature not up to his own distinguished position. Every day he was visited in his hut by the prettiest slaves in the compound, and the Mansa had given him various captives, so that his harem consisted of a dozen or more concubines.

"Well, what are you looking at me like that for?" Tiekoro asked Malobali.

The boy lowered his eyes and started to go away, but Tiekoro called him back. "Come here," he said.

Malobali came back toward the mat spread outside the entrance to Tiekoro's hut. Tiekoro was wearing a sulfur-colored embroidered caftan that he'd bought from some Fez merchants. It was made of a silky material with threads of gold. On his shaven head was perched a smart skullcap of coffee-colored lace which matched the short scarf around his neck. He had a huge string of prayer beads in his hand, made of yellow stones with occasional

streaks of white. He had rubbed his cheeks with some Hausa
perfume, and the cloying smell made Malobali feel sick.

Tiekoro looked at his young brother.

"Do you know what?" he said slowly, his eyes bright. "I've
decided to send you to Jenne, to the Koranic school there. It will
improve your temper to feel the cane whenever you leave a word
out of your recitation of the suras."

"Jenne?" stammered Malobali. "But I don't want to go to
Jenne."

"Don't want to, don't want to!" Tiekoro sneered. "Since
when has a little good-for-nothing like you been allowed to say
what he wants and what he doesn't want? You're going, and
soon."

This was mainly a threat to frighten Malobali, but the young
boy took it seriously and looked around in despair. A few months
back he had been just one child among the others. Then he'd
learned about his mother's origins, and now he had his elder
brother's hatred to contend with. What had he done to deserve
all this?

He made for Nya's hut. If he hadn't restrained himself he
would have rolled on the ground and howled, in one of his usual
fits of rage. But he knew that would do him no good. The other
children in the compound, seeing him go by so serious and silent,
wondered what had happened.

Nya was sitting outside her hut. She had just bathed Ali Sunkalo and was rubbing him all over with shea butter. He was a
rather delicate little thing and his grandmother had offered to
take care of him. Malobali squatted down in a corner and watched
Nya lavish upon another child the attentions that had once been
his. A lump came into his throat. Who was behind all these upheavals? Tiekoro. Tiekoro.

"*Ba,*" he managed to say, "is it true I'm going to be sent to
Jenne?"

Nya looked at him quickly. He thought he detected guilt in
her glance.

"Nothing's settled yet," she said. "Tiekoro thinks that now
all the boys in the family ought to learn to read and write Arabic.
He says Islam is the religion of the future."

"I don't want to be a Muslim!" Malobali protested fiercely.

Nya sighed. "Islam frightens me too, I must admit," she said. "But Tiekoro says . . ."

Tiekoro, Tiekoro! Always him! Him again! Malobali couldn't endure any more. He rushed out of the compound and straight down to the river.

Segu! The high walls of clay. The sparkling and tumultuous river. The canoes on the banks, painted red and yellow. Segu. His world. On market days he would go along with Nya, her slaves following with big calabashes. People would whisper, "What a beautiful child!" And then, to propitiate an always jealous fate, they would murmur the words that warded off illness and death. Every afternoon he used to run to the square in front of the Mansa's palace to listen to the griots. These days they were celebrating the peace with Kaarta which had given Segu a new queen. Malobali would elbow the other children aside and stand in the front row of onlookers. The trumpet and drum would speak to one another, then the thin voice of the flute would answer the full, majestic voice of a man. And did Tiekoro mean to deprive him of all that? Very well, he'd run away, to the ends of the earth. Everyone would look for him in vain. They'd panic. They'd weep. But it would be too late. He'd already be far away.

Malobali was not the only one to suffer as a result of Tiekoro's behavior. Nadie was certainly even unhappier than he. To begin with she'd told herself it was a passing mood, due to the adulation and admiration of his family, and his restoration to wealth and honors. She thought she knew Tiekoro: arrogant, selfish, susceptible to flattery, extremely sensual, but good-hearted. She was sure the years they had spent together had formed bonds between them that nothing and no one could break. All she had to do was wait, say nothing, be there when he pulled himself together. But gradually doubt, anguish and terror had overcome her. She was certain Tiekoro was becoming alienated from her for good. She didn't really resent his accepting the wife offered him by the Mansa—he couldn't refuse such an honor. But she had other reasons for despair. He didn't talk to her any more. He preferred his mother's cooking to hers. He tried not to meet her eye. One day, unable to bear it any longer, she went into his hut. He was sitting

in the doorway being served a meal by a slave girl from Mande*
who had been sent to him by the Mansa that same morning. She
was good-looking, naked except for a string of blue beads around
her waist and bangles on her ankles, indicating that she was a
virgin. Nadie remembered her own first meeting with Tiekoro
in the Moor's compound, their lovemaking. Why hadn't she
screamed, protested, roused the neighborhood? No doubt because
she already loved him . . .

When he saw her come in, Tiekoro exclaimed angrily, "What
do you want?" and Nadie, incapable of saying a word, fled. Surprisingly, the slave girl looked on with a sympathetic expression.

While Nadie had had the impression, in Jenne, that she was
useful, she was convinced, in Segu, of the exact opposite. Neither
Tiekoro nor her children needed her. Even if she had stayed lying
down in her hut all day there would still have been plenty of
food—grain, poultry, game, fish. Fabrics from Europe and Morocco would have gone on piling up in the calabashes, with gold
and silver jewelry, amber and coral beads. The work of the slaves
and the gifts of the Mansa would still have filled hut after hut
in the compound with sacks of cowries and gold dust, and the
horses would have gone on whinnying in the paddocks. As for
affection—Tiekoro didn't want anything more to do with her.
Her two little boys, being treated with all the attention due the
eldest sons of a firstborn son, seemed not to care about her. They
slept with Nya; she bathed them and gave them their meals. If
they stumbled, hundreds of hands stretched out to help them up.
If they cried, hundreds of lips were ready to kiss them. Out of all
the women they now called mother, could they even recognize
Nadie?

The only one left to her was Awa Nya, for a girl always belonged to her mother.

At that moment Nya came through the doorway, stooping
slightly because she was so tall, with Ali Sunkalo trotting behind
her. Nya and Nadie didn't hate each other: Nya was merely doing
her duty as a mother, concerned for the good of her sons. Although the family council had given her to Diemogo after Dou-

* Mande or Mali, an empire at its height in the fourteenth century, com-
prising parts of present-day Guinea and Mali.

sika's death, it was no secret to anyone that he and she didn't really live as husband and wife.

Nadie hastily found a stool for Nya. Nya lowered her heavy hips onto it, and after they had exchanged the customary greetings she began to speak, slowly, choosing each word.

"I have to tell you," she said, "that Tiekoro's marriage is going to be celebrated soon. As the bride is the daughter of one of the Mansa's sisters, there will be a very large dowry. I didn't want the royal family to look down on us, and Tiekoro to go to them like a pauper."

Nadie knew all about these negotiations and preparations, but all her limbs began to tremble and she broke into a cold sweat. "Why doesn't *koke* tell me about it himself?" she stammered.

"Why should he?" Nya answered harshly. "What obligation is he under to you? Isn't it kind of me even to keep you?"

Nadie was stunned, but she realized that what Nya said was true. She looked this way and that, as if to take the universe to witness. But no one, nothing, seemed to care. The sun remained like the yolk of an egg in the bowl of the sky. The acacias were covered with odorless flowers. The children ran about naked. Women were pounding millet, unseen behind their walls. Life went on, a life in which she no longer had any place. Nya's voice brought her back to earth.

"This is what I've come to suggest," she said. "You could, of course, remain in Tiekoro's service . . ." She hesitated slightly on the word, but went resolutely on, "but there's a *woloso** I consider as my son—Kosa. I've talked to him, and he is ready to marry you. He will pay the dowry, and you'll both go and live on the family land at Fabougou."

If Nadie had been less overwhelmed with grief she would have guessed at the fear these words were designed to hide. No, she wasn't so paltry and despised as she thought. On the contrary, everyone was afraid she might mean too much to Tiekoro, and that the legitimate wives might have reason to resent her presence. That was why they wanted to send her away, wanted to throw her into the arms of another man. But she was suffering too much to understand such schemes. Her bosom heaved with

---

* House slave as distinct from a prisoner of war.

the thumping of her heart; her teeth were clenched as if she was about to die; she couldn't utter a word. She gave Nya such a look that she too remained speechless.

Nadie managed to stand up, hoist Awa Nya onto her back, and walk to Tiekoro's hut. All sounds had suddenly died out, and she had the strange impression that she was walking in broad daylight but in the silence of night. She went in. Tiekoro was just finishing dressing, fastening the strings of his loose white cotton drawers.

"I'm late," he said quickly. "I ought to be at the palace by now . . ."

Nadie leaned against the wall.

"I'm sorry, *koke*," she said, "but I've got to talk to you."

"Didn't you hear?" he said with exasperation. "I'm late. It's council day today."

Tiekoro himself was suffering. He knew that however much he tried to deceive both his body and his heart, he would irrevocably come back to Nadie. But he hated this dependence. If only she had been a relative of the Mansa, or the daughter of a noble family! But she was only Nadie, whom he had savagely possessed in the stench of excrement and urine of that privy; Nadie, who had known his secret troubles, his humiliations and his poverty in Timbuktu and Jenne. To love her took him back to a part of his life and of himself that he wanted only to forget. But seeing the desperation on her face he softened.

"Very well," he said. "Come and see me when I get back from the palace."

But she pressed him.

"When you go to see the Mansa," she said, "you often stay all afternoon and part of the night."

He put on his heel-less slippers and took a large European umbrella from a corner of the room.

"No, no," he said. "I'll be back before the night prayer. Make me some of your cakes and we'll spend the night together."

He went out. Left alone, Nadie feverishly collected the clothes scattered about on the floor, rolled up the mat on which he had slept with another woman, then started sweeping energetically with a bunch of *iphene* leaves. She hoped this would help her recover control of her body. After a while she was able to leave the hut, go back to the women's courtyard and join in the day's activities.

Meanwhile, in the palace, the council was all assembled. The princes of the blood and the heads of the leading families were all seated on their skins or mats. Da Monzon, surrounded by his slaves and his griots, lay on the dais smoking his pipe. Tiekoro stood waiting for Tietigui Banintieni to indicate, on the Mansa's behalf, that he might speak.

Then he bowed slightly and began.

"Master of energies," he said, "I have heard that Amadou Hammadi Boubou has just sent emissaries to Ousmane dan Fodio in Sokoto to ask if he might declare jihad or holy war. Ousmane dan Fodio granted his request and blessed some standards for him, one for each of the countries to be conquered. But he left out two, which means that two countries will not be seized by Macina."

Da Monzon sat up, forgetting to draw on his pipe.

"Which countries are they?" he asked.

"Ousmane did not say," said Tiekoro. "So it's anyone's guess."

Twenty pairs of eyes were fixed on him, and he resumed amid a general silence.

"Ousmane dan Fodio is a saint," he said, "but his sons are greedy. I will lead a delegation to Sokoto, bearing gold and ivory and cowries, and I am sure I can persuade them that Segu is one of the countries the Fulani of Macina are to spare."

At this there was an outcry. The master of war, supported by many princes of the blood, shouted that it wasn't Segu's habit to beg to be spared, but rather to fight, leaving dead and wounded on the field. Tiekoro heard all this with contempt, then turned again to the Mansa, as if counting on his intelligence alone.

"We're not talking about the usual kind of war, where the object is loot and murder. This is a holy war. The God you all refuse to submit to is on Amadou Hammadi Boubou's side and helps him in every battle. You can't win against him. You can only negotiate for your survival."

The idea of saying such things in the presence of the Mansa! Of casting doubt on the might of Segu! Anyone else would have paid for such temerity with his life. But Tiekoro was looked on as a soothsayer, a seer. An anxious silence hung over the council chamber. After a moment Da Monzon spoke again.

"Aren't you supposed to be getting married, Tiekoro?" he said. "Are you going to leave your new wife to go on a mission?"

Tiekoro bowed.

"I will do as you wish, master of our lands and our goods."

This form of words, too, was insolent, implying that souls belonged only to God. But Da Monzon did not take offense. The courtiers whispered that he was smitten with Tiekoro as with a woman, and that he'd regret it in the end. Wasn't he giving him one of his relatives in marriage? The Traores were noble and rich, admittedly, but even so! There were many who were against Tiekoro because of his superior airs and his strange and elaborate clothes. They patiently waited for him to fall from an even greater height than his father!

The council broke up, but Tiekoro stayed on with Da Monzon and his favorite griots. The Mansa was worried. Even though he agreed with Tiekoro he too thought it humiliating to negotiate for peace. He had made an alliance with the Kulibaly of Kaarta— mightn't it be better to raise armies of *tondyons* and attack the Fulani? At the same time he was seized by a superstitious terror. He recalled Tiekoro's words, coming after the predictions of Alfa Seydou Konate:

"This is not the usual kind of war. God helps Amadou Hammadi Boubou in every battle."

It wouldn't have taken much to make him convert to Islam, but the thought of his subjects' wrath held him back.

"When do you leave?" he asked Tiekoro.

Tiekoro pondered. "In a few weeks' time the rainy season will be over," he said. "The Joliba will be back in its bed. I'll set out then."

The chief griot, who was jealous of Da Monzon's partiality for Tiekoro, secretly wondered why a man about to be married should show so little repugnance at the thought of parting from his wife. What man hadn't wished to stay as long as possible between the loving thighs of a virgin? This was a mystery that would bear investigation. There was nothing like some affair with a woman to ruin a man, and Tiekoro was a ladies' man.

Tietigui Banintieni sniffed around Tiekoro in his mind, turning him over and over as a wild beast would an unfamiliar prey. What sort of man was he? What did he want? What lay hidden behind his conversion to Islam? Where did religion end and play-acting and calculation begin? Because he lived by men's credulity, Tietigui was used to sizing them up easily, and the difficulty he encountered in trying to see through Tiekoro vexed him. Not entirely bad, but certainly not good. Attractive. Irritating. Not at all in the same category as the old soldiers and courtiers who surrounded Da Monzon and never thought of anything but filling their compounds with gold and cowries, and their huts with wives. In short, an enigma.

CHAPTER

5

In spite of her sorrow, Nadie had fallen asleep. She went to the doorway of the hut to try to make out what time it was.

The night was dark and damp. Rain had fallen in sheets. The earth had drunk its fill and now gave off heavy vapors toward the sky. The trees were still, exhausted by the storm. So Tiekoro hadn't kept his promise. He hadn't come back. In the entrance to the hut, in the shadows, the bowls full of the cakes she had made so lovingly seemed like symbols of his desertion. She was seized by a kind of rage, a sort of murderous madness. It wouldn't have taken much for her to go and seek him out like one of those shrews who plague their husbands with scenes. But Tiekoro wasn't her husband. She had no rights over him.

Behind her, Awa Nya moaned in her sleep. Nadie went and picked her up, clasping her savagely to her. This little one, at least, was hers. No one could separate them. Hardly knowing what she was doing, she went out into the courtyard, where her naked feet sank into the mud and made sucking sounds at every step. Walking straight ahead, she found herself outside the compound. The street led away into the darkness, and the voices of the spirits could be heard whispering.

"Where's she going, at this hour, with her child?"

"Isn't it Diosseni-Kandian's daughter?"

It was a long time since Nadie had been called that: ever since the *tondyons* from Segu had set fire to her village, destroying and scattering her family. Suddenly the past rose up before her. Nothing good could come to her from Segu! She should have realized that as soon as she crossed Tiekoro's path. She turned at random to the right, along a narrow street full of the gleaming eyes of perhaps imaginary animals. But she was not afraid. The world of the invisible held nothing more horrible than the world of the living, and then she would be reunited with her father and mother. She came to the south gate of the town, which opened not on the river but on the bush, where the dark fields of millet were saturated with water. Segu was now surrounded by a vast refugee camp, for the city itself could not hold all the Bambara who had come there from Macina, Femay, Sebera, Saro and Pondori. The whole area was made up of a tangle of straw huts like those of the Fulani nomads, together with hastily built mud boxes, and shacks made of woven branches. Gangs of idlers came from these hovels and attacked the houses of the better off. Such behavior was unusual in Segu, and two of the offenders had been executed the previous week—at the entrance to the town—so that their impious blood might not sully its soil.

The outlines of men appeared under the mahoganies, but they retreated, alarmed at seeing a woman walking about at night with a child.

Nadie walked straight ahead, driven by the desire to put as much distance as possible between herself and Segu. Segu, the home of injustice and perfidy. Her feet made a slapping noise in the mud, the damp grass clawed at her legs. A fine rain began to fall, then a strong wind started to blow from behind her.

At one point Nadie curled up at the foot of a tree, but when white mists began to mingle with the black of the sky she got up and went on. Gradually men and women appeared in the fields. In a swamp they were planting rice; elsewhere they were cutting millet; or, again, women were busy roasting the kernels of shea nuts in clay ovens. A little farther off could be seen the roofs of huts, dark as animal skins. Yes, life could taste as sweet as fruit. But it hadn't been like that for her!

She came upon a well—a round opening, surrounded by half-dried-up branches twined together. At first she thought only of quenching her thirst. She had been walking for hours, and although the air was cool her tongue had grown furred with dried saliva. But as she leaned over to pull up the goatskin bucket suspended from a long cord of *da*, she saw the water sparkle below. A gust of cool air blew into her face like a call, and she remembered the story Siga used to tell her when they lived in Timbuktu.

"She's thrown herself down the well! She's thrown herself down the well!"

A thin body. Pointed breasts like a young girl. A gently curved belly. But she, Nadie, wouldn't leave a child behind to be a scapegoat: she had her frail and vulnerable little daughter with her. She took Awa Nya off her back and put her between her breasts, gazing passionately into the sleeping face. Soon they would meet again in the world of the spirits. The family were bound to be upset by her death, and would offer up many sacrifices for her, and she in return would work for their well-being.

She leaned again over the well. At this time of year the water was not far down. You could see it moving, lapping the earthen sides; its coolness was like a sweet breath.

Nadie climbed over the balustrade of branches, and for a moment the life instinct was too strong. She remembered Tiekoro's body close to hers, the smell of his sweat when they made love, the clear laughter of the children, the sting of the sun. She clutched at the branches. But they couldn't take her weight, and slowly gave way. As she fell toward the black water, held back and borne up briefly by her skirts, she was filled with a sense of resignation. It was what she had wanted; she had only herself to blame. She held Awa Nya tight.

They organized a search party to look for Nadie.

Forty or so men rode in all directions. Tiekoro, who had dashed his head against a tree in an attempt to kill himself, lay delirious in his hut, watched over by his mother and surrounded by the most celebrated fetish priests. The women in the compound were speechless: they all felt they were involved, responsible. Perhaps if anyone had smiled at Nadie as she pounded millet, or spoken to her as she sat with them at night, the tragedy of her disappearance might have been avoided. One act of sympathy might have saved her from despair. But no word had been spoken.

In the town, tongues wagged. What was wrong with this family, the Traore, that they should have all these violent deaths, disappearances and calamities of every kind visited upon them? The people who knew them wondered if it mightn't be better to stay away. Those who didn't know them congratulated themselves on having kept their distance. Most people hadn't known Nadie, and outlandish stories were told about her. She was a Moor from Timbuktu, a Moroccan from Jenne, who had left her own country and family to be with Tiekoro. On the whole, people felt sorry for her, even though love carried to such a pitch did seem rather disturbing. What would happen if all the women stopped accepting the fact that their men might remarry and have concubines?

The news reached the Mansa's palace, and Princess Sounou Saro, who had been promised to Tiekoro, was upset. Was she going to marry a man who tried to dash his brains out because a concubine went away? She went to see her mother, who agreed with her. But what was to be done? The dowry had already been paid, the day of the wedding was fixed. The two women sent for Tietigui Banintieni, who was never short of ideas. They remained in conclave for a whole afternoon in one of the rooms in the palace.

Meanwhile, toward the end of the day, one party of those sent out to look for Nadie reached the village of Fabougou.

The village was in an uproar, for they had pulled the body of a strange young woman from the well, and with it, more cruel still, the body of a little girl only a few months old. The local soothsayer had predicted the most terrible catastrophes: it was a sign that the whole region would be destroyed, first by the Fulani and then by hordes of men even more dreadful.

Yes, the gods and the ancestors were abandoning the Bambara.

Tiefolo, who was leading the party of searchers, dismounted and knelt down by Nadie. She hadn't been in the water long enough to be disfigured, and her face was peaceful and gentle as ever. Tiefolo remembered how he had met her a few months earlier, when he had gone to Jenne to announce Dousika's death.

He had just come out of prison and was still suffering from his wounds and the blows he had received. She had crouched down beside him, applying to his wounds a dressing of leaves that she herself had prepared.

"Does it hurt?" she'd asked.

Then she'd supported his head with her hand and given him a warm potion to drink.

He'd asked what it was. She had smiled.

"Inquisitive! Just go to sleep! Do you think women give away their secrets?"

And now she was dead. She had had the audacity to end her own life, to commit the most dreadful crime. What would become of her spirit, and that of her daughter? He tried to imagine her last hours: the unbearable sorrow, the loneliness, the fears. They were all guilty, not only Tiekoro.

Behind him the village chief asked: "Do you know her? Is she one of your people?"

Tiefolo looked up.

"Yes," he said. "She's my eldest brother's woman."

As she had committed the worst of crimes, it was dangerous to touch her. The chief fetish priest hastily chose two gravediggers, and they wrapped her in a mat and buried her as far away as possible from the fields belonging to the village.

CHAPTER

6

You've got a head as thick as a donkey's tail!"

"It's not that! I want to learn to read, but why do I have to sing the praises of your God at the same time? He's not my God!"

Siga collected his writing things and started to get up, but Sidi Muhammad held him back.

"Some tea?" he proposed.

Siga sat back and said sulkily:

"But tell me—why do people have to learn to read by using the Koran?"

"Don't blaspheme, if you please," said Sidi Muhammad, casting up his eyes to heaven.

Then, to cut short the argument, he ordered tea. He lived in the casbah of the Filala in Fez, and was a saddler by profession. He knew his ancestors had come as slaves in the days of Yacoub el-Mansour, and he thought they were of Mossi* origin. Having seen Siga pass by his booth every morning on his way to the Elkettan *souk*, he'd spoken to him and they had become friends. Although he wasn't rich, Sidi Muhammad lived comfortably on the fruits of his labors and lived in a pleasant one-story house of carefully worked brick, with mosaics, a courtyard and a tiled

* Ethnic group occupying present-day Upper Volta (Burkina Faso).

portico. Sidi Muhammad's friendship had been very important to Siga. In fact, he regarded his life as divided into two parts—the time before he knew Sidi Muhammad, and the time afterwards.

When they had drunk their tea, Siga rose.

"I must get back," he said.

Sidi Muhammad shrugged. He really didn't understand his friend, working so hard and living a life of almost monastic austerity. But without further protest—he knew it would be useless—he gathered up his woolen burnous and went along the street with Siga as far as the Bab el-Mahrouk gate.

In 1812, Fex seemed to be at the height of its glory. It was made up of two different parts: Fez Jdid, or New Fez, built by Yacoub ben Abd el-Maqq el-Merini; and Fez el-Bali, or Old Fez, which extended down the slope of the valley of the river Fez. From the beginning Siga had been lost in admiration for this jewel of a city. He'd at once realized what relativity meant, and that Segu, hitherto regarded by him as the finest city in the world, was really only a large village. Here there were marble monuments, stone palaces, mausoleums, medersas or Muslim colleges, mosques vying with one another in ingenuity and grace with their tiled roofs poised delicately on forests of pillars, and gardens with fountains made of precious transparent stone. In the midst of a leafy park, the Qarawiyyin university had eighteen portals covered with plaques of engraved bronze, patterns and inscriptions. Its octagonal cupolas, its capitals, the vaulting of its arcades and the friezes around its portals were the elegant expression of what seemed a more than mortal genius. Feeling extremely humble, Siga watched the students—Arabs, Berbers, Spaniards, converted Jews, black Sudanese—throng through the gates, and understood the fascination of learning. One day he plucked up his courage and went into the patio, and was amazed at the multicolored florescence of the walls—gold, purple, turquoise, sapphire and emerald.

Siga and Sidi Muhammad parted near the Bab el-Mahrouk gate. Siga had to go to his master's house in Fez Jdid, not far from the royal palace. It was a sumptuous dwelling, dating from the time of the Merinides, and Mulay Idris, Siga's employer and a relative of Abdallah in Timbuktu, was certainly one of the richest men in Fez. He owned some weaving shops working in silk, and in brocades that were made into women's belts, hangings and standards for the sultan's escort. He also employed a number of embroiderers who produced tablecloths and cushions, and all these treasures were sold in the *souks* of the Qaiceria. He was a believer, austere in appearance, but fond of money and of a series of very young wives. He treated Siga justly but without kindness, and there was a kind of unintentional contempt in the way he spoke.

Siga went through carved double doors into the house, and by the fountain with its majolica tiles in the central patio. Mulay Idris seemed to be waiting for him, and came quickly out of one of the first-floor rooms to greet him.

He was talking to a couple of haggard, swarthy Arabs whose clothes were covered with pinkish dust from the desert—caravaneers, apparently. With unusual affability he invited Siga to sit down.

Siga obeyed, somewhat intrigued. Green tea was served, with fresh dates, and then Mulay Idris broke the silence.

"Our two friends here have come from your home, Segu, and they have a message for you. Allah's will be done, Ahmed—your father is dead."

Siga didn't know what to say. He wasn't sure he felt any grief. He had left Segu long ago and it all seemed so far away! And anyhow he'd never been very fond of Dousika, who'd never bothered much about him and had treated him chiefly as Tiekoro's servant. Then he thought how afflicted Nya would be, and of the family's distress, and he did feel something. Mulay went on, still speaking kindly: "Would you like to go back to Segu? I'll provide the money and any horses you may need."

"What's the point?" Siga shrugged. "Even the fortieth-day ceremonies are over by now, I should think, given the time it takes to get here."

"But perhaps it would comfort your mother to see you?"

His mother? Nya had been the best of stepmothers, but she'd never been a mother to him. Siga asked permission to go up to his room. So Dousika was dead! He had passed too soon, without waiting for him, Siga, to prove himself. Now Dousika would never know what his son was really worth, this son whom he had regarded as a bastard. Siga's heart was flooded with bitterness.

In Fez he had learned the ferocity of social distinctions. True, in Segu there had been nobles, craftsmen and slaves, and everyone married within his own caste. But it seemed to him that people hadn't looked down on one another. Even Timbuktu, where he had been struck by the arrogance of the Armas and the ulemas, could not be compared with Fez, which was a conglomeration of antagonistic social groups all doing their best to exclude the others from power. The *chorfa*, the nobles, hated the *bildiyyin*, the descendants of Jewish converts, and both despised the common people, who were themselves divided into factions. A long way behind all these came foreigners, the *harratin*, or half-castes, and the black slaves. Here Siga had come upon the notion of race, which had still been rather vague in Timbuktu. Because he was black he was automatically looked down on, bracketed with the armies of slaves with whose help, a century before, Sultan Mulay Ismael had held Arabs, Berbers, Turks and Christians at his mercy.

Until he met Sidi Muhammad, Siga hadn't had a single friend in Fez. He hadn't crossed the threshold of any house but that of Mulay Idris, hadn't exchanged a smile or had a drink with anyone. That was how he came to be seized with a burning desire to show what a Bambara, a son of Segu, could do. First he had to learn to read and write, then to acquire the secrets of all the marvelous new techniques he saw around him so as to be able to take this knowledge back home. So every day he not only applied his clumsy fingers to calligraphy but also went and watched the masons, the makers of mosaics, the men who sculpted in plaster, the cabinetmakers and those who made lanterns, masterpieces of chased metal. Through Mulay Idris's connections he had been able to spend a few months with a tanner belonging to the famous family, the Oulad Slaoui, and had been initiated into the complex processes involved in the making of Moroccan leather goods. There were plenty of oxen and cows, sheep and goats in Segu— couldn't the same thing be done there?

There was a knock at the door. It was Maryam, Mulay Idris's first wife, who, though sometimes haughty in her manner, had always been very kind to Siga.

"I hear you have lost your father," she said. "May Allah's will be done. Don't stay here brooding—come and listen to a musician playing the viol."

Siga obeyed. He didn't really like the sort of music they played in Fez, but he was grateful to his hostess for her kindness. He followed her along a covered balcony that ran around the house overlooking the patio, which was itself surrounded by a spacious gallery embellished with arches and colonnades. The viol player stood near the fountain in the middle. The women of the household, shrouded in veils, were already gathered around. Little trays of dates, honey cakes and sugar candy were being handed among them.

A little boy with black skin but light curly hair stood in front of Siga smiling broadly and holding out a letter. Siga unfolded it and read, with some difficulty:

"Are you blind? Can't you see I love you?"

He stared in bewilderment at the boy, who grinned more broadly still and ran off.

Since dawn Siga had been at work in the Elkettan *souk*, where his employer had a shop that sold cotton goods made up from the yarn Abdallah sent from Timbuktu. It was no trivial matter to arrange the wares to best advantage, attract customers, discuss transactions with them and conclude a good bargain. Siga didn't have a minute to himself! Fortunately, Sidi Muhammad's booth was not far off, near the intersection of the Semmarin, and he used to send Siga cups of tea, and sometimes a cup of the strong coffee with thick muddy grounds that was drunk with slices of lemon.

Leaving his shop for once unguarded, Siga followed the child through narrow streets shaded with reed screens and already full of people. The little boy ran along with the obvious intention of being overtaken, darting in and out of shops selling slippers, jewelry and birds, and clutching at the burnouses of passersby. Then suddenly he stopped and Siga grabbed him by the collar.

"What does it mean?" he said. "What does it mean?"

The little boy grew suddenly serious and stared at Siga with golden-yellow eyes like those of a cat. "It's my sister Fatima," he said.

Siga looked around in terror.

"Where?" he cried.

"Come to our house tonight with your friend Sidi Muhammad," he said. "My sister Yasmin is getting married, and you won't be recognized as foreigners among all the people." Then he gave an address, and fled.

For a moment Siga stood there like an idiot, turning his head this way and that. Then he ran to Sidi Muhammad's, in his haste almost knocking over two or three water carriers with their goatskin containers. Sidi Muhammad was putting the finishing touches to some harness for the sultan's family, for he was a recognized expert at his trade. Siga handed him the note and panted out what had happened. His friend didn't seem at all surprised.

"About time too," he said.

Since his arrival in Fez, Siga had had no dealings with women except for the prostitutes in the public brothels: he was too proud to risk being rebuffed by a woman because of his color. Two or three prostitutes who lived near the Bab el-Chari'a gate were always glad to see him, and there he took his pleasure practically without seeing the woman who groaned and writhed beneath him. And now he suddenly learned that here in this foreign and almost hostile city a girl had noticed him, among all the other men who were rich, educated, handsome and sure of themselves. He could have gone down on his knees to thank her. But what was this unknown girl like? What color were her eyes? What sort of smile did she have?

Meanwhile Sidi Muhammad was scratching his frizzy mop.

"The address isn't far from here," he said. "It's in Zekkar er-Roumane. And judging by the name I'd say she's the daughter of a matchmaker, a woman called Zaida Lahbabiya. An illegitimate child, of course—matchmakers aren't allowed to get married themselves."

None of this meant anything to Siga, who knew little about the social customs of Fez. What mattered was that an unknown woman loved him and had had the temerity to say so. Finally Sidi Muhammad handed back the note.

"Try to make yourself look nice," he said, "and meet me here at six o'clock."

How could one possibly describe Siga's day? He floated on air, he imagined the wildest schemes, he sang old Segu songs he thought he had forgotten. He'd have liked to call the whole world to witness and shout at the top of his voice, "A woman loves me! A woman loves me! Me! Me!"

For a moment he did feel anxious: what if she were old or ugly or had a hump? But he soon dismissed the thought.

He shut up shop in the middle of the afternoon. It was the end of the winter. Poor people were wearing burnouses of rough wool, while the more fashionable paraded about in clothes made of materials imported from Europe, wearing dark red caps wound about with voluminous turbans that went around their heads twice. The children were muffled up in bright-colored woolens, and though the little girls were mostly at home with their mothers, little boys were to be seen everywhere, scurrying along with their writing tablets under their arms.

Siga decided to go to the baths. This was a feature of the life here that he had come to like. To pass from the cold room to the hot room, where skillful hands washed you, then to the third room, where everyone sweated together and rich and poor were no longer distinguishable amid the smell of the dung-fueled boilers—it was intoxicating! Sometimes students from the Qarawiyyin would start to declaim: "Fez, they are trying to rob you of your beauty. Is it your zephyrs or a mere breeze that gives us rest? Is it your cool clear water or money that flows? Yours is a land of rivers, as well as of crowds, markets and streets."

In the baths, people talked to complete strangers, brought close to one another by their nakedness. But this time Siga didn't linger—he was afraid of being late for his appointment. Though he usually paid no attention to what he wore, he now dressed with the utmost elegance in a tight jacket with dark blue sleeves, a fine linen shirt, a brown caftan and a black wool burnous with black embroidery.

A wedding was no small matter in Fez. The dowry might not be so large as in Segu but it was still an orgy of presents: ducats, lengths of silk and linen, heavy brocades, necklaces and bracelets of filigree gold and especially silver, made by the best craftsmen. When Siga and Sidi Muhammad arrived at the house of the mysterious Zaida Lahbabiya the party had only just begun. The patio and the first-floor rooms were full of men, while the women were still on the second floor. The air was ringing with the sound of horns and viols, laughter and the poets' songs of praise.

What a fine house it was! If Sidi Muhammad was right about her profession, matchmaking must bring Zaida a great deal of money. There was a large patio, and a mezzanine floor between the first and second floors. The balustrade around the galleries was decorated with geometrical patterns set in slanting panels. There were white marble paving stones on the floors, and delicately molded rose windows over the doors. No one was surprised at the appearance of Siga and Sidi Muhammad among the guests: among all those men, laughing and chatting, it would have been hard to pick anybody out.

Zaida Lahbabiya soon made her appearance: as a matchmaker she was allowed to meet men unveiled. She was a tall black woman with only a trace of Arab blood and sparkling eyes: rather terrifying, in fact. She wore very heavy makeup and her short black hair was decorated with silver coins. Her large hands and feet were dyed with henna, and her body gave off a perfume of pepper mingled with mint that was simultaneously sweet and exciting. She looked Siga in the eye, and his heart turned to water. Did this formidable mother know why he was here? If so, wouldn't she have him thrown out like a yokel? Or worse, denounce him publicly? What could he say in his own defense?

But Zaida had already passed by without stopping, like a heavily laden canoe going down the river. Siga realized that in a way she was the real heroine of the occasion—not her daughter, her future son-in-law or his parents. She ostentatiously handed out ducats to the members of the orchestra who had just installed themselves on the patio. She clapped her hands, and servants brought in trays of mutton and couscous. She danced a few steps.

Suddenly Siga felt a hand on his. It was the boy he had seen that morning, dressed in his best, his hair carefully combed and parted on one side. He put his slender finger on his lips, and signaled for Siga to follow him.

—

For Siga, love was like the first showers of the rainy season. The dry season seems as if it will never end. The earth is cracked and crumbled. The grass is scorched. The sap has dried up in the trees. And then clouds gather over the fields. Soon they burst. Naked children run out to catch the first drops of rain, still hot and few and far between. And then everything grows—rice, millet, gourds. The nets fill with fish. The herdsmen water their flocks. How had he managed to live without Fatima?

Siga would wake at night to ask himself that question, and it was with him in the daytime too, in the *souk*, during his reading lessons, in the baths, at meals. He took no interest in anything else—food, drink or work. For the first time Mulay Idris had to chide him about the running of the shop, and Maryam complained about his room being untidy. Sidi Muhammad told him he'd never learn to read.

Fatima was nothing like the women Siga had sometimes dreamed about. She was as black as her mother and her little brother, but with silky hair and gray eyes. And she was very tiny, her hips and breasts scarcely curved. How was it possible to get such delights from so ridiculously small a morsel of flesh? And yet Siga had never enjoyed such pleasure with the buxom creatures with which he used to have his fill. But now the pleasure was of the heart. Of the soul. Siga never tired of hearing Fatima tell him: "I'd been to buy some slippers in the Essebat *souk*, and was on my way home with the package under my arm. And then I saw you . . ."

"And fell in love with me. Just like that? Why?"

"Because you looked sad . . . lonely."

At this point Siga always smothered Fatima in kisses.

There was only one flaw in the picture: they had to meet in secret at the house of a helpful friend in El-Andalous, for Fatima lived in terror of her mother.

Zaida's ancestor had come to Morocco as a slave in the days of the Sultan Mulay Abdallah, in the year of the great earthquake that devastated Fez. She had worked as a dresser in the old *fassie**

---

* Word derived from the name of the city of Fez.

family whose name she bore, preparing every bride for her departure to the marital home. This function had evolved into a definite profession, supplemented by embroidery work in the intervals spent waiting for the return of spring and the wedding season. Matchmakers' privileges were then handed down from mother to daughter. They also organized the exhibition of newly born infants, and recited at circumcisions forms of words known only to themselves. Under the present reign of Sultan Mulay Slimane, the "guild" of matchmakers, all of them descended from black slaves, had seven leaders, of whom Zaida was the most influential. She was rich. She owned so much jewelry that she hired it out at exorbitant fees to families who didn't have enough of their own to decorate their brides. She knew the sultan and was often received at the palace. When she went through the streets of Fez el-Bali everyone recognized her and greeted her by name.

"What are you afraid of?" Siga asked Fatima. "That she'll think I'm too humble for you? I'm the son of a nobleman in Segu, and my family can send her a caravan of gold if she likes."

Fatima shook her head.

"She mustn't ever find out," she said earnestly. "Not ever."

But Siga wanted to shout his love from the housetops. He wanted to have children. He wanted to move into a nice house in the Filala casbah, near his friend Sidi Muhammad. Why couldn't he?

Siga arranged the lengths of cotton, and his thoughts went around in the same old circles. Why did Fatima refuse to introduce him to her mother? Because he was black? No, that was impossible—she was just as black as he was. Because he was a bad Muslim? If so, he was ready to go and grovel five times a day in the Abou el-Hassan mosque. Because she thought he was a pauper? If so, he'd send a message to Diemogo and prove the opposite.

Suddenly a whiff of perfume met his nostrils, a strange perfume of pepper mingled with mint. And he heard a slightly husky voice sensually softening the harsh Arabic tongue:

"Well," it said, "it's taken me long enough to find you!"

Siga swung around, and nearly fainted. Or ran away. For there before him in a heavy dark robe, her face half covered by a fancy veil, her hair dotted with sequins, stood Zaida, Zaida Lahbabiya herself, Fatima's mother. In his terror he dropped the piece of cotton cloth he was holding, and she gave a deep, throaty laugh which made her bosom heave.

"Do I really frighten you so much?" she said.

Siga wasn't a child. He knew that wasn't the way an angry mother spoke to her daughter's sweetheart. This was an attempt at seduction. Too many women of easy virtue had looked at him like that, trying to guess the weight of his body and the size of his penis. The thought only added to his horror.

"What do you want?" he stammered.

Zaida laughed louder than ever.

"Don't you know?" she said. "The other day, at my daughter's wedding, you disappeared in a flash. When I looked for you, pfft, you'd already gone. I've had to move heaven and earth to find you."

"Tell me what you want," repeated Siga, with a dreadful feeling that he was being stupid. "Whatever it is I'll try to give it to you."

Zaida moved near enough to touch him.

"I'm sure you will," she said. "You know my address. I'll be expecting you tonight."

CHAPTER

7

How many men have made love to mother and daughter at the same time, and had as much pleasure with both?

It wasn't the same kind of pleasure, of course. When Siga left Fatima he felt happier, lighter, polished and refined like a precious stone that has been in the hands of a jeweler. When he dragged himself from Zaida's bed he hated both her and himself. Thinking back on her voraciousness, he said to himself, "If she goes on like that she'll have my balls off!"

He lived in constant dread lest the mother find out about his relationship with the daughter or the daughter find out about his relationship with the mother. Sleeping little and spending all his seed, he was tired, absentminded and negligent. Mulay Idris was always having to grumble at him. One day he called him into his office.

"Listen," he said. "You've been here for several years now, and until lately I've only had to congratulate myself on having you work for me. But recently you've changed beyond belief. I'll give you one last warning. If you go on like this I shall have to send you back to Abdallah in Timbuktu."

What was he to do? Break with Fatima? Impossible. Break with Zaida? He hadn't the strength.

The fact was that Zaida, quite apart from her exceptional skills in bed, was also a marvelous character. She was full of stories, true or imagined. According to her, Sultan Mulay Slimane had been madly in love with her and wanted her for his harem. According to her there was a gazelle-skin manuscript in the Qarawiyyin containing poems in praise of her. She said there was a portrait of her in the palace of a nobleman in Cordova in Spain. Irritated as he was by all this, Siga never tired of hearing her talk. He would be dying with laughter as he fell back between her wide open thighs, and there was something playful in their first embraces.

What was he to do?

On his way back from Mellah, the Jewish quarter, where he had delivered some brocade to a rich merchant whose daughter was getting married, he sat down one day in the Lala Mina gardens. A few yards away a street entertainer was singing a love song, accompanying himself on the tambourine. Further off, two beggars were displaying some dancing monkeys dressed in red. It was a familiar sight, and Siga paid no attention. Suddenly an old man sat down beside him, dressed poorly in an old burnous and a cap without earflaps. He offered Siga his snuffbox, and when he refused, took a pinch himself and spoke.

"You look very miserable, young man!" he observed.

Siga sighed. It is well known that in times of great trouble one confides in whoever comes along. Siga was no exception, and he told the old man everything. When he had finished the old man wagged his head.

"What it is to be young!" he said. "I was in a similar position once myself, before I got to be as decrepit as I am now. I was staying with my uncle in Marrakesh . . ."

Siga was beginning to regret his outpourings, and the old man's tale was tedious. He was getting up to go when the other held him back, saying:

"Run away! That's the only thing you can do!"

Siga sat down again.

"But what about Fatima?" he said.

"Take her with you. Abduct her. Put the Sahara between you and the mother."

It was certainly a bold idea! Siga realized the old man was saying aloud what he himself didn't dare put into words.

"But I haven't finished my apprenticeship . . ." he said.

The old man laughed.

"It's as if someone confronted with death said, 'Wait, I haven't finished my apprenticeship.' Life is an endless apprenticeship."

Siga buried his head in his hands. Imagine running away, going back to Segu! But would Fatima agree to go with him? If not, should he really abduct her? He couldn't do that without accomplices, in this foreign place. He turned toward the old man to explain his objections. He had gone. He realized it was an ancestor in disguise who had come to show him what he should do, and a great calm swept over him.

He stood up. Just as he was about to leave Fez, he realized how much he loved it. He had never grown fond of Timbuktu, but Fez had gotten into his blood like a woman. He would never forget it wherever he went.

He passed by the old mosque of the Red Minaret and through the Bou Jeloud gardens, and slowly returned to Fez al-Bali. Children's voices were chanting the first suras. The whole city lay stretched out at his feet, with a chain of lofty mountains beyond. Had he used his time here to advantage? Perhaps he'd been shut out of the place's inner life because he didn't share its religion. He didn't prostrate himself in its mosques, or attend its medersas, nor had he ever mingled with the crowds going into the Qara- wiyyin to hear the great commentators on the hadiths, come from all over the world, especially Andalusia.

When he saw Fatima again he found her in tears. Her mother had beaten her again. Siga smothered her in kisses. Then, when he'd made her drunk with pleasure, he decided to sound her out. Would she agree to go with him? But she was only a child, not yet fifteen. She'd been able to get a love letter written and sent to a man, because this was something romantic and bold, typical for a girl of her age. But it was quite another matter to ask her to take her life in her own hands!

Siga decided to act alone, and quickly worked out a plan. In all the years he'd worked for Abdallah in Timbuktu and then for Mulay Idris, he'd received board and lodging but no wages. So he must get what he was owed. With these he must load a caravan with cotton goods, silks threaded with gold, brocades and em- broidered fabrics. The world was changing. In Segu, even those who weren't Muslims would like to buy such novelties. The women would take up the fashion. He'd open a big trading house. As well as fabrics he'd sell Timbuktu salt and kola for good measure. Better still, he'd open a tannery.

What would he need for that? An open space where you could dig holes. There was plenty of space in Segu, and the Joliba would supply plenty of water. The sun would do the drying. He could make the sort of soft leather slippers, yellow or white, that Fez exported to all the Muslim countries. Siga could see himself employing dozens of *garanke*, Bambara leather workers, for he himself, as a nobleman's son, couldn't lower himself to such an occupation. Yes, he'd show everyone what he could do, this son whose mother had thrown herself down the well!

While he was already counting up his sacks of gold and cowries, he found himself quite close to the school of the coppersmiths with its humble minaret, amid the rubbish that the inhabitants of the quarter always left lying about. He hurried on to Sidi Muhammad's shop.

He found his friend deep in conversation with a customer ordering a saddle for a thoroughbred as if it were a woman. Siga tried to hid his impatience. At last the wretched chatterbox left and Siga, without stopping for breath, told Sidi Muhammad of his decision.

There was a long silence. Then:

"Zaida's very sharp," said Sidi Muhammad. "Probably the most intelligent woman there is. If you disappear with her daughter she'll put two and two together, tell the sultan, and get all the travelers and caravans going to Segu stopped. You'll be back here in less than a couple of days and in chains."

There was a good deal of truth in what he said. Siga gazed at him in despair.

"Have you got a better idea?" he asked.

Sidi scratched his head in his usual way. But his rough manners concealed great shrewdness.

"Another route," he said finally. "You must go by another route."

Siga stared.

"Do you know of one?" he asked.

Sidi Muhammad slowly poured himself some tea, and said: "The sea."

"The sea? Where's the sea in Fez?"

Sidi Muhammad sighed, as if discouraged by such stupidity.

"There isn't any. But a few kilometers away, near Kenitra, there is. And I've got an uncle there. Boats leave from there for all over the world."

Siga went slowly back to Mulay Idris's.

When night fell, darkening the whitewashed walls, the people liked to gather in the squares until the loud call of the muezzin with his "Allah Akbar!" sent them back home for the last prayer of the day. Vendors of almonds, mint and grilled corncobs tried to make the most of the time left to them, and public storytellers would sing of the foundation of the city. Siga made a detour via Bab el-Guissa where every day a poet declaimed the verses of Abou Abdallah el-Maghili to an attentive crowd: "O Fez! May Allah revive your soil with dampness. May He send down rain from generous clouds. O paradise of this world, surpassing Hims* with your glorious panorama . . ."

Siga's cheeks streamed with tears as he listened. He was going away, going on his travels again! But he was weeping for his own weakness also, for he knew that at midnight he would hasten back to Zaida's bed.

Siga emerged from the washerman's hut where he'd been hiding since the previous day. According to his calculations his friends—or rather Sidi Muhammad's—should be arriving soon. Had they pulled it off? He knew the main obstacle to the success of the enterprise was Fatima herself. She might take fright, panic, refuse to go with them! If Siga had had a fetish priest within reach he would have paid him anything to know what had happened.

Everything had gone well so far. Mulay Idris had paid what he owed him with princely calm, then, taking back with one hand what he gave with the other, had undertaken to provide him with high-quality merchandise. In reality he seemed to welcome the voluntary departure of someone who no longer suited his convenience. Only his wife Maryam had been surprised.

---

* Hims (or Homs): Syrian city trading in textiles and, like ancient Emesa, famous for its Temple of the Sun.

Siga had managed to conceal his intentions from Zaida, lull-
ing any mistrust with caresses that were more passionate every
night. Sidi Muhammad and his friends were to grab Fatima as
she came home from Koranic school. No one was likely to interfere, as the custom of pretending to abduct the bride before
marriage was not yet entirely extinct. Then the little group would
leap on the horses that had been tethered under the olive trees
of Lemta, and off they'd go through the Bab el-Guissa gate. Nothing could be easier!

But Siga was apprehensive. He believed Zaida to be capable
of anything. Of moving heaven and earth to find him and punish
him for his perfidy. As long as he was alive he could never rest.
He walked down to the river, which together with a dozen or so
springs provided the city with running water. On the other bank
rose an orange grove, without either flowers or fruit against the
gray late winter sky. Then he went back and squatted down again
in the hut, almost ready to curse the love that had thrown his
orderly existence into such a mess. At the same time he knew
that this disarray was the only thing that gave his life meaning.

So he was going back to Segu. What changes would he find
there? His father was dead. Had Tiekoro returned from Jenne?
Siga realized that the grudge he bore his brother was still there.
Tiekoro didn't deserve the wife he had! When he thought of
Nadie, Siga's heart softened. He had ordered a special length of
brocade for her, to be woven with gold and silver thread and
decorated with metal spangles. Legitimate wife or not, he intended to honor her!

He thought he heard the sound of horses on the road, and
hurried out. But it was only a group of donkey boys and their
heavily laden beasts returning from the slaughterhouses. He went
inside again and, tired of fretting, unrolled his mat and tried to
sleep. When he was upset, old nightmares always took possession
of Siga's spirit. So scarcely had he closed his eyes than his mother's corpse, streaming with water, appeared beside the well. A
slender body. Pointed breasts like those of a young girl. Gently
curving belly. The terrified and pitying circle of women. But this
time the setting was different. Instead of taking place in Dousika's compound the scene was set in a rain-soaked plain dotted
with shiny-leaved shrubs. The opening of the well was sur-

rounded by branches, and the fetish priest crouched nearby, praying the earth not to be angry but to go on yielding its fruits.

"Let not this evil, barren death turn you against us!"

Siga mingled with the crowd of onlookers, and saw not one
body but two. Two women, young and frail, and between them
a little girl. He elbowed his way toward the front of the group
but the others kept forcing him back as if on purpose, and he
couldn't see the faces of the women, while all he could see of
the child was its chubby feet and pearly toenails. What is more
absurd than the death of a child, than the falling of the unripe
fruit before the ripe one?

"Why did they kill themselves?"

No one knew. They belonged to that dangerous race of
women who love too much, who put their own feelings before
the rules of society.

"Which of them took her child with her?"

"She was right. A daughter always belongs to her mother."

The murmur of women's voices died away. Siga shoved
harder and managed to get a glimpse of a round cheek and white
teeth revealed by curled back lips. Nadie. It was Nadie. A cry of
terror stuck in his throat, than crawled slowly upwards and rang
out. Nadie. It was Nadie.

As he started up, helpless, tortured, a hand shook him by the
shoulder, and he opened his eyes upon darkness. People were
laughing.

"That's a nice way to welcome your wife!"

The darkness dissolved into the laughing faces of Sidi Muhammad and some other men in woolen caps.

"She's dead, she's dead!" Siga moaned.

"No, she's not!" guffawed the men.

And they stood aside to make way for Fatima, shapeless,
shrouded in blankets like a bale of merchandise, still frightened,
but jubilant.

It took some minutes for the shadows to disperse and for Siga
to realize it was only a dream. Eventually he returned to reality,
but the impression had been so strong it canceled all joy and
hovered over him like a bad omen. With the others, especially
Fatima, looking on disapprovingly, he poured himself a stiff
brandy.

Sidi Muhammad and his companions had brought with them olives, onions and biscuits of hard wheat. They all had something to eat.

So—the first part of the plan had succeeded. Now came the second part—going up the river by boat to Sebou, then on to the Atlantic. The first part of the route had been in frequent use ever since the days when commander of the faithful Abou Inan had launched his warships on it. As for the Atlantic Ocean, that was said to be black with masts sailing in all directions toward Spain and along the coast of Africa as far, so they said, as the mouth of the Joliba.

When Siga found himself alone with Fatima he was not as happy as he had expected to be: he was still overwhelmed by the memory of his dream. It was as if Nadie's spirit, before plunging into the country of the invisible, had wanted to bid a last farewell to those who had loved her. Moreover, Siga realized that Fatima was only a little girl, to be led through life by the hand. She was already missing Ali, her younger brother.

"Who will the poor boy play with when I'm not there?" she wondered. "And he'll forget to say his prayers. Like you, Ahmed—you're not a good Muslim and you'll roast in everlasting fire!"

Anyone seeing the sea for the first time feels his heart turn over. Its smell makes him catch his breath. Faced with that great unfolded shroud, he enters the dimension of infinity and death. Having seen Lake Debo on the way to Timbuktu, Siga had thought the sea would be no surprise to him. How wrong he was! He scanned the horizon. What lay beyond that gray curve? No doubt the lands of men with light skins like the Arabs or white skins like the Spaniards, who looked down on men whose skins were black. Siga had come to understand that a black skin made you a creature apart. But why? However much he turned the question over and over in his mind he could find no answer. The Bambara were as strong, proud and creative as any other people. Was it simply the question of religion? If so, he clung to his gods and his ancestors out of sheer defiance. He would remain a drinker of alcohol and a worshipper of spirits, no matter what.

Fatima and Siga went from Kenitra to Sale, once a busy port trading with Spain in oils, leather, wool and cereals, but now like a great graveyard full of gray tombstones. They steered clear of Rabat on the other bank of the river—they'd been told it was swarming with slave traders—and went on to Muhammadia.

Now Siga had left Fatima behind at the inn, for she hadn't stopped crying since that morning. She had suddenly awoken to the fact that she wasn't going to have the marriage of her dreams, with a sumptuous trousseau, furniture, and a personal slave of her own. Though Siga kept telling her he would provide her with all these things in Segu, he was beginning to wonder what view she would take of their clay houses there, their calabashes, their mats and their unrefined habits. No, they didn't possess all the material goods enjoyed by the people of Fez! He sighed and set out for the quay, where the low-roofed warehouses were full of sacks of rice and wheat, baskets of dates and olives. There were also *fekkarines*, blue-glazed earthenware pots that bare-chested men were carefully packing in straw.

Sidi Muhammad's friends had told the truth: the Atlantic was covered with ships. Their crews were sluicing the decks. Siga saw a black man sitting on a pile of rope, and told him of his plan. The other just tapped himself on the forehead.

"You must be mad!" he said. "No boat goes as far as that. You propose to go down further than the mouth of the Senegal River and then strike inland? Why didn't you go by caravan?"

"That's my business," answered Siga curtly. "Do you know of a ship going south?"

The sailor pointed out a rather unprepossessing brig.

Captain Alvar Nuñez, born in Andalusia, had knocked about the coast of Africa trying his hand at the slave trade, but since the confounded English began stopping and searching all the slave ships he had switched over to more lawful cargoes. He looked in surprise at this handsome black man, dressed like someone from Fez and speaking perfect Arabic.

"What are you doing so far from home?" he asked.

Siga had no wish to talk about himself, and merely presented his request. He was ready to pay whatever was necessary to be taken to the mouth either of the Senegal or of the Gambia River.

Alvar Nuñez took his pipe out of his mouth.

"A few years ago," he said, "I wouldn't have given much for your chances of staying free in those parts. But now everything's changed. I'm only here for repairs—I'm really on the way to Bonny near the Niger delta to take on palm oil. Did you say you had some gold dust?"

Siga bounded down the ladder to the quay. No, the gods and the ancestors had not abandoned him! Here he was, only just arrived in Muhammadia and he'd found a ship, and a captain who didn't seem too bad a fellow. To celebrate, he went into a tavern. Men of all colors—swarthy Arabs, white-skinned Spaniards, blacks, pallid Jews—were consuming the drinks that help people forget their daily cares: brandy, rum, wine, gin. There were also a few women, wearing makeup but no veils. Siga sat down at a table and was just lighting a pipe when a man rushed up to him.

"Jean-Baptiste!" he cried. "Everyone's been mourning you— we thought you were dead!"

Disagreeably surprised by this, but trying not to show it, Siga thumped on the table. "I'm not Jean-Baptiste," he said, "but I'll buy you a drink!"

The man sat down. He seemed taken aback. He told Siga how, with his master, a completely mad Frenchman called Isidore Duchâtel who wanted to transform Cape Verde into one huge botanical garden, he was on his way to the Beni Huareval region to get flower seeds and orange, lemon and mulberry slips. In Gorée he'd known a Bambara slave called Jean-Baptiste who looked exactly like Siga.

"Jean-Baptiste!" said Siga with a shrug. "The Muslims always saddle us with their names, and so do the Christians. What was the name his father gave him? Do you know?"

The man looked at a loss. "Tala, I think," he said. "Or was it Sala?"

Siga leaned forward.

"Naba," he said tensely. "Are you sure it wasn't Naba?"

C H A P T E R

8

Naba could feel his brother's thoughts fluttering around his face through the stinging sun; then it settled on his brow, as soft and caressing as a butterfly's wing. He drew on his pipe of *maconha*, and after a few puffs his spirit grew light and porous, detached itself from his body, and went forth to meet people and things.

That was how he had met the soul of his father as it left his body; he had gone with it for a while before it plunged into the invisible. In the same way, he knew now that the family was in trouble, though he didn't know whom they mourned. It was something to do with a well. A thin figure. A rain-soaked landscape.

He drew at his pipe again to find out which of his brothers it was who was thinking of him.

It wasn't Tiekoro, the beloved eldest brother: his spirit was still scouring the bush, in the depths of grief, thinking of nothing. It wasn't Tiefolo: they met every day in his dreams. So it must be Siga, the slave's son, child of the woman who threw herself down the well, the one who was always left out in the cold. Where was he? Not in Segu: Naba could see a wall of seawater, whipped higher still by the wind.

Above his head, among the dark green foliage, fruits seemed to proffer themselves: oranges. Two days ago he had gone out into his garden and the fruit was still indistinguishable from the leaves. And now, suddenly, a galaxy of suns. Yes, indeed, this soil was rich and fertile, glad to bring forth, like a woman. Naba stood up and looked around him. Dense vegetation gave way to fields of sugarcane, covered with a mauve veil of blossom. Far away, as if stippled by heat and distance, lay the outline of the *chapadas*, mountains whose peaks had been pounded flat. Naba put up an arm and carefully plucked a single orange. Tomorrow he would come back and take possession of the whole harvest.

Manoel Ignacio da Cunha was the owner of this *fazenda* or plantation in the province of Pernambuco, not far from Recife in the northeast of Brazil. Da Cunha, having enough slaves already for the cane fields, had not bought Naba, but he had bought Ayodele, the little Nago girl whose protector Naba had become. Naba had been purchased as part of a lot by a Dutchman who was trying his hand at cattle raising in the arid Brazilian hinterland, the *sertão*, and who was not afraid of difficult customers. But a few months later Naba had mysteriously turned up in Manoel's *fazenda* one mealtime and gone straight to the Nago girl, now called Romana. Manoel was superstitious, and on his wife's advice he never touched Romana again from that day on, though he loved her dearly and she was already pregnant by him.

What had happened in the *sertão*? Naba had never said: he hardly ever spoke. He just came and went in a big straw hat, knee-length cotton trousers and a shapeless jacket, a pipe of *maconha* in his mouth. The slaves said he was mad and a bit of a sorcerer—not bad, but capable of unleashing evil forces. As he had an extraordinary knowledge of plants they consulted him whenever a child had a swollen stomach, a woman suffered from a running ulcer, or a man had something wrong with his penis. Naba did just as he pleased, protected by his reputation as a madman. He cleared a square of land to the east of the mill and the cane fields and made it into a fruit and vegetable garden. Everything grew there—tomatoes, eggplants, carrots, cabbages, papayas, oranges, lemons. As if he knew the land didn't actually belong to him, Naba used to leave two full baskets of fruit on the veranda for the *senhora* every time he picked one of his crops. Ayodele sold the rest in Recife, where people were always short of fresh food. Not only did they depend on the arrival of ships from Portugal, but since the upheavals caused by Napoleon had driven the court of João IV of Portugal to take refuge in Rio, all the food tended to go there.

Naba had taken Ayodele back, just as if she hadn't slept for months in the Great House, as if the child she was carrying wasn't Manoel's at all. The slaves never stopped talking about it. Couldn't he see that the child was a mulatto?—quite different from the little black children of his own that she would have later on. During their three years of life together, Ayodele managed to give birth to a son every nine months and each time she became more beautiful. The slaves hated her. After having been the master's whore, she now gave herself airs of respectability and even helped to organize a brotherhood in the *fazenda* called "The Good Lord Jesus of Aspirations and for the Redemption of Black Men," based on one which already existed in Bahia. The women were particularly hard on her.

Naba took the path that cut across the cane fields to the grounds and the Great House or *habitation* at the top of the hill. In the Great House lived Manoel and his wife Rosa; Rosa's sister Eugenia, who had come to live with them after her husband died of syphilis; fifteen or so children, legitimate and illegitimate, white and mulatto; a dozen domestic slaves; a priest, sacked from his church because of his passion for little black girls; and a schoolmaster come from Rio to teach the children to write. Naba couldn't wait to show Ayodele the first orange of the season: he wanted her to share with him the unique moment when the seed, set in the earth's warm vulva, appears at last after silent labor, plump and perfect as a newborn baby finally revealed to its impatient parents.

At first sight Manoel's house looked rather grand. It was built of stone, with a tiled roof, an upper storey, and an attic floor above that. On the first floor was what was called the yellow drawing room because of the color of its silk curtains; it also had a rather fine Aubusson carpet on the floor. On the same level there was also a pair of smaller drawing rooms, one green and the other blue. The latter contained a piano which Eugenia and Rosa would sometimes play, and was therefore called the music room, when people didn't choose to call it the Chinese room because of a Chinese sofa inlaid with mother-of-pearl. There was a billiard room too, where Manoel entertained his friends, also planters, and a huge dining room where the somewhat primitive furniture consisted of stools and benches around a large table with candlesticks on it. Black and white tiles paved the floor of the vestibule and went halfway up the walls. A wooden staircase led up to the bedrooms on the second floor, and a very steep ladder to the rooms in the attic where Manoel's favorite slaves slept.

Yet despite the jacaranda wood furniture, the bronzes and the carpets, the whole place had a grubby look, due perhaps to the exuberance of the tropical climate. The smell of the tubs of night soil, hidden under the stairs and emptied by a slave when they were full, permeated the whole house despite the aromatic herbs that little slave boys burned all day long in every room. Rosa and Eugenia glided through the place like ghosts in their severe black gowns, their long black veils hanging from the combs in their shining coiled hair and their shoulders draped in black shawls. The slaves said Manoel slept with both of them, and this would explain their gloomy, tense expressions.

Ayodele was in the kitchen, surrounded by a crowd of children. She was making *pamonhas*, corn cakes—you could smell them already—and looked up at the sound of footsteps. No one knew better than Ayodele that Naba wasn't mad. No one knew better than she the kindness, delicacy and generosity of his heart. For her he was a quiet strength, a dike against her passions. She smiled at him as he showed her the orange, as proudly as if it were a nugget of gold from Ouro Prêto in southern Brazil.

"Will it be a good crop this year?" she asked.

He nodded.

"Will it bring us in a lot of money?" she insisted.

He smiled now.

"Why do you want to calculate, *iya*?"* he said. "Can't you leave the gods to do it for us?"

She did not react to this reproach.

"I'm going to ask the master for the day off to go into Recife," she said, then scolded the children, who had taken advantage of this conversation to dip their fingers, already sticky with cane juice, into the batter.

Slavery turns a human being either into an apathetic lump

* Yoruba for "mama."

or into a wild beast. Ayodele was not sixteen when she was torn
away from her family, and even now was only just over twenty.
But her heart was that of an old woman, older than that of the
mother who bore her, older even than her grandmother's. Her
heart was bitter, bitter as *cahuchu*, the wood that weeps, which
the *seringueiros*, the rubber gatherers, stabbed with their knives
in the forests. Without Naba she might have gone mad, or put
an end to herself, weary of carrying her child in self-hatred and
self-contempt. But without saying anything he had conveyed to
her that she was only a victim, and his love had kept her alive.
But a man's love was not enough. There was all the rest. First of
all the country itself, with its hateful beauty—the royal palms
challenging the opaque blue sky; the lakes, with their profusion
of green transparent water lilies and orchids with torn and bloody
lips. And then there were the people: on the one hand the slaves,
sunk in passivity; on the other the masters, eaten up with syphilis
and scratching at their scabs and sores with their long fingernails.

But for some time now Ayodele had been cherishing a hope.
She had learned of the emancipation societies that the slaves in
Bahia and Recife were organizing with the object of returning to
Africa. With the help of black *ganhadores* or money-makers, and
blacks and half-castes already freed, they were setting up funds
into which they paid any money they could save. Whenever one
of them had deposited half the amount his master demanded in
order to free him, the fund made up the rest. Then he would try
to get Portuguese passports for himself and his family—a process
involving bribes and deals of all kinds. Some families had already
gone back to Africa and settled in various ports in the Bight of
Benin, especially Ouidah. Ayodele had saved up the money from
the sale of Naba's fruit and vegetables *real* by *real*, and got in
touch with a *ganhador* called José. All that remained to be done
was complete the bargain.

Recife owed its name to the rocks that defended the entrance
to its port and beaches. It had been in the hands of the French
and the Dutch, but was now once more in the possession of the
Portuguese, who had founded it in the sixteenth century. Each

of the occupying powers had left its own traces behind, so that the town was a jumble of buildings in different styles.

Ayodele made for the Nago Tedo quarter.

This was a collection of thatched mud huts arranged in compounds, so that you might easily have thought yourself in Ife, Oyo* or Ketou in the Bight of Benin. There, on the outskirts of the town, the population consisted only of blacks—Nagos for the most part, but also Hausas, Bantus, freed slaves and half-castes. They plied every kind of trade: there were tinsmiths, potters, water carriers and charcoal burners. Their wives squatted at street corners selling cakes, fruit and vegetables. Children either naked or in rags swarmed about the muddy streets full of holes. The air reeked of pimento and malaguetta as well as of the palm oil used for cooking.

The house of José the *ganhador* stood out from the rest by its pathetic attempt at elegance. It was built of clay like all the others, but had three rooms and a veranda. The first room was a shop where José sold charcoal. The second was a drawing room with a sofa and two chairs, all fitted with antimacassars tied on with ribbons in the Portuguese manner. The third room was a bedroom, containing a bed fitted with a mosquito net.

José himself was a peculiar character, a Nago from Oyo. Because of his extreme good looks the Portuguese had used him as a woman, and he had finally adopted their vice himself. He lived amid a small court of young men who rolled their hips provocatively as they walked. But his proclivities had made it possible for him to earn money and live in semifreedom. At first sight one hardly took him for a man at all, slim as he was and covered with lace, and with trinkets and pendants hanging from his ears and neck. He outlined his beautiful eyes with kohl. But their expression was troubled, for José the *ganhador* was sadly conscious of his degradation, and his heart was full of hatred toward the white man.

Dismissing two half-naked youths who had been polishing his nails, José offered Ayodele a chair. They were from the same village, and she began by asking him anxiously if there was any news from home.

---

* Towns in present-day Nigeria, once powerful kingdoms.

He sighed.

"I went aboard a ship and talked to the captain. Things are bad."

Ayodele clenched her teeth.

"When will it all end?" she asked bitterly. "When will our people be able to drive the white men into the sea?"

José shook his head.

"That's not the question," he said. "The English have put an end to the slave trade, and soon there won't be one slave ship on the sea. No—there's another danger, now, from the north."

"The north?"

"Yes—the Fulani have invaded our towns. They're setting them on fire and killing our women and children."

Ayodele was dumb with astonishment for a moment, then exclaimed: "The Fulani? But they've always been our neighbors!"

"Ah, but Islam!" said José. "They've been converted to Islam, and they think it's their mission to convert all of us, by fire and sword. Jihad, they call it."

There was a moment's silence.

"All right," said José at last. "Now, let's talk about you. The emancipation society has agreed . . ."

Ayodele was so overwhelmed with happiness she couldn't even utter a word of thanks.

"But some members had objections. Naba's a Bambara from Segu—are you sure he wants to go with you to Benin?"

Ayodele shrugged.

"Segu or Benin—aren't they both Africa? Isn't getting away from this infernal country the only thing that matters?"

José made a gesture that might have meant anything.

By this time, nearly a dozen families had managed to overcome the insurmountable obstacles and embark on ships bound for one of the ports on the Bight. But José knew he himself could never go. What would his people do—his father and mother, brothers and sisters, the whole community—if he went back among them with the vice the Portuguese had sown in his blood? They'd stone him to death and bury each of his limbs at a different crossroads, so that he might not soil the ground which real men walked upon! He wasn't a Nago anymore. He wasn't even a human being. He was only a good-for-nothing pervert.

Meanwhile, Naba had gone to deliver his fruit crop to one of Ayodele's regular customers, a Dutchman called Ian Schipper who had stayed on in Recife in spite of his country's reverses. He lived in the rue de Cruz in a tall narrow house with wooden shutters. As always, Naba was enchanted by the sight of the port with its raftlike *jagandas* and heavy-rigged ships. He stood for a long while watching the sea, smooth at first, then suddenly raging and drawing back into a wall several yards high.

As he began to walk on, a man came up to him, his head close shaven, wearing a long, loose white robe. After looking to the right and left, he handed Naba a paper that when unfolded revealed a series of Arabic characters.

"Allah is calling you, brother," he whispered. "Come and pray with us this evening in Fundão."

Madness took a heavy toll among the blacks in Pernambuco, whether they were slaves or *ganhadores* or had been emancipated. So Naba paid no attention to the man. But he had liked its cabalistic signs and put the paper away in his jacket, promising himself he would copy them.

When he arrived at José's, where Ayodele had asked him to meet her, he found them deep in conversation. José was telling Ayodele about the revolt that had taken place recently in Bahia. The plan had been a clever one. The rebel slaves were to light fires in various parts of the town to distract the attention of the police and the army and lure them out of their barracks. They were to take advantage of the ensuing confusion to attack the military quarters, seize the arms there and massacre all the colonial masters. Once they were masters of the city they intended to join up with the slaves from the *fazendas* inland. But at the last moment they were betrayed, and the fine plan came to nothing.

José lowered his voice.

"They say it was the Muslims who were behind it all, and that they meant to slaughter all the African Catholics, too."

Ayodele shrugged.

"Are we ever really Catholics?" she said. "We just pretend, that's all."

José laughed. But they both felt the same anxiety. If the "Muslim" slaves were planning to massacre the "Catholic" slaves,

didn't that show that the dissensions of Africa had been transplanted into the world of slavery? When the only real enemy was
the Portuguese master, the white man?

Naba slept very badly that night.

Each time he was about to drift into slumber, the tear-stained
face of Nya appeared to him, followed by that of the stranger who
had approached him in the streets of Recife—now covered in
blood, with a wound in his forehead. When Naba tried to get up,
invisible hands held him down, digging painfully into his flesh.
At last he awoke, with the taste of ashes in his mouth, and went
out into the little garden attached to his shack to have a few puffs
of *maconha*. But that night the herb seemed to have lost its magic
power to make him relax. He sensed dangers approaching, like
dim, undistinguishable shapes.

He could hear sobs and the sounds of a whip, and breathed
in the smell of the *urubu* of death.

As he stood gazing into the darkness his second son, Kayode,
came and joined him. Kayode doted on his father. He immediately
asked to be told a story, and Naba began a story taken from the
inexhaustible epic of Souroukou.

"Souroukou fell down a well," he said, "and she wanted to
see whether she hadn't broken a tooth. But she was so stunned
by her fall that she put her hand up her anus by mistake. 'Oh!'
she cried, 'I haven't got a single tooth left!'"

The little boy let out a peal of laughter, then asked: "How
many languages do you speak, *baba*?"

Naba smiled in the darkness.

"You could say three. Two are the languages of my heart—
Bambara and Yoruba. The other is the language of our servitude—
Portuguese."

The child pondered.

"How many languages shall I be able to speak?"

Naba stroked the little head, with its knobby curls.

"I hope you'll only speak the languages of your heart," he
said. Then he took the child in his arms, rocked him a little and
put him back to bed.

"Go to sleep now," he said.

The *senzala* consisted of two rooms with floors of beaten earth and only the barest minimum of furnishings, as Ayodele saved every *real* that Naba earned. There was a closet that Naba had made himself to hold kitchen utensils, frying pans and saucepans blackened by use. There was also a table and a broom. The second room contained some hammocks bought from the Indians and a few straw mattresses.

Ayodele was asleep in one of the hammocks with Babatunde, her youngest child. The other hammock was occupied by the eldest boy, Abiola, Manoel's son. Naba was creeping out again on tiptoe when by the smoky light of the lamp he noticed that Abiola couldn't sleep either. He went over and spoke to him softly.

"Well," he said, "it looks as if all the family's been drinking coffee tonight!"

The child shut his eyes. He hated Naba. He hated his black brothers: they reminded him that his mother was a slave and he was half Negro himself. He hated being called Abiola, when his baptismal name was Jorge. Jorge da Cunha. For he was the master's son. Why didn't he live in the Great House, then, with the master's other sons? Why did he have to live in this mud and wattle hut? And now he was hearing them talk about going back to Africa, that barbarous place where human beings were sold like cattle if they were lucky enough to escape being eaten! No! Never! He would do all he could to prevent it.

Naba didn't insist. He knew how Abiola felt.

He had tried more than once to talk to Ayodele about it, but he was afraid of hurting her. Hadn't she already suffered enough from her connection with Manoel? And a child was like a plant, anyway. If you gave it plenty of love it would grow up straight in the end, straight up toward the sun.

He went outside again into the darkness, dotted at intervals by the denser shapes of the other shacks. Not a sound. The sweet smell of cane juice came wafting from the mill, tempered by the wind. And the wild smell of the earth, untamed even between the sugarcanes. But what was that black shape there at the top of the breadfruit tree?

Was it death?

Was it the *urubu* of death?

CHAPTER

9

Manoel turned his head and screwed up his eyes, to size up the small boy. He was a darkish mulatto with fine curly hair and a wide mouth tinged with mauve that was trembling with fear.

"Are you sure?" said Manoel.

The child nodded.

"If you don't believe me, have the house searched," he said. "Then you'll find the papers I've been telling you about. He's a Muslim, and he knows the Muslims in Bahia."

If someone else had been involved, Manoel would have shrugged the accusations off. The slaves on his *fazenda* prayed morning, noon and evening, going through the rosary and the Salve Regina with their masters, lighting candles, burning consecrated palms and fervently reciting, "I believe in the Holy Cross!"

But the one involved was Naba, who had taken away from him a woman he still desired. So he said, "Go and fetch the *feitor*."*

The boy didn't move.

"Well," snapped Manoel, "didn't you hear what I said?"

The boy fell on his knees.

* Overseer.

"If I've told you the truth," he begged, "will you keep me with you? I'm your son, master—why don't you let me be with you?"

Manoel was surprised and vaguely pleased. He had thought the boy completely attached to his mother.

"Of course, of course," he assured him. "Your place is here."

The boy sped off.

Manoel Ignacio da Cunha was typical of a whole generation of Portuguese. He came from a veritable family of adventurers who had emigrated to Asia, Madeira and Cape Verde. Manoel had found Cape Verde too cramped and come to Pernambuco. After some time spent as an ordinary farmer bringing his sugarcane to the owner of the mill, he had grown rich and was now contemplating going to live in Recife, leaving his *fazenda* in charge of an overseer.

He was very worried by what Abiola had told him, and went up to see his wife Rosa, who was in bed, as yellow as the Indian pillow on which she lay. She listened to him intently, her heart jumping for joy in her bosom, which was decked out with consecrated medals, scapulars and reliquaries. At last she had an opportunity of getting her revenge on Ayodele!

"I don't think it's him," she said. "He's only a harmless lunatic. It's her—her! I've noticed she's been disappearing as often as five times a day. Attending her witch's sabbath!"

Manoel knew these were merely the fantasies of a jealous woman, but after what had just happened in Bahia, where Muslims had planned one of the most ingenious rebellions of recent times, one couldn't be too careful. He went downstairs, where he found the *feitor*, straw hat in hand. Joaquim was his right-hand man, the one really in charge of the running of the *fazenda*. He listened to his master in horror.

"He's not a Muslim," he said. "Though I don't say he isn't a sorcerer. But how could he foment a revolt? He never speaks to anyone!"

Then the two men looked at one another. The *feitor* had something against Ayodele, too: one evening when he tried to fondle her breasts she had slapped his face. He and Manoel understood each other without words. Joaquim set out for the *senzalas*.

A search of Naba's house did indeed bring to light a paper

with Arabic words written on it, and some green leaves covered with the same characters.

Taking three hefty slaves along with him, the *feitor* went to arrest Naba. He was in his orchard, a pipe of *maconha* in his mouth, and he offered no resistance even when his legs were fettered.

When the news of his fate spread through the *fazenda* there was consternation. Everyone said he was innocent, and recalled how he had cured one person and helped another. But they did blame Ayodele. It was she! Hadn't she tried, along with the people in Bahia, to set up that brotherhood for the "Aspirations and Redemption of Black Men," whose purpose was to emancipate slaves? Didn't she have dealings with the emancipation societies in Recife? Dozens of men and women went to the *feitor* and even to Manoel himself to swear on the cross that they'd seen her groveling in the dust, holding a string of ninety-nine Muslim prayer beads half a yard long.

The *feitor* and Manoel agreed to take no notice of these denunciations. Naba's arrest created a serious problem. He wasn't a slave, or at least not one of Manoel's, even though he lived on his *fazenda*. Did he have to be regarded as a free man? No, because a Dutchman had once paid good money for him, and was still there somewhere in the *sertão*. He was a runaway, then? In that case, why had Manoel let him live on his land all these years? It was all too complicated. Naba was locked up in the cell attached to the Great House, to be sent to Recife the following day.

Meanwhile Ayodele had been absent from the *fazenda*. It was Sunday, the day of rest, and immediately after mass, ever anxious to make some money, she had loaded an oxcart with baskets of oranges and vegetables and gone off to sell them in the neighboring *fazendas*. Then she'd stopped to wash her children's clothes in the clear water of the rio Capibaride, which wound through the fields before flowing into the rio Beberibe and on to Recife. When she got home she found the hut empty and the children in tears. A sympathetic neighbor told her what had happened.

She rushed like a madwoman to the Great House and flung herself on her knees in front of Manoel, who was sitting in a hammock on the veranda.

He looked at her, the woman who had defied him so boldly, now in tears at his feet.

"There's nothing I can do," he said. "It was your own son who denounced him. And then we found proof."

Ayodele writhed on the ground.

"Take me, master," she cried. "That's what you really want!"

This vexed Manoel. He wanted people to think he was executing justice, not revenge.

"Do you want me to have you whipped?" he shouted.

But she went on imploring, and as she raised her head and looked at him he thought how stupid he was not to have taken advantage of her offer.

"Let me go to Recife, then," she begged, "to defend him!"

He nearly laughed. A slave woman, a Negress who could scarcely speak Portuguese, wanting to go and plead in the royal law courts. He shrugged.

"Go to the devil if you like!" he said.

Naba's trial took place in an already unpropitious atmosphere.

In the last ten years or so there had been many uprisings by slaves and freed Africans in Bahia and Recife as well as on the *fazendas*. They divided public opinion. Most Brazilians regarded them as proof of the blacks' perverseness and cruelty. Others saw them as just retaliation against inhuman masters. For a handful of liberals and intellectuals they were noble protests by oppressed human beings against the usurpation of their liberty. The wars and other troubles in the Bight of Benin had recently brought a large influx of prisoners from Africa who helped to inflame feeling among the slaves, especially the Muslims who, whenever the slave ships arrived, managed to find out about the victories of their coreligionists across the sea.

And now news had come that in San Domingo, an island in the West Indies, the slaves had taken up arms and waged a regular war of liberation against the French. At that all theories about the blacks as "harmless overgrown children" collapsed. The naive creatures relegated to the back of the church so that their smell might not incommode the priest or the rest of the congregation, and who sang in chorus:

> *I go to bed with God and with Him I get up*
> *With the grace of God and the Holy Ghost.*
> *And if I should die, light my way*
> *With the torches of the Holy Trinity*

—these naive creatures, these "overgrown children," were suddenly striking fear into their masters.

Naba appeared in court wearing the prisoner's uniform of a coarse cotton shirt and nankeen trousers, and seemed not to understand what was going on around him.

When asked to swear on the Bible, he said nothing. When asked "Are you a Muslim?" he only laughed. When told to choose between Catholic rosary and Muslim prayer beads, he stood motionless. The same thing happened when he was asked to choose between a picture of St. Gonçalves of Amarante and a piece of paper with Arabic calligraphy. No link could be established between him and the Muslim slaves in Bahia, where he had never set foot. The court even went so far as to examine him and his sons to see if they had been circumcised. They had been, but it was merely an African custom. As a last resort the judges steered the trial toward black magic, and here the evidence was overwhelming.

If Naba made no effort to defend himself, it wasn't because he didn't understand that his life was at stake; it was because he was weary. Ever since that fateful hunting expedition had parted him from his own people, he had lost interest in everything. Neither his plants nor his fruit trees, neither Ayodele nor even his sons had been able to reawaken his zest for life. He missed the soil of Segu; the smell of the Joliba at low water, when the banks were studded with oyster shells; the *to* his mother made with baobab leaf sauce; the bush fires at noon. Long ago, in Saint-Louis, he had tried to die. But he'd been saved. Now he was at the end of his tether. He felt some remorse when he thought of Ayodele, but then he told himself she was young and beautiful and some man would console her. He was tempted to live only when he thought of his sons, Olufemi, Kayode and Babatunde—especially the last, whose name meant "Father has come back!" Born after Dousika's death, he was a reincarnation of his spirit. But what use was a father who was a slave? What sort of example could he give to his children? He would never hold Babatunde's hand and take him hunting lion with bow and arrow.

> *The yellow lion with tawny glints*
> *The lion forsakes the flocks of men*
> *And feeds on that which lives in liberty . . .*

He would never make him a *karamoko*. So what was the point?

What was the point of life without liberty? Without self-respect? You might just as well be dead.

José the *ganhador* didn't remain inactive during the trial. He got his emancipation society to send a petition for mercy to João IV in Rio. Unfortunately it arrived just as another revolt had been uncovered: a search of the huts of Antonio and Balthazar, two Hausa slaves belonging to Francisco des Chagas, had revealed four hundred arrows, cord for making bowstrings, guns and pistols. So João ordered the courts to be extremely severe. Every slave found in the street or away from his master's premises after nine o'clock at night was to be imprisoned and given a hundred lashes.

Knowing nothing of all these events, Ayodele was optimistic till the last moment. The memory of her years with Naba kept going through her head, from the day he came up to her with his bag of oranges in the slave house in Gorée, to his departure for the *sertão* and then his reappearance on Manoel's *fazenda*. He hadn't looked at her gourdlike belly. He had just smiled, unfolded his handkerchief and showed her two pink and yellow guavas. Then, for her, he'd built the house by the cane fields.

Naba had covered her shame.

Naba had reconciled her with herself.

It was hot in the courtroom. The judges spoke in a language Ayodele couldn't understand, the Portuguese of the educated classes, so different from the jargon interspersed with African words used by Manoel and the *feitor*. She couldn't see Naba. They were separated by chairs and benches, men and priests and judges. She had already lost him.

Suddenly, José, who was sitting near her, took her arm, and she realized the verdict had been delivered. They went out into the blazing sun.

There was nothing to be said.

Where were they going? She collapsed on the San Antonio bridge, just slid quietly, almost furtively, to the ground, like an animal that has held out till its strength is utterly exhausted. An animal or a slave. Sometimes a man or woman would collapse like that, without a groan, on the *fazenda*. As they were quite near the hospital, the Santa Casa de Misericordia, José and his friends took her there.

There was nothing to be said. There was nothing to be done. A sorcerer, or a Muslim, it hardly mattered which, had been sentenced to death. For the greater glory of God.

A black had been sentenced to death. For the greater peace of the whites.

For Ayodele, life was for a long time reduced to a blue square of sky, the taste of licorice water, the occasional pain of bloodletting from her arm, and the white caps of the nuns like great seabirds. Then one day she recognized the faces of her children—Olufemi, Kayode and Babatunde. Where was Abiola? Then she remembered, and wept.

How was she to learn to live again when there was no more reason for living? Speak of tomorrow when there was no future, watch the sun rise when there was no more light? One morning a priest came to see her. Father Joaquim was one of those mystics who liked the company of heretics and the underprivileged. He made her repent her sins. Soon she was being called Romana again. Soon she received Holy Communion.

The first time she took communion she had a vision. The heavens opened and the Virgin Mary, holding the infant Jesus in her arms, threw her a rose. Father Joaquim and the nuns were very pleased.

At last she was strong enough to leave the hospital. And it was then that Father Joaquim and the nuns told her. As the partner of a *feticeiro*, a sorcerer, who had caused a public scandal, she had been declared persona non grata in Brazil, and she and her three children were to be deported to Africa.

The boat they were to sail in, the *Amizade*, was anchored off

Cobres Island. Besides Romana, the passengers consisted of a number of Malé who had again caused bloodshed in Bahia, together with some black families who had managed to buy their freedom and passports. The deck was crowded with bodies, trunks, bundles, bottles, musical instruments, birds in cages— all the paraphernalia of poverty. Ayodele's children, whom the nuns had taken away from José because of his abominable vice and kept in their orphanage at the Santa Casa while their mother was ill, gazed at the coast of Brazil, the gold of the beaches contrasting with the dark green fringe of palms. Except for Baba, who was too young, they had lumps in their throats. Where was their father? What had changed their mother? They couldn't recognize her in this austere, hollow-cheeked woman dressed all in black, who never spoke of anything but God.

CHAPTER

10

The *urubu* of death, invisible to the eyes of ordinary mortals, alighted on a tree in the compound and flapped its wings. It was exhausted. It had flown over miles and miles of sea, fighting against spray and air currents, then over dense forests swarming with a thousand different forms of fierce and violent life. Finally it had seen a tawny stretch of sand below and realized that its journey was nearly over. Then the walls of Segu appeared.

The *urubu* had a mission to perform. Naba had died far from home. His body lay in foreign soil and had not received the proper funeral rites. So his people had to be told he was in danger of having to wander forever in the desolate waste of the damned, unable to find reincarnation in the body of a male baby or to become a protecting ancestor, later a god. The *urubu* preened its feathers, got its breath back, and looked around.

It was morning. The sun had not yet answered the call of the earliest pestles and mortars, and still slumbered on the other side of the sky. The huts huddled together and shivered. But already the chickens were cackling, the sheep bleating, and from beneath the awnings of the open-air kitchens the smoke arose in white puffs. The women slaves were starting to prepare the morning porridge, while the men went to the bath huts, whetted their *dabas* on stones, and got ready to go out into the fields. The *urubu* looked with interest at all this activity, so different from that in the *fazendas*, where long before daylight the ox carts, preceded by the earsplitting sound of their axles, went up to the sugar mill laden with men in rags. There, working on the land was degradation. Here men only asked the earth for what was necessary to live. The landscape was different, too. There it was sumptuous and baroque, like the cathedrals the Portuguese built to worship their gods. Here it was bare, with the grass often as short as the pelt of an animal; but it was beautiful, too. The *urubu* hopped onto a low branch, facing the hut belonging to Koumare, fetish priest to Dousika's family. It was a wise move, for Koumare came out to divine what sort of day it was going to be, and didn't fail to notice the creature perched among the leaves.

Koumare had known for some time that the will of the ancestors concerning one of Dousika's sons was approaching fulfillment. One day when he was throwing his cowrie shells on his divining board they had told him so. But they wouldn't reveal anything more, however much he asked them. The coming of the bird was the sign it was all over. He went back into his hut, chewed some of the roots that allowed him to hear the speech of spirits, then took three stalks of dried millet out of a bowl. Then he went out under the tree, stuck the stalks into the earth, put his ear to them, and waited for instructions. They were not long in coming. Above his head the *urubu* had shut its eyes. It was going to sleep all day. Koumare went back to his hut, waved away his first wife's offer of gruel, put on a European blanket against the cold, and went out of the compound.

Segu was changing. Why? Was it because of the influx of merchants offering goods once rare and expensive, now quite common? Muslim robes, caftans, boots, European fabrics, furniture from Morocco, hangings and tapestries from Mecca. . . . It was Islam that was eating away at Segu like some incurable disease. The Fulani had no need to come any nearer—their breath had already fouled everything! Their jihad wasn't necessary any more! Everywhere there were mosques, their muezzins shamelessly bawling down their sacrilegious summons. Everywhere there were shaven heads. In every market people fought over talismans, powders, a whole lot of rubbish wrapped up with Arabic labels and therefore considered superior. And the Mansa wasn't doing anything about this new religion!

Koumare went into what used to be Dousika's compound, now in the charge of Diemogo. He had to get a white cock and a white sheep from Diemogo, and then find out which tree Naba's umbilical cord was buried under. Diemogo was talking to the leader of a group of slaves just going off to clear a piece of hitherto uncultivated land belonging to the clan. He glanced at the fetish priest anxiously. What new calamity brought him here?

The family was already sorely tried. Tiekoro had not left his hut since Nadie's death, and he was as weak and sickly as an old man. Princess Sounou Saro, his promised bride, feeling humiliated, had sent the dowry back by the royal griots, together with such presents as she had already received. Tiekoro's mission as ambassador to the sultanate of Sokoto was given to someone else. Nya, affected both by the recent tragedy and by her son's misfortunes, was not well either. She was getting thin and haggard and seemed to take no interest in anything. Without her supervision, everything went to rack and ruin. It was no use looking to the other wives: they had always been under the thumb of Dousika's *bara muso*. Diemogo went over to Koumare, who took him aside and told him what had happened.

"The ancestors have sent a messenger to me," he said. "One of Dousika's sons needs my help."

Diemogo trembled.

"Tiekoro?" he asked.

"Don't seek to know secrets too heavy for you," answered the other severely. "I need a white cock, a sheep without markings, and ten kola nuts. Have them all sent to my compound before nightfall."

Then he went to find the tree he needed for his ritual. As he was going through the compound he passed a hut where slaves were going busily in and out. It was Nya's hut. She had been taken ill with a violent pain near her heart and had collapsed unconscious. Koumare thought with wonder of the strength of mother love and the intuition that went with it. It was just as powerful as the knowledge that came from intercourse with spirits.

—

Nya lay on her mat, her eyes closed, surrounded by women, co-wives, slaves. Every now and then she would pant like an animal. Two healers applied dressings of leaves to her forehead, rubbed her limbs with lotions, or tried to make her drink. In a corner a couple of fetish priests were consulting their cowries and kola nuts. When they saw Koumare, their uncontested chief, they rose respectfully.

"Help us, Komotigui,"* said one of them.

"Her life is not in danger," Koumare replied soothingly.

Then he crouched down by the patient.

He knew what she had been through since she'd been widowed. The family council, doling out Dousika's wives, had given her to Diemogo, for whom she had never had any respect and whom she considered, rightly or wrongly, as opposed to the interests of her own sons, especially those of Tiekoro. But from then on she owed him total submission and obedience. She couldn't refuse him her body. And now, on top of all these troubles, she had been mysteriously warned of Naba's death! Koumare decided to intercede for her with the ancestors, to try to lessen her sufferings. Meanwhile he took some powder from a goat horn and inserted it into her nostrils: at least she would now have a dreamless sleep.

Then he went out again. At the far end of the compound, near the paddock where the horses were kept, stood a group of trees, the tallest of which was a baobab, its branches covered with birds. Koumare walked around it three times, muttering prayers. No, the umbilical cord wasn't there. A white egret appeared, skimmed along the ground for a while, then swooped up like an arrow and alighted on a tamarind tree growing against the wall of the compound a few yards further on. Koumare saluted this messenger of the gods and the ancestors.

Nya slept all day, a deep sleep like that of childhood. When she opened her eyes, night had fallen. She found her pain was the same, but silent, like a presence that would never go away.

Her son Naba was dead. She could feel it, even though she

* Master of Komo, i.e., high priest.

didn't know where or how he had died. She saw him as he was when a baby, a little boy, always trailing behind his elder brother. Then she saw him as a hunter—her heart used to quake when Tiefolo took him into the bush. They often stayed there for weeks at a time. Then one day the sound of whistling would announce their return. The animals they had killed would be cut up while they were still warm: antelope, gazelles and warthogs. The heads and feet would be sent to Koumare, who had made the arrows that killed them; she herself received the animals' backs as her symbolic share. But those days were gone, gone forever. What sorrow, for a mother, not to know what earth covered her son's dead body! She turned onto her side, and the women watching over her bestirred themselves.

"Would you like some chicken broth?"

"Let me massage you, *ba*!"

"*Ba*, do you feel better?"

She indicated that she did. At that moment Diemogo entered the room and everyone else withdrew. Diemogo and Nya had never liked one another: he thought she had too much influence over Dousika. The reason why the family council had made them husband and wife was to try to resolve these tensions, to force them to forget personalities and think only of the family and the clan. But until now they had had as little as possible to do with one another. Diemogo only spent the night with her so as not to cause her too much humiliation.

Now he felt a pity for her that resembled love. She was still beautiful. Beautiful with the characteristic arrogance of the Kulibaly, whose totem was the *mpolio* fish. He laid his hand on her brow.

"How do you feel?" he said.

She gave a fleeting smile. "My hour is not yet come, *koke*," she answered. "I shall still be making your gruel tomorrow . . ."

He wasn't used to such mildness from her; she usually treated him like an enemy. Perhaps for the first time, he looked at her body with lust: her still-firm breasts, her wide hips, her long thighs visible through her *pagne*. All this had belonged to his elder brother, but now was his. For he was the master now—of lands, property, cattle, slaves. His heart, usually free of pride, swelled within him, and he was filled with an intoxication that merged into desire.

It was very dark now. All the noises of the compound had ceased apart from the crying of a child, trying to delay the sleep that marked the end of playtime. A drum could be heard in the distance. Diemogo, surprised at the vigor of his member, went nearer to Nya. It was as if another person had gotten inside his skin, taking over his heart and his sex. He lay down beside her.

"Let me sleep with you," he whispered. "A man's warmth is still the best cure."

She turned toward him, offering herself with a naturalness he had never seen in her before, and when he rather shyly touched her breasts he found them hot and ready. He entered her.

And so, that night, thanks to Koumare, Naba's wandering soul found its way back into his mother's womb.

PART THREE

A FRUITLESS
DEATH

CHAPTER

1

What awful weather! It had been raining for weeks, months. The tops of the trees were almost scraping the low murky sky, black as the saucepan lid of a bad housewife, while their roots struck ever deeper into the womb of the soft, fat, muddy earth. Morning was like noon or evening, for the sun never rose. It hadn't the strength to answer the call of the women's pestles and mortars and lay sluggishly behind thick screens of cloud. Malobali went back into one of the huts hastily built of branches.

"Shouldn't we go on, all the same?" he asked his companions.

One of them looked up at him.

"That's enough from you, Bambara," he said. "You're not the leader of the escort, as far as I know."

It was true. With a sigh, Malobali sat down and went through his clothes in search of a kola nut. He didn't find one.

"Has anyone got some snuff or a kola nut?" he asked.

One of the men handed him a snuffbox.

Malobali and his companions were dressed in cloth jackets adorned with all sorts of gris-gris and with Muslim amulets in their triangular leather pouches. Their cotton trousers had strings of animal tails around the waist, and their high leather boots, once red, were now shabby and stained. As the men were indoors they had taken off their monkey-skin caps, with chin straps decorated with cowries. They were part of the army of the Asantehene, supreme chief of the Ashanti kingdom.

Malobali took some snuff, then curled up on the floor to try to sleep. Around him the damp air was made thicker by the smells of sweat and dirt emanating from so many unwashed bodies. But Malobali didn't look down on his companions because they were dirty: he was dirty, too. He'd almost forgotten the time when he was a petted child in Nya's hut, the son of a nobleman, of a man of influence. Now he was only a mercenary, selling his services to the Asantehene in return for board and lodging, and occasionally a share of the loot. He wasn't the only one. The king's armies contained sixty thousand men who were not Ashanti—captives, tributaries, foreigners of all kinds. These armies had conquered all the states around Ashanti: Gonja and Dagomba in the north, Gyaman in the northeast, Nzema in the southeast, and had even crossed the river Volta and taken Akwamu and Anlo. The only people who still opposed Ashanti hegemony—the Fantis, strongly supported on the coast by the British—had just been defeated.

Malobali couldn't sleep, so he got up and went over to his friend Kodjoe, the one who had lent him his snuffbox.

"Get up, you bastard, and come for a walk!" he said. "Perhaps we'll find an animal to kill."

Kodjoe opened one eye.

"Has it stopped raining?" he asked.

"What a question! Does it ever stop raining in this rotten country?"

Another voice made itself heard.

"If you don't like this country, Bambara, clear out. No one's stopping you. Go home!"

But it was only a joke. Malobali and Kodjoe left the hut without answering. All around them the forest was so dense it was almost dark. All sorts of plants intertwined with one another, from the bamboos and giant ferns growing out of a carpet of moss and mushrooms to the iroko trees whose tops formed an almost unbroken vault. At every step you fell over lianas creeping up tree trunks in complex arabesques, and climbing plants armed with hooks and tendrils like so many snares. At first Malobali had hated this murky universe smelling of death and corruption, and he still found it depressing, for at every turn he thought he caught sight of the malevolent shape of some angry spirit. And, though he would have liked not to believe in anything, he found himself muttering prayers against illness and sudden death.

Kodjoe stooped to pick up enormous snails with purple flesh, a local delicacy which filled Malobali with disgust. Kodjoe was an Abron from the kingdom of Gyaman, which had fallen into the power of the Ashanti a century earlier. But his mother, a Goro, had taught him to speak a language similar to Malobali's, and that was what had first brought them together. Finally they had found that they shared the same attitude: a kind of contempt, almost hatred, for the human race.

Kodjoe sat down on a root, a huge excrescence that plunged into the soil again a few yards further on, and looked up at Malobali.

"I've got something to tell you," he said. "If we get to Cape Coast, I'm never going back to Kumasi."

Malobali dropped down beside him.

"Are you mad?" he said.

"No. I've got a plan," answered Kodjoe, tapping his brow. "The future lies on the coast, with the English, the whites. Wasn't it because of them that the Fantis were able to hold out so long against the Ashanti? They've got arms, seagoing ships, money— and they know about the new plants. The Asantehene, Osei Bonsu, trembles before them and tries to get into their good graces."

Malobali stared at him in wonder.

"Don't tell me you mean to enter the service of the whites?"

Kodjoe picked a wild berry and started to chew it.

"I want to learn their secrets. I want to learn to write."

Malobali shrugged.

"Become a Muslim then—you can learn to write that way!"

Realizing there was no point in arguing, Kodjoe got up and started to walk on. For a while Malobali followed silently, deep in thought. Then, "The English won't take any notice of you, either, unless you're converted to their religion!" he said.

Kodjoe looked around.

"In that case I'll be converted!" he answered.

Malobali could never hear the word "conversion" without

thinking of his hated brother Tiekoro. It was Tiekoro who had made his life what it was. Tiekoro had driven him out of Segu as surely as if he'd actually banished him.

After Nadie's suicide Tiekoro himself had hovered for some time between life and death. Then he got better. But instead of beginning his new life with humility, he had paraded his ordeal, calling the whole world to witness. Ah, how he had suffered! And why? Because he had been a miserable sinner. But now he was resolved to do penance. Dressed all in white, with a string of prayer beads in his hand or wound around his wrist, he sat himself down on his mat and never left it except to go to the mosque. People soon started coming to see him, some asking for a prayer, others for advice, others again just wanting him to touch them. His reputation for saintliness had somehow grown and spread to Jenne, Timbuktu and Gao. It even reached the ears of Amadou Hammadi Boubou, who had adopted the title of sheikh and had a town built for himself called Hamdallay. He invited Tiekoro to go there to discuss the best way of converting the Bambara to Islam.

One morning Tiekoro was preaching to a handful of the faithful, as was now his habit.

"God is Love and Power. Creation comes from His love, and not from any constraint. To hate what is produced by God's will, acting out of love, is to oppose God's will and challenge His wisdom."

The sound of his voice had provoked such a mixture of anger and nausea in Malobali that he had leapt onto a horse and ridden straight out of Segu. At first he only meant to go to Tenenkou and see his mother. He had an account to settle with her, too! Then he met some kola-nut merchants going to Salaga and went with them. One thing led to another and he ended up in the Asantehene's army.

To be converted! To deny the gods of one's fathers, and through them their whole culture and civilization—this struck Malobali as an unforgivable crime. He would never commit it, even under torture.

Malobali and Kodjoe came to a little clearing planted with yams and sweet potatoes, the first sign of human life they had met with since they left Kumasi four days ago. They were just beginning to dig up some of the tubers, disregarding the fact that they did not belong to them, when a girl appeared, holding a basket. She was very young, with small but rounded breasts and long legs.

"Leave them alone," she called in a shrill little voice. "Or else give us some cowries for them."

Malobali started to laugh.

"Why do you say 'us'?" he said. "I can't see anyone but you."

"Our village is just over there," she said, pointing to a path.

"Why are you so frightened then?" he asked.

While Kodjoe sat sniggering on a root, Malobali went over to the girl. She was pretty, with a jet black skin and a delicate pattern of tribal scarifications on her cheeks. Desire stirred in Malobali.

"What's your name?" he asked.

"Ayaovi," she said, after a moment's hesitation.

Then she turned and fled. Malobali rushed after her. At first she had inspired in him only the vague and easily mastered desire he felt in the presence of any pretty girl. But pursuit made it more acute. As Ayaovi ran, her naked buttocks bobbed up and down and the sweat pouring down her back made her skin shine. She disappeared behind a tree, reappeared between two ferns, then tripped over a vine. Malobali threw himself down on her as she lay in a patch of leaf mold. Realizing, from the shape of her body, how very young she was, he was almost moved to let her go with nothing worse than a fright.

But she started to insult him so volubly that his ear, still unused to *twi*, the Ashanti language, could not make out the words, and this angered him. He was just about to slap her to make her stop when she lifted her head as swiftly as a snake and spat right in his face. It was too much. He had to punish her, and he had only one way of doing it. As he roughly pushed her legs apart it occurred to him that she must be below the age of puberty, and he realized the enormity of what he was doing. But she flashed him a look of defiance unusual in anyone so young. So he penetrated her. She shrieked, and Malobali knew he would hear that earsplitting cry until his dying day. It was like the death cry of a terrified child, a child calling on the gods to witness the cruelty of adults.

He felt a little pool of blood under his suddenly wilting mem-

ber. He almost got up and begged her forgiveness, but he was
seized by some malignant force that came from he knew not
where. With some difficulty he finished penetrating her, then lay
still, not daring to look at her. A hand tapped him on the shoulder.
It was Kodjoe.

"Don't forget your friends!" he said.

Malobali made way for him.

Unlike all the other campaigns of recent years, especially
those against the Fantis, Malobali's expedition was entirely
peaceful. Its object was to escort a white man by the name of
Wargee to Cape Coast. Wargee had arrived at the Asantehene's
court after an incredible journey that had taken him from Istanbul
to Tripoli and Murzuk, then from Kano to Timbuktu, Jenne and
the trading town of Salaga, before he ended up in Kumasi, the
Ashanti capital. Osei Bonsu, the Asantehene, famous for his great
courtesy to foreigners, was having him escorted to the coast so
that no harm might befall him. Once he reached the coast the
English would help him get home. Where did Wargee come from?
What was he doing in Africa? Neither Malobali nor his companions cared. They just did as they were told, and by common accord
kept well away from Wargee.

For Malobali, who had never seen any whites before unless
you counted the Moors he met with on all the trade routes, Wargee and his like were a different species, as intriguing and incomprehensible as women or animals. He couldn't understand
their admirers, for he saw in them a danger worse than that of
the Fulani and all the other Muslims combined.

When Malobali and Kodjoe got back to their hut the soldiers
had lit a fire that produced more smoke than light and gave off
no heat at all. The wood was wet.

"Well, what have you brought?" asked one of them.

Kodjoe emptied his bag: a few snails drawn back into their
thick black shells, and some sweet potatoes. The others laughed.

"A fine supper that'll make!" said one.

Kodjoe sat down and smiled mysteriously.

"Perhaps we found better game, too," he said.

At that, those who were drowsing woke up and those who

were lying around the edges of the room came nearer, while Kod-joe began to describe Ayaovi's charms in detail. This angered Malobali, who was still overwhelmed with shame at what he had done.

"Shut up, Kodjoe!" he said. "There are some things one doesn't boast about!"

And he left the hut. He could hear the others' comments behind his back: "The Bambara's mad!"

Malobali's life had been a series of reprehensible deeds ever since he left Segu. Not just because he killed the Asantehene's enemies or took them captive. No, war was war, and that was what he was paid for. But too often his arms had been turned against the innocent. With Kodjoe and a few others he would go into the Ashanti villages themselves, where peaceful peasants were scraping the mud from their feet as their wives pounded *fou-fou* paste. Then they would rape and steal and set the place on fire just for the pleasure of feeling equal to the gods, replacing the happiness and peace of a moment before with despair. Once they had murdered an old man just because he had looked so ugly with his face contorted with fear.

Suddenly Malobali's past attitude disgusted him.

What should he do? Go back to Segu?

The rain, after stopping for a moment, had begun to fall again in big drops that were at once hot and refreshing. In his mind's eye Malobali saw Ayaovi's face. How old must she be? Not more than ten or eleven. Normally, once a rape was over, Malobali forgot about his victim. So why this shame and remorse? He started to wander about at random in the rain, and bumped up against someone in the dark. It was the *safohene*, captain of the escort.

"Oh, it's the Bambara!" the other exclaimed. "Tell the others we start again at dawn."

"About time!" said Malobali. "A bit longer here and we'd be growing roots!"

The pleasantry annoyed the captain, who had often been ir-ritated by Malobali's behavior. He swung around.

"I'm the one who gives the orders here, don't forget," he said curtly. "The white we're escorting is an old man. He finds the forest hard going."

And certainly it wasn't easy! The soldiers had to hack away the grasses, vines and giant roots that lay in their path. Sometimes they sank up to the knees in the spongy ground, and only the ropes linking them together saved them from being completely bogged down. Not to mention the reptiles, and the insects that clung like leeches to their faces, necks and shoulders.

At any other time Malobali would have taken no notice of this snub, but that evening it struck him as a humiliation. He went back into the hut.

The men were baking the sweet potatoes in the embers and grilling the thick flesh of the snails on a spit. Gourds of palm wine were passing from hand to hand.

Malobali went and sat in a corner, his back against the damp wall. How much longer could he endure this coarse, limited existence? How much longer would he eat this primitive food, listen to these vulgar jokes?

"Hi, friend," he said as Kodjoe approached, "tell me about your fine plan."

"I knew you'd be interested!" was the laughing reply. "There are several possibilities. There's a garrison of trained men in the fort at Cape Coast who are dying to attack the Ashanti. We could offer them our services."

"Commit treachery, you mean?"

Kodjoe waved the word away.

"And there are priests in and around the town—missionaries, they're called—who employ people in their fields and teach them to read and write. Someone told me they even send some of them to study in their own schools in England. If you like we could try them."

As Malobali didn't seem very enthusiastic, Kodjoe went on.

"Or else we could go into trade."

It was Malobali's turn to jeer.

"Trade in what?" he said. "The English don't want any more slaves."

Kodjoe shrugged.

"But there's still the French, the Portuguese, the Dutch. You just need to be clever, that's all. Or else we could deal in palm oil. The whites use it to make their soap. . . . Or in hides. Or in elephants' tusks."

Malobali heard all this in amazement, wondering how Kod-joe, whom he had thought as frivolous and pleasure-seeking as himself, could have worked it out. He suddenly felt a kind of respect, a sentiment unusual for him. He himself felt dull-witted in comparison, and his self-contempt increased.

He turned toward the mud wall—the wattle was crawling with insects—and tried to sleep. But he only succeeded in seeing Ayaovi. What a stupid, senseless thing to do! At the moment of penetration his member had almost refused, and he'd had to urge it on like a lazy horse by thinking of the girl's insults. He imag-ined her returning to her father's village—her tears, her halting confession. From her description her people would be able to tell her assailants were the Asantehene's men, and they'd be too ter-rified to do anything. So this crime too would go unpunished. The only thing to do was start a new life! Settle on the coast! Settle on the coast—why not?

Malobali huddled against the wall. The raindrops pattered softly down on the roof of leaves.

CHAPTER

2

In June 1822 the town of Cape Coast was regarded by some as the finest spot along the stretch of the African seaboard known as the Gold Coast. Its wide, well-kept streets were lined with magnificent stone houses belonging to English merchants who had been there for decades. The local population lived in a kind of suburb not totally devoid of charm, with its huts of dried mud beneath coconut and other palms. But the most impressive building was undoubtedly the fort. It had changed hands ten times, passing from the Swedes to the Danes to the Dutch before being firmly held by the English. The building was triangular and surrounded by a thick wall. Two of its sides faced out to sea, guarding the approaches through the fixed black eyes of seventy-seven cannon, which though rusted by the sea air were still in working order. Until recently the English had used the fort as a distribution point for slaves on their way to the Americas, and they had rarely left the place except after ships berthed there, to trade with the people along the coast, especially the Fanti. But gradually their influence had spread and they had set themselves up as defenders of the Fanti against their enemies inland, the Ashanti. This did not stop the latter from subduing the region and installing their own resident there. Ever since they had abolished the slave trade the English were champing at the bit inside the fort, waiting for their government to decide what relationship it meant to entertain with the new Ashanti masters.

Why didn't they attack these barbarians? Why didn't they ensure unhampered trade by occupying the whole region?

This was certainly the view of MacCarthy, the new governor of the fort, and when he was told of the arrival of a small band of Ashanti warriors he almost thought of having the cannon fired. What stopped him was the information that among them was an elderly white man in the uniform of the Royal Africa Company. He was suspicious, and told his guards to let no one enter the fort but the old man, an interpreter and the war chief.

Malobali and Kodjoe went to look for a tavern. After the dampness of the forest the sea air seemed dry, and left a salty film on your lips which made you thirsty. It also, strangely, made your eyes fill with tears. The tavern was a brick building that looked very elegant to Malobali amid its clumps of coconut palms. More important, it had a fine supply of gin, rum, schnapps and French wines.

The man who ran it was a mulatto. Mulattos were becoming common throughout the coast since Europeans had started to come there in large numbers. In the early days the Danes, Swedes and English had contracted various forms of marriage with African women, and sent their children, especially the sons, to school in their own countries. Then, as the custom spread, the most they ever did was pay allowances to the mothers.

The tavern keeper filled their glasses and asked:

"Who's the white man with you?"

Malobali shrugged and let Kodjoe explain.

"It seems he was born in a place called Kisliar, and was sold as a slave."

"Really! Do you mean to say white men are sold as slaves too?"

Kodjoe joined Malobali at his table. The tavern looked out over a white sandy beach, dotted here and there with the rotting trunks of coconut palms and the remains of old fishing boats. A European ship was anchored in the offing, surrounded by a mass of little boats belonging to local traders. In them you could see bales of cloth with red, green, white and blue stripes; strings of brass and coral bracelets; barrels of spirits—all the apparently trivial things for which men will fight. Kodjoe signaled to the tavern keeper to come and fill their bowls again, and as he leaned over to do so, said, "You're half a white—do you know about the whites' affairs?"

The other laughed.

"It depends," he said.

"About work, for example," Kodjoe went on. "We've had enough of the army."

The man looked out to sea and frowned.

"Everyone comes to the coast and wants to work for the whites," he said. "It's getting difficult. But there is the mission. You look a bit old to me for catechists, but you can always try."

As Malobali was trying to conceal his repugnance, the man said to him, "But you're not an Ashanti. You look like a Fulani to me."

Malobali hated to be reminded of that half of himself, connecting him with a mother he regarded as having abandoned him. He scowled.

"That means you may find work more easily!" whispered Kodjoe to placate him.

The fact was that the intrigues of the English and the Fantis had made the mere name Ashanti hated from the river Ankobra to the Volta. Especially as the Asanthehene was harsh in his treatment of subject countries, imposing heavy taxes, harassment and humiliations of all kinds.

Kodjoe and Malobali decided to go and look for themselves.

A wave of missionary zeal, inspired by the Methodists, was sweeping through Cape Coast. Proselytism, previously confined within the fort and to the dozen or so mulatto children its staff produced year in and year out, was now attacking the local population. A huge gray stone church was rising in the middle of the town, while the mission itself more discreetly stood half hidden on the road to Elmina. It was not very prepossessing: just a straw-thatched rectangular shanty with a garden in front containing some pathetic attempts at flowers and vegetables. A handful of little boys were chopping logs under an awning, while a chorus of thin voices chanted some incomprehensible prayer and an army of black swine rooted around in the earth.

The missionary himself, no doubt intrigued by the arrival of two Ashanti warriors on his doorstep, came out onto the veranda. He was a mulatto! Dressed in a heavy black robe and wearing a sort of chaplet around his neck with a huge cross at the end. But a mulatto just the same!

Malobali and Kodjoe exchanged glances. No—they didn't want anything to do with this half-black. There was no more to be said. They turned on their heels.

How exciting it was to walk through a town in the uniform of a conquering army! The shopkeepers protected their wares and the men protected their wives, whose only thought was to surrender their bodies. The children rushed out of the compounds yelling and clapping their hands. But all this, which had once delighted Malobali, now left him cold. As he looked around him he remained unimpressed by Cape Coast, almost despising it for its lack of a past, of traditions. It owed its existence only to the will of the whites—to the Portuguese who had liked the anchorage, which they called Cabo Corso, and to the other Europeans who had come later and fought to establish a fort there. In those days Cape Coast had no wall; it was there for the taking like the women the whites took, made pregnant, and abandoned. With its plain right angles and commercial buildings, it was completely lacking in mystery. Was it really a town at all? No, it was only an entrepôt marked forever with the infamous brand of trade in human flesh.

As the captain had dismissed the company, Malobali and Kodjoe went to the house of the Asantehene's resident, Owusu Adom, who was responsible for carrying out the decisions of the Ashanti government. He was of royal blood, the Asantehene's nephew, and lived in the midst of a large court. He had his own stool or sacred symbol of authority, and his temporary residence was filled with people carrying fans, scepters, elephants' tails, litters and swords, together with linguists, eunuchs, cooks and musicians, in an attempt to re-create the royal palace in which he had grown up.

His captain, Amacom, showed Malobali and Kodjoe a hut where the rest of the troop were already lodged. They were all in good spirits, for Amacom had sent in bowls of palm wine and dishes of *fou-fou*, together with soup of red palm oil.

"So that's the end of our fine plans!" mocked Malobali as he washed his hands.

Kodjoe rolled his eyes.

"Do you think I'm so easily put off?" Kodjoe said. "There must be plenty of missionaries whose two halves are white. If not, we'll try something else."

Meanwhile, in Kumasi, it was a day when the Asantehene gave audience. Asantehene Osei Bonsu had succeeded his elder brother Osei Kwame, whom the council had deposed because of his sympathies for Islam. He was short but very strong; his magnificent eyes sparkled with intelligence.

He was seated on his throne. Beside him, also on a throne, was the golden stool, symbol of the Ashanti kingdom, decorated with three large and three small bells of brass and gold. Osei Bonsu was dressed in a *kente*, a sumptuous woven *pagne* which left one of his shoulders bare. He wore loose sandals on his feet, for they must never touch the ground. On his arms and ankles were finely chased gold bangles depicting all kinds of animals. His smooth neck, straight as a tree trunk, was hung with a profusion of gold necklaces and breastplates, together with Muslim amulets in their leather cases. High priests stood about him, and two servants plied big ostrich feather fans. He was listening intently to his head linguist as he interpreted the words of a village chief from the region of Bekwai, now groveling respectfully in the dust before the royal dais.

A serious offense had been committed.

A girl under the age of puberty had been raped on the way to one of her parents' fields in the forest. In other circumstances her parents might have said nothing, for the guilty party was a soldier belonging to the Asantehene's mighty army. But the girl, Ayaovi, was their only child, born after six brothers and three sisters had died, and she was the only one the gods had left to them. They demanded that justice be done. When the head linguist stopped speaking the high priests gave their verdict without more ado. The crime was an offense against the earth itself. If it remained unpunished, the earth would not rest: the hunters would catch no more game; the crops would not flourish. Chaos would reign.

Who had committed the crime?

The *kontihene*, the commander in chief, stepped forward. According to the child's description the soldier in question was not

an Ashanti but one of the mercenaries from the north—a Fulani
or a Hausa. He had been in the neighborhood of Bekwai about a
week before. From all these facts, the *kontihene* swiftly deduced
that it could only be Malobali, the Bambara in Wargee's escort.
So he must be brought back to Kumasi to be punished.

In the days of Osei Tutu, the founder of the kingdom, such
a crime would have been punished by death. But Osei Bonsu had
introduced a certain mildness into Ashanti ways; his motto was,
"Never use the sword when the way of negotiation is still open."
He ordered the family bringing the charges to be housed in a wing
of the castle, and to show his sympathy told his treasurer to pay
them a *dommafa*, an Ashanti measure, of gold dust. The priests
and sages were full of praise for his benevolence.

The Ashanti kingdom, whose capital was Kumasi, was also
called the kingdom of gold. In the rainy season the nuggets were
laid bare and the Asantehene's agents had only to shovel them
up. The country also had inexhaustible mines at Obuase, Ko-
nongo and Tarkwa, hence its king's nickname, "He who sits on
gold." Yet despite the wonderful prosperity symbolized by the
ornaments in which he was decked, Osei Bonsu was sad and
careworn. He was worried about the English!

After buying slaves by the boatload, here they were abolishing
the slave trade! Why? What did they want now? What was he
going to do with his prisoners of war? Was he to let them grow
up among his own people, to strangle them like weeds in the
field? Was he to kill them like dangerous beasts? Moreover, no
matter how many gestures of goodwill he made toward the English they persisted in backing all the rebellions that arose against
him. Why did they want to destroy his kingdom?

As always when he got into this kind of mood, he decided to
consult the gods and the ancestors. Had he been guilty of some
negligence? No—every day the royal stools were sprinkled with
blood. At the recent Odwira festival, chicken and mutton cooked
without salt or spice had been offered up together with the flesh
of the yam, as bright and tender as that of a young woman. Then
the doors, windows and arcades of the palace had been smeared
with a mixture of egg yolk and palm oil. . . . Osei Bonsu sent for
the Muslim Muhammad al-Gharba. While he wasn't at all
tempted to convert to Islam like his elder brother, he had the

highest respect for the Muslims' knowledge and accorded them an important place at court and in the country at large.

Some were members of his privy council. Others were ambassadors to the Muslim countries in the north. Others again were responsible for his correspondence with kings and merchants in distant parts. A whole quarter of Kumasi was occupied by Muslims and known as Asante Nkramo.

No one quite knew where Muhammad al-Gharba came from. Some said he was from Fez, and it was generally held that he had once been in the entourage of sultan Ousman dan Fodio. He was no vulgar soothsayer or scribbler of amulets. If he read present and future and gave Osei Bonsu the benefit of his gifts, it was in the name of Allah and to convince the king of His power.

Osei Bonsu turned toward him eagerly as he entered.

"I've just heard the English have sent a new governor to the fort at Cape Coast," he said. "They haven't informed me, and he hasn't sent me the customary presents."

Muhammad sighed.

"You are too good, Son of the Sun," he said. "The English are a false and perverse race. All they want is power, access to your gold and the monopoly of your trade. It's impossible to discuss anything with them. Attack them—attack them and destroy them before it's too late."

Osei Bonsu shuddered.

"Too late?" he said.

"It is written, master," Muhammad al-Gharba said quietly, trying to mitigate the gravity of his words, "the English will destroy the power of Ashanti and lay hands on the stool of gold."

Such sacrilegious words were punishable by death. But Osei Bonsu knew this was not impertinence and that he should trust his adviser.

"Pray, Muhammad," he said, "and ask your god to be with us. If you can persuade him to adopt our cause . . ."

He paused. What can you offer a man who lives only in the spirit? He was filled with a sense of helplessness and dejection. If it was written, what was the use of struggling? If it must happen, it must.

But not everyone felt like that. Little Ayaovi was happy. Ever since she had arrived in Kumasi with her parents three days ago she had been in a state of constant delight. What a wonderful place! Her father had taken her to see the kumnini tree, the one that kills pythons, planted centuries ago by the founder of the kingdom, Osei Tutu. The town, only a village then, wasn't yet called Kumasi. But the kumnini tree had grown there and shown all the Ashanti that this must be their capital. As for the palace, it was a town in itself with all its buildings, arcades and court-yards full of trees reaching to the sky.

In the presence of all this beauty Ayaovi almost forgot her trouble, her shame, the cruel wound inside her. After all, she was only eleven. Hopping from one foot to the other she started to chant a singing game she and her friends used to play back in the village. Then she stopped. She ought not to be indulging in such childish things now. She would soon have a husband. And what a husband! She remembered Malobali's face. Rough, of course, and distorted with desire. But handsome—so handsome. He wasn't just one of those soldiers who marched through the country with a gun on his shoulder, a machete at his waist and a cudgel in his hand. He was nothing like the man who was with him—she had forgotten what *he* looked like already! Malobali was the only one who mattered. If only the men sent to find him might do their job properly and bring him back quickly!

Sometimes Ayaovi was slightly worried. Hadn't she lied on oath, accusing only one man? She remembered the words of the priest as he killed the sacrifice:

> *Earth,*
> *Supreme being*
> *I rely on you*
> *Earth*
> *Let not evil triumph.*

Yes, she had lied. But she shook off the thought. After all, she was only eleven! She threaded her way through the courtyard full of soldiers to one of the gates, and looked out into the main square at the tulip trees with their scarlet flowers, at the royal palms and the only slightly less arrogant kapok trees that covered the ground with gray threads. Her mother had followed at Ayaovi's heels. She had had no rest since the tragedy, reproaching herself for not having taken better care of her child. The soldiers should have raped *her*, who knew all about men's bodies, not her fragile little girl, scarcely more than a child!

Her husband scolded her. What was she crying for? It wasn't the first time men had abused little girls. The guilty party was supposed to offer up a sheep to be sacrificed to the earth, which the priest sprinkled with blood to obtain its forgiveness. Then, when the girl reached puberty, the rites were performed and the marriage celebrated. That was all! And soon Ayaovi would have a husband, and what a husband! A warrior belonging to the royal armies! The Asantehene would be bound to present him with some land where they could grow oil palms. And the chorus of little girls accompanying the bridal pair would sing:

> *May God give you sons and daughters!*
> *And may he give you long life!*

The ancestors always knew what they were doing. Something good always comes out of something evil.

CHAPTER

3

Run, Bambara, run! They're after you!"

The shout roused Malobali from a half sleep. He began to sit up. The voice came again.

"Run, Bambara, run!"

His body still numb, his spirit half out of his body, he crawled over to the clothes he had tossed into a corner of the room. The woman beside him woke and protested.

"Where are you going?" she asked.

He silenced her with a slap, slipped on his trousers and made for the gate. It was dawn. The sky was gray between the coconut palms, and you could hear the monotonous surge of the sea. A tumult of voices in one of the courtyards proved that Malobali hadn't been dreaming. There was a silk cotton tree by the wall of the compound. He hoisted himself up onto the wall by its lower branches and jumped nimbly down into the street. Then he started to run.

A man who is running for his life has no idea of his surroundings. He is nothing but a set of muscles at work, a pair of lungs husbanding their strength, a heart at full stretch. Malobali kept running, and nothing around him mattered. He kept on running, and the rows of huts gave way to a landscape of coconut palms, some upright, some broken in half by the wind and lying on the sand. He kept on running, and the streets changed into a neglected road wide enough for two or three men to walk abreast. He kept on running, and the sun rose and drove its thorns into his head and back.

At last he keeled over exhausted in the sand. How long had he been running? And why? He couldn't have said. A few yards away he could see the sea, still pale green, soon to be sparkling. It seemed to taunt him. He wiped away the sweat that was streaming down his forehead and making his eyes sting, like tears. After a while he tried to compose his thoughts. Why should they have come to arrest him? What had he done?

He'd gotten drunk, but no more than usual. There hadn't been any ruckus. As for the woman who had let him into her bed, she had simply liked the color of his gold and anyone could have had her. So what was it all about?

Had the Fantis broken the truce and declared war on the Ashanti with the blessing of their protectors the English? In that case, why should he run away? What he had to do was join the rest of the army and fight. Malobali was too bold and determined a character to resign himself to flight. He turned back toward Cape Coast. But he took the precaution of getting rid of his soldier's uniform, keeping only his loose drawers and a dagger hidden at his waist.

There were two roads from Cape Coast. One led eastward to the fort of Elmina, which had once belonged to the Portuguese and then to the Dutch, and westward to the half-abandoned fort of Mouri. The other road led to the river Pra and the Ashanti country. Malobali decided to approach the town by the route leading from Elmina, little used because of the uneasy relations between the occupants of the two forts. He was approaching the entrance to the town when he saw a small group of men leaving it. He recognized them as Ashanti warriors, and was just going to call out and join them when caution held him back. He cut across a patch of scrub and posted himself at a street corner.

Kodjoe was being dragged along by a dozen or so soldiers. His hands were tied behind his back and his legs fettered as if he were a criminal or a convict being taken out to execution. He had a wound on his head, and the blood from it had dried on his cheeks in a horrible reddish patch that stood out against his black skin. He looked dazed, stunned.

Malobali was stunned too. Why were they arresting Kodjoe? What had he done?

Then he understood. The rape. The little girl in the clearing. That was the only explanation.

The girl's parents must have overcome their fear and appealed to the Asantehene's unsleeping justice. Malobali's first impulse was to try to help his friend. But what could he do, half naked against all these armed men? He continued to crouch there in the grass. Then his sense of helplessness mingled with his sense of shame, and he vomited at length. A colony of hungry ants appeared.

What was he to do?

The town wasn't safe. If he went to see the resident he would surely meet with the same fate as Kodjoe. He was overcome by a kind of fatalism. Hadn't he wished for a new life? And the mocking gods had made him as naked as an infant again. Not since he was a baby in Segu had he been so vulnerable.

About noon he began to feel pangs of hunger. In the course of his adventures he had learned to snare birds, to light a fire with a couple of stones and to make salt out of ashes. As he was whittling some branches he heard a voice say: "May the gods take away my sight if it isn't the Bambara!"

Malobali leapt up. The speaker was a toothless old man, his legs covered with ulcers but apart from that apparently quite robust. His only garment was a cotton loincloth around his waist, which failed to conceal an enormous hernia.

"*Papa*," he said respectfully, "how do you know me?"

The other threw back his head and laughed, displaying a purple uvula.

"How do I know you? The whole town's talking about you! . . . Do you know what's happened to your friend?"

Malobali sighed.

"I saw him go by," he said.

The old man laughed more heartily than before.

"The best part is," he said, "that it wasn't really him the *kontihene* sent for! You were the only one the girl mentioned."

"Me?"

"Yes! You must have made quite an impression on her! And

imagine what she'll say when she sees Kodjoe! But he said he was guilty."

Malobali laughed too. But when he recalled Ayaovi, her slim body and smell of green leaves, he felt some regret. Then he pulled himself together.

"*Papa*," he asked, "what ought I to do now? You're old enough to be my father's father. Tell me what to do."

The old man squatted down, took a kola nut from his loin-cloth and opened it. He studied the red-veined flesh, then said, "Run away! That's all you can do. Run away. The sea is covered with ships."

The sea covered with ships? But where were they bound for? To lands of servitude and sorrow—Jamaica and Guadeloupe. And Malobali, born on the edge of the desert, had always thought of the sea with repulsion and terror. It was a sort of deceitful land that gave way beneath you and plunged you into secret chasms.

Looking up to question the old man further, Malobali found he had disappeared. Then he realized he was an ancestor come to show him what he should do, and he was filled with great peace.

He avoided the town and went toward the beach, with its usual feverish coming and going between the land and the European boats anchored offshore. Though not tenderhearted Malobali could not help thinking of all those who had passed through the coast, desperate and in chains. He knew the Asantehene opposed the English, who had declared the slave trade illegal. But this decision, which ought to have made them more congenial to Malobali, only struck him as suspicious. What lay behind it?

For a moment Malobali wondered whether he might not go back to Segu. Segu—how he missed the place where he was born! When would he swim in the waters of the Joliba again? But then he remembered Tiekoro, and Tiekoro's voice, proud even in its humility, and again it nauseated him.

"I must speak to you again of charity," he recalled it saying, "for it grieves me to see that none of you really possesses this goodness of heart. And yet what a grace it is!"

No, no, he couldn't stand that! He made resolutely for a part of the beach where a good-looking young man was supervising the unloading of a canoe.

"Who do you work for?" he asked him.

"Mr. Howard-Mills," said the youth with a pleasant smile. "I'm collecting some goods for him."

"Is he an Englishman?"

"No, no—a mulatto!"

"A mulatto!" Malobali exclaimed. "Those wretches are getting a foothold everywhere."

The young man looked resigned.

"What do you expect?" he said. "The whites favor them because they're their children. Mr. Howard-Mills is very rich. You're not from these parts yourself, are you?"

Malobali took him by the arm.

"Don't you worry about where I'm from. Just help me get out of here."

All around them files of porters were carrying merchandise of all kinds toward Cape Coast. The young man launched the canoe, signaled to Malobali to jump in, and started to paddle energetically out toward the ships, which seemed like symbolic stools of new gods with the sea stretching like a royal carpet at their feet. Looking back you could see the dark outline of the trees along the coast, and the massive shape of the fort. The whites had come, cadged a little land to build their forts, and then because of them nothing was ever the same again. They had brought with them things never before heard of here, and people had fought over them, nation against nation, brother against brother. And now the whites' ambition knew no bounds. Where would it end?

The canoe drew alongside a ship, a fine-looking three master. As he was about to climb up the ladder to go on deck, Malobali almost drew back. He didn't even know what he was letting himself in for! Then he pulled himself together. Hadn't the ancestor himself told him this was what he must do?

—

When the Asantehene's resident, Owusu Adom, heard that Malobali had disappeared he suspected the English of having a hand in it. Only they could have given him refuge and allowed him to flee by letting him onto one of their ships offshore.

Owusu Adom was all the more furious because in all the time he had lived at Cape Coast he had never once been invited inside the fort, either by the old or by the new English governor. The present insult was directed not only at him, but through him at the royal person of the Asantehene himself. So he decided to leave Cape Coast at once for Kumasi.

He set out the next morning. At the head of the procession came slaves armed with cutlasses to hack away the vines, roots and branches obstructing the way. They were followed by two men each carrying by its tip one of the golden swords symbolic of Owusu Adom's office. Then came priests, councillors and the rest of the resident's staff. He himself was carried, by men chosen for their ability to cover long distances, in a stout litter surrounded by musicians playing trumpets, horns, drums and bells. They made so much noise that birds fled their nests, and snakes slid through the grass in terror to their holes.

Gradually the procession was joined by traders who'd just completed their business on the coast. Tongues wagged. The English and the Dutch weren't buying any more slaves. At least, not openly, for there was always some illicit slave ship offshore. But, thank God, there were still the French. They paid slowly and were difficult to deal with, but greedier than all the others! Their ships thronged Elmina and Winneba. What would happen to everyone if the slave trade was stopped? Dealing in palm oil and timber from the forests would be no substitute. Everyone stood to gain from slavery, not only the kings. Even minor chiefs could sell convicted criminals, and as for ordinary folk, they could sell the people who couldn't pay their debts!

They also discussed Malobali and Kodjoe. It wasn't the rape of a little girl that shocked them, but the way it had been done. Two fellows sharing one girl like that! The number of sheep that would have to be sacrificed to appease the earth for such a crime! In a way they were glad one of the pair had gotten away. Otherwise, what a dilemma for the judges! Which of the two would have to marry the girl? Some said it ought to be the first to penetrate her, others said it should be the second, as the other had merely prepared the way.

Then everyone fell silent: they were entering the forest. The roof formed by the irokos and mahogany trees intermingled with the vault of the sky. It was a depressing place. The forest was the home of the gods and the ancestors, the place where they most often manifested themselves. Was it not on the edge of a forest that the gods, appealed to by the high priest Okomfo Anokye, had sent down the stool of gold onto Osei Tutu's lap, thus marking him out as the object of universal veneration? Was it not in a forest that the stools of the kings were kept? Was it not in a forest that the high priests met for all their most important consultations? The forest is like a woman's womb, out of which come life and hope.

When it got too dark to go on, some slaves cut low branches and swiftly put up shelters, while others lit fires and the musicians gave a regular concert. Then a linguist sprang into the middle of the improvised circle to tell the story which most pleased the ear of all Ashanti: the story of the founding of the kingdom and the adventures of Osei Tutu.

"It is from the sky that the Ashanti people descended, from the womb of the moon, the moon-woman who wants power to be handed down through the women. So King Obiri Yeboa was worried when his sister, Princess Manou, after being married for five years, had no children. Who would succeed to the throne? One day the queen mother summoned Manou before her and said: 'I don't think you're barren—at least that is what the high priest says. So you are to go with him and do whatever he tells you.'

"Manou obeyed, and nine months later—beat the sacred drums that celebrate a birth! sound the ivory trumpets!—she had a son. The high priests, examining the child, soon saw which ancestor was reincarnated in him, and gave him the name of Osei, followed by Tutu, for Tutu was the god of abundance who had just given Manou her wish.

"And Osei Tutu grew and grew . . ."

Somewhere above the trees the moon rose, piercing the dense foliage with her rays as if she too wanted to hear the familiar story. Wasn't she involved in it? Osei Tutu was really her son,

even though in the course of time the sun had usurped her position in the universe, claiming to be the father of all living
creatures.

"When Osei Tutu was ten years old, the king his father sent
him to stay with his uncle in the kingdom of Denkyira. The
exchanging of young princes was a guarantee of peace, for what
king would not hesitate to declare war when he knew his enemy
held his heir hostage?"

The gathering, the moon and Owusu Adom all listened to
the linguist's story. And confidence was restored. The Ashanti
nation was immortal. The English, that people of the sea with
cold pale skins the color of evil spells, would never be able to
destroy it.

Meanwhile the priests listened to the sounds of the forest and
interpreted the signs of the invisible. They sensed that great
events were in preparation, and that in this very place a strange
and fearful story would be written that would eclipse that of Osei
Tutu.

CHAPTER
4

Malobali could feel the eyes of the elder of the two white men wandering over his face, lingering, scrutinizing, tenacious as a fly on the slit belly of a carcass at some street corner. Malobali couldn't hear him or even follow the movements of his lips, but he knew what he was saying: "I don't trust him. He's too old for a start. At his age, conversion is never anything but superficial and dictated by self-interest."

The other man answered with his usual gentle inflexibility.

"You're wrong, Father Etienne. He's hardworking and extraordinarily intelligent. His progress in French and carpentry has been exceptional. As for his piety, you can take my word for it."

Malobali wondered which of the two he hated more—the first, who saw through him, or the second, who thought he knew him so well. He looked down at the plank he was planing.

Father Etienne raised his voice, uttering each syllable distinctly so as to be understood.

"Samuel—come here!" he cried.

Malobali obeyed, and stood there as he'd been taught, head bowed and hands hanging down the seams of his trousers. The two priests were sitting on the veranda of the modest straw-thatched hut. One of them was bald and rather fat. The other was thin, almost emaciated. Both had red faces and kept fanning themselves. But what really terrified Malobali was their eyes—pale, transparent, but with an unbearable flame in their depths like that of a forge. Every time they rested on any part of his body it was as if he were being burned, and he was always amazed afterwards to find his flesh intact.

"Father Ulrich tells me you are about to receive the body of our Lord Jesus Christ. Are you quite ready for this incomparable honor?"

Malobali managed to assume a mask of the utmost solemnity.

"Yes, Father," he said.

"We shall bestow the sacrament on you in Ouidah. We leave for there tomorrow. There are many Christians there. The family of the Lord is increasing."

Malobali feigned a smile of delight. Then, in spite of himself, he looked up and met the eyes of the priest. The hatred in his glance was the equal of that in his own. It meant: "You are a fine beast, proud and cruel. You have blood on your hands. But no matter—play the game you've chosen to play. We shall see who gets tired first."

"Very well, Samuel," said Father Ulrich, with his customary unctuousness. "You may go now. I think you have more washing to do . . ."

Malobali turned on his heel, inwardly raging. So this was what he had come to: performing the services of a woman for this white man without a woman, without balls.

He collected a calabash of dirty linen from under the kitchen awning and started out toward the lagoon. Sometimes, when he thought of his present situation, Malobali wondered if he wouldn't have been better off as a slave in the Americas. There at least you did a man's work, on the land. He passed by the church, made of tree trunks with a roof of branches, where the services were attended by a congregation of perhaps three or four people who had agreed to be baptized in exchange for a few cotton garments. Then he took the grassy path that led away from the village to the lagoon.

The mission was outside the village, on a piece of land granted the missionaries by King De Houezo. In it lived two priests, Father Ulrich and Father Porte; the latter was at the moment in Sakete in the vain hope of bringing about some conversions. Father Etienne, the older of the two who had been discussing Malobali , had just arrived at the mission after living for many years in Martinique.

Sometimes, when he was not blinded by hatred, Malobali would briefly feel a kind of admiration for these men: driven by some ideal they had left their own country and people to live here, indifferent to solitude and danger and at the mercy of a king who could drive them out at any moment. Their only contact was with the French slave traders who anchored outside the harbor. And sometimes a French traveler in search of sensation would come to observe life on the coast.

But most of the time there was no room in Malobali's heart for admiration, only for despair and helpless rage. How thoroughly the earth had taken its revenge on him for Ayaovi's rape and his own flight! How completely the pleasant-looking young man he had entrusted himself to at Cape Coast had duped him! How much had he been paid for betraying him? After he'd taken him to the ship he'd talked at length with its captain, and scarcely had he started to paddle away again in his canoe than Malobali had been knocked on the head, bound, thrown among the bales of merchandise, and left there half dying of hunger and thirst. After a few days the ship had stopped again.

Through the mist of his fever and hunger Malobali had made out a village and the massive outline of a fort standing out against the forest along the coast. A boat was lowered into the water, and two men paddled the captain swiftly toward the fort. Malobali realized what fate they were preparing for him. He was to swell the numbers of the slaves soon to emerge from inside those stone walls.

How did he manage to break some of his bonds, jump in the sea, and escape the cruel tyranny of his jailers? No doubt some ancestor had taken pity on him. He had found himself on the sand—naked, chilled to the bone, weak, terrified. And being looked at by a white man. The white man had bent over him, then picked him up in his arms like a child and carried him to his hut. There he had nursed him day and night, refusing to give him up to any of those who tried to claim him. Yes, the white man had saved his life.

And yet he hated him as he'd never hated anyone before. Not even Tiekoro. He hated him because immediately, though Malobali didn't know how or why, he had established a relationship of dependence between them. He was the master, Malobali only the pupil. By pouring a drop of water on his forehead he had changed Malobali's name to Samuel. He forbade him to use his own "vile jargon" and taught him French, the only language he considered worthy. He routed out all the beliefs Malobali had hitherto lived by. He left him not a moment's freedom. The prison he'd built for him was the strongest and subtlest of all jails, for you couldn't see its walls!

Malobali had often thought of killing him. Once he'd even gone up beside the bed where Ulrich lay, sweating and pale under his mosquito net. To plunge a knife into his throat and watch his blood bubble out—that was the only way for Malobali to redeem himself, to become a man again. But Ulrich had opened his eyes. His blue eyes.

So should he run away?

But in which direction? Before he'd gone ten paces the Gouns and Nagos of the village of Porto Novo would have caught and bound him so as to traffic in his flesh. He hated them, too—a greedy, cruel race who ever since the days of King De Adjohan had sold their own children! How many captives were crammed into the fort, brought from the interior and treated like animals! And slavery was not the only thing to be feared. Often the *lari*, eunuchs employed in the palace as servants, disemboweled pregnant women just for fun, decapitated children and rolled their gory heads across the marketplace, while the princes of the blood sowed desolation through the kindgom!

Malobali came to the edge of the lagoon. It was worst when women were there. They would start to laugh as soon as he appeared, dressed up in the red uniform jacket and narrow trousers the priest had given him. They split their sides when he undid his bundles of linen and clumsily attempted to wash it. As he couldn't speak their language he couldn't insult them as they deserved, and of course he dared not hit them! Fortunately the banks were deserted this morning. The dense vegetation grew right down into the water and continued under it, emerging here and there as sinister purple flowers like things decaying. Other parts of the lagoon had grayish beaches, broken up by the hooves of animals.

Malobali crouched down, then took off his uniform jacket
and stretched out. The sky above him was cloudless. Somewhere
on the earth—was it to the north? to the east? to the west?—
Nya was thinking of him and weeping. She never stopped begging
the fetish priests to intercede with the ancestors to ensure him
a good life. Well, they hadn't succeeded, the fetish priests! He
was in hell, the hell Father Ulrich was always talking about.

The religion with which the priest tried to indoctrinate Malobali struck him as totally incomprehensible and abstract, containing none of the sacrifices, libations and offerings he was used
to. Worse still, it condemned all manifestations of life, like music
and dancing, and reduced his existence to a desert in which he
wandered alone. Sometimes when Father Ulrich was talking to
him Malobali would glance to right and left to try to catch sight
of the omnipresent god the priest kept referring to. But there was
only silence and emptiness.

What was he to do?

Once again Malobali asked himself the question and could
think of no answer. In the distance a *calao* rose from the top of
a tree.

The safest way from Porto Novo to Ouidah, known in the
region as Glehoue, was by boat along the coast. The two priests
and Malobali, with four men to paddle them, made the journey
in two and a half days. The town of Ouidah had passed into the
control of the powerful king of Dahomey, who had installed his
vodoun, his gods, there. Ouidah was reached from the coast by
a short road used for years by slaves destined mainly for Cuba
and Brazil, and by the Europeans—Portuguese, Dutch, Danes,
English and French—who all had forts there and schemed against
one another for the king's favor.

On entering the town the two priests, like all strangers, had
to go and see the *yovogan*, the king of Dahomey's representative,
and explain the purpose of their visit. They had learned that there
was a large Catholic colony in Ouidah, made up of Africans—
former slaves, now freed and back from Brazil—and Portuguese
and Brazilian traders. The last Portuguese priest to live in the
fort had died, and Portugal, weakened by wars and by a recent

loss of their colony in Brazil, could no longer send out missionaries. God is God—what does it matter if he is served by Portuguese or by Frenchmen? So Father Ulrich and Father Etienne
had come to offer their services to this flock without a shepherd.

Dagba, the *yovogan*, was so huge he could hardly walk. Surrounded by fan bearers, he sat on a tall wooden chair wearing an
immaculate cotton *pagne* and rows of cowrie necklaces. Malobali, used to the splendors of the Asantehene's entourage in Kumasi, looked around him with some scorn. A straw-thatched hut
looked out on a carefully swept courtyard and was full of an
apparently random jumble of objects that were in fact the symbols of Dagba's high office.

Dagba graciously gave the priests permission to stay in the
town, and as a crowning piece of affability ordered a slave to take
them to Senhora Romana da Cunha, a former slave returned from
Brazil, where in accordance with the custom she had taken the
name of her master. She was the leading light of the Christian
community.

The two priests and Malobali aroused great curiosity as they
went through the streets. The people of Ouidah had been used
to the comings and goings of white men for years, but these two,
with their black robes, wide belts, and crosses around their necks
bore no resemblance to the men they were accustomed to in their
full-skirted coats, buttoned waistcoats and short-top boots. Malobali too intrigued them. People wondered about his ritual scars.
Where was he from? He was neither a Mahi nor a Yoruba. Was
he an Ashanti?

Ouidah was a pretty town with good roads and neat compounds clustered around the temple to the god Python, the symbolic heart of the city inherited from its first inhabitants, the
Houedas. Not far from the temple was a market selling all kinds
of wares, including local produce like fresh and smoked meat,
corn, cassava, millet and yams, together with European goods
such as brightly colored cottons, English kerchiefs, and above all
alcohol—rum, aguardente and cachaça. Ouidah was different
from Cape Coast in that the forts of the Europeans were in the
town, a gunshot away from one another so that each could see
what the others were up to.

Romana da Cunha lived in the Maro quarter, which was inhabited exclusively by former slaves from Brazil, known as "Brazilians" or Agoudas, and the real, white Brazilians and Portuguese with whom they shared a religion and certain customs. Romana had gotten rich by doing the washing of the European slave traders, and she lived in a big square house surrounded by a balcony with windows and finely fretted wooden shutters.

As a clear indication of her religion, she had covered the north front of the house with *azulejos* depicting the Virgin Mary with her precious burden in her arms, and over the door was a carved cross. A little boy with grown-up manners opened the door to the visitors and asked them to wait while he went and called his mother. After some time Senhora da Cunha made her appearance.

She was a small, rather frail woman, still young, who would even have been pretty were it not for her expression, which was at once austere and exalted, melancholy and pious, frightened and inflexible. A black linen kerchief half covered her forehead, and a black gown made like a sack concealed her hips, thighs and breasts, which one guessed to be round and firm. Using her son as an interpreter, she mumbled that she was very honored, her modest house didn't deserve such distinction. Then she opened a pair of double doors onto a room furnished with armchairs, a heavy chest of drawers, and a table decorated with shiny metal candlesticks. Meanwhile Malobali had been waiting tactfully at the entrance to the compound, but now, at a sign from Father Ulrich, he came forward and greeted their hostess.

When Romana looked at him her face changed. An expression of incredulity was followed by one of panic. She stammered out some words that her son imperturbably translated: "Where is he from? What does he want? Who is he?"

"He's Samuel, our right-hand man," said Father Ulrich soothingly. "He is a child of God, too."

Romana convulsively turned her back on Malobali, saying, "You stay outside."

Malobali, beside himself with anger, obeyed. Who was this woman? What right had she to talk to him like that? Nothing but a wretched slave who had usurped the name of her master, abjured her own gods, renounced her ancestors. He nearly changed his mind and went into the house to taunt Romana and ask the reasons for her rudeness, but he restrained himself.

All around him there was a great commotion. The news of the two priests' arrival had spread through the town in no time, and all the Catholics came running: whites, mulattos like those Malobali had seen at Cape Coast, but mostly blacks wearing flowered robes and speaking a Portuguese sprinkled with a few words of English and French and punctuated by sweeping gestures.

Romana came out into the courtyard again. She had offered to put up Father Etienne and Father Ulrich until they went on an embassy to the king of Dahomey to get permission to build a mission. She put her best rooms at their disposal, with mosquito nets on the beds and fine Holland sheets. She studiously avoided looking at Malobali, who wondered if she meant to accommodate him too or whether he would have to take refuge in the streets.

As he stood sadly under an orange tree, a young girl came up to him.

"Bambara?" she asked softly.

He nodded, and she signaled for him to follow her. Surprised, he did so.

They went back at a run to the center of town, within sight of the forts. She signaled for him to wait, and disappeared inside one of them.

After a few minutes she reappeared, together with a soldier. Before the other drew near or opened his mouth Malobali had recognized him as a Bambara. The two men threw themselves into one another's arms. When he heard the sound of his own language again, Malobali had to wipe his eyes against the stranger's uniform to avoid shedding tears, humiliating tears, fit only for women. At last they drew apart, though they still held hands as if they couldn't bear to be entirely separated.

"*Tie*," said the soldier, "I'm Birame Kouyate."

"I'm Malobali Traore."

A Bambara! Sing *bala, fle, n'goni*! Beat the *dounoumba*! A Bambara! He wasn't alone any longer!

The girl who'd brought Malobali was standing tactfully to one side.

"Who's that?" asked Malobali.

Birame smiled.

"Modupe,"* he said. "And no one ever deserved the name

*Yoruba name meaning "I give thanks."

more. As soon as she heard you were a Bambara she thought of
bringing you to me. She's a Nago, and lives in the Sogbaji quarter
near a girl I'm going to marry."

But Malobali had to be getting back. What would the two
priests say if they noticed their "right-hand man's" escapade?
What would Romana say if she noticed her maid's absence? But
now balm had been poured into his heart.

When they got back to Romana's no one paid any attention
to them, for there was another visitor, a very important person-
age, the most important man in the country after King Guezo
himself. Francisco de Souza was a Portuguese known as Chacha
Ajinakou. He had come to Ouidah as bookkeeper to the ware-
houseman at Fort San João d'Ajuda, but when the Portuguese and
the Brazilians withdrew he had stayed on and become the chief
authority there, getting spectacularly rich from the slave trade.
He was the exclusive slave agent, and no ship could take on a
single slave without his permission. The fact that he was a fervent
Catholic didn't prevent him from having a regular harem and
losing count of his children. He was dressed with a negligence
surprising in a man of his rank. On his head was a velvet skullcap
with a tassel that kept falling over his eyes. He was explaining,
through his son Isidoro, who could stammer a bit of French, that
it was an insult for the priests not to stay with him. But Father
Etienne, who was good at soothing injured feelings, spoke skillfully and at length on the subject of Martha and Mary, the lowly
women whose house was chosen by our Lord, and Chacha Ajinakou quieted down. He promised to use his influence with King
Guezo—who was greatly in Ajinakou's debt because he'd helped
him to the throne at his brother's expense—to get the priests
received at court as soon as possible and have their request
granted.

Soon the maids, Modupe among them, brought in dishes of
food quite unknown to Malobali: *fechuada*, a mixture of tomato
juice, onions, fried meat and cassava flour, made according to a
recipe from Bahia; *cocada*; and a Brazilian sweet called *pe de
mouleque*.

It wasn't the first time Malobali had found himself among
strangers; for months he had been knocking around far from
home. But it was the first time no one had shown him any hos-

pitality, the first time he'd been treated as a pariah. Ignored. Neglected.

Why?

Because no slave ship had taken him to a land of servitude to bring him into dubious intimacy with the whites? Because he hadn't come back aping their manners and professing their faith?

And now they were all folding their hands and starting to sing the Hail Mary, the shrill voices of the children outsoaring those of the adults. Father Ulrich beat time with his hand and tried to moderate the enthusiasm of his new flock. Malobali's eyes met those of Romana. She had exchanged her black robe for a long iridescent gown caught by a belt at the waist, with puffed sleeves and six bands of lace around the neck. Ridiculous as this getup seemed to Malobali, at least it suited her and underlined her youth, especially as her pleasure at the priests' visit animated all her features. But she looked quickly away from Malobali, leaving him bewildered. Why did this woman hate him? He hadn't even known her yesterday.

As he was thinking this, Modupe stooped and offered him a bowl of food. She, unlike her mistress, wore an expression of adoration and already total submission. Malobali knew that she was his as soon as he wanted her.

All in all, this visit to Ouidah looked quite promising. On the very first day he'd found the friendship of a man and the love of a woman.

C H A P T E R

5

"A*go!*"*

Malobali opened his eyes and recognized the shape beside him as that of Eucaristus. He smiled and beckoned to him, for a strange friendship had grown up between the child and the adult, mingled, in the latter, with great pity. When Malobali remembered his own freedom, gaiety and games in Dousika's compound, and compared all this with the education of Eucaristus, smothered in clothes, beaten with a paddle for the least little thing, made to pray on his knees for hours on end and mumble interminable, almost incomprehensible formulas, he was tempted to go to Romana and tell her what he thought. But what right had he to do so? All he objected to was just a way of life he knew nothing about.

The child still stood shyly in the doorway.

"Mother wants you to chop some wood," he said.

Malobali sighed. He sensed that despite his efforts he was heading toward a violent confrontation with Romana. Father Etienne and Father Ulrich had set out to see King Guezo two weeks ago, leaving Malobali behind for the time being as he could be of no use to them. And Romana had started to treat him like a servant: "Samuel, do this! Samuel, do that!"

*Fon word used to call the hearer's attention.

At first he had complied, out of courtesy, because he was a guest. But he soon realized that for Romana it was quite a different matter. She wanted to humiliate him. Why?

He got up, and without bothering to dress, wearing only a loincloth around his waist, went out into the courtyard, where an axe lay by a pile of wood reaching nearly to the eaves. Swallowing his anger, Malobali set to work. With great, powerful strokes, sweat streaming down his back, he split the trunks and branches. He had disposed of a good third of the pile when Romana came out of the house. She seemed to be possessed by some extraordinary fury, shrieking and uttering incomprehensible words. She rushed at Malobali, snatched the axe away from him despite the risk of hurting herself, then flung it away. Malobali was dumbfounded. What was the matter? What had he done wrong? The noise had brought all the little maids out from under the awning where they were getting the washing ready, and those who had been sweeping the rooms soon came running, too. Malobali wiped the sweat from his forehead and confronted Romana.

Seeing her shouting and yelling like that, he felt really sorry for her. She must be suffering. But why? Modupe had told him her husband had died in Brazil in circumstances she never referred to, and that now she wanted no other spouse but Christ. Was it the memory of the dead man that tortured her and made her so inhuman? For a moment her cries ceased, and Malobali noticed the beauty of her almond eyes, the childish mouth usually twisted and bitter.

"What do you want?" he asked gently.

Eucaristus, who had flattened himself, terrified, against the wall of the house, now stepped forward.

"She says you're to put some clothes on. She doesn't want naked savages here—hers is a Christian house," he stammered.

This was the last reproach Malobali expected. Since when had a man's body been an object of scandal? He burst out laughing, turned on his heel, and went back to his room.

Matters might have rested there. But no.

Apparently enraged by Malobali's nonchalant return to a room he occupied only out of the kindness of her heart, Romana went into the house and came out again with the paddle used to chastise her children. She then went after Malobali. Perhaps she didn't really mean to use it? Perhaps it was only bravado?

When Malobali saw her advancing on him with the paddle in her hand he was stupefied. How low had he sunk that a woman dared threaten him like this? He was overwhelmed with rage. He was about to throw himself on her, knock her down, kill her perhaps, when a voice reminded him of his difficulties in the Ashanti kingdom after the rape of Ayaovi. What would happen if he now committed murder?

He shoved Romana aside, broke the paddle over his knee, and went out.

Modupe joined him in the street. First of all she gave him his clothes, the cause of all the trouble, and then again, like a benevolent spirit, guided him through the streets. Though it was still very early the town was astir. Women were heading for the markets, where craftsmen had already started offering their wares to passersby—gourds with patterns carved on them, pottery, woven baskets, cloth. Lines of slaves hurried toward the newly planted palm groves just outside the town, or to the fields whose produce fed the population. Traders wended their way toward the port.

Modupe and Malobali went by the Python temple, then entered the Sogbaji quarter where Modupe's family lived.

They were from Oyo and specialized in weaving. They were comfortably off and independent but had thought fit to entrust one of their daughters to Senhora Romana da Cunha, a Nago like them and highly respected in the community. It would never have occurred to Modupe to complain about the blows or other ill treatment she might receive; she put them down to her mistress's desire to give her a good education. But her love for Malobali had given her courage. After going through a series of courtyards in the family compound, she boldly threw herself at her mother's feet, and told her, weeping, what had happened, emphasizing the fact that Malobali was related to Birame. The first impulse of Molara, Modupe's mother, was to avoid doing anything that might vex the powerful Romana. But the traditional hospitality of her people got the better of her. As the Yoruba proverb said, "If the soothsayer consults the god of divination every day, it's because he knows life is full of changes."

And who could tell whether one day one of her own sons or some other member of her family might not be far from home and in need? So she told one of her maids to bring Malobali some fresh water and an ample breakfast of plantains and beans, and waited for her husband to come home.

Francisco de Souza, alias Chacha Ajinakou, was in the habit of acting as arbiter in quarrels that arose among the Agouda community, officiating as judge and councillor in the house he had built in the Brazil quarter. First he heard Romana da Cunha's account, because she was the one who considered herself wronged. Then he listened to Malobali's side of the case, as presented by Modupe's respectable family. He understood why they chose to appeal to his authority.

Chacha's was a fine house. A dozen rooms furnished with European armchairs, tables, chests of drawers and beds fitted with mosquito nets opened onto a square courtyard planted with orange and fig trees. Beside the house was a *barracon*, a sort of vast open warehouse divided by fencing into quarters for the slaves who were brought there from all over the country. There were about a hundred of them waiting for a ship to arrive to take them away, and their wretched forms could be seen lying about prostrate, in every attitude of dejection. But no one in Chacha's entourage, he least of all, paid any attention to them.

He took a pinch of snuff and stared at Malobali, trying to appraise him as another male. How foolish women were! How could Romana have thought she could strike him with impunity? He turned toward Isidoro, Chacha's son, and delivered his verdict.

"When Father Etienne and Father Ulrich left Samuel at Senhora da Cunha's house, they did not say he was to be her servant. Samuel is a Catholic, he has been baptized and cannot be treated as a slave. But it must be admitted that by going about indecently clad in the house of a respectable woman he did put himself in the wrong. Nevertheless, this did not give Senhora da Cunha the right to threaten him with a paddle. To make sure such incidents do not recur, I shall take Samuel under my roof until the servants of God return."

He then recited three Our Fathers and three Hail Marys,

echoed by all those present. Modupe had tears in her eyes. She had been hoping Malobali would be entrusted to her own family; in which case, instead of stolen kisses, what nights they would have had! Malobali, for his part, was very pleased with the verdict, and went and shook hands enthusiastically with Chacha and his son and with Olu, Modupe's father. Then he went and bowed to her mother as he might have done to Nya, in one of those eminently graceful actions that won him so many women's hearts. Olu, with whom he had gotten on immediately, had given him some Yoruba clothes, and wearing these his former majesty and nobility were restored.

After the verdict Romana and Eucaristus withdrew. The little boy slipped his hand into his mother's, which he found, to his surprise, burning hot.

"It's all for the best, Mother!" he said.

Romana scarely heard him, for Malobali was right—she was in torment. Since Naba's death and her own return to Africa she had never looked at another man. Her heart was a chapel dedicated to Naba, and she kept reliving in her imagination all the events that had led up to his terrible end. The Muslim rebellions in Bahia. Abiola's betrayal. The trial. She had never confided in anyone about all this; she knew that as soon as she began to speak of it the dikes of sorrow would break and she might go mad. But she had three sons to bring up.

As soon as Malobali appeared, all that had changed. Her heart, which she had thought as hardened as smoked meat in the market, had started to throb again. She had been tortured by desire. In her delirium she thought she was seeing Naba again, but younger and more handsome. And yet strangely the same. Her feminine intuition, sharpened by jealousy, had told her at once what was going on between Modupe and Malobali, and how she went to him during the siesta when they thought the rest of the household was asleep. At first she had thought of going and informing Modupe's father. Then she was ashamed of herself.

And now what had she done? Through her own stupidity she had deprived herself of the sight of him. He would no longer go through the courtyard with his long, nonchalant stride, or greet her in his faltering Yoruba. She wouldn't see him in the morning, drinking his corn porridge standing up. But worst of all, it seemed to her, was that everyone must know her secret; everyone must know she was madly in love with this man, this stranger, this servant of the priests—and, to top it off, younger than she was, too!

They reached her house, and Romana went to her room to cry in peace. But she had reckoned without the Agouda community. There was an endless procession of people with names like d'Almeida, de Souza, d'Assumpcao, da Cruz, do Nascimiento ... They all considered themselves insulted by the verdict. Shouldn't that Negro have been punished for going about naked in a Christian woman's house? Everything was exaggerated: by the end of the morning, Malobali had attacked the maids, made obscene gestures to Romana and beaten the children.

There was talk of appealing to King Guezo, who had always been partial to the Agoudas. Perhaps for the first time there was a spirit of revolt against Chacha.

When night fell Romana could bear it no longer. She sent a little maid to Malobali, asking him to come and see her.

As for Malobali, he had no way of guessing the feelings he inspired in Romana. He was surprised to get her message, and wondered what the woman who had caused him so much trouble already wanted with him now. He went out into the darkness.

Somewhere in the town someone had paid his tribute to death, and Malobali could hear the sound of the funeral choir.

> *The snake that passes on*
> *Relies on the dead leaves*
> *To hide its little ones.*
> *But you, on whom have you relied?*
> *To whom have you left us*
> *As you go to the land of the dead?*
> *O kou, O kou, O kou!**

The song struck Malobali as a bad omen, and he nearly turned back. But he went on, and when he got to the Maro quarter he saw that Romana's house was practically in darkness. The maids had gone to their rooms in the outbuildings on the far side of the courtyard. The children were in bed. The only room that was lit,

*Fon for death.

by stearine candles, was Romana's. It was sparsely furnished with mats and gourds, for she kept her best furniture for the public rooms. She had taken off her Portuguese clothes and wore Yoruba dress—a short woven *pagne* fastened at the side and a low-cut tunic beneath which her body suddenly appeared free and young. She was bareheaded, her thick black hair finely and beautifully braided. She really didn't know herself what she expected of Malobali, and when she saw him so near her she nearly fainted. It seemed to her it was Naba who had just come into the room. Naba, young and strong, as no doubt he had been before captivity had destroyed him, was bringing her his fruit and his love. But Malobali remained silent and perplexed. At last he spoke, searching for words in the labyrinth of an unknown tongue.

"What do you want?" he asked her. "If what you have to say is good, why wait for night to say it?"

Romana turned away.

"I wanted to ask you to forgive me," she said.

Malobali shrugged.

"No need to talk about that. Chacha Ajinakou has arranged matters."

There was a silence. Then Romana plucked up her courage.

"I wanted to ask you to come back here to live. By our Lord, I won't treat you badly anymore."

Malobali smiled.

"In my country," he said, "we say that anyone who trusts himself to a woman trusts himself to a river in flood. Despite your promise you will get angry again."

When she heard him say "in my country," she almost said, "My dead husband was from Segu, too." The words trembled on her lips. But it would be treachery to speak them, to speak of the dead to the man who was inflicting on the deceased the most cruel of outrages, since he was stealing the heart and senses of his widow. So instead she said: "At least come back to see the children. They're all so fond of you. Especially Eucaristus."

Malobali went toward the door.

"I'll come back, senhora," he said. "I'll come back."

Troubled, angry with himself, anxious, Malobali made for the fort, to meet Birame. Why wouldn't the woman leave him in peace?

Birame's history had been quite different from that of Malobali. He was from Kaarta and had been captured by the Tuareg,
who took him to Walo.* There he had been one of the recruits
who worked for Governor Schmaltz in his experiment in agricultural colonization in Senegal. Later he had knocked around
in various places, always with French people, and had finally
ended up, again with them, in the fort at Ouidah. When they
were recalled by their government he had stayed on with the
other Bambara, dealing in slaves and hoisting the flag to let passing traders know there were captives to be picked up. In fact, he
was more or less one of Chacha's men.

"Come and live here," he said when he'd heard what had
happened. "There's room for everyone here."

"No," said Malobali, shaking his head. "Chacha has said I
can live with him, and I don't want to seem ungrateful."

Birame made a face.

"Be careful of these Portuguese and Brazilians," he said, "and
above all of the blacks. They're a rotten bunch of whited apes
who look down on everyone and think themselves superior.
Avoid them like the plague!"

Malobali was still thinking about Romana. With any other
woman he would certainly have guessed her secret. But he
couldn't understand Romana's attitude—the mildness after so
much violence, the smiles, the looks. Utterly confused, he helped
Birame empty several gourds of aguardente.

Soon all the Agouda community and the whole of Ouidah
had something to talk about.

Chacha Ajinakou became immoderately fond of Malobali.
This was an unusual thing, for Chacha was an arrogant man who,
when he wasn't in bed with one of his wives, hardly saw anyone
but the captains of slave ships. He employed Malobali in his
dealings in slaves. The English had banned the trade more than
ten years ago, and forced many other countries to follow suit.

---

*Kingdom situated in present-day Senegal.

The French had recently done so. And yet the traffic in slaves was not lessening; whole boatloads still sailed to Brazil and Cuba.

So Malobali was to be seen being rowed out to the slave ships, coming back with their captains, and taking them first to Dagba, the *yovogan*, and then to Chacha's house. He was to be seen eating at the same table as Chacha and the slave traders, and going with them to inspect the human cattle whom he himself had made presentable beforehand by means of various tricks.

In short, it wasn't long before Malobali was hated.

Why? Because he was involved in the slave trade? Certainly not. Practically everyone in Ouidah had something to do with it. Because he was a foreigner? That wasn't the reason either. In this narrow strip of land between the rivers Coufo and Oueme, there were Ajas, Fons, Mahis, Yorubas, Houedas and so on, not to mention Portuguese, Brazilians, Frenchmen, and even Englishmen from Fort William. Languages intermingled, gods were exchanged, customs of all kinds existed side by side. So what did people have against him? They disliked him for being arrogant and for being attractive to women; for drinking too much; for winning too much at card games he said he'd learned on his travels; for thinking that Segu was better than any other place on earth. In that case, why hadn't he stayed there?

Things took a turn for the worse when the two priests came back from Abomey, brimming over with gratitude to King Guezo for having granted them a piece of land outside the town. They asked for their servant back, but Chacha refused, saying Malobali was too good for what they wanted him to do.

At that there was a fine outcry!

The priests accused Chacha of trading in human flesh, a commerce unworthy of a Christian, rebuked Malobali, and finally gained their point. Henceforward Malobali divided his time between helping to build the church and working in the palm groves of the planter, José Domingos.

For a new trade had started to develop, parallel to the traffic in slaves, and it was already making fortunes for merchants on the Gold Coast and especially on the "oil rivers."* The commodity they dealt in was palm oil.

*Name given to the water courses of the then-uncharted Niger delta.

Now Malobali could be seen taking droves of slaves out of the town to the palm groves and supervising their work. This consisted of climbing up the trees tied to a rope and carrying an axe between their teeth; then knocking down bunches of nuts and either loading them into canoes or carrying them overland in baskets.

Malobali went on living with Chacha. The two men could be heard late into the night playing billiards, drinking rum and exchanging pleasantries with the captains of the slave ships. Isidoro, Ignacio and Antonio, Chacha's three eldest sons, were jealous, and talked about Bambara black magic.

It seemed a good period in Malobali's life. After the dangers, killings and rapes of the soldier's life and the frustrations of being the priests' servant, he now enjoyed complete freedom. Moreover, he was getting rich with the palm nuts José Domingos let him have in exchange for his services, for he sold them to women who crushed the kernels to make red oil. Two Frenchmen, the Régis brothers, had recently arrived in the town, and talked of converting the fort into a private trading post. Oil could be stored there and sent to Marseilles, a town in France, to be made into soap and machine oil. In the long run it would be more lucrative than the slave trade.

Malobali hesitated. Chacha claimed he could get King Guezo to grant Malobali some land on which to build a house. Then he could marry Modupe. But he was thinking more and more of going back to Segu. He scented danger in the dry, scorched smell of this country, in its lagoons and mangrove swamps. And somewhere that danger was lurking, like an animal waiting for the moment to leap out on him and bury its fangs in his throat.

Someone told him that Adofoodia, in the north of the kingdom, was only ten days' journey from Timbuktu. He couldn't rest till he found out exactly where Adofoodia was, and how to get there.

Once you got to Timbuktu you were practically in Segu.

CHAPTER

6

Eucaristus touched Malobali on the arm.

"Tell me a story," he said.

Malobali thought for a moment, then began:

"Souroukou and Badeni met. Badeni thought Souroukou was his mother. So he ran after her and started to suck. Souroukou tried to get free and took hold of Badeni by the head. But all her own sexual organs came away in Badeni's teeth. 'Oh,' she cried, 'Badeni sucks too hard!'"

Eucaristus burst out laughing. When Malobali talked like that, a dim memory of his father would come into his mind. He'd been so young when his father died—scarcely three years old. And since then his mother never uttered his name, as if he'd been buried in some accursed place where trees and plants and bushes are allowed to grow and no one ever weeds or clears the ground. When Malobali told him stories he seemed to see again a tall imposing man who was very gentle and more affectionate than his mother. He seemed to hear the sound of a language that was not Yoruba. What people had his father belonged to? He dared not ask Romana: he knew she'd answer with a blow from the paddle or a slap on the mouth. He leaned his head on Malobali's shoulder.

"Now tell me the story of when you were born," he said coaxingly.

Malobali laughed.

"That's not a story," he said. "The very day I was born a white man was at the gates of Segu, asking to see the Mansa. Where was he from? What did he want? No one knew. The fetish priests thought he was an evil spirit in disguise, because his skin was the same color as an albino's . . ."

"Why are people afraid of albinos?" asked Eucaristus.

At that moment a maid came into the room.

"*Iya* wants you, Samuel!" she said.

Romana was inside the house. She had clearly just had a bath: her skin was oiled and shiny and gave off a faint perfume. She looked at Malobali.

"You come and see Eucaristus," she said reproachfully, "and you don't even come and greet me!"

"I thought you were asleep, senhora," he said, smiling apologetically.

She signaled for him to sit down.

"I want to suggest a business deal," she said. "A partnership. I know you're doing very well in the palm oil trade. I'd like to become a partner."

"What do you mean?" he asked. Stupid fellow, he didn't realize how little she cared about palm trees, palm oil, or anything to do with them!

"Well," she went on, "I'd like you to undertake to deliver between three and five basketfuls of nuts to me here every week. I've got enough servants and slaves to do the rest."

Malobali thought it over. He had no wish to enter into too close an association with Romana. Her presence filled him with a kind of terror. Her extreme irritability bothered him because he dared not put it down to the only cause possible.

"You know I'm not my own master," he told her. "I'll have to speak to José Domingos."

"He hates me," she sighed.

He shrugged.

"Why should he hate you?" he asked.

"Because they all hate women and look down on them and don't like them to take any initiative."

This was completely incomprehensible to Malobali, and as he could find nothing to say Romana went on.

"Life is very difficult, you know, for a woman without a husband."

Now Malobali was back in his depth.

"But why do you stay like that? he asked. "You're . . ."

For the first time, perhaps, he looked her straight in the face and saw how fragile she was. He finished his sentence sincerely.

"You're beautiful," he said.

"As beautiful as Modupe?" she countered.

He could no longer be in doubt. He had seen too many women swooning over him not to understand now. He leaped up as if he'd just come face to face with a snake in the bush.

"*Iya*," he mumbled, "Eucaristus is waiting for me. I must go and tell him the end of the story."

He had called her *iya* to try to summon up her self-respect, but he pronounced the word wrongly, stressing the first syllable and not pitching the tone. She stood up and threw herself on him, crying: "Someone else used to say it like that!"

Malobali put his arms around her. Out of habit he was just about to do what was evidently expected of him when he had an intuition that with this frail body strange and dangerous emotions were entering into his life: passion, possessiveness, jealousy, fear of sin. He pulled himself together, thrust her firmly back on her mat and left.

Eucaristus, watching from under the orange trees, saw him stride away.

When Romana realized she was alone she was petrified at first. So—she had offered herself, broken the seventh commandment, profaned her husband's memory . . . and been rejected. She let out such a cry of horror that the little maids doing the washing in the yard of the compound and all the children and neighbors heard it.

It pierced Malobali's ears, too, and lent his feet wings. He started to run for dear life. People came out of their huts to see this thief in flight.

At last he found himself on the beach with fine white sand underfoot, and dropped down on a mossy palm trunk eaten away with salt which gave under his weight. Lying offshore were a schooner and a sloop. If only he could go and start a new life in Brazil, or Cuba—anywhere!

Malobali looked his life in the face and hated it. To him, it was like a whore in some filthy hut with whom he was doomed to share the rest of his life.

As he sat there a man approached, and after observing him, asked, "Aren't you Samuel, José Domingos's partner?"

Malobali turned his back. He wasn't going to be taken in again by the advice of ancestors pretending to be sympathetic but in reality bent on destroying him! But the man persisted.

"We could go to Badagry if you like," he said. "Or Calabar. That's where the future lies! In three months from now we could be dressed in silk and velvet like Chacha Ajinakou himself."

No! If he had to leave here it would be to go home. But would he ever get away? He realized he had put himself more in the wrong by refusing to make love to Romana than he would have done in yielding to her. How would she avenge herself?

A boat set out from shore, full of poor wretches in fetters who were about to be thrown into the belly of the sloop. The wind wafted to Malobali's nostrils their smell of sweat and suffering.

Meanwhile a horde of angry Agoudas were swarming into Chacha Ajinakou's courtyard. Chacha came out in a dressing gown, for he'd been in bed, sleeping off some overindulgence in aguardente. Francisco d'Almeida, a mulatto who'd come back from Bahia the previous year, raised his string skullcap respectfully and said: "Give us Samuel, Chacha. He has raped Senhora da Cunha."

Although he was in a very bad humor, Chacha burst out laughing.

"Who told you that?" he said.

"There are witnesses, Chacha!"

Chacha shrugged.

"Witnesses?" he said. "In that case it wasn't rape."

But he ordered a slave to go and find Malobali so that he could explain. Just as the slave came back alone to say he had disappeared, Malobali appeared in the courtyard.

"Samuel," Chacha said to him. "These people are here on a very serious matter. It seems you raped Senhora da Cunha."

Malobali looked up and stared at Chacha in bewilderment.

"Who told them that?" he cried.

"The senhora herself!" cried Francisco, with a look of hatred.

"And the whole neighborhood heard her shrieks as she tried to defend herself. Even little Eucaristus saw you running away afterwards."

Chacha intervened at this point.

"We'll take him to Dossou," he said. "He'll put him to the question."

Malobali sighed.

"No need," he said. "I'm guilty."

There was an uproar. Some made as if to attack him, others shouted insults, while others broke branches from the fig trees in the compound with which to beat him. But Chacha calmed them down and called for silence.

"In the kingdom of Guezo," he said, "no one takes the law into his own hands. Take him to Dossou—he will decide on the punishment."

Dossou was the representative in Ouidah of the minister of justice, the *ajaho*, who himself lived in Abomey in constant contact with the king. Dossou acted as a kind of examining magistrate, dealing with minor affairs; when they exceeded his jurisdiction he sent the plaintiffs to Guezo in person. Dossou lived not far from Dagba, the *yovogan*, in a house of rather modest appearance when compared with the splendid dwellings of the Agoudas. Perhaps that was why he hated them. He came out into the courtyard, thinking about the cinder-baked yams and calalou one of his wives had cooked for him.

"Can't it wait till tomorrow?" he asked his visitors irritably.

Then he ordered two slaves to tie Malobali's hands behind his back and put him in the little hut adjoining his own which did duty as a prison. The Agoudas had no choice but to disperse and go home.

Malobali squatted in a corner of the dark, damp little hut. The slaves had barred the door with the trunks of coconut palms. He couldn't quite understand what was going on inside him. He felt a kind of lethargy, as if he no longer had the strength to strive against his fate. He had escaped from Ayaovi only to find himself pitted against Romana. There was another feeling too, confused, complex—a sort of pity for Romana. Was he going to humiliate her publicly by saying she was a liar? He had seen Chacha's smile.

It meant: "Fancy going and raping Romana! What a ridiculous thing to do!"

He remembered the plaintive question: "As beautiful as Modupe?" He ought to have said yes and taken her in his arms! Instead of which he had run away like a coward. What punishment might be imposed on him for rape? In Segu it wouldn't be considered a very serious offense since Romana wasn't a married woman or a little girl. But he didn't know the customs in Dahomey.

Didn't people say convicts were often taken to Abomey and sacrificed to the spirits of the royal ancestors in great religious ceremonies? In other cases they were sent to a marshy region called Afomayi, where they worked on the king's lands for the rest of their lives. And then Romana was an Agouda, a member of a powerful social group with influence at court. So he might well fear the worst.

In the dark of his prison Malobali could hear the voices and laughter of Dossou's wives and children in the courtyard of the compound. If he were sentenced to death or forced labor, who, here, would care? No one, apart from Modupe. And Modupe wasn't yet sixteen—she would forget him. Even in Segu, Nya would tire of waiting for him to return, and devote herself to the children Tiekoro would doubtless beget with some other wife, not Nadie. What was life? A fleeting passage leaving no trace on the earth. A series of trials whose meaning you didn't understand. Father Ulrich used to say it all had but one aim: to purify a man and make him like Jesus. Was he right?

The mosquitoes began their hellish dance around his face. Next day he would be brought before the judges to be tried. Meanwhile he must sleep. Not for nothing had Malobali been a soldier, used to snatching sleep in the midst of battles and raids. But scarcely had he shut his eyes than his spirit left his body to wander through the invisible world.

It flew over the dark stretch of the forest and the tawny pelt of the sands and landed in Segu, in the late Dousika's compound.

They were celebrating a birth. Nya lay on her side clasping a baby, a son called Kosa, a name meaning "business concluded," and so given to a child of an older mother. What greater happiness can a woman have than to bear a child when she is past her youth?

Nya was radiant. It was with the face of her youth that she looked at the infant, as it slept with a drop of milk still on its lips. Then suddenly the child opened its eyes, adult eyes, deep and black, full of real malice. It stared at Malobali and asked: "Will you have as much luck as I . . . Naba . . . ?"

The dream was so striking that Malobali woke up, gasping for breath. What did it mean? Malobali had scarcely been more than seven or eight years old when Naba disappeared; he hadn't really known him and hadn't mourned him. So he had rarely thought of him. This sudden shocking confrontation with an infant claiming to be his reincarnation could have but one meaning. Naba was dead. But why that ill feeling, that aggressiveness? What harm had he, Malobali, done his elder brother?

Malobali turned these thoughts over and over in his head. In the morning the slaves moved the palm trunks aside and Father Etienne entered.

He was the last person Malobali expected to see! Father Ulrich, perhaps; but Father Etienne! Still under the influence of his dream and the anguish it had inspired in him, Malobali huddled in a corner and groaned. What did the priest want? To gloat over his misfortune?

Father Etienne crossed himself several times, then said:

"Kneel down, Samuel, and say the Lord's Prayer with me."

As always when under the maleficent gaze of the two priests, Malobali could only obey. He sought for the words devoid of real meaning for him but so important to them.

"I know you haven't sinned—that you are innocent of the crime of which you are accused," said the priest.

A flame of hope sprang up in Malobali's heart.

"How do you know, Father?" he asked.

Father Etienne folded his hands again.

"Yesterday evening I heard Romana da Cunha's confession," he said. "Samuel, do you know the parable of the pearls cast before swine? It's a pearl you have there, unworthy swine. But perhaps God in his unfathomable wisdom has decided to bring about your redemption by this means. By contact with her you will be purified. She will make you walk in the way of the Lord."

Malobali looked at the priest in bewilderment.

"What do you want me to do, Father?"

"I want you to marry her, Samuel," the priest answered, "that the love you have lit in her may work for the salvation of you both."

"I want to explain. I don't want you to think I throw myself at all and sundry . . ."

Malobali put his hand over Romana's mouth, but she put it firmly away and went on.

"Let me speak," she said. "I've had this weight on my heart for too long, and I must get rid of it.

"I was born in Oyo, the most powerful of the Yoruba kingdoms. My father was an important court official—an *arokin*, a griot, responsible for reciting the royal family trees. We lived in the palace. Then one day, as the result of quarrels and the intrigues of his enemies, my father was dismissed from his post, and our family was scattered. I don't know what became of my brothers and sisters. I was sold to some slave traders and taken to the fort at Gorée. Can you imagine what it is like to be separated from one's parents, torn away from a life of luxury and well-being? I was scarcely thirteen, still a child. So in that fearful fort, surrounded by poor creatures doomed to the same hell as I was, I never stopped crying. I wanted to die, and certainly would have if a man hadn't come to me. He was tall and strong, carrying a bag of oranges over his shoulder. He gave me one, and it was as if the sun, which for weeks had refused to rise for me, had reappeared in the sky.

"For my sake, to protect me, that man made the terrible crossing. Through terrible storms he would stay by me and sing me lullabies in a language of which all I could understand was its gentleness. In the hold the white sailors used to rape the black women, and I could hear their groans mingling with the roar of the sea. Samuel, if hell exists, it must be like that.

"Then we arrived in a big town on the coast of Brazil. Can you imagine what it's like to be sold? The crowd around the platform, staring at you while your muscles, your teeth, your sexual organs are examined. The sound of the auctioneer's hammer! But alas, Naba and I were separated."

"Naba? Did you say Naba?" breathed Malobali.

"Let me go on," said Romana. "I'll answer your questions afterwards. I was bought by Manoel da Cunha, who took me to his *fazenda*. Naba went north, into the *sertão*. And then my real martydom began. For, as I soon realized, I hadn't suffered anything up till then, because he had been with me. But now I was on my own. Alone. And I hadn't been on the *senzala* two nights when Manoel sent for me. I had to submit to a man I hated, and he planted his seed in me . . ."

"Stop, stop. Don't talk about it—it hurts you too much."

"No, I must go on. A hundred times, a thousand, I wanted to kill that child. The old slave women knew of plants and roots which could have made me expel that fetus, the symbol of my shame, in a stream of red liquid. But something prevented me. And one day Naba reappeared. In the kitchen, just as I was serving a meal. Without saying a word he took me in his arms. And I felt cleansed, absolved . . ."

As she stopped to get her breath back, Malobali begged: "Tell me about that man, Romana. . . . Did you say he was called Naba?"

"Yes," she answered, "and I must tell you about him so that you don't think I'm depraved, falling in love with just anybody! He was a Bambara from Segu, like you. His *diamou* was Traore. His totem was the crowned crane. He wasn't fifteen when he killed his first lion, but one day some 'mad dogs of the bush' caught and sold him . . .

"And when I saw you come into my house with the two priests I thought God in his unfathomable goodness had given him back to me. I was about to fall on my knees to thank him. But, alas, I realized my mistake! Once again fate was mocking me and making me suffer. For I must tell you the rest of my story. They killed him, Samuel—they killed him!"

"They killed my brother?"

"Your brother?"

"Yes—he was my brother. The story you've just told is the story of my family. Because of it my mother's hair went white, my father died before his time, and nothing has been the same with us ever since . . ."

Malobali clasped Romana to him, marveling at the foresight and perseverance of the ancestors. For she was lawfully his after the death of his elder brother. But with so many seas and deserts and forests between them, how could he have entered into possession of her without their help, without the series of adventures they had so patiently concocted? From Segu to Kong. Then to Salaga. From Salaga to Kumasi. Then to Cape Coast. From Cape Coast to Porto Novo. And finally from Porto Novo to Ouidah.

Oh, how he would love her now! To make her forget. Already, because of him, she had recovered her beauty, her youth, and soon she would be cheerful again, too. He wouldn't rest until he brought the laughter back to her lips. And to the lips of her children. He stroked her soft breasts, her slightly curving belly, made bold to touch the secret down of her sex—all the garden, the fine land he would now plow beneath the consenting gaze of the gods and the ancestors.

Modupe? He drove the thought from his mind. What right had she compared to the claim of his elder brother's widow? That was a sacred and imperative duty which could not be avoided.

He held Romana in his arms and satisfied her desire to be possessed.

CHAPTER

7

If all the rusted cannon of Fort Saint-Louis de Gregory, Fort São João Baptista de Ajuda and Fort William had begun to roar against the town at the same time, it wouldn't have caused more of a shock than the announcement of Malobali and Romana's marriage. People saw the hand of the priests in it. But what could have been their objective? They knew too well that Malobali's Catholicism was only a veneer, and that after a couple of months Romana would probably have a couple of co-wives inflicted on her. The Agoudas couldn't understand how she could exchange the fine Brazilian name of da Cunha for that of Traore, which reeked to high heaven of barbarism and idol worship. Everyone felt sorry for Modupe, who said nothing. Great sorrows are silent.

The wedding took place at the end of the dry season. The missionaries, with the help of the slaves Chacha put at their disposal, had done well and built quite an imposing church, a large rectangular hut thatched with straw. The roof was supported on pillars made of iroko trunks, joined together halfway up by a fretted wall. The altar stood on a dais against a palisade on which a cross had been painted with vegetable dyes. Benches for about a hundred people were set on either side of a central aisle. Behind the church was a building that served both as a school and as a house for the priests.

To please Romana, Malobali went to an English merchant

who was staying at Fort William on his way to the oil rivers, and bought a frock coat, a pair of tight trousers and a black silk cravat. Romana herself had bought a mauve silk dress with pagoda sleeves and a shawl that came down to the ground. Her three sons—Eucaristus, Joaquim and Jesus—were dressed all in black, carrying little silver-knobbed sticks. Chacha Ajinakou acted as Malobali's witness.

One incident spoiled the smoothness of the proceedings. Scarcely had Father Ulrich finished his homily on the beauty of human love, a reflection of the love of God, than a big python uncoiled itself from a branch up in the roof. It swayed its head back and forth in the air, then slid silently to the ground just by the choir boys. Dagbe the Python, incarnation of the Supreme Being! What had he come to announce? Some took it for a good omen, some for a bad. Everyone was troubled.

All the inhabitants of Ouidah came out of their houses to see the procession of the Agoudas, and they were torn between hilarity and admiration. How hot they must be, swathed in silk and velvet, out in the sun! Had they forgotten the color of their skin, that they dressed themselves up like whites?

The procession wound into Chacha's house, and all the slaves in the *barracon*, aroused from their prostration, crowded forward to see the bridal pair. Chacha had them served additional rations. In the house itself large tables were laid with services of Chinese porcelain, beautiful cut glass and silver trays heaped with every kind of food. There were Brazilian dishes, of course: fechuada, cousidou, cachuapa, and prion. But local dainties were provided, too: acassa balls, pots of calalou, fish from the sea or the Wo marshes boiled whole, and great heaps of shrimps, yams and cassava. Bowls of millet beer made the rounds, together with aguardente, gin, aquavit, port, French wines and pints of stout. The captains of the slave ships were there, sharing in the banquet. Even the *yovogan* Dagba put in an appearance, surrounded by his dancers and musicians.

Perhaps the happiest people there were Romana's children, sitting at the foot of one of the tables. They thought they could see a new life dawning for them. Their mother was transformed. She was smiling and indulgent. Their father was restored to them in the shape of his brother. It was much more fantastic than the

Brazilian folk tales their mother used to tell them! With their new father, no more beatings with the paddle, no more chanting of dozens of rosaries and Hail Marys. They wouldn't have to sing any more such songs as:

> *African peoples in the dark*
> *You are no longer doomed to scorn and hatred*
> *No longer abandoned as if you were accursed!*

or,

> *Let us walk in the footsteps of Jesus.*

There would be no more boring reading and arithmetic lessons!

Long before the other guests, they realized there would be a struggle between two ways of life, two cultures, two worlds. And they naively believed they could guess which would win.

During dessert, musicians burst in carrying over their shoulders green and yellow streamers, the national colors of Bahia. They were the Agoudas' slaves, and they beat on little square drums, scraped saws with metal sticks, clacked bits of wood together, clapped their hands—in short, kicked up a terrible din!

The Bambaras present, Birame in particular, looked on in amazement. If all the Agoudas were interested in was perpetuating the memory of Brazil, why hadn't they stayed there? Here they were, proclaiming those were the happiest days of their lives. Had they forgotten they had been slaves? And that they'd chosen to come back to Africa? Had they forgotten they'd often fomented revolts over there? What a strange reversal!

Toward the end of the afternoon, after a last sermon, the two priests withdrew and the atmosphere grew more free and easy. Jeronimo Carlos got up and did an imitation of the frenzied motion of the bull, the *boi a ou boi*, while his brother João played the "careta" or masked man. The children set off firecrackers, which terrified the natives of Ouidah, unfamiliar with these and other entertainments learned from the whites.

The evening continued with a ball. All the Agoudas could remember the balls given by their former masters in Recife or Bahia or on the *fazendas* on the day of the harvest festival or *botada*, when all they had done was bring in the dishes. But now it was they who danced to the music of waltzes and quadrilles, with an abandon perhaps unknown to the Portuguese. Nostalgia and a sense of wrongs righted at last combined to lend a special atmosphere to the celebrations and draw all the guests together.

The party ended with a fireworks display. For a long while the bright patterns unfolded over the straw roofs of Ouidah, between the coconut palms of the coast and out over a sea as dark as the sky.

The early days of the marriage were a revelation to Malobali. Perhaps because he had possessed so many women he had never really paid attention to them. They had only been docile bodies whose warmth he liked but which he forgot immediately afterwards. But with Romana he discovered for the first time that a woman was a human being, whose complexity disconcerted him. He soon recognized in Romana an intelligence keener than his own, and would have been inclined to admire her if at the same time she had not been so dependent on him. A rough word, a gesture of impatience, was enough to make her burst into tears. Any sign of indifference sent her into a panic, and she was capable of spending hours asking him what she had done wrong.

For Malobali, love had always been an act as simple and satisfying as eating or drinking. With Romana it became a drama, a fascinating and perverse game, a theater of cruelty whose signs he could not decipher and in which he found himself involved almost against his will, almost afraid. He couldn't understand either why Romana desired him so fiercely, or why she seemed to repent it so much.

On the material plane the couple prospered. Chacha, who wasn't interested in the trade in palm oil, persuaded King Guezo to grant Malobali a monopoly in the sale of it to Europeans, to the Régis brothers in particular. Malobali bought all the red oil produced by the women, paid a tax on it to a royal official and then resold it to the merchants. He was soon so rich that he started a barrel-making business, employing Agoudas who had learned carpentry in Brazil. Wooden barrels were superior to the earthenware jars that had been used hitherto: they didn't break and were easier to handle.

Romana had always been grasping. Naba used to chide her about it. And this side of her character had developed during the long years when she had had to bring up her children alone and had constantly feared for their future. She bought a tin chest in which she amassed not only gold dust and cowrie shells but also the gold and silver coins she got from some merchants. She kept the key of the chest between her breasts, for she was afraid of Malobali's fits of generosity and his tendency to spend a fortune on drink or cards. This too was why she tried to keep him away from Chacha and Birame, though there was a good deal of jealousy involved here too. She resented the time Malobali spent away from her; the pleasure he might experience anywhere else; his freedom. She would have liked to keep him in the compound where she could see him, like one of her children. And when he was there she kept nagging him to notice her.

When did the rift between them begin? It really started on the wedding night itself, when Malobali was forced to give more than he had. Soon anything might provoke a quarrel. The Agoudas, for example, whose amusements struck Malobali as childish and affected, and whose arrogance toward the natives he found unbearable. Or the Bambara, whom Romana regarded as coarse and depraved, the enemies of the true God. She especially hated Birame, because he was a Muslim and she saw Islam as a murderous religion that was putting Oyo, her native country, to fire and sword, and had been the cause of Naba's unjust death. The children were another bone of contention, especially Eucaristus. Romana had found out that the English missionaries sent young Africans to London to learn to be priests, and she wanted to ask Father Etienne to do the same for Eucaristus. She already pictured her last-born dressed in a long black robe, his rosary at his waist like a weapon of God, a cross around his neck and a crowd prostrating itself at his feet. But Malobali only talked to the boys about Segu, that den of idol worship, and called them the Bambara names he had given them.

To avoid these squabbles, followed by even more exhausting reconciliations, Malobali, who until then had hated exerting himself, flung himself into his work. Gradually the only things he talked about to Romana were the measuring of palm oil, its treatment, how to sell it to the best advantage and how to eliminate competitors. The worst of it was that moon succeeded moon and Romana didn't have a child, although she had had four sons before! It seemed to Malobali her body was like a field that has lain fallow too long and can no longer nourish seed.

In her distress Romana went to see a *babalawo*. He was from Kétu, and had a great reputation among the Nagos in Ouidah. She found him sitting on a mat with his instruments of divination in front of him: the sixteen palm nuts, the sacred chain and the powder. He fixed her with his glittering eyes and made her recite the ritual words:

> *Ifa is the master of today,*
> *Ifa is the master of tomorrow,*
> *Ifa is the master of the day after tomorrow.*
> *To Ifa belong the four days*
> *That the God created on earth.*

Then he threw his palm nuts onto the wooden divining board with its triangular border and picture of Eschu the messenger. Romana's heart beat fast. But Ifa's representative reassured her, reciting a long, obscure poem ending with the word Olubunmi.*

When did Malobali find his way back to the house of Modupe, who, comforted by the predictions of her own *babalawo*, was patiently awaiting his return? When did he begin to look upon her as his only true wife? No, the ceremony in the church at Ouidah meant nothing. There had been no presents handed around. The gods and the ancestors had not been invoked, appeased, asked to afford their protection. The choir had not sung the traditional blessing:

> *May this marriage be happy!*
> *May it last come what may!*
> *May its fire endure!*

Segu! Segu! He must go back to Segu! What was the point of

---

*Yoruba for "God will provide."

hanging on here among strangers? With a wife who wore him out but didn't produce a child? What was happening in Segu?

The reign of Mansa Da Monzon was sure to be continuing in greatness and victory. Why wasn't he, Malobali, there to share in its triumph? If only he could rest his head in Nya's lap!

"Mother, your hair has gone white while I have been away. I haven't been there to see the wrinkles gather around your mouth, and I find you more frail and vulnerable than I remembered. Mother, can you forgive me my faults?"

Malobali told Modupe about his plans.

"I'm not sure how to get there," he told her. "I shall have to ask the Hausa merchants—they know all the routes."

Modupe's eyes filled with tears.

"Can I tell my mother about it?" she asked.

Malobali took her in his arms. He was aware of all the sacrifices she was making for him. Although most of the Agoudas, in spite of being Catholics, had two or three wives, he knew he could not: Romana would never permit it. So although he lavished presents on her family, he had never been able to marry Modupe, and he knew she suffered from this humiliation, this false position.

"We'll be married in Segu," he told her gently, "among my own people. Then my family will send your family a caravan of presents. Can you see it arriving in Ouidah? The people will all rush out and say. 'Where are they from? Who are they for?'"

At last he managed to make her smile. Yes, he must put his plan into execution without delay. Birame too had had enough of living in foreign parts. He would certainly join in any scheme to return to their native country.

Romana's house had undergone considerable changes. In the courtyard Malobali had put up a mud-walled building, one side of which served as a store for barrels of palm oil waiting for transport overseas, while the other was used as a shop, with French scales and measures to weigh the jars of oil brought in by retailers. All morning there arose a babble of women's voices, their owners suspicious of the whites' system of weights and measures, always claiming they had been cheated and threatening to complain to King Guezo himself. Eucaristus, who could now write with perfect ease, kept the accounts, sitting at a table covered with inkpots, pens of various colors and sealing wax. His set, serious young face and the cabalistic marks he made on his papers intimidated everyone, and he was spoken of everywhere as a prodigy. The cooperative workshop was built on a piece of land nearby, and employed ten workmen who spent the whole day cutting, planing and polishing, while slaves brought in tree trunks from the neighboring forests.

But when Malobali got home all was quiet, for it was very late. The only noticeable feature was the bitter smell of palm oil mingled with that of newly cut wood which clung to everything in the compound. He went into the bedroom and Romana saw with relief that he wasn't drunk. He filled his pipe with Bahia tobacco and put it in his mouth. But he didn't light it because he knew Romana hated the smell. And she, reduced to being content with what she could get, rejoiced in this sign of consideration. Then he said gravely: "*Iya*, I'm thinking of going to Abomey."

"Abomey?" she said incredulously. "What do you need to go there for?"

He had his answer ready.

"I want to have a palm plantation of my own," he said. "I want my own slaves to gather the nuts and extract the oil. It would be more worthwhile for us than buying from retailers."

Romana was silent for a moment. Then: "Extracting palm oil is work done by free women, not slaves," she said. "Some of them belong to influential Fon families. Do you think they'll let you do what you propose?"

"That's why I have to have an audience with the king himself," said Malobali.

Romana sighed.

"Malobali," she said (he had forbidden her to call him Samuel), "don't forget you're a foreigner!"

Malobali shrugged her objection aside.

"Yes, but I'm married to an Agouda, and King Guezo adores them! And what if I am a foreigner? Aren't the Portuguese and the Brazilians foreigners too, and yet they rule the roost!"

If she had said, "Yes, but they're white!" he would have been furious, so she only answered, unenthusiastically: "If you think that's the right thing to do . . ."

He started to get up, and she couldn't help murmuring:
"Won't you stay with me?"

Malobali thought quickly. If he wanted to lull her suspicions and be free to arrange his departure, it would be best to satisfy her desire. He went over to her, and as he did so he noticed she had anointed herself with a scented cream that the Hausas sold. He suddenly felt sorry for her, and his compassion created the illusion of desire.

Why hadn't Romana accepted her position as a woman? Why hadn't she let herself be led, instead of trying to lead him and impose on him a way of life he hated? It was so sad to let happiness slip like that!

Romana had her own explanation of the difficulties that had arisen between Malobali and herself. It was Naba. Mild and tolerant though he had been in his lifetime, he now could not endure to see his widow in his brother's arms. No matter how often Malobali told her it was the custom among the Bambara, and that Nya, his mother, had been given after Dousika's death to Dousika's younger brother Diemogo for the good of the community, Romana detected a tinge of incest in it all. So she spent most of her time in prayer, covered the altar with flowers, and sang hymns passionately imploring the Lord to have mercy on her.

In short, she was more tortured after her marriage than before. She got thinner and thinner, and the matrons of Ouidah pursed their lips. The ancestors had their reasons for not blessing this marriage, as the God of the Christians, who had given it His blessing, would soon learn to his cost. But that night, assuaged for once, she stroked Malobali's arm and whispered: "To obtain an audience with Guezo you'll have to make him some handsome presents, especially as he only likes things from the white man's countries. Tomorrow I'll open the chest, and you can take out as much as you want."

These words, designed to please him and show she was submissive, only irritated Malobali. Shouldn't it have been he who said, "*Iya*, tomorrow I'm going to open the chest—I've got some big expenses ahead of me"? Wasn't that how it had always been between Dousika and Nya when there was some important family ceremony to organize? He collected his clothes in the dark and got up.

"Where are you going?" she begged.

He went out without answering.

Once out in the courtyard he lit his pipe and inhaled deeply. It was a mild night. A faint crescent moon lurked behind the branches of a silk cotton tree. Should he really go away? And leave behind Naba's children, in other words his own, decked out in borrowed names, brought up in ignorance of their own language and traditions, worshipping a foreign god? Wasn't that a crime for which he would have to answer to the family? How could he ever explain it to them? How could he look Nya in the face if she knew he had found Naba's sons and not brought them back to Segu?

Malobali was trying to quiet his conscience, when Eucaristus appeared out of the shadows. He must have been waiting for Malobali to come back, waiting with the door ajar. Of the three boys he was the one most attached to him, the most sensitive, the one who suffered most from not having a father.

"Tell me a story," he said.

Malobali stroked the little round head.

"All right!" he said fondly. "A man and his son were having a meal. A hungry stranger came along, so they invited him to share. The stranger sat down and helped himself to a huge handful of food. The child cried out, '*Baba*, did you see what a big mouthful the stranger took?' The father rebuked him, and said, 'Be quiet—did he say he was going to take another one?' Who do you think made the stranger go away—the son or the father?"

Eucaristus, who knew the answer, pretended not to. Then he asked: "What am I—an Agouda, a Yoruba or a Bambara?"

Malobali clasped the boy to him.

"Sons always belong to their fathers," he said. "You are a Bambara. One day you'll come to Segu. You've never seen a town like it. The towns here were created by the white men—they were born out of the trade in human flesh. They're no more than vast warehouses. But Segu! Segu is surrounded by walls, like a woman you can possess only by force."

Eucaristus listened, and his imagination was set on fire. No, he didn't want anything to do with the future his mother was preparing for him. He didn't want to become a priest, a man without wives. He wanted to hear the girls tinkle the bells on their ankles and sing in chorus for him, as full of admiration and fear as Yoruba hunters facing a leopard:

> Prince, prince, giant among men
> Your embrace brings death
> You play and you slay
> You break every heart
> The death dealt by you is sweet and swift.

A cloud passed over the crescent moon and for a moment the sky was dark. The smell of the sea reached them, drowning that of the orange trees which grew all over the compounds. Malobali sighed. He would go; he had made up his mind. But in the very moment of leaving Romana he imagined what his life would be like without her, and he was sad. Would Modupe be able to fill the gap she left?

Eucaristus sensed that Malobali's thoughts were far away, and he wanted to hear more about Segu.

"Tell me about the day you were born," he said, "and the white man at the gates of the town."

"You've already heard it a hundred times."

"I know," the child said coaxingly, "but you've never told me whether your mother herself took it for a bad omen."

"My mother?"

Malobali stood up. He was nearly thirty now. He had knocked about the world, seen many places, held many women in his arms. But the pain was still there, sharp as ever. Nya's words still rang in his ears: "I am your mother, because I'm your father's wife and I love you. But it wasn't I who carried you in my womb."

Where was she, the woman who had abandoned him? "Absent, cruel mother! Do you know you doomed me to wander forever, looking for you?"

C H A P T E R

8

After Ouidah, sand gives way to soil. There is more vegetation, the trees are more bushy. Then you enter a dense forest that lasts as far as Ekpe. After Ekpe comes Lama, a muddy depression of clay and marl with a permanently low water level. Then the route climbs steeply upwards for a while, after which the ascent becomes more gentle, leading finally to a plateau facing south, with scalloped edges. The vegetation here grows gradually thinner until there is nothing left but tall grasses and clumps of palmyra and silk cotton trees.

The journey had started badly for Malobali.

To begin with, he had given in to Modupe's tearful pleas and let her family in on the secret. This meant that the least indiscretion—and one was always possible—would be enough to alert Romana to his trip to Abomey. And then, Dagba the *yovogan* had told him he concerned himself only with the king's relations with the whites. Malobali was a black, married to a local woman, and thus perfectly free to go anywhere he liked so long as he paid the taxes due to the various *denou*, the custom posts. Dagba had given him the right to travel on horseback, with a parasol and a retinue of armed servants like the Dahomey chiefs. This was an honor Malobali could not refuse, but it made him hopelessly conspicuous, whereas he had planned to lose himself among the traveling merchants to cross the river Zou to Adofoodia, whence he'd been told it was very easy to get to Timbuktu. He would wait there for Modupe to join him, escorted by Birame. It was all very dangerous and uncertain.

On entering Abomey, Malobali was surprised by the size of the town, and especially by the size of the king's residence, the Singboji palace, which covered an area as big as the whole of Ouidah. It was surrounded by enormous fortifications and a wide ditch, and held about ten thousand people. These included the king, his wives, his children, his ministers, his troop of female soldiers, the Amazons, his warriors and an army of priests, singers, craftsmen and servants of all kinds. The buildings occupied by Guezo were rectangular, but the tombs of the dead kings, also inside the palace precincts, were round, with thatched roofs so low that people entered on their hands and knees. The tombs stood to the east of a central alley called Aydo Wedo, or rainbow. The quarters of the "mothers of kings," still called "mothers of panthers" and exercising considerable influence at court, were to the west. The sound of music rose ceaselessly from a variety of instruments—horns made of elephants' tusks, drums, bells— and from the voices of hundreds of girls known as "the king's birds." Their chirping accompanied him wherever he went.

Malobali was to spend a night or two in the Okeadan quarter with a family related to Modupe's. Here he intended to get rid of his escort, paying them handsomely and sending them back to Ouidah. By the time they got there and people started to wonder at his absence he would be approaching Timbuktu—at least he hoped so. Now it so happened that a man called Guedou often visited the same Nago household into which Malobali hoped to marry. He was a member of the famous *leguede*, King Guezo's secret police. Noticing the furtive way Malobali parted with his escort and the haste with which he went to his room without being introduced to the family, his instinct told him this stranger had something to hide. He took one of the host's children aside in the shade of a wall.

"Do you know who that man is?" he asked.

The child made a face.

"I think he's an Ashanti or a Mahi. He's not a Nago, anyway."

Guedou frowned. An Ashanti? A Mahi? If so, he was an enemy anyhow!

Relations between the Asantehene of Kumasi and the king

of Dahomey had never been good, and a year or so earlier Guezo had intimated to MacCarthy, governor of the fort at Cape Coast, that he would be glad to see the English seize the Ashanti kingdom. As for the Mahis, they were hereditary enemies whom all Guezo's generals urged him to destroy. The king was known to be preparing another expedition against Houjroto, his neighbors' capital, for he needed captives for the slave trade and to serve as sacrifices for the great feast of the Atto, when the king handed out presents to his subjects. It was a good season for spies!

Guedou therefore hurried to his superior, Ajaho, who combined the functions of minister for religion, court chamberlain and head of the secret police.

How busy the streets of Abomey were! With whites slumped in litters, being carried along by bearers. With fetish priests, their heads shaven, naked from the waist up, strings of cowries around wrists and ankles, their eyes outlined with red and white paint made from kaolin and laterite. With lines of girls in silk and velvet *pagnes* going to the Dido fountain to draw water for offerings to the dead kings.

When he reached the Ahuaga quarter Guedou found Ajaho had gone to the Singboji palace for an important meeting of ministers. The palace opened onto the square and the town through a number of gates. Guedou carefully avoided the Hongboji gate, reserved for the queens' comings and goings and guarded by eunuchs, and went through the Fede entrance. The council was over, and Ajaho was deep in conversation with Hountonji the jeweler, who was sitting on a block of wood with his feet in the dust, his body bathed in sweat and wearing only a strip of cloth held in place by a belt of vines. Ajaho himself was a fine tall man, one of the kingdon's seven "wearers of felt hats." He was dressed in a loose white silk *pagne*. Guedou quickly told him of his suspicions about Malobali, and Ajaho, far from laughing at him, listened attentively. For it was a serious matter. He thought for a while, then said: "Guezo is only interested in the Mahis—he wants to teach them a lesson. They killed two or three of his white friends who wanted to visit their sacred woods. He completely neglects the Ashanti. I think, however, that it's from them an attack is most likely to come. Because of the English blockade they have practically no outlet to the sea, and they'd like to get

hold of our port at Ouidah. Be careful, Guedou—don't let that
man out of your sight!"

Guedou didn't need telling twice. He left the palace, crossed
Singboji square in the direction of the main market, then turned
west making for the Okeadan quarter. The sun was getting ready
to go to rest in the river Coufo. The heat had abated, and a cool
darkness was beginning to fall from the sky. The women were
leaving the markets, followed by little girls carrying all the bundles of pimentos, gourds full of palm oil, smoked meat and maize
that remained unsold. Guedou wondered how to find out who
the stranger really was; he couldn't just go up and ask him. Suddenly he had an idea. Millet beer loosened men's tongues. He
was a frequent visitor at the house. He could turn up at mealtime
and be generous with the beer. He went into the Ajahi market.

"I don't understand our kings," said Malobali, his voice rather
thick. "They adore the whites. After welcoming the Portuguese
with open arms, now Guezo only has eyes for the French—the
Zodjaguis. When I was at Cape Coast it was the English who
were the favorites. Don't they see that all the Whitebodies are
dangerous? I myself . . ."

Guedou was interested in just one word.

"Were you at Cape Coast?" he said. "Forgive my curiosity,
but what country are you from?"

Malobali was about to tell the truth when it struck him it
would be best to remain incognito. How did he know Romana
hadn't sent spies after him? Guedou, watching him intently, noticed his hesitation.

"Forgive me," he said, with feigned politeness. "I'm being
indiscreet."

"Indiscreet? No," Malobali answered, shaking his head. "I'm
an Ashanti from Kumasi. For a long time I wore a soldier's uniform, then a few years ago I went into trade. I sell kola nuts to
the 'blackeners of tablets' in the Hausa country, and that's where
I'm going now."

This didn't ring true, though Guedou couldn't have said why.
But he dropped his inquisition for the moment and went back to
the original subject.

"You're right about the whites," he said. "What is it about them that attracts our kings? Their guns and gunpowder? Haven't we got bows and arrows? Their alcohol? Aren't corn and millet beer just as good? Their silks and velvets? I can tell you *I* prefer our clothes made from raffia."

They both laughed, and emptied another bowl of millet beer.

"They say the whites refuse to prostrate themselves before Guezo," said Malobali.

"I've seen it with my own eyes," said Guedou. "And that's not all. The king invited them to the great feast of the Atto, and just as the sacrifices were dispatching the captives toward the gods and the ancestors, the whites made a public display of their disapproval and disgust. Some of them even left the royal dais."

"What did Guezo do?"

Guedou shook his head sadly.

"Nothing, of course. The whites can't understand our honoring our own great ones. Imagine if, when your Asantehene Osei Bonsu died, the priests hadn't sent his wives and slaves and favorites with him to keep him company!"

And then Malobali made a mistake. It was understandable enough. He was half drunk, weary after many days' journey, tense and anxious as to whether his plans would succeed. When he heard what Guedou had just said he exclaimed without thinking: "Is Osei Bonsu dead then?"

Guedou looked him straight in the eye and said simply: "It's at least two dry seasons since Osei Yaw Akoto took his place on the golden throne."

Then he went away.

There are times when a man gets tired of struggling. Against himself. Against fate. Against the gods. "Oh," he says to himself, "let come what may!" Worse still, something inside him wishes for trouble and agitation to end, and wants only peace. Everlasting peace.

It seemed to Malobali that for years he had been fleeing some obscure but omnipotent force from which he only escaped in order to fall victim to it later on. He had avoided the consequences of raping Ayaovi only to fall into the toils of the missionaries. Then into those of Romana. Now he was trying to escape from her. Where would that land him?

And while every instinct told him to distrust Guedou, to leave this house after having made such an awful blunder, to resume his journey, he was incapable of doing anything. No matter how much he reminded himself of Modupe's longing breasts, Nya's face, or the smell of the earth in Segu when the sun warmed or the winter rains soaked it, he just stayed there inert, his mind and his body numbed. Meanwhile Guedou hurried as fast as he could to the Singboji palace.

Ajaho was with his friend Gawu, a prince of the blood renowned for his valor in war. The two men were passing a snuffbox back and forth between them, and emptying bowls of rum from Ouidah. Only the king was really supposed to drink it. And yet they were not at all merry. They were talking of what the whole court was gossiping and worrying about: the white men's influence on Guezo.

"Who'd have thought Guezo would fail to inherit the character of his father King Agonglo?" said one of them.

"Has he forgotten he's descended from Agasu the panther?" said the other.

Guedou gave a little cough to call attention to his presence, and Ajaho turned to him.

"Well?" he said.

Guedou knelt on the fine white sand, brought from Kana, and said quietly: "What would you say to an Ashanti who didn't know that Asantehene Osei Bonsu went to his ancestors two dry seasons ago?"

The three men all looked at one another.

"Very strange!" said Gawu ironically.

There was a pause, the Ajaho gave an order.

"Take some men and arrest him! Bring him before me tomorrow morning!"

Already thinking of promotion, Guedou asked, "Where am I to put him?"

In Abomey, prisoners were assigned to the various jails according to their rank. There were cells for princes and princesses inside the palace and others in different quarters of Abomey for ordinary people. But the Gbekon-Huegbo prison had a particularly sinister reputation. It was said that prisoners there had their necks fixed in iron collars connected by chains to the jailers outside their cells. The jailers tugged on the chains when they felt like it, and sometimes, when they were in a particularly jocular mood, they pulled so hard they broke an unfortunate prisoner's neck. The corpse was then disposed of under cover of night. Then the family of the victim could not shave his hair or cut his nails, nor wash him with warm water and anoint him with sweet-smelling balm so that he might present himself properly for admittance by Sava the gatekeeper into Koutome, the city of the dead.

It was to Gbekon-Huegbo that Guedou took Malobali.

"After all, do we know who he is? He came here with missionaries, then left them. He seduced our women. If the men of the *leguede* have arrested him they must have their reasons."

This was roughly what everyone in Ouidah said when they heard Malobali had been arrested. No one rushed to Abomey to swear to his identity or guarantee his respectability. Chacha said he'd become so arrogant he must have acted insolently at court. Father Etienne and Father Ulrich didn't lift a finger. For one thing, they were afraid of offending the king. Moreover Malobali had always been a cause of dissension between them, with Father Etienne distrusting him and Father Ulrich confident of being able to bring his soul around to God. As for Modupe's family, they called in a *babalawo* who prescribed potions and ointments designed to drive the memory of Malobali out of the girl's head. To complete the cure, he advised her people to send her to stay with an uncle in Ketou. The Bambara in the Fort, led by Birame, remembered they were foreigners, dependent on other foreigners, the French, and that if he felt like it Guezo could drive them all into the sea. In short, no one stood up for Malobali.

No one except Romana.

Romana couldn't understand why she had to go through the same ordeal over and over again. Always to see the man she loved imprisoned for a crime he didn't commit. What sin was she herself expiating? Were the Yoruba gods, the Orisha, punishing her for having abandoned them and changed her name from Ayodele, "Joy has entered my house," to Romana? Then she blamed Father Joaquim who had converted her, and the nuns in the hospital Santa Casa de Misericordia in Recife.

Then she blamed herself for having loved and desired Malobali as one should love and desire God alone, and for having betrayed because of him the fidelity she owed her dead husband. She was in so agitated a state people feared for her life. The whole Agouda community, who had so often criticized her, gathered around her mat.

The *babalawo* and the *bokomo* sat under the orange and fig trees and cast their palm nuts and cowries onto their divining boards, reciting litanies known only to them. Father Etienne and Father Ulrich looked on, not daring to drive them out, and gave the patient communion whenever her condition permitted.

Then, just as everyone thought she was at death's door, Romana regained consciousness, and asked for a bowl of water. Then she said feverishly: "I must go to Abomey. I must save him."

It took a week for someone in good shape to walk from Ouidah to Abomey, for only the king and visiting whites were allowed to be carried in litters, and horses and mules were reserved for important dignitaries. Could a woman, weakened by illness and half mad with grief, walk all that way? To everyone's surprise Birame and the other Bambara, as if stricken with remorse, offered to go with her. Romana's maids and the wives of the Bambara stuffed bags full of grilled corn, millet flour and acassa balls, and provided gourds full of fresh water.

The little group started out in the morning. Birame took Molara, his young bride, with him. At the gate of the town stood a statue of Legba, the spirit of evil. It was a clay statue with a monstrous penis and an expression of the utmost wickedness. Romana's heart was filled with terror. It seemed that Legba was looking at her and telling her any attempt to save Malobali was vain. He had his prey in his clutches and would not let him go.

Soon afterwards they went through a region of palm plantations, and when she saw the slaves climbing the trees or busy with the clusters of nuts that had fallen to the ground, Romana remembered Malobali. In the early days of their marriage when he came back sweating from the fields she used to give him *acaraje*, a Brazilian dish he was very fond of. Then he would join her in her bedroom and say, laughing, as he took her in his arms: "Love in the afternoon! You learned that from the whites!"

The whites! Yes, it was their customs, their religion, that had come between her and Malobali. She hadn't known how to play the game of submissiveness, respect and patience like her mother before her. She had wanted to speak to him as an equal, to give him advice, to run him. And in the end she had lost him. For she knew now it was her he was running away from when he fled to Abomey. Her and her alone.

While these thoughts were swirling confusedly through Romana's head, Birame and Molara were enjoying the spectacle on the road from Ouidah to Abomey, the most frequented route in the kingdom. They tried to tell the difference between the Frenchmen and Englishmen, but failed. All they saw in either case were faces the color of clay, yellow hair and eyes glittering like those of beasts of prey.

Dahomey was a prosperous country. As far as the eye could see there were fields of corn, little hills covered with the curly green hair of yams, others dotted with white puffs of cotton. Slaves, like colonies of ants, carried water from the wells in big calabashes.

Once the whole party had to stand back among the grasses at the side of the road when a dignitary went past, preceded by his singers, dancers and musicians and sheltered under a huge parasol held over his head by slaves. Some said it was Prince Sodaaton on his way to replace *yovogan* Dagba, who had displeased King Guezo.

Those who knew what Romana was going through looked at her with pity. But they kept their distance. Wasn't misfortune contagious? When Zo, fire, wants to burn down a tree, doesn't he also set the grass and bushes ablaze around it?

Finally, one morning they arrived at their destination. The town was in a state of suspended animation: king, dignitaries, soldiers and Amazons were all away at the siege of Hounjroto, capital of the Mahi country. But Romana, as an Agouda, had influential connections. Ever since the time of King Adandozan, "Brazilians"—half-castes, blacks and former slaves—had swarmed to the court at Abomey to serve as interpreters, cooks, doctors and so on. So it wasn't long before she found out which prison Malobali was in.

CHAPTER

9

The siege of Hounjroto had lasted three months.

Two of King Guezo's brothers had died as prisoners there and he wanted revenge. So as soon as his troops were in control of the town they set it on fire and razed it to the ground. The old men were disemboweled, the younger ones, with the women and children, were taken away into captivity.

The conquerors entered Abomey at dawn through the Dossoumoin gate, facing the rising sun. The soldiers led the procession, followed by the king in his litter and surrounded by dignitaries on horseback. Guezo wore his campaign outfit—a red tunic and a *pagne* passing under the right arm and fastened on the left shoulder. He wore his cartridge pouch around his waist, and on his head a wide-brimmed cap covered with protective amulets. In his right hand he held a buffalo horn full of gunpowder. The Amazons formed the royal guard, separating the men from the queens who wanted to accompany their husband. Next came the eunuchs, who guarded the queens against any contaminating contact or breath. Then followed the endless line of captives, their hands tied behind their backs and their legs in fetters.

The common people weren't too sure what the Mahis had done, nor why they must all soon fall to the executioner's knife or go as slaves to Cuba or Brazil. But since the drums were beating, the soldiers singing and the horns sounding, all amid a smell of gunpowder and dust, the crowd was happy. To top off the excitement the soldiers fired their guns, and a roar of enthusiasm rose skyward.

Romana, supported by Birame and Molara, had dragged herself to the square opposite the Singboji palace. She could scarcely see, but stared at Ajaho in the hope of making out what kind of man he was, for she meant to throw herself at his feet when she could obtain an audience. He must believe her. If not he must give her *adimu*, the potion that would show she was telling the truth. Birame took her by the arm and pulled her away.

"Come, Ayodele," he said, for like Malobali he never called her by her Catholic name, "there's nothing we can do here. Let's go and wait for Ajaho at his house."

He led her through the festive crowd to the Ahuaga quarter. Then quiet returned. The women went back to their market stalls, the weavers to their looms, the dyers to their vats. Near the Adonon gate the makers of royal parasols and their numerous apprentices chatted and laughed in expectation of the forthcoming celebrations when, in the joy of victory, Guezo would be lavish with food and drink and throw handfuls of gold and silver to the crowd. The feasting would last for days!

Romana, Birame and Molara didn't have long to wait. Ajaho was a conscientious official and wanted to find out what had been going on in his absence.

With instinctive coquetry Romana had dressed in one of her finest Brazilian gowns. The upper part of the bodice was of worked muslin with a broad lace jabot from neck to waist, and the full circular skirt was edged with white arabesques. A shawl made of colored strips of cotton hid her right shoulder. She had bound a big kerchief of white net around her head. Ajaho was charmed. He listened to her without interrupting, then said, with a wink at his entourage: "Why should a man with a wife like you want to leave her? You must be mistaken—the man you believe to be your husband is only a Mahi dog passing himself off as an Ashanti."

Romana threw herself at his feet.

"Have him brought face to face with me, lord," she implored, "and you'll see whether he has the heart to persist."

A strange business! Ajaho sent Romana away, telling her to

return the next day. As they left the Ahuaga quarter Romana and Birame passed by the Adonon gate again, and there they met a town crier ringing his bell and followed by two drummers. They stopped to listen.

"Citizens of Abomey! The Master of the World, the Father of Riches, the Cardinal Bird who does not set light to the bush, bids me announce that the 'customary celebrations'* will begin tomorrow evening. The Master of the World will distribute cloth and money among his people after messages have been sent to the dead kings."

Romana shivered. Messages to the dead kings—that meant sacrifices. If she did not succeed in saving Malobali, he would be one of the messengers!

Further on they met some whites in their litters, leaving the town in haste. They could not bear the sight of the human sacrifices that Guezo would invite them to witness as guests of honor from the royal dais. Birame spat at them as they went by.

"Hypocrites!" he said. "In their own country they slaughter one another by the hundreds of thousands with those guns of theirs. And they come here and turn up their noses."

Some men who heard him expressed warm agreement and struck up a conversation. Everyone was sure the whites would destroy Dahomey by doing away with both the slave trade and the sacrifices to the kings. Romana heard nothing of all this. She was deep in prayer. She appealed not only to Jesus Christ, the Virgin Mary and the saints in paradise but also to the powerful Yoruba Orisha whom her parents used to appease with palm oil, fresh yams, fruit and blood. Which one had she offended? Ogun, Shango, Olokun, Oya, Legba, Obatala, Eshu . . . ?

Guedou unwedged the plank barring the entrance to the cell and recoiled before the horrible stench. No wonder—the man had been left in his own excrement for three months, and that odor mingled with the reek of rotten scraps of food, dead animals and the polluted air in the narrow passage.

He signaled for two of his men to enter.

*Observances in honor of dead kings and divinities.

"Untie him," he ordered.

What they brought out into the light of day was a bag of bones covered with a thin skin broken with ulcers and scaly as a snake's. His hair and beard had grown like weeds, and a whole colony of displaced fleas and bugs scattered in fright. The man's eyes, hurt by the light, fluttered like moths encountering a torch. At the sight a kind of rage seized Guedou, who had thought he was doing his duty but now realized he had been a torturer. He aimed a great kick at the man.

"If you're a respectable Bambara, why didn't you say so?" he cried. "Why did you pretend to be an Ashanti? Quarrels with women are settled under the tree, not in prison."

But Malobali was incapable of defending himself: For a long time he had been almost unconscious, his spirit detached from his body and fretting against the bonds still tying it to earth. The men gathered around him as Guedou went on with the same fierce resentment as before: "Apparently he's even a friend of Chacha Ajinakou's. Ajaho's going to send him one of the king's doctors before he's given back to his wife. And she's an Agouda!"

These allusions to Chacha Ajinakou and the Agoudas only indicated the enormity of the misunderstanding. But why hadn't the man defended himself?

The royal doctor soon arrived, and when he first saw Malobali he thought he was dead. Then a film of sweat on the skin showed him his error, and he opened the leather bag that contained his powders, plasters and unguents, together with the gris-gris that helped them work. But whatever he did Malobali remained unconscious, unable to stand or react to the human voice. All the doctor could do was have his hair, beard and nails cut, and cover his body with bandages to prevent the spread of infection. He then withdrew. It was scarcely more than a corpse that was handed over to Romana.

A woman gives birth to a premature infant which is imperfect. The family wants to get rid of it and thus be reconciled with the gods who have thus manifested their wrath. But the woman refuses and grows fond of the uncomely infant, preferring it to her other children. She looks anxiously for the slightest spark of life in its eyes and interprets its grimaces as smiles. At last, as a result of such love, the little creature takes on a human form. So it was with Romana and Malobali. Apparently indifferent to the smell of his open wounds, his vomit and his defecations, she tended him and managed to find all the things the *babalawo* and doctors asked for, however difficult. No sacrifice was too great. Someone advised her to get in touch with Wolo, one of the royal *bokono* who sometimes consulted the oracle for the benefit of common mortals. With the help of an Agouda called Marcos, one of Guezo's cooks, she managed to get into the royal palace and into the round room to the right of the entrance where the old man was. Wolo meditated for a while before entering into communication with the spirits, then began the séance. But the longer he manipulated his instruments the more troubled and disconcerted he seemed. He gave the impression that he was having a long argument with an invisible interlocutor, using threats and persuasion alternately. At last he fell into a preoccupied silence, and then delivered his verdict.

Sava, keeper of the gates of Koutome, city of the dead, had let through the spirit of Malobali, which had been wandering in the other world. But this seemed to be a mistake, and Wolo had ordered Sava to free the spirit and give it back to the living. But Sava argued that the doctor called in to treat Malobali had shaved his head and trimmed his nails at night, rituals performed only upon corpses. So Sava had been within his rights. Wolo did not despair of persuading him in the end, but it would take a long while.

For the first time Romana gave way to discouragement. She had already spent a large part of her fortune. Her children were far away, and who knew how they were faring in Ouidah? She herself was in a strange city given over to the joy of victory that meant nothing to her. Even the patience of her companions, Birame and Molara, was wearing thin; they were beginning to think Malobali was taking too long to die. For a moment Romana thought of killing first him and then herself, like a royal spouse following her lord: then she was ashamed of such thoughts, which offended both Christian and Yoruba beliefs.

In the Ajahi market where Romana sat, girls were selling millet and corn. Chickens, their legs tied together with straw, cackled unceasingly. Were they telling stories as sad as those of human beings? Romana propped herself up against one of the

iroko pillars supporting the roof of the market. From a nearby
stall came the smell of ginger and other spices. A woman laughed,
showing dazzling teeth. Life went on. Romana wished she could
die. She feebly dragged herself to the part of the market where
they sold four-legged animals and bought the black sheep Wolo
had asked for. Bystanders watched intrigued as the frail woman
seemed to be led away by the huge animal.

When she got back to the Okeadan quarter she found everyone in great excitement. Malobali had sat up and asked for a drink
of water. Now they were feeding him a little corn porridge. He
looked at Romana.

"Where have you been, *iya*?" he asked plaintively.

His once-athletic body was only half its former size. His skin,
though always carefully oiled, was seamed with scars, some of
them not quite healed and oozing pus. The rather brutal face,
which so many women had turned to look at, was partly emaciated and partly swollen, as if it had been beaten at random by
the hammer of some mad blacksmith. But he was alive. Romana
gave thanks to the gods and clung to him.

These were undoubtedly the happiest days of their life. Romana had always dreamed of having Malobali to herself, something formerly impossible because of other women, drinking
companions and fellow roisterers. But now no one else wanted
him. She alone could take him in her arms, seek contact with
his body, follow unwearyingly his scarcely audible words. Anyone who went near their room heard a murmur like the gentle
music of flutes when the moon is high and the shepherds lie in
the grass by their flocks. They shrank from going in, and left food
and necessary medicines outside the door, tiptoeing away in wonder. Was there such a thing as perfect love? Could the hearts and
bodies of a man and a woman really merge into one?

A few weeks after the sacking of Hounjroto, while the people
were still digesting the good things Guezo had had distributed,
Sakpata, goddess of smallpox, waxed angry. None could say what
had caused her wrath. Had sacrifices been neglected? Had prayers
been skimped? If so, by whom? Whatever the cause, one fine
morning Sakpata grew furious and filled Abomey with her stink-

ing breath. She strode from the Okeadan quarter where the Nagos lived to the Ahuaga, Adjahito, Dota and Hetchilito quarters. She passed over the tomb of King Kpengla* and entered the royal palace, knocking down both guards and Amazons, who had been conversing peacefully, their muskets laid at their feet. She skirted around the "house of the pearls," built in honor of the dead kings, avoided the dwelling of Agasu the panther, ancestor of the Fon kings, and in a fit of temper burst into the throne room, where Guezo, surrounded by dignitaries and princes of the blood, was listening to the paeans of his praise singers. Prince Doba, one of Guezo's sons, fell mortally sick at the king's feet, his face suddenly red and swollen, his eyes full of putrid tears. Sakpata gazed at Guezo maliciously.

"I'll spare you this time," she hissed. "But I'll be back—you shan't escape me!"

Then she rushed out again to the populous districts of the town.

Molara, Birame's young wife, was in the Ajahi market when she heard that Sakpata had entered the town. She had just been buying palm oil, cassava leaves and smoked fish from the Wo marshes and was looking for some curds for Malobali. She immediately hurried back home, for when Sakpata was angry it was best to stay indoors, send visitors away and avoid the neighbors. In no time the markets were empty, and so was the square outside the Singboji palace, usually thronged with people waiting to see the princes and the king himself arrive for meetings. The streets filled with terrified folk seeking potions against the disease. Everywhere priests of the goddess could be seen hastening to her temples to try to appease her with prayer and sacrifices. But evidently they didn't succeed, for by the evening there were already two hundred and fifty corpses. Hardly had a family finished laying out one dead body than another member succumbed. There was no more room for graves in the compounds. Soon funeral mats, white sheep and poultry were no longer to be had. Some people went to nearby towns in the hope of getting them there and profiting from the sorrow of the bereaved. A scrawny chicken came to be worth two bags of cowries or three jars of palm oil.

*King of Dahomey from 1775 to 1789.

Sakpata raged even more furiously on the second day, and people began offering explanations. Sakpata was a Mahi goddess introduced by Guezo. Was she displeased because her people had been defeated by those of Abomey? Was she showing her dislike of the country to which her worship had been transplanted? Was she objecting to the king's having appointed Misaju as high priest? In short, sacrilegious thoughts were brewing.

In the Okeadan quarter everyone was anxious about Malobali. He had started to eat again and could walk a few steps unaided, but he was still vulnerable: at the goddess's first summons he might go and join the train of her followers. Romana gathered together a store of tamarind leaves and berries, reputed to be a sovereign remedy. Birame and Molara, who had just had a child, were less worried about their baby than about Malobali, and when someone recommended an infusion of mahogany roots as a preventative, Birame went all the way to Kana to get some.

Sakpata's following continued to grow. Every family in Abomey was in mourning, when suddenly Malobali had another attack of fever. Romana, panic-stricken, called in a doctor who had just saved a neighboring family's children. But he was unable to give an opinion, and merely prescribed plasters of baobab leaves. By the evening the fever had abated and everyone breathed again. But three days later it returned worse than before.

Romana, who had gone to draw water, heard a loud cry, and running back to the room found Malobali arched like a bow, his body eaten up with pustules that had descended as suddenly as locusts on a field. His eyes brimmed with milky tears. A few hours later he died in her arms.

What was Malobali thinking of as he went to Koutome? Of Ayoavi, whom he had raped, thus bringing down on himself the wrath of the earth? Was it not perhaps the earth avenging herself now through another goddess? Or was he thinking of Modupe, whom now he would never marry, who now would never give him sons. Or of Romana, the pearl, cast before the swine? No— he thought of the only two women who had ever really mattered in his life: Nya and Sira. What were they doing when he closed his eyes for the last time? Did they feel a sudden pang in their hearts and look up anxiously at the sky through the palmyras?

Or did they just go on their way through the sandy courtyards of their compounds, giving orders to their servants?

"Mother, I'm dying, and you don't know!"

At the very instant that Malobali's spirit left his body forever, Sakpata's ire ended. She had raged and swept through the town for forty-one days and nights, exhausting her priests. The number of her worshippers had tripled because of her show of strength. Her statues had been erected at all the gates of the city, and on the graves, now more numerous than the houses, her favorite foods were offered up.

Meanwhile, in the Singboji palace, apprehension reigned. Had not Sakpata promised to come back for King Guezo himself? The royal antechamber was constantly filled with priests trying to predict when she would return. All day they cast their palm kernels on their divining boards, but nothing was revealed to them.

CHAPTER

10

After Malobali's death Ayodele lost interest in everything. She was just thinking of dying when she realized she was pregnant. A child! The treasure she had hoped for in vain all through her marriage to Malobali was now being bestowed on her after his death. She remembered the words of the *babalawo* she had consulted years ago. He had concluded the interview by saying, 'Olubunmi,' which means 'God will provide.' So that was the name she gave the child. What irony, that God should afflict her with one hand and favor her with the other. However, she was a Christian, and accepted it. She endured her pregnancy bravely. But for a woman like her, children are not enough to give meaning to life. Although we did everything we could, her spirit was yearning for Koutome and trying to get through its gates. One morning we found her dead on her mat. As she had no milk my wife Molara had been suckling the child, so we kept him, and when I decided to return to Segu I brought him back for you. He belongs to you."

Birame was silent for a moment, and nothing could be heard but the weeping of women and the sighs of men. But what cure is there for death but a child? The only one who did not share this feeling was Nya, who had just learned of the death of two of her sons. She lost control of herself: "What about the rest? My two sons' other children? What have you done with them?" she cried.

Diemogo signaled for her to be silent, but not unkindly, since a woman is never mistress of what she says, especially when she is suffering. Birame resumed his story.

"Ayodele's family was from Oyo. We thought it had been scattered in the religious strife there, the wars between the Muslim Fulani and the Yoruba. Then a man arrived in Ouidah, who was her uncle on her father's side—in other words, her father. He had been a slave in Jamaica, and after being enfranchised settled in Freetown. He was rich and said he could take charge of the three eldest boys. We could not stop him."

Nya threw herself down on the ground with all the other women. Diemogo was torn between the wish to show gratitude to a guest who had after all brought one child home, and sorrow at having lost three others.

"But why?" he asked Birame. "Why did you let him take them?"

Birame hung his head.

"Forgive me," he said. "I was anxious at the thought of this long journey, through countries fighting for slaves, and afraid what happened to Naba might happen again to his other sons. Olubunmi is only a baby, and Molara carries him on her back wherever she goes."

Perhaps for the first time it occurred to the family to take a look at the little boy. Not yet a year old, he was plump and chubby-cheeked and gazed seriously at them all, as if he realized how crucial a moment this was.

Then someone exclaimed: "But Olubunmi isn't a Bambara name!"

"What does his name matter?" said Diemogo soothingly. "The main thing is that he's alive."

Then, turning to Birame: "We've been unfair to you. We should be thanking you and showering you with presents instead of criticizing. But that's the usual fate of messengers—to be blamed for the bad news they bring."

Birame sighed.

"I'd have avoided it if I could, believe me," he said. "But it's the will of the gods."

The family council was gathered in the main courtyard of the compound. Diemogo sat in the middle, surrounded by the other

men of the family. The women were there too, grouped around
Nya, enveloping her in their sympathy. Was not she the chief
victim of this tragedy? What had she done to have to endure such
trials? But their pity was not unmitigated. Was she not holding
in her arms the child of her middle age, Kosa, a token of the gods'
goodwill? And how beautiful she was! All the sorrows she had
faced had left her eyes sunken and replaced the rather arrogant
brilliance of their youth with a gleam of affectionate indulgence
toward other people's follies. There were folds around her mouth.
But instead of making her look bitter they only added to the slight
weariness, generosity and benevolence of her expression.

Nya looked at Tiekoro as if inviting him to speak, for as yet
he had said nothing. He occupied a peculiar place in the family.
While Diemogo was the *fa*, the head appointed by the council,
Tiekoro was indisputably the family's spiritual guide. He had
emerged with credit from the ordeal of Nadie's suicide, for he
had acknowledged his share of responsibility and done open penance. He had gone to Hamdallay, the capital of Macina, to discuss with Cheikou Hamadou the possibility of promoting Islam
in the kingdom of Segu, and this had lent him an aura of wisdom
and efficiency. To crown it all he had performed the pilgrimage
to Mecca the previous year, and on the return journey had stopped
in Sokoto, where the sultan had lavished honors upon him and
given him a wife. The whole clan was now proud of having a son
famous all over the world.

Tiekoro stood up. His prestige was increased by the magnif-
icence of his dress—a silk tunic and trousers with a richly embroidered bolero; a heavy turban, one end of which he often drew
over his face and over which he had thrown a white scarf. He
joined his hands together and turned to Birame.

"Far from criticizing you," he said, "I thank you, and ask all
the family to join me in so doing. Have you not brought the best
of news? Is not death a cause for celebration? Does not only a
heathen lament our fleshly fate, forgetting the joy of the soul,
the lamp of the body, when it merges with the light of the divine?
There is no god but God . . ."

As he spoke, Tiekoro's voice gradually swelled until it
drowned all other sounds: the crackle of burning branches, the
rustle of leaves disturbed by the wind, the bleating of sheep in

their fold. As he listened to his brother, Siga felt a lump form in his throat and rise up to burst in his mouth, filling it with the bitter taste of hatred. The hypocrite! The hypocrite! Everyone knew it was his cruelty and injustice that had driven Malobali out of the compound, forcing him into the hazards that had ended in his death. And yet here he was, showing not the slightest remorse, sermonizing away and explaining everything to the greater glory of God. What sort of a god was it that asked a mother to rejoice in the death of her sons? Siga would have liked to take Nya in his arms and say: "Weep, beloved mother—there is no more light in the house, and the sweet birds of happiness have flown. Weep, but do not forget I am here beside you."

But Siga was honest enough to admit it wasn't only what Tiekoro said that irritated him, but also the way everyone looked at his brother. Especially the women, and his own wife in particular. In fervent admiration, as if the gods themselves had decided to visit the earth and sweep through it in dazzling procession. Couldn't they see what an affected rascal he was?

Now Birame was standing up and symbolically handing Olubunmi over to Diemogo, who lifted him up over his head. He was a beautiful child. But the Yoruba blood added to his father's Fulani blood helped to make him look quite foreign already. Molara, who had suckled him for ten months but whom no one had asked what she thought about it all, was weeping quietly. Birame rebuked her in a low voice. Why was she lamenting when their journey had ended happily and the little orphan had been restored to his own family?

At a sign from Nya the slaves brought in bowls of *dolo* and threw fresh logs on the fire. Then the women withdrew, leaving the men to talk and drink among themselves. Birame was soon assailed with questions.

"Did you say Dahomey?"

"Did you say there are lots of whites there?"

"And Fulani? Are there Fulani there?"

"And Muslims? And mosques?"

Curiosity took over. Soon the extraordinary adventures of Naba and Malobali would only be a couple of exotic elements in the general family heritage.

Siga said nothing. He had scarcely known Malobali, as most

of his adolescence had been spent in Fez. Back in Segu, he had
found him in rebellion against his elder brother, but Siga himself
had taken no part in these quarrels. How he regretted it now!
Perhaps he might have prevented Malobali from setting out on
the adventures whose tragic end now plunged the family into
mourning! But they were all responsible, all of them! It had been
unfair of him to blame only Tiekoro.

Tiekoro began questioning Birame. "Do you think the main
danger in Dahomey comes from the whites?" he asked. "How is
that? Is it because of their religion? Or do they have political
ambitions?"

Birame was a simple soul and quite incapable of answering
such questions. Tiekoro was obviously taking pleasure in his intellectual superiority. Siga was sickened and looked away.

Contrary to what Siga thought, Tiekoro was suffering tor-
tures. He now felt responsible for Naba's and Malobali's deaths
as well as Nadie's. He would have liked to throw himself on the
ground and howl like a woman at a funeral to rid himself of his
anguish and remorse. But the personality he had adopted years
ago, that of a sage preoccupied by God alone, clung to him. He
couldn't stop himself from saying the words, making the gestures
and adopting the attitudes of his double. In reality, who knew
what was going on in his mind?

His whole life was one long dialogue with Nadie. Sometimes
he would accuse her of not having trusted him, not having waited
for the pride that clouded his spirit to disperse. Then he would
beg her to forgive him and assure him of her love. And now here
were two more shades come to join the first and assail him in
their turn. In his distress, he went over to Diemogo and said:
"Shouldn't we let Malobali's mother know?"

Diemogo was vexed. Once again Tiekoro was cutting the
ground from under his feet. For shouldn't he himself have thought
of it? His irritation made him morose.

"How do we know where she is?" he answered grudgingly.

Tiekoro shrugged.

"It shouldn't be difficult to find out," he said. "We know she
lives in Macina and that she remarried. Her husband's a man

called Amadou Tassirou who's quarreled with Cheikou Hamadou over the brotherhoods. He belongs to the Tijaniya and Cheikou Hamadou belongs to the Qadriya."

Even now Tiekoro couldn't help being pedantic and subtly showing Diemogo how ignorant he was about the questions that divided the world around him.

Diemogo looked down to hide his expression.

"And who do you advise me to send?"

"I would undertake the mission myself," said Tiekoro.

Diemogo stared at him in astonishment.

"You mean you'd leave your *zawiya*?"*

"I'll only be gone a few weeks. I have to be away in any case— the Mansa's asked me to go and talk again to Cheikou Hamadou in Hamdallay."

Until that morning Tiekoro had thought of refusing the mission. He had changed his mind because he saw in it an unexpected opportunity to exorcise his remorse and helplessness. He would be able to approach Sira, talk to her about the dead Malobali, act the part of a comforter.

"When are you thinking of leaving?" asked Diemogo.

"Tomorrow morning," he answered.

Diemogo watched him go with feelings akin to hatred. Tiekoro always came between Nya and himself. For a while he'd hoped their son Kosa would bring them together. But alas, no. Nya never forgot that she was Tiekoro's mother first, and only his interests and whims mattered. She had insisted on his being allowed to start his *zawiya*. Walls had to be knocked down to make room for it, and parts of the courtyards had to be altered to accommodate the students who kept streaming in from all over the kingdom. There were now no fewer than a hundred or so children droning out prayers from early in the morning, scribbling on tablets and singing of their faith in Islam. If only they contributed to the expenses they entailed! But no, Tiekoro thought it scandalous to ask any payment for teaching the word of the true God. So until the fields they cultivated brought in harvests, the Traore family had to feed them! Feed that bunch of heretics! Had Tiekoro forgotten the Muslims were their ene-

---

*Koranic school for teaching and meditation.

mies? But whenever Diemogo tried to raise the question Tiekoro would stop him disdainfully.

"God provides for plants and all creation to flourish," he would say. "He will never let us want for anything!"

Didn't Nya realize the presence of the *zawiya* was enough to anger the gods and the ancestors and make them unleash the most dreadful events on the family? Perhaps poor Malobali had paid with his life for his elder brother's apostasy and the family's culpable tolerance of it! Once again Diemogo told himself to exert his authority and bring the matter of the *zawiya* before the family council.

Meanwhile Tiekoro was on his way to the Mansa's palace to tell the king he was leaving for Hamdallay the following day.

The Bambara and Fulani armies had not confronted one another directly for some years. But news had recently arrived that the famous Macina lancers had leapt onto their horses once more and conquered Timbuktu. The Fulani were forcing the Tuareg to become sedentary and cultivate the land, and the rest of the inhabitants to pay heavy tribute. There were revolting stories of how merchants were compelled to hand over their gold and other valuables; of even Muslim women being raped; of herdsmen being held for ransom. This created a new situation in the region. What would become of the commercial relations between Segu and Timbuktu? What officials had Cheikou Hamadou caused to be appointed; who were the new civil and military leaders? These were the questions for which Da Monzon wanted Tiekoro to seek the answers.

The palace guards knew Tiekoro and lowered their spears for him to pass through. Tiekoro never entered the palace without remembering the humiliating fashion in which his father Dousika had been dismissed from the king's council. In a sense he had already avenged him. So why this bitterness still in his heart? He went through the series of seven antechambers to the room where Da Monzon received private visitors.

Da Monzon had grown very old. After nearly twenty years on the throne he looked worn out by too many military exploits and too many weighty decisions concerning Segu's relationships with Kaarta and its attitude toward Islam, the slave trade, and the recently expanded commercial dealings with the north. It was whispered that the main reason for his aging was his excessive love of women and his attentions to his eight hundred wives and concubines. He was sitting on a red leather chair with legs carved in the shape of lions, which, like his black velvet slippers embroidered with golden flowers, he had bought from a trader on the coast.

After bowing and paying his respects, Tiekoro came straight to the point.

"Master of energies," he said, "I leave tomorrow to carry out your decisions."

Da Monzon was astonished.

"I am happy to hear it," he said. "But what made you change your mind? As recently as yesterday you were undecided."

Tiekoro summarized Malobali's story for the king, then added: "So I shall take advantage of my journey to go and inform his mother, Sira the Fulani."

There was a profound silence. Even the musicians put down their flutes and poised their drumsticks. What could be worse than meeting your death in a foreign land? How terrible was the fate of the Traore family! What crimes had they committed to deserve it? Those who disliked Tiekoro were inclined to think his conversion had brought down a curse upon his family. But his gifts were needed and such dislike could not be expressed openly. Tiekoro was sensitive to this atmosphere heavy with stifled and half-articulated thoughts. He would have liked to be loved, and he was only being used. He would have liked to be admired, and he was only feared.

Da Monzon broke the silence.

"Tomorrow I shall send presents to your family," he said. "Tell Diemogo we all share his grief."

"What do you want?" asked Siga roughly when he recognized Tiekoro.

Tiekoro didn't let himself be put off.

"I wanted to tell you I'm leaving tomorrow for Macina and shall be away for several weeks," he said.

Siga shrugged, indicating it was all the same to him, and Tiekoro looked at him sardonically, as if greatly amused by this attitude.

"I could be of great help to you," he said.

"How?" answered Siga.

Relations between Tiekoro and Siga had never been good, but by now they had reached rock bottom. For one thing, Siga was racked with jealousy and resentment. While Tiekoro had had no difficulty in opening his *zawiya* in the family compound, Siga's project of starting a tannery had been rejected with horror. Were the Traore, nobles born to cultivate the land, to imitate the *garanke*, men from the caste of leather workers? Was Siga mad? Not content with having brought back the foreign woman who looked down on everybody, did he now want to dishonor the family? Then there had been the painful affair after which Siga had left the compound to go and settle on some family land at the eastern end of the town. As he had kept the real reasons for his departure secret, he was regarded as an ungrateful son, and Nya lost no opportunity of comparing him with his elder brother. He tried to drive these thoughts from his mind as Tiekoro leaned toward him.

"You don't understand," Tiekoro said. "The important thing is to impress other people. To make yourself respected. Feared."

"Keep your sermons for the pupils in your *zawiya*," exclaimed Siga, losing patience. "But is that what you really say to them? Don't you talk to them just of charity and love?"

Tiekoro put out his hand in a soothing gesture.

"Siga," he said, "I want to help you. Sincerely. Cheikou Hamadou has just destroyed Timbuktu. The influential Moroccan families have fled. Trade is disorganized. Caravans no longer leave for the Maghreb because there's no more gold or cowries. Isn't now the right moment for a man with some ingenuity to step in and make his mark—to supply all the articles that every Muslim needs?"

Siga shrugged.

"Let's not talk about it, Tiekoro," he said. "You know what the family thinks of my ideas!"

"All right then," answered Tiekoro contemptuously, "go on doing what you hate—farming. Perhaps that's all you're good for!"

He got up to leave, but Siga held him back.

"How could you help me?" he asked.

"All I need do is mention you to the people I know in Ham-dallay and other places," said Tiekoro, "and orders will come flooding in. And money will bring respect!"

This forthrightness shocked Siga. But it was no more than the truth. All those years of apprenticeship in Fez; all those plans and dreams! Instead he had become a farmer again, sweating and toiling in the field allocated to him by the family council, too poor to employ slaves. He looked his brother straight in the eye.

"What are you trying to make up to me for?" he asked.

"You know very well I've nothing to reproach myself with!" replied Tiekoro arrogantly.

It was true! On one score at least he was completely innocent. It wasn't his fault if he struck Fatima as the only civilized person in this "den of fetishists and barbarians." It was religion that had drawn her to him at first, but gradually she had come to entertain other feelings, led on by her inherited taste for amorous intrigue. Siga remembered the note that had been handed to him one morning in Fez: "Are you blind? Can't you see I love you?"

Well, she'd sent other notes to Tiekoro! Perhaps she didn't really have adultery in mind—perhaps she just wanted to revive the dangerous games she missed from earlier days. If she'd been a Bambara girl Siga wouldn't have hesitated to send her back to her family, but she was a foreigner who had left her own people far away and come here for love of him. Wasn't it his own fault if she was morose and disappointed? Was that the future he had promised her? Ever since their arrival in Segu, Siga had seen his birthplace through Fatima's eyes and regretted not having taken fuller advantage of the splendors of Fez. "A town to which the dove has lent its collar and the peacock its plumage," an old man used to sing at Bab El-Guissa, and the crowd hung on his words. Was it the fate of every human being to long for what was far away?

He clapped his hands to summon a slave girl and ordered some mint tea. As she went to make it he turned to his brother.

"Very well," he said. "But if you do speak to the people you know and get me some orders for slippers, how am I going to make them?"

How ashamed he felt, asking advice from someone who had wounded him so often! Tiekoro put on a typical air of self-importance.

"You've got a perfect right to ask Diemogo for your share of gold and cattle. The cattle will provide you with hides. The gold will pay your workers' wages."

"You know what he'll say," answered Siga, discouraged again. "A Traore becoming a *garanke*, a trader!"

"No, he'll agree this time," said Tiekoro. "This evening I'll speak to our mother."

Again Siga felt resentful. How blind and unfair mother love is! All Tiekoro had done was take the trouble to be born first, and whatever harm he caused—and he really did cause trouble—everything he did found favor in Nya's sight. And he, Siga, would never be anything but the son of the woman who threw herself down the well!

The slave came back with a copper tray and some little glasses painted with flowers. Manufactured goods from Europe and North Africa were finding their way little by little into Segu. It was not unusual to see well-born young men in boots bought from some trader. Many families had silver dishes in their huts, and the Mansa proudly displayed to his friends a service of fine Chinese porcelain that he never actually used. Tiekoro was right. One ought to take advantage of the disruption caused by the capture of Timbuktu by those fanatics from Macina.

Siga's old dreams rose again from their ashes. He saw himself bare to the waist, steeping, dyeing, cutting out skins, giving orders to a crowd of slaves. He would have a shop, too, selling not only leather goods but also silks and brocades. Yes, he had lacked perseverance; he had yielded without protest to the family conservatism. But the world around the nobles in Segu was changing, and changes were to be seen even within the family itself. Naba had been taken to Brazil. Malobali had gone with the caravans to the Ashanti kingdom and found death in Abomey, a journey of days and nights away from home. Both of them had left sons who only half belonged to the clan, and who nurtured alien desires and aspirations. And perhaps, after all, wasn't Tiekoro the most intelligent among them? He'd foreseen the inevitable victory of Islam and become not only its first convert but also one of its chief propagators. A clever bet! Siga almost sympathized with his brother, and, looking at him covertly, was struck by his expression of suffering. The light from the shea butter lamp cast a halo around his face, outlining features hollowed by fasting. Every day he grew more like one of the zealots in Timbuktu who never went out in the street without ostentatiously telling their beads, and who said their prayers wherever they happened to be to demonstrate that God must not be kept waiting. But his huge black eyes, now still, now darting, destroyed the harmony of his countenance. You couldn't meet them. They gave a frightening hint of what was going on inside him.

PART FOUR

THE FERTILE BLOOD

C H A P T E R

1

Tiekoro sent for his son Muhammad.

"Cheikou Hamadou does us a great honor," he said. "He's written asking me to send you to him to complete your religious education."

Muhammad occupied a special position in Tiekoro's household and in the whole compound. He was his first male child borne of Maryem, the wife the sultan of Sokoto had bestowed on him after his return from Mecca. She had given birth to three daughters and Tiekoro had begun to despair of having a worthy heir. For although he loved them in his own way, he couldn't forget the status of Ahmed Dousika and Ali Sunkalo, Nadie's children. After all they were the sons of a slave. As for Maryem, she was related to a sultan and had been brought up amid wealth, luxury and high living, so Muhammad was almost a royal child.

Ever since he'd been born, however, Muhammad had been the butt of all the hatred and jealousy people dared not express toward his father, and he was a sensitive, introverted boy who clung to his mother's skirts. The thought of being parted from her made him so desperate he plucked up the courage to protest.

"But aren't the Fulani of Macina our enemies?" he asked.

Tiekoro glared.

"Say that again and you'll regret it, you wretch!" he cried.

"Aren't they our coreligionists, our brothers in Allah, the only God?"

The boy dared say no more. But he knew how much the Bambara hated the "red monkeys," the "blackeners of tablets," the "*bimi*," as the Bambara called the Fulani who had so often humiliated them.

"When must I go?" he stammered, fighting back his tears.

"When I tell you to," answered his father.

As the boy turned away, hugging his tunic around him and outlining his slender body, Tiekoro's heart smote him. He called him back, tempted to throw off his usual coldness and put his arms around him.

"It's for your own good I'm accepting this offer," he would say quietly. "Islam will conquer—it's already triumphant. Soon the world will belong to those who can write and read books. Our people, despite all their human virtues, will be regarded as backward and ignorant."

But as the boy came back toward him all he managed to say was, "When you're in Hamdallay, go and see your grandmother Sira."

"Have we got relations in Macina, then?" asked Muhammad, staring. He knew little of the complexities of family genealogy.

Tiekoro nodded. As he sat down again on his mat his second wife, Adam, brought him his morning gruel. After Nadie's death he had greeted the breaking off of his engagement to Princess Sounou Saro with joy and gratitude. His only desire was to live alone and never to take a woman in his arms again, spending the rest of his life in expiation for his sin. Then the sultan of Sokoto had given him Maryem. And Cheikou Hamadou had given him Adam, a girl belonging to his own family. There was also the relationship that had somehow started up between him and Yankadi, the slave who was bringing up Nadie's sons! And so, without meaning to, he found himself the master of two wives and a concubine and the father of about fifteen children! But each new birth in his household, far from giving him joy, filled him with shame, because it illustrated the abyss between aspirations and instincts. That was why he now looked with irritation at Adam's swelling belly, and told her the gruel was too runny.

Tiekoro got up and went to his *zawiya*. It now numbered two hundred pupils, all from the most aristocratic families of Segu, each one calculating that it might be wise to give at least one son some knowledge of Islam.

Every day followed the same pattern. First the reading of the Koran, then the commentaries, either legal or theological. After the midday meal came recitation from the Holy Book, ending only for the afternoon prayer. Then the boys went and worked in the millet fields or the kitchen gardens they tended on the Traore family's land. Tiekoro, who had always refused to work on the land, didn't go with them, but began to tell his prayer beads and then went to the mosque where he discussed religion with the imam until it was time for the last prayer of the day. Then Tiekoro would go back to the compound where, before returning to his own hut, he would call on Nya, who consulted with him about all that was going on: betrothals, marriages, name-giving ceremonies and dowries.

Tiekoro enjoyed those hours spent with Nya in the peace of the evening. Now that he'd lost Nadie, Nya was the only person who loved him without reserve. And when he talked to his mother he felt he was talking to Nadie, for not only did he not love Maryem and Adam, but he had the impression they saw through him and despised him. They thought he was nothing but a hypocrite, a hypocrite greedy for honor and glory, for whom invoking the name of Allah was just another way of attracting attention and whose piety only concealed ambition!

As he entered the *zawiya* the youngest pupils, who despite the rigorous routine of prayers they had to follow were after all only little boys, were shouting, chasing one another and rolling in the sand in imitation of battles and violent sports. When they saw him they all froze. Those who were on the ground got up and hastily dusted off their *boubous*. Rows were formed; dozens of pairs of eyes were fixed on the ground. Tiekoro hated the impression he made on the youngsters; sometimes, in his exasperation, he would cuff the cheeks, forehead or eyelids of those who'd been too docile. He went into the part of the enclosure set aside for the second class and sat down on his mat. One by one the children came and sat around him.

Muhammad, his eyes swollen, was among the last. He'd prob-ably run to his mother to mingle his tears with hers. It was cer-

tainly time to part him from Maryem—she was making him soft.
Time to make a man of him! Of course the family would be
annoyed with him for making a favorite of one of his own children. He could already imagine their comments and the resentment of Ahmed and Ali, whom he'd married off to girls of good
birth but not much wealth and who had to labor in the family
fields. He thought of Adam's anxiety about her own sons. But
above all Tiekoro was concerned about the political consequences of his decision. Tensions between the Fulani and the
Bambara were getting worse. The Mansa talked of launching a
major offensive against Macina, and was getting in stores of guns
and powder and urging an alliance with the king of Kaarta. People
would look askance on his sending his son to Macina. But could
he refuse such an honor to his family? Wasn't it a recognition of
his—admittedly distant—relationship with the sultan of Sokoto?

Coming back to earth, Tiekoro scrutinized the anxious little
faces turned toward him.

"How many of you have followed the advice I gave you yesterday?" he asked.

The class stirred. Obviously no one knew what he meant.

Then Alfa Mande Diarra stood up.

"I did, master," he said. "I wrote the divine name of Allah
on the wall opposite my bed so that it would be the first thing
I see when I wake up."

Alfa Mande belonged to the royal family. He was a son of a
brother of the late Mansa Da Monzon. Tiekoro gave him special
treatment, exempting him from working on the land and giving
him two days a week off to go and see his father in Kirango in
the vain hope that Alfa Mande would attract other royal pupils.
None of Mansa Tiefolo's sons had followed, and Tiekoro had
never been granted the audience he asked for with the new king.
Gone were the days when the late Da Monzon used to consult
him about everything and send him as his emissary to Moslem
cities! People now thought about nothing but war! Didn't they
realize that even if they killed the Fulani of Macina down to the
last man, Islam had still come to the region to stay? To take root
like an everlasting tree that ignored the rigors of the dry season
and remained green when all the surrounding bush turned yellow! What dense and dull fellows they were!

Tiekoro congratulated Alfa Mande, who was undoubtedly one of his most brilliant pupils, and went on: "Yes, write the divine name on your walls. When you get up, speak it with fervor from the depths of your souls, so that it may be the first name to issue from your lips or to strike your ears. And when you go to bed . . ."

As he spoke he caught Muhammad's eye, and it seemed to him the boy saw through him, clearly recognizing his hypocrisy and vanity. As if to numb his own thoughts he continued more loudly: "If you persevere, the light contained in the secret of those four letters will eventually be shed over you, and a spark from the divine essence will inflame and irradiate your hearts. . . ."

But in fact there was nothing in Muhammad's look that need have troubled Tiekoro: he was too young and too respectful to think of judging his father. Others did it for him. Tiefolo, Diemogo's eldest son, was one of them.

Tiefolo never forgot it was he who had gone to find Tiekoro in Jenne after Dousika's death, and he never ceased regretting it. He had meant well, endeavoring to fulfill the dead man's wishes and promote the unity of the family. If only he'd known he was simply bringing about the ruin and humiliation of his own father!

He couldn't bear seeing Diemogo reduced to the role of Tiekoro's factotum. He couldn't bear the presence of the *zawiya*, and listening to all those litanies in praise of a god his own people didn't believe in. His life had become nothing but a feverish speculation as to how to rid the family of Tiekoro. When his first wife, *bara muso* Tenegbe, came and told him what she had heard, he looked at her with incredulity.

"What's this you're telling me?" he said.

Tenegbe didn't answer. She was a very beautiful woman from Kaarta, related through her mother to the late Mansa Fula-fo Bo, "Bo the Fulani killer," still well remembered by all. Tiefolo thought Tenegbe's hatred of Islam and consequently of Tiekoro must be misleading her, and he shrugged.

"Impossible!" he said. "He has no respect for our family or our kingdom, but he wouldn't do that!"

"You'll believe me when you see Muhammad on the horse taking him to Hamdallay," said Tenegbe simply, and left.

Tiefolo, perplexed, went out into the courtyard. The end of the rainy season was approaching. The leaves of the mahoganies and tamarinds were bright green and the women's kitchen gardens were in flower. Soon the walls of the huts would have to be replastered and the roofs repaired. It was the time of year when every healthy man feels his blood coursing joyfully through his heart. A few weeks from now, when the work in the compound was finished, Tiefolo would go hunting in the bush. But instead of the joyful anticipation he should have felt he was full of anguish and exasperation. He strode toward his father's hut, determined to act for once.

Diemogo was giving orders to the head slave about some field work. As Tiekoro knew nothing about such things, it was the only area in which Diemogo enjoyed a certain amount of independence.

Tiefolo went over to his father, waited respectfully until he deigned to turn to him, returned his greetings, then said: "Is it true, what I hear? That he's going to send Muhammad to live with our enemies in Macina?"

Diemogo shrugged helplessly.

"So Nya tells me," he said. "He's got her so confused she thinks it a great honor for our family."

"An honor?" cried Tiefolo. "People will think we are traitors and spies!"

Spies . . . as he spoke, a plan began to form in Tiefolo's mind. Spies? Abruptly he took leave of his father and went home. He changed into more elegant clothes and left the compound.

Segu's opulence at that period made it easy to see why Cheikou Hamadou's Fulani were so anxious to get their hands on it. Of course the "red monkeys" only talked about the propagation of Islam, but everyone knew they wanted to seize Segu's wealth and control its markets. The Bambara, driven out of Jenne by religious persecution, had brought back with them new techniques in masonry, and the houses now looked like veritable palaces, with tall geometrical panels over the doors and regular friezes around the walls. Every market bore witness to the diversity of trade in the kingdom: there was rice, millet, mead, cotton, perfumes, incense, hides, dried and smoked fish and imported goods so plentiful they had become quite common. A few years earlier the women had snapped up these things; now they no longer glanced at them. Only gunpowder, weapons and brandy were sought after these days, but their sale was strictly controlled by the Mansa.

Tiefolo crossed the square surrounding the royal palace. He knew it was the day for the king to receive visitors, and no one could forbid him access. Some workmen were busy on the outer walls, daubing them with ochre paint made of mud and kaolin, stopping up cracks and pointing up the friezes. The royal weavers were installed in the second courtyard, and long white snakes of cotton cloth seemed to be attacking the looms. A little way off the slaves were gathered around a jester drumming on gourds with ringed fingers. Tiefolo frowned. Another Fulani? The red monkeys were everywhere!

Mansa Tiefolo had succeeded his brother Da Monzon, who had continued to taunt him even after his death, for Tiefolo was less handsome, less strong, less admired by women than he, and never managed to be more successful on the battlefield. He was lying on his oxhide, propped by one elbow on a leather pillow decorated with arabesques. He was listening, bored, to a griot expounding a problem being put forward by two plaintiffs. His keen eye lighted on Tiefolo Traore as he entered.

"Hey," he called mockingly, "isn't this Daddy-Mosque's brother honoring us with his presence?"

For such was Tiekoro's nickname.

Tiefolo did not answer, but lowered his brow into the dust, waiting to be asked to speak. But as his turn approached he grew more and more doubtful about what he proposed to do. Shouldn't he have told his father about it first and got his consent? But no— Diemogo would only have asked him to call a family council, which once again, under Nya's influence, would have decided in Tiekoro's favor.

Was it right to bring family quarrels before the king? Yet this was more than a family matter. Tiekoro's decision about Muhammad might put the interests of the whole kingdom in danger. Tiefolo was still debating with himself when Makan Diabate, the chief griot, called his name. Tiefolo, taken by surprise, could only stammer to begin with, but gradually he managed to state his case.

He was well aware of the respect due to an elder brother. That was why he had accepted Tiekoro's conversion, together with the new ways and ideas it entailed. It had been more difficult for him to accept two foreign, Fulani sisters-in-law, one from Sokoto and the other from Macina. Harder still to accommodate himself to the transformation of the family compound into a place for impious meetings and prayers. And now his brother intended to send one of his sons to Hamdallay, to the house of Cheikou Hamadou himself! So, he was wondering, might not his brother be a spy employed by a foreign power? How else was one to explain his close and privileged links with the kingdom's chief enemy? As Segu's interest had to come first, he had decided to confide his anxieties and suspicions to the Master of Energies and of the Waters.

As Tiefolo spoke everyone admired his bearing and the nobility of his features and tended to take his side, for Tiekoro's demeanor was disapproved of by all. But opinions were divided. Should brother denounce brother? Couldn't the matter be resolved under the palaver tree in the family compound?

When Tiefolo finished there was a long silence. A warm breeze came in through the openings of the reception room and music could be heard from one of the palace courtyards.

"Namesake," the Mansa said at last—for his name too was Tiefolo, "this is a very delicate matter, and I realize it must be hard for you to talk about it . . ."

As he spoke the king scrutinized Tiefolo, trying to figure out his motives. Was he really concerned about Segu? Didn't people say Tiekoro had taken away all Diemogo's authority, and might not the son be defending the interests of his father? If Tiekoro was convicted of spying and punished, who would benefit? And yet Tiefolo's face radiated sincerity. He wasn't trying to harm his brother—or at least that wasn't his only motive. He was really distressed, and in his helplessness he was appealing to his sovereign as a last resort. But the Mansa wasn't a man to act on impulse.

"Don't oppose him," he said. "Let the boy go to Hamdallay. If anyone in the family is tempted to object, keep them quiet.

We shall see that he is watched, and shall find out what he's hiding."

Mande Diarra, a prince of the blood and a councillor with great influence at court, spoke: "I know Tiekoro Traore and dislike him as much as the rest of you. But why should he betray Segu, *fama*? What can the Fulani offer him that we do not have here? Land? He has plenty already. Gold . . ."

Tiefolo interrupted, paying involuntary homage to his brother.

"If Tiekoro is a traitor," he said, "it is certainly not for material advantage. It can only be a matter of religion. He sincerely believes his Allah is the only true God and that it is his mission to glorify Him."

After leaving the palace Tiefolo went out of his way to call in at Siga's compound. To stop his wife Fatima from carrying out her threat to return to Fez, Siga had built a house that people were always coming to look at, making a detour on their way to the market where medicinal plants were sold. It was made of clay brick like the other houses in the town, but built with its back to the street, turned entirely in on itself around a circular courtyard with a fountain. Each of its two storeys had a gallery with arches and colonnades running around it and the main rooms opening on to it. The floors of the courtyards, galleries and some of the rooms were covered with fine white sand that Siga had brought at great expense from a special creek on the Bani River. But most surprising of all was the tannery, built onto one side of the house. For a whole dry season Siga could be seen, bareheaded like his slaves, digging vats and pits with round stone borders and drainage channels. Nearby were two sheds for drying and storing the hides. For these Siga had come to an arrangement with the butchers but as the hides were untreated he had to salt them himself and steep them in a warm bath to swell them slightly before washing them over and over again. Unfortunately this impressive system had produced no results! Had Siga miscalculated the slope of the ground in relation to the vats and pits? Had he underestimated the difficulty of getting regular supplies of hides, or the opposition of the *garanke*, who declined to cooperate with a man who did not belong by heredity to their profession? Whatever the reason, Siga's tannery produced neither slippers nor boots nor belts nor harness. One year when salt was so scarce in Segu that the Bambara women used ashes from the fire to season the food, whole stocks of hides were hopelessly spoiled, and the stench spread through the streets of the town as far as the palace gates.

After that, Siga made what living he could from selling a few slippers to a merchant in Jenne, and occasionally sending brocades to his former master in Fez. He also farmed a field that the family had allotted him at Tiekoro's insistence.

Tiefolo never went into Siga's fine house without feeling he was entering the temple of a capricious god who had refused at the last moment to grant his worshippers' prayers. Everything possible had been done to please him—the altars covered with milk, fruit and blood, the ritual words pronounced, and the beating of the drums meticulously carried out. But the god had not come down. Why? Fatima was in the patio with two slave girls who were also Siga's concubines, as he was too poor to have any more wives. It seemed to Tiefolo she had grown even fatter, and although he was used to thinking of corpulence as a sign of prosperity and beauty in women, he did think she had carried it far enough. She looked at him out of gray eyes still beautiful despite the puffiness of her features.

"He's in bed," she said in a plaintive tone. "He's had a fever since the morning."

Her Bambara was still atrocious after nearly ten years: it was a symbol of her refusal to become integrated into her husband's country. Then she went back to the stuffed dates her brother sent her regularly, together with henna and other cosmetics, as if they were things one couldn't possibly do without. Tiefolo went up to his brother's room. Siga had aged prematurely and looked at least ten years older than Tiekoro, as if the latter's youth had been preserved by his life of prayer and fasting. Siga's hair was going gray. A ragged gray beard covered his cheeks, and he had the bloodshot eyes of a habitual *dolo* drinker.

"I thought you'd gone hunting!" he said in surprise. "Don't tell me the antelopes and warthogs haven't called you away yet?"

"There are things more important than hunting," the other

replied. "It's time order and authority were restored in the family."

Then he told him about Tiekoro and what he had decided for Muhammad. Siga only shrugged.

"Hasn't he the right to do as he likes with his own son?" he said.

He saw what Tiefolo was getting at. But he was tired. His life seemed to him like the canoe of a Somono fisherman moored on the banks of the Joliba, when the waters rose again after the rains. A slight pull of the current freed it from the mud, and it gently zigzagged downriver, brushing against beds of reeds and getting momentarily caught in oyster beds. When he remembered the dreams and illusions that had enlivened his days and nights in Timbuktu and Fez, he wondered what had become of the young man he once was. Defeated. Destroyed. Dead, just as dead as Naba and Malobali. Of course he could always try to find excuses: no one had understood or supported him; his wife had not come up to his expectations. But he knew that the real cause lay in a mysterious flaw in his blood. After a fit of coughing he said: "Don't count on me to help you destroy Tiekoro. You won't succeed, anyway. The gods are on his side."

Tiefolo laughed.

"Gods!" he said. "What gods?"

CHAPTER

2

The town of Hamdallay—whose name meant "Praise to God"—was founded in 1819, and masons from Jenne took three years to build it. It was divided into eighteen districts and surrounded by a wall with four gates. Above it floated a sort of mist, made up of the breath of the faithful praising Allah. There were no fewer than six hundred Koranic schools in the town, where the pupils were instructed in the hadith, theology recitation and spiritual exercises; auxiliary subjects like grammar and syntax were taught in separate colleges. Hamdallay was a very austere place. Policing was in the hands of seven marabouts, and anyone found in the streets an hour after the last prayer of the day was arrested and had his identity checked. Each person thus detained had to recite his family tree and give the date of his conversion to Islam before explaining why he was in Hamdallay. Hygiene and cleanliness were rigorously maintained. Urinating in the street was forbidden, as was spilling the blood of slaughtered beasts. Women selling milk had to cover their wares and have a bowl of water nearby in which to wash their hands.

Muhammad shuddered as he passed by the great tamarind tree near the north gate under which executions were carried out, and again as he went by the central prison and the place where other punishments were inflicted. The city inspired in him nothing but fear. The men with whom he had made the journey had told him Cheikou Hamadou's pupils lived on public charity, begging from door to door for their food, sleeping on the bare floor and never washing, as a sign of humility. The boy was terrified: he could already see himself crawling with fleas, bugs and other insects. A disciple took him to Cheikou Hamadou's compound and handed him over to the beautiful Adya, one of his wives.

Without knowing it Muhammad was going through the same suffering his father had once done in El-Hadj Baba Abou's courtyard in Timbuktu. But Cheikou Hamadou was not El-Hadj Baba Abou. Muhammad was introduced to a man of about fifty, quite tall, with a kindly, vivacious expression. He was very simply dressed in a tunic made of seven strips of cotton and tanned leather sandals, with a dark blue turban seven times the length of his forearm. He smiled at Muhammad.

"*As salam aleykum,*" he greeted him.

Muhammad lowered his eyes.

"*Wa aleyka salam. Bissimillahi,*" he replied.

"Do you speak Arabic?" Cheikou Hamadou asked him, still speaking very gently.

"A little, master," said Muhammad.

"'Master?' Call me father," he replied. "That's what I ought to be to you."

Muhammad had always associated piety with arrogance, and learning with severity on the weakness of others. How different this man was from his father! Was this the leader whose armies were feared in Bambouk, Kaarta and Mande, not to mention Segu? The only weapon he carried was his prayer beads. Muhammad fell on his knees.

"Father," he said, "may Allah grant I never disappoint your affection."

At that moment Abdulay, Cheikou Hamadou's younger son, entered.

"Take good care of this boy," said his father, turning toward him. "His father illuminates the name of Allah among the infidels in Segu. Without his efforts it would be a kingdom of darkness."

Then he indicated that the audience was over.

It was enough to dry Muhammad's tears and make him look to the future serenely. For the first time he realized he was the son of an important man, and he reproached himself for having feared him much more than he loved him. His father was a saint and he hadn't known it.

Meanwhile Abdulay was taking him to the western part of the compound, where the pupils lived. Some forty boys between the age of eleven and fifteen were in a kind of dormitory; all of them were painfully thin and had the tight shiny skin that goes with malnutrition. Their *boubous* were tattered and dirty, their feet bare. What struck Muhammad still more were the scratches and scars on their arms, legs and hands, as if there had been an epidemic of smallpox or mange. The words of his fellow travelers suddenly came back to him, and his anxiety returned. Abdulay introduced him briefly.

"Here's your brother Muhammad Traore. He's from Segu."

Then he left. When he must have been a good distance away there was a general uproar, the boys imitating all kinds of animals and dancing and skipping about wildly. You'd never have thought you were in a place devoted to teaching the word of God. One boy capered about obscenely in front of Muhammad, saying: "Traore from Segu—Bambara, eater of dogs and tainted meat, drinker and fornicator . . ."

What was he to do? Say he was only partly Bambara, that he was half Fulani, related to the sultan of Sokoto? But that would be tantamount to denying his father, and he couldn't do that. Should he fight? He was frail, and usually got the worst of it. So he said proudly: "What do you mean—a Bambara? Does Allah recognize race? I am a Muslim, your brother in Him."

A silence indicated that he had made his point. After a moment a boy of about his own height came over and introduced himself.

"I'm Alfa Guidado," he said.

His features were so delicate you wondered whether he wasn't a girl who to satisfy some whim had cut off her hair and dressed in boy's clothes. His skin was as fair as a Moor's; he had slanted, flashing eyes, full red lips and a beauty spot near the left corner of his mouth. His father was one of the seven marabouts responsible for policing the town, a man so pious he had freed himself from the need to eat several times a day and was satisfied with a bowl of curds once a week.

"Are you the son of Modibo Oumar Traore?" asked Alfa
Guidado.

Muhammad was taken aback. Was his father so very famous?

"Bori Hamsala isn't a bad chap," Alfa went on, "even if he
does make fun of people. He's always ready to share what he's
given to eat."

What he's given to eat? Muhammad pricked up his ears. Was
what he had been told true? Alfa looked at him with a kind of
pity.

"Don't you know," he said, "that while we're seeking God
we have to live by begging, no matter how rich our parents? The
days are over when your mother used to bring you a bowl of gruel,
and you slept on a nice clean mat under a thick blanket. Good-
bye ease, joy, pleasure! Our martyrdom is about to begin. But
what a martyrdom! And in what a cause!"

Meanwhile Hamdallay was in turmoil over a visitor quite
different from Muhammad Traore. This was El-Hadj Omar Saidou Tall, a Tukulor from Futa Toro. Five years earlier he had
been completely unknown, but now he came with his immense
reputation for saintliness and Koranic learning. He had made several pilgrimages to Mecca, visited Sokoto, lived for several years
in Cairo and been to the tombs of the prophets Abraham and
Jesus in Palestine. Everywhere he went he performed miraculous
cures. Why had he come to Hamdallay? Perhaps Cheikou Hamadou's fame had attracted him? Perhaps he had heard people
praise the administrative, fiscal and military organization of Macina, and had come to pay homage to a brother in Allah? But
Cheikou Amadou's entourage was still worried. Numerous
prophets were said to have predicted that El-Hadj Omar would
found an empire which would include Nioro, Medina, Segu,
Hamdallay and other cities at present free and proud. Hadn't the
Almami, the Fulani religious leader of the Fita, said: "On his own
he will build more mosques than you can imagine"?

Cheikou Hamadou himself was quite serene. He thought El-
Hadj Omar had come to meditate at the tomb of Saint Abd el-
Karim who had died the previous year while visiting Hamdallay.
Anyway, a man of God like himself was never troubled.

Soon after El-Hadj Omar's arrival Muhammad and Alfa were begging at the millet-straw fence surrounding the compound of Bourema Khalilou, member of the Grand Council, governor of Macina and one of the highest authorities concerning things in general. The maids filled the boys' bowls with *tatiri masina*, which made a nice change from the millet husks they usually got at the most pious houses! Muhammad was about to devour these unhoped-for dainties when Alfa stopped him.

"No!" he cried. "Don't you know you have to take it back to the refectory and share it with the others?"

During the weeks he had been in Hamdallay, Muhammad had been nothing but a hungry, perpetually empty stomach, rumbling with worms. Hunger prevented him from thinking, praying, sleeping. When he shut his eyes it was only to dream of the hot tasty dishes cooked by the women in the compound in Segu. He hadn't known then how well off he was! His mouth filled with bitter saliva that overflowed onto his chin and mingled with his tears. A hundred times he had been tempted to run away—to go back to Segu, to the warm shelter of Maryem's arms and his games with his younger brothers! Why should he go on suffering like this? One noon he had fallen down, overcome with hunger and the sun, and longed to die there like a dog, far away from home. What would Tiekoro say if they came and told him, "Your eldest son is dead"? Would he see then how harsh and unfair he had been?

Muhammad's trouble was having Alfa Guidado as his friend. If he had joined up in the same way with Bori Hamsala, Alkayda Sanfo or Samba Boubakari, who spent all their time thinking up ways of getting food, everything would have been different. But Alfa was as pure as he was handsome. He was like a balm made of musk, with a perfume that doesn't fade. A gift from God. The masters had to correct his tendency to exaltation and mysticism, but Cheikou Hamadou loved him and often sent for him to talk about religious matters. Just by looking at him Alfa made Muhammad feel ashamed of being trapped in the flesh, with a stomach, a belly and innards like the dogs forbidden the town and relegated to herding the flocks. Sometimes Alfa would hand Muhammad his bowl, saying: "Here, you have it—I don't need it."

But coming from him the words had no arrogance. He was simply stating a fact.

A shed had been put up behind Cheikou Hamadou's compound to act as a refectory. When they had finished their round of begging, the disciples would go there, passing the mosque on the way.

The mosque in Hamdallay had no minaret or any other architectural ornament. The walls were seven cubits high and surrounded a covered area preceded by a spacious courtyard where the ritual ablutions took place. There were twelve rows of pillars marking out the aisles set aside for readers of the Koran, copyists crouching over rare manuscripts and makers of shrouds, these last intended to remind everyone that death had its place in the midst of life.

There were no such buildings in Segu. True, there were more and more mosques there, but they were still very unobtrusive, as if Allah had agreed to stoop to conquer. So every time Muhammad passed this proud edifice in Hamdallay his heart beat faster with fear and respect.

The disciples met in their refectory, and after the division of the spoils Muhammad gazed sadly at the food that was left for him. Once again he'd have to fill himself up with water. Just as he was putting the last melancholy mouthful of rice in his mouth, his mentor Abdulay came in.

"Hurry up," he said to Muhammad. "El-Hadj Omar wants to see you."

There was a stupefied silence. How was it such a distinguished visitor could take notice of little Muhammad Traore from Segu? If they hadn't had such respect for Abdulay they'd have thought he'd gone mad!

Muhammad rose quickly, went and washed his hands, and followed Abdulay. He dared not question him, and the beating of his heart nearly deafened him. They went into the compound, across the room where Cheikou Hamadou's fabulous collection of manuscripts was kept, then entered the Grand Council room, also called the Hall of Seven Doors because there were three entrances to the north, three to the south and one to the west. It was a magnificent chamber with tiny openings to admit light and ventilation. The vaulted ceiling was made of wooden arches springing from a third of the way up the walls according to a technique borrowed from Hausa-land.

Cheikou Hamadou was surrounded by several companions, but there was no mistaking which one was El-Hadj Omar. He was a handsome man of about forty and his magnificent dress, contrasting with the extreme simplicity of his host's garments, reminded Muhammad of his father. He wore a white embroidered tunic, an Arab burnous of a sky-blue linen ornamented with gold braid, and a heavy black turban that brought out the hieratic dignity of his features. Muhammad couldn't take his eyes off the saber in its big leather sheath that hung at his waist. It seemed to him the very symbol of this pious conqueror who waged war in the name of God.

"Here is our son, Muhammad Traore," said Cheikou Hamadou, smiling.

El-Hadj Omar smiled too—a smile at once courteous, even affable, yet at the same time slightly mocking and tinged with the satisfied appraisal of a beast of prey.

"Come here," he said in a melodious voice. "Don't be afraid!"

Muhammad crossed the interminable space that separated him from the great marabout, his eyes fixed on the cuffs of the other's boots, made of leather soft as cloth. Then he looked up— and nearly fainted under the piercing glance directed at him. He felt as if this man could decipher the secret geography of thoughts and instincts of which he himself knew nothing.

"Why are you afraid of me?" asked El-Hadj Omar.

"I'm not afraid of you, master," Muhammad just managed to utter.

Hardly had he spoken than he regretted what he'd said. What boldness! What impudence! Yes, he ought to be afraid of so grand a spirit—he himself, a mere speck of dust, ought to be dazzled by the man before him! As he sought desperately for a way of repairing his blunder, El-Hadj Omar went on: "I want to tell you I have the highest possible esteem for your father, Modibo Oumar Traore, who possesses the great light of religion and sheds it around him. I am going to Segu when I leave Hamdallay, and as a sign of my friendship I shall stay with him there. No house could suit me as well as his."

Naive as Muhammad was, he knew of the controversy raging

around his father and realized the effect in Segu if he had such a guest in his house. News of it would reach even the Mansa's palace! But what an honor for their family! A man who had been the guest of the most illustrious rulers! A saint! A prophet! In his excitement he could find nothing to say, and withdrew feeling he had been awkward and stupid throughout the interview.

It was quite by chance that Muhammad got to know his relatives in Macina. Tiekoro had spoken of his grandmother, Sira, but since his arrival he had forgotten all about her, busy as he was trying to get used to this austere town where even the singing of griots was forbidden, and to the Macina dialect of the Fulani language, so different from the Sokoto version his mother spoke.

One day he and Alfa were begging at a compound not far from the Damal Fakal gate. For some days a treacherous wind had been blowing through the streets of Hamdallay, already damp as the city was built in an area formerly subject to flooding. And so between every litany he was shaken by a fit of coughing. Suddenly a woman came out of an enclosure, seized him by the arm and said angrily: "No, God doesn't require women's children to die for him!"

Despite his protests she dragged him inside, and he was too hungry and cold to refuse a bowl of hot millet gruel and some flavored curds.

"You're not a Fulani, are you?" the woman said.

"No," he answered, "I'm a Bambara from Segu."

"Segu?" breathed the woman, her face devoid of expression. "Have you by any chance heard of Malobali Traore, son of Dousika?"

"He was my father," said Muhammad.

The woman dissolved into tears, and a few minutes later Muhammad and Alfa were meeting the whole family.

Sira had not had an easy life. For one thing, she had never stopped missing Segu, though she had left there of her own accord. Then she had never loved her husband, Amadou Tassirou, even though she had served him faithfully and borne him four children. Something repelled her in this man, always fiddling with his prayer beads and talking of God, who threw himself avidly on her body at night and was always taking younger and younger concubines, as if hoping through them to rejuvenate his own blood. When he died she had refused to be handed over to his younger brother, and to avoid scandal had come with her children to Hamdallay, bringing a few cows which her husband's family still laid claim to. Thanks to their milk she was able to bring up her children: she set up a stall in the market amid the other women, and sold the best *kodde* of them all. The passing years had robbed her of her beauty but not of her courage and determination, and it almost seemed as if the gods had made peace with her when Tiekoro came and told her of Malobali's death in a distant country.

Death in a foreign land! Oh, a bad death! What was Malobali looking for, all over the world? His mother. His mother, with breasts drier than a baobab seed! She had killed him as surely as if she had tied three stones around his neck and thrown him down the well.

Sira was delirious for days and nights. Then she recovered, for death may not be compelled. She recovered, but from then on she was only a silent, absent-minded old woman, fumbling to light a fire or milk a cow, cutting her hands when she tried to chop baobab leaves. M'Pene, her eldest daughter, took her to live with her, and everyone was surprised to find that no grandmother was ever better at gently quieting or bathing a baby.

Now she gazed at Muhammad with eyes that sorrow had bleached of color.

"Are you Olubunmi?" she said quietly.

M'Pene and everyone else who was present realized everything was all mixed up in her old head.

What balm it was to Muhammad's heart to have found some relatives! Sira frightened him a little, but when he looked at M'Pene he saw his father's features again. What a marvelous thing is blood! Like a river that irrigates distant lands but never forgets it source!

Muhammad showered M'Pene with reproaches.

"Why didn't you ever come to see us in Segu?" he asked.

"My mother would never have let me," she said.

"All right—but now I shall take you there and introduce you to all the family . . ."

Sira's sons, Tijani and Karim, looked on with amusement. That part of their mother's life didn't concern them. They were Fulani, Fulani of Macina. But they took to this new little relative—who looked like a *bimi*. As for young Ayisha, Tijani's eldest daughter, her heart was wrung with pity, for she'd seen a suppurating sore on Muhammad's ankle, inadequately covered with a dressing of leaves.

C H A P T E R

3

Fa, *fa!* You can't allow him to
have this Tukulor marabout stay here with us. You know the
Fulani and the Tukulor are related, and that he's just been in
Hamdallay. How do we know he hasn't been plotting with Cheikou Hamadou against Segu? Even if he hasn't, that's what everyone will think!"

But Diemogo was only a feeble old man.

"I can't do anything about it," he said, shaking his head. "Nya
has convinced everyone it's a supreme honor for our family!"

Tiefolo got up. There was no point in wasting any more time
by this old fellow's mat—action was what was needed. Should
he go to see the Mansa again? He hadn't much cared for his lukewarm reception a few months ago, and his cautious words: "Let
the boy go. We'll take care of the rest."

And what had they done? Here was Tiekoro imposing this
marabout on the family! Everyone who had heard of him said he
was more fanatical than Cheikou Hamadou, for he belonged to
another brotherhood that considered it their duty to kill the infidels and drive idolatrous kings from power. Was the whole family blind? Did no one see the danger?

Tiefolo had just come back from hunting when Tenegbe told
him what was impending, and he hadn't stopped to cut up his
catch and share it in the ritual manner.

He must go and see all the men in the family and call a family council where Nya and her son would be in the minority. If that failed, he would have to go back to the Mansa.

Tiefolo began with Siga, whom he found in his tannery. There seemed to be a revival of activity there that morning. Slaves naked to the waist, and wearing only a rag below that, were running about between the vats. Siga was talking to some *garanke*, drawing models in the sand as he did so.

"Well, this is new!" exclaimed Tiefolo. "Where have the orders come from?"

"How could I refuse?" answered Siga, looking down with embarrassment. "I haven't had any work for months."

For a moment Tiefolo didn't understand. Then, "The Tukulor marabout!" he cried incredulously.

Siga nodded.

"Forty pairs of slippers and forty pairs of boots for him and his companions. As many again for his sons and the sons of his companions. He paid in advance, half in gold and half in cowries. How could I say no?"

Tiefolo turned way. He wasn't a violent man but he felt a terrible anger rising up in him, and if he didn't master it it would make him throw himself on his brother as if he were one of the animals he pitted himself against in the bush. What is a man if he can't resist the temptation of material goods? Siga had sold himself for an extra handful of gold and a few more cowries. He was ready to join those who would bow down before the marabout and back up Tiekoro and his plans. Then Tiefolo's wrath was succeeded by disgust and nausea. His eyes filled with tears.

"Be realistic, Tiefolo," said Siga. "He's a man of importance. All the kings have paid homage to him."

"Does that allow him to dethrone the Mansa?"

"Who's talking about dethroning?" said Siga, shrugging. "The Mansa could be converted . . ."

It was too much! Tiefolo preferred not to hear any more.

As he strode through the streets of Segu he met Soumaworo, a fetish priest whose services he resorted to whenever he went hunting and on all other important occasions in his life. Soumaworo drew him aside.

"I was just coming to see you," he whispered. "This morning, as I was thanking Sanene for bringing you back safe and sound from the bush, he told me something . . ."

Sanene was the patron spirit of hunters.

Soumaworo lowered his voice still further.

"Death is upon your family," he said.

Tiefolo restrained himself from shrugging. Diemogo was failing fast—all Segu knew that.

"It's not what you think," Soumaworo whispered. "There's nothing surprising about the death of an old man. Sanene is quite firm: it's to do with your brother Tiekoro."

Tiefolo shuddered. Were his evil thoughts turning into poison against his brother?

"Soumaworo, what is this you're telling me?" he said.

The other fixed him with his hot red eyes, in which the white could scarcely be distinguished from the pupil.

"I don't know anything about the circumstances of the death in question," he said. "Sanene didn't reveal them to me. Do you want me to question him and try to ward it off?"

Tiefolo remained silent for some time. He seemed to be looking at the walls of the huts, but in fact he saw nothing. His blood was seething within him. It was as if he held in his hands not only the fate of the clan but also the future of Segu, whose survival depended on his answer. The responsibility paralyzed him. If Tiekoro went, Islam would have no champion either in the compound or in the kingdom. Friction would die away. Unity would be restored. The faith of the ancestors would be respected once more. He looked at the river, sparkling like a snake at the end of a narrow street, and said in a low voice: "Let the will of the gods be done."

Then, ashamed to meet Soumaworo's glance, he turned his back on him and hurried away. Suddenly he was filled with a great peace, as if now he was delivered, free to idle and stroll about as he wished. He went into the cattle market and looked at the Macina horses grazing and pawing the ground. He loved horses; they were so different from the animals he tracked in the bush; they could establish strange relationships with men, relationships ostensibly of submission on their part but in fact of total independence and mutual respect.

"How much are you asking?" he said to the vendor, a young Sarakole.

"Too late," answered the other. "A representative of the Tukulor marabout has taken the lot. He'll need more horses when he leaves Segu, and he's making arrangements in advance."

Tiefolo choked back the fury rising again within him.

"Haven't you got any others?" he said.

"Have you forgotten how many people have decided to go with him and become his disciples?" said the other. "Apparently there are more than eight hundred of them already."

"Segu isn't Macina!" Tiefolo burst out. "Wait and see what sort of a reception we'll give your marabout here!"

As he left the cattle market he ran into one of his slaves.

"Master!" cried the man, throwing himself on the ground. "Half a dozen of us have been looking for you. The Mansa wants you urgently at the palace. Hurry—they say he's in a terrible rage!"

It was true. The Mansa was like a lion rushing furiously into the bush. His slaves, councillors and even his griots stood at a respectful distance as he railed at Tiefolo, abandoning all thought of dignity.

"I ought to have you thrown into irons! You Traore—you're a bunch of rogues and traitors. Your brother's preparing to welcome the Tukulor marabout into your compound, and you don't run to warn me!"

Tiefolo, prostrate before him, at last managed to get a word in.

"Master of the world," he said, "I only got back yesterday from hunting. I didn't even stop to cut up the animals—"

"May they make you impotent, sterile, or give you a hernia! Do you talk to me about hunting when my throne is in danger?"

The curse the king had just pronounced was so awful that the already oppressive silence grew even deeper. Makan Diabate was brave enough to give his master a look of reproach. Then Mansa Tiefolo calmed down. A slave rushed forward and proffered his snuffbox, another hurried to fan him, a third to wipe the sweat from his brow. Makan Diabate signaled for Tiefolo to speak up for himself.

"Master of the world," he began, "I came to see you a few months ago, and what did you say? 'Let the boy go. We'll see to the rest.' Could I foresee you'd do nothing to oppose the plans of my brother and his friends?"

There was an implicit criticism in his words, and the councillors looked anxiously at this madman who seemed not to know what he was saying. But Tiefolo was so dignified that the Mansa didn't protest. On the contrary, he seemed to be taking the measure of the man kneeling before him, still dressed in his hunting gear: a pointed cap covered with gris-gris; a full tunic caught in at the waist by a wide belt studded with cowries; short trousers leaving bare a pair of handsome calves scratched by the thorns of the bush. Yes, Tiefolo was right to reproach him. He hadn't treated him well on his first visit, when he'd subtly hinted that he mistrusted his motives. But now the Mansa was convinced that El-Hadj Omar and Cheikou Hamadou were in league to destroy him and were relying on help from inside Segu. He'd been told of things El-Hadj Omar had said in Hamdallay which suggested that an expedition was being prepared against him.

"My father, the great Monzon," he said, "always maintained that the path of guile is surer than the path of force. The Tukulor marabout will come to Segu and stay with your brother—I shall not oppose it. I shall receive him in my palace. But once he comes in, the gods alone know when he will go out again, and how. I wish you to report to me every evening and tell me every single word the Tukulor exchanges with your brother."

Tiefolo withdrew.

As he went through the courtyards he felt disgusted with himself. Should one brother betray another? Spy on him? Repeat what he said? Here he was, a nobleman, behaving like a slave forced to use the vilest of means to rise above his condition. Then he remembered Soumaworo's words, and while they had comforted him at the time they now filled him with anguish. If only the ancestors would grant that he might have nothing to do with this death! As some griots hurried to his side he pushed them roughly away. This was unusual, for he liked to be reminded of his exploits in the bush and of the lion he had killed when he was ten years old. The griots obeyed him, but he could hear them singing mockingly behind his back:

> Hunter, hunter,
> If you boast I shall not praise you
> Are you not he who slays the elephant
> Pursues the buffalo
> And kills the sun-colored giraffe?
> But hunter, hunter,
> If I don't sing of you
> Who are you?
> Does not the word make the man?

By the mosque at Somonos' Point, Tiefolo met Tiekoro and was so embarrassed he almost turned back. He scrutinized his brother's face for the shadow Soumaworo had spoken of, but all he could see was the countenance of one evidently proud and pleased with his life.

Tiekoro had always looked on Tiefolo as a boor who covered himself with gris-gris to track down animals that had never done him any harm; his reputation for bravery was for him tantamount to a reputation for stupidity. But Tiefolo was the eldest son of his father's younger brother, and so he ought to try to get along with him. Tiekoro smiled politely.

"Did your *bara muso* tell you I was looking for you yesterday?" he asked.

Tiefolo stared down at the dust.

"I know what you wanted to say to me," he said.

His coldness was quite perceptible, but Tiekoro answered quietly, as if talking to a rather dull child.

"*Tie*," he said, "I know what you think. But you must accept it—there is no god but God. Allah will conquer all this region like a blinding sun, and our family will be blessed for having contributed . . ."

"If you want to preach, go in there!" said Tiefolo rudely, pointing to the mosque.

Tiekoro stood for a moment watching his brother walk away, then with a sigh he entered the courtyard of the mosque.

While the Bambara of Segu resolutely refused Islam, the same was not true of the Somono of the city, who had close connections with the big maraboutic families in Timbuktu. So Tiekoro was hoping to include them in the arrangements for El-Hadj Omar's reception. However, instead of the enthusiasm he expected he met with a sullen countenance from Alfa Kane, the imam of the mosque, who was drinking green tea with his assistant, Ali Akbar.

"Do you know this El-Hadj Omar is a follower of the Tijaniya?" he asked.

"What does it matter—Tijaniya, Suhrawardiya, Shadiliya? We're all Muslims, aren't we?" replied Tiekoro.

"So you say," came the answer.

There was a pause. It was nearly time for *zohour*, the second prayer of the day, and the faithful were beginning to arrive one by one or in groups, taking off their slippers and placing them carefully in a row along the wall. Then the voice of the muezzin rent the air. Tiekoro could never hear the call to prayer without being moved to the core. He remembered the first time he had heard it ringing out over the walls of Segu and felt that God was speaking to him, him personally, a wretched creature with scales still over his eyes. He shuddered.

"O God," he thought, "how I long to come to you!"

But Alfa Kane brought him down to earth again.

"I want nothing to do with the Tukulors' visit," he said. "I tell you—because of him, brother will fight against brother, Muslim will shed the blood of Muslim. You were afraid of Cheikou Hamadou, but it's this one you ought to fear."

And, drawing around him his immaculate white robe, he went off into the mosque.

What should Tiekoro do? Follow and make him explain? But, deep down, Tiekoro wouldn't be sorry to be the only one to play host to the great marabout. He'd show what a Traore could do. He had plenty of gold and cowries and saddle horses. His paddocks were full of sheep and poultry. The storehouses were overflowing with millet, and they didn't know where to put all the sweet potatoes. El-Hadj Omar's arrival should be the climax of his life as a believer!

—

Basically Maryem, Tiekoro's first wife, and Fatima, wife of Siga, had nothing in common. The first was related to a sultan and the founder of an empire; she had been born in a palace and surrounded by slaves to wait on her hand and foot. The second was the natural daughter of a Fez matchmaker—a profitable but certainly not a distinguished profession. The first was energetic, used to giving orders and to being obeyed, while the second was indolent and rather querulous. One was the wife of a man whose reputation was beginning to spread beyond Segu, while the other's husband was an undutiful son whose name some of the family wouldn't even utter.

Yet the two women were such friends they couldn't spend a day apart. From morn till night, slave girls ran back and forth between them with dainties, and children were sent with messages and presents.

What bound them together was their hatred of Segu, their contempt for the Bambara and their religion and customs, and the need to keep talking about it. Fatima was cured of the mad attraction she had once felt for Tiekoro when she heard his wife describe his behavior down to the last detail with a hatred as burning as love. She didn't hate Siga herself, though she did feel cheated and completely taken in, like a golddigger who finds his nuggets are only clay. She consoled herself with her ten children, tender and affectionate and all of them so handsome! As her husband was too poor to have many slaves she looked after her children herself, so her life had been nothing but feedings, basins of gruel, toothaches, fevers, diarrhea and teaching infants to walk and talk. As Siga let her do as she liked, she had brought them up to believe in Allah and sent them as soon as they were old enough to a Koranic school for Moorish children on the other side of the river.

The news that El-Hadj Omar was coming reconciled the two women to Segu. They began to badger the seamstresses to make them new *boubous*. Fatima's brother had sent her some lengths of silk interwoven with gold thread from Fez, and she hadn't yet had it made up. Maryem had some richly chased jewelery that usually lay unused in bowls in her hut. There was just one thing that bothered her. Would Tiekoro send for Muhammad to come with the Tukulor, and would she have her son home again? Fatima tried to make her see reason.

"It wouldn't be a good thing for him to come back in the middle of his service," she said.

"Service?" cried Maryem. "You talk as if he were a soldier!"

"Isn't he a soldier of God?" asked Fatima quietly.

Maryem was ashamed to have laid herself open to such a reproach. But religion was one thing and mother love was another. Muhammad was her only boy, and it was torture to think of him going begging in a town where she'd been told the women went about veiled and widows had to stay shut up at home for fear of arousing old men's lust. She waved away Fatima's offer of some stuffed dates. She didn't like sweet things; the only concession of that kind in Sokoto was the way they mixed curds with honey. Fatima took a bite of the brown and green sweetmeat.

"They say there's been a quarrel between the Tukulor marabout and Cheikou Hamadou," she said. "El-Hadj Omar intended to stay in Hamdallay until the end of the dry season, but he's had to leave early."

"Who told you that?" said Maryem, staring.

"The Moors at the Koranic school my boys go to. They've had orders from the Kounta in Timbuktu not to go and welcome him when he arrives."

"But why?"

Fatima shrugged.

"How should I know? Just one of those quarrels, I suppose— over brotherhoods, over power, over prestige. Men's quarrels!"

Maryem resolved to ask Tiekoro about it. But she'd be lucky if she could find a suitable moment, so busy was he with preparations for the marabout's visit. These included replastering the huts where the Tukulor and his entourage were to stay, covering the floors with Moroccan carpets, burning sweet-smelling essences to perfume the air, collecting presents fit for El-Hadj Omar, and checking supplies of millet, rice and poultry. Maryem was never alone with him. The only person Tiekoro consulted about this visit was his mother! They would talk about it for hours and then she would give orders, supervise, cavil and scold. How could an old Bambara woman who'd never even crossed the Joliba know how to treat a *moqaddem*?

The wind wafted the stench of Siga's tannery across to them.

"At least all this will have brought him some work!" said Fatima scornfully.

"What if I told you," said Maryem, "that despite the fact that he's an idol worshipper I have a lot of respect for Siga? People just don't appreciate him, that's all. He's too honest—he doesn't know how to scheme and calculate and scratch other people's backs."

She was obviously thinking of Tiekoro.

"You're not being fair," Fatima protested. "I believe Tiekoro sincerely loves God and works for His greater glory. Has he told you how he was converted, all by himself, just following his own intuition? And how he made his family accept his vocation?"

"For years I've never heard anything else," said Maryem impatiently.

A slave handed her some tea.

So things were going badly, were they, between the Tukulor marabout and Cheikou Hamadou? Perhaps she ought to tell Tiekoro and warn him to be careful. Their son was in Hamdallay, and he mustn't fall a victim to quarrels they knew so little about here in Segu. But would Tiekoro listen to her? He'd made up his mind to work for the greater glory of God and of the Tukulor marabout. And, incidentally, of himself.

CHAPTER
4

Idol worshippers though they were, the good people of Segu mustered along the streets to watch El-Hadj Omar and his retinue go by. They looked on him as a magician who had performed prodigies. Didn't people say he'd brought water back to a well that had run dry? Called down rain on a town under siege and so prevented it from having to surrender? Hadn't he healed the sick and brought the dying back to life just by the laying on of hands and the speaking of a few words? They compared these miracles with those worked by the fetish priests of Segu, and even the most reluctant spirits had to admit they outdid them. Barren women, believing a look from the visitor would enable them to have a child, jostled with cripples, people suffering from scrofula and the victims of incurable diseases for places at the front of the crowd. Those afflicted with blindness wormed their way among people's legs, whining appeals for forbearance, while smart fellows, exploiting the intense heat, offered gourds of water for a cowrie apiece. The *tondyons* were patrolling the streets, but the Mansa had instructed them not to interfere with the innumerable spies scattered throughout the town.

Tiekoro, after informing the Mansa of the illustrious guest's arrival, had gone out to meet him at Sansanding with a small band of slaves and Soninke coreligionists; he'd been unable to persuade the Somono to accompany him, for they had had a letter from Sheikh El-Bekkay in Timbuktu saying, "On the pretense of reviving Islam this man will cause the death of many innocent people."

Suddenly the Joliba grew black with canoes, horses with flying manes and rafts full of cows, sheep, baskets of chickens, men and women. The crowd gathered outside the walls gave a loud cry: "They're here!"

Then those who had so far stayed inside rushed out to see the new arrivals, and the *tondyons* had great difficulty in holding them back.

El-Hadj Omar's procession was made up of about a thousand people—pupils, supporters, servants, women and children. He had been preceded by the detachment of Macina lancers that Cheikou Hamadou had given him as an escort. They wore coats of mail, high boots of soft leather and huge black silk turbans. But the *tondyons* regarded them as enemies and wouldn't let them enter Segu-Sikoro, so they dismounted and camped on the banks of the river. It was almost impossible to catch a glimpse of El-Hadj Omar himself, partly because there were so many people around him and partly because they deliberately hid him from view. Who could tell from what quarter danger might come in this impious city, this den of idolators? It was easy to shoot an arrow from a rooftop, or a bullet from a gun immediately abandoned in the dust. So the inhabitants of Segu were reduced to craning their necks and asking each other every time they saw a haughty face, a large turban or a braided burnous, "Is that him? Is that him?"

The beauty and elegance of the women, some of them said to be princesses from Syria, Egypt and Arabia, took everyone's breath away. The crowd wondered at their long black hair, flowing like silk from beneath their veils, and at the color of their skins, warmer and less pallid than that of the Moors. The Tukulor women had the same graceful elegance as their Fulani sisters and could only be distinguished from them by their finery: necklaces made of oblong beads strung on cotton threads; jewels on their foreheads, beneath their kerchiefs; fretted and filigreed bangles, made of fine gold alloyed with copper, all the way up their arms! There was no doubt about it: this was a much finer procession than that of the Mansa Tiefolo when he left his palace. The old folk said there hadn't been any really good-looking men in Segu since the days of Monzon, son of Makoro—they were all under-sized fellows, like the *bimi* who had never been completely conquered.

Tiekoro galloped along beside the great marabout. He felt as if his heart were about to burst with happiness, pride and grat-itude to God for allowing him to know such a day. As the Tukulor were leaving Macina, Amirou Mangal, war chief of the Jenne region and an octogenarian respected throughout the kingdom, had asked a favor of El-Hadj Omar: to say the prayer for the dead over him. And the old man had been wrapped in a shroud and rolled up in a mat like a corpse, so that the marabout might perform the rite. How Tiekoro would have liked to do the same! Never to see the sun rise again after this day that no other could rival in felicity! Only one thing was missing: Nadie. How happy she would have been too! How far he had come since the stinking courtyard where he had bestridden her like a beast! And since the dreary hovel in Jenne! He hoped El-Hadj Omar's stay beneath his roof would not end without his guest bestowing on him some title that would put a crowning touch to his reputation. Some-thing worried him. Like all those who had studied in Timbuktu he belonged to the Kounta Qadriya. Should he arrange to be in-itiated into the Tijaniya? Yes, but then mightn't he offend Chei-kou Hamadou? He sighed and spurred on his horse, which was lagging behind.

Then suddenly the sky, bright blue as on any other morning in the dry season, was cleft by shafts of lightning, followed by such violent claps of thunder that the walls of several compounds collapsed and a wide crack appeared in the north front of the Mansa's palace. The crowd let out a yell of amazement, and a thousand faces looked up at the inscrutable heavens, from which fell scalding torrents of rain as red as a wounded man's blood. It lasted only a few minutes, and the inhabitants of Segu might have thought they'd been dreaming had it not left visible traces on their clothes and bodies. There was no need for a fetish priest or expert in the occult to interpret these signs. The Tukulor mar-about would bring bloodshed to Segu. When? How? The crowd fled in disorder before the horses' hooves, which echoed like the drums of victory. Admiration gave way to terror. People were ready to criticize the Mansa for allowing El-Hadj Omar to enter the town.

Tiekoro looked in dismay at the red stain on his burnous. Though he had rejected the superstitions of his own people he felt it was the ancestors who had just shown themselves. Suddenly, as he looked at the deserted streets, he was afraid. At that moment El-Hadj Omar turned and smiled at him, and for the first time he noticed the cruelty of that face with its acute angles and slanting planes. He was certainly a luminary, destined by God to play a great role in Islam. But at what price? How many corpses would there be? How many funeral dirges would be sung?

They were arriving at the Traore compound. Slaves rushed forward to take the horses and the baggage and relieve the women of the children they carried on their backs or hips. Meanwhile others were putting the finishing touches to great dishes of couscous, to be served with sweets and fruit drinks since Islam forbade all fermented beverages. The jars of water had been flavored with mint leaves or ginger. White and red kola nuts were set out in little baskets. The welcome was perfect, yet Tiekoro felt dissatisfied and anxious. He remembered how Maryem had tried to warn him. But then he never listened to her: she was too beautiful and too well born, and would have lorded it over everything, himself included, if he'd given her the chance. But now he'd better talk to her as soon as possible . . . if, with the marabout here, he had the time.

"Modibo Oumar Traore," said the marabout, "there are two kinds of infidel—those who worship idols and pagan divinities instead of the true God, and those who mix infidel practices with those of Islam. Are you sure you're not one of the second kind?"

Tiekoro was speechless, and the Tukulor marabout went on, with a benevolence that contrasted with the gravity of his words.

"Not directly, of course! But by allowing those who live under your roof to act in this way. You know the dictum, 'Islam mixed with polytheism is nothing.' Can you swear to me that your brothers and their wives and children do not worship idols? Or even the boys you teach in your zawiya?"

Tiekoro hung his head. What could he say? He knew very

well that the Islam practiced by his family and even by his pupils was only superficial. But he thought it would gradually deepen, put down roots and eventually change their hearts. The marabout kept on: "Anyone who practices *muwalat** with infidels becomes an infidel himself!"

Tiekoro fell on his knees.

"Master," he said, "what must I do?"

El-Hadj Omar did not answer directly.

"Did you know Cheikou Hamadou is not what he seems? Not what you think he is? He has seized the property of Tijanists in Macina by an act of injustice and aggression. The kingdom is rife with family struggles and intrigues of all kinds. It's a corruption of Islam."

There was a silence. They were in a large hut with a roof of leaves, the floor covered with a Moroccan carpet, the walls with brocaded hangings depicting arcades of alternate red and green decorated with Arab calligraphy. Stearin candles mingled their light with that of shea butter lamps set on little stools covered with monochrome embroidery. The smell of incense and aromatic herbs swamped that of the green tea being served on chased copper trays by slaves specially dressed for the occasion in white silk *boubous*.

"Oumar Traore, have you read the *Jawahira el-Maani*?"† asked El-Hadj Omar.

Tiekoro had to admit he had not.

"Read it carefully. Steep yourself in what it says. Then come and see me," said the marabout.

"Where, master?" asked Tiekoro.

"I'll let you know when the time comes," was the answer.

Tiekoro was shattered. The event he had waited for with such excitement was turning out to be a failure. The Tukulor marabout was not praising him for all he had accomplished alone among a pagan people. On the contrary, he was blaming him for his laxity and tolerance. What did he expect him to do? Murder his brothers and sisters, his mother and father, in the name of jihad? Not only was the marabout not going to confer any honor

---

* Solidarity.
† *The Pearl of Meanings*, a treatise by Ahmed Tijani.

upon him, he was treating him like a schoolboy! Tiekoro could
have defended himself and listed all his achievements, but he felt
tired, bitter and disappointed again. Why was life no more than
a bridge from disillusion to disillusion?

"Call me to yourself, O God!" he implored inwardly. "Let
me be wrapped in seven garments and a shroud, rolled up in a
mat and buried lying on my right side. Why should you deny me
that?"

It was time for the last prayer of the day, and the people went
outside to prostrate themselves in the direction of Mecca. In the
courtyard Tiekoro noticed Tiefolo standing with his arms folded,
surrounded by his sons and younger brothers. He realized it was
not by chance that they'd come to show their opposition to the
presence of the Tukulor marabout beneath their roof.

"As I told you, Oumar," said El-Hadj Omar, turning to Tiekoro with his inimitable smile, "whoever practices *muwalat*
with infidels becomes an infidel too."

As Tiekoro was about to prostrate himself a slave touched
him on the arm. In his exasperation, anxiety and sorrow he would
have shouted at the man and struck him, but the other exclaimed:
"Forgive me, master—but there are messengers from the Mansa!"

A delegation was waiting in the first courtyard: royal griots
in green velvet tunics lined with red or dark indigo blue silk;
members of the council dressed in white with ceremonial canes
in their hands; slaves bare to the waist, laden with gifts. What
particularly struck Tiekoro was the number of gris-gris they wore
on their arms and legs and around their necks and waists, as if
to make sure there was no mistake about which side they were
on. Segu was rejecting Islam.

It was councillor Mande Diarra who spoke for them.

"Here are presents from the Mansa to your guest. The Mansa
wishes him to come and see him tomorrow at the palace. You
are to come too, of course."

Now Tiekoro was even more worried. Seeing how intransigent the marabout appeared to be, would he agree to meet a king
who worshipped idols?

"El-Hadj Omar is at prayer—I can't interrupt him. I'll send
you his answer tomorrow morning," he stammered.

Mande Diarra glanced at his companions.

"Traore," he said, "have you gone out of your mind? Your sovereign summons you and you hesitate to obey?"

Too many things had happened since that morning, and Tiekoro was too confused to be diplomatic.

"I have no sovereign but Allah," he replied roughly.

There was a terrified silence. If Tiekoro had profaned a cult or broken a taboo or oath it wouldn't have been as bad as publicly denying his allegiance to the Mansa. Mande Diarra, who had always regarded Tiekoro's conversion to Islam as a symptom of madness, took pity on him and whispered: "Ask forgiveness for what you've just said, Tiekoro Traore! I have enough respect for your family to persuade myself I didn't hear it."

But Tiefolo and his sons, and his brothers and their sons, had drawn close, and it was becoming a point of honor. Tiekoro gave a haughty glance around him, and without another word went and joined his coreligionists at prayer.

As he pressed his forehead to the fine, carefully swept sand, he again wished for death. What sort of a life was this? Outwardly perhaps a success, but inwardly full of regrets and frustrations. What are wives, sons and daughters, full storehouses and many cattle if the spirit is as bitter as the bark of the mahogany? And how can the spirit not be bitter when it has to drag its fleshly envelope around with it?

"Free me, my God!" begged Tiekoro again. "Let me come to you at last and know beatitude!"

He had thought Islam would be a refuge, freeing him from the practices that had repelled him in the religion of his fathers. But now men were about to spoil his refuge too, like naughty children who break everything they touch. Qadriya, Suhrawardiya, Shadiliya, Tijaniya, Mewlewi . . . had not Allah said, "Leave men to their vain pastimes"?

Meanwhile the marabout's companions had finished reciting their prayers, and as Tiekoro remained prostrate El-Hadj Omar thought he was meditating on their recent conversation and went to his hut without disturbing him. Tiekoro, looking up, saw a shape in the shade under the trees of the compound. Was it death? At last? But the shape moved. It was only Siga. All Tiekoro's ill humor returned.

"Now you come!" he said curtly. "Are you turning apostate again?"

"Tiekoro," whispered Siga urgently, "take care! A plot is being hatched against you. If you go to the palace tomorrow with the marabout, the Mansa will have you arrested. You've still got time to escape—if you leave Segu at once, at dawn, you can be safe in Macina."

Siga knew he was wasting his time. Tiekoro was too proud to run away from danger. On the contrary, danger would only stimulate him. Tiekoro took Siga's arm, and the younger brother was surprised by the simple friendliness of the gesture.

"Walk along with me, will you?" said Tiekoro.

Segu was locked in darkness, but its sounds came through all the more clearly. Behind every wall voices whispered about the extraordinary events of the day. Everyone expected the worst—some prodigy on the part of the marabout, reducing the town to ashes or swelling the waters of the Joliba so that they swept away all the houses, together with the inhabitants and their animals.

Siga sensed his brother's distress, and not knowing what to say suggested: "Come and have a drink with me at Yankadi's! Muslim or no, there are times when a man needs a drink."

Tiekoro leaned more heavily on Siga's arm.

"If anything happens to me," he said, "take Maryem as your wife—she gets on so well with Fatima. And above all take care of Muhammad—I can tell he's like me . . . he'll never be happy."

Siga tried in vain to find words of comfort, but he knew his brother was in dire peril. They came to the Joliba, a dark ribbon between the sleeping boats of the Somono fishermen. On the other bank they could see the gleam of the Macina lancers' campfires turning the bush into an unreal landscape.

"Do you think your Allah is worth the trouble?" asked Siga, softly.

"Don't blaspheme!" said Tiekoro, but not angrily.

"It's not blasphemy," said Siga. "Don't you ever doubt?"

Tiekoro shook his head in the darkness, and Siga put it down once again to pride. But Tiekoro was telling the truth: if there was one thing that really existed in him it was faith. Of course it had never stopped him from being a miserable sinner, but it filled him as the blood filled his veins. It was faith that made his heart beat and moved his arms and legs. He had known Allah was the only true God ever since the day, on that street corner, when he'd been intrigued by the call of the Moors' muezzin and gone into the mosque to find an old man writing verses from the Koran.

He sat down on a boat.

"Yes, take Maryem as your wife," he said again, in a voice that was calm and detached. "Let the family decide about Adam and Yankadi, but insist about her. I'll go in peace if I know she's with you."

Siga was moved to tears by this mark of esteem, belated though it was. He looked at his brother and realized that what Koumare had once said was true. Tiekoro's fate and his own were as inseparable as night and day. Or as sun and moon, for they both fill the world with light and life. Tiekoro had been crowned with honors, but he'd also been afflicted with great sorrows. And he, Siga, had been a patient, ordinary drudge, experiencing small disappointments and small joys. But now they were both left empty-handed. Beaten.

Beaten? Was Tiekoro really beaten? Siga looked at the Macina campfires across the river, and they seemed to him symbolic. The fire of Islam spread by the Fulani and the Tukulor would in the end set Segu ablaze. It was this conviction that gave Tiekoro his self-assurance and pride. He had been the first to see what was coming.

The two brothers went back into Segu. *Dolo* drinkers were emerging from the taverns, talking over the events of the day. In their drunkenness, they multiplied the size of the marabout's escort by four, the number of his wives by a hundred. According to them a whole wing of the royal palace had crumbled, and clots of blood poured down from the sky. The day had given them food for their imagination, for their need to wonder, to be surprised, to be afraid.

CHAPTER

5

When the town, and then the whole kingdom, heard that the Mansa had arrested El-Hadj Omar, together with some of the Muslims in his suite and Tiekoro Traore, the king, who had never been loved, immediately enjoyed a wave of popularity. People were reminded of the great days of previous reigns when the *tondyons* were always winning victories, and came back laden with booty and strings of captives staggering along behind their horses. A crowd gathered in the palace square. But nothing filtered through the walls. Everything seemed as usual. The masons were already repairing the breach made by the thunder the previous day, slaves were carrying food and water to and fro, merchants and artisans came and went through the gates.

No one knew exactly what had happened. Some said the Mansa had asked the Tukulor marabout and his host to go to the palace, and when they refused had had them brought there by force and clapped into irons. Others said they had come to the palace of their own free will, and that the king had then had them thrown into prison. Their crime? They were plotting to overthrow the Mansa, of course. At a given moment the squadron of Macina lancers were to have called upon other soldiers concealed across the river, and then all the inhabitants of Segu were to have been forced to make the horrible profession of faith, "There is no god but God!" or else have their heads chopped off, bang!

When the news got out, Nya left the women to howl and writhe in the dust; she went into her hut and dressed with the greatest care. She put on a *pagne* of stiff dark indigo, bead and amber necklaces, and in her graying hair an ornate headdress. When she went out into the courtyard everyone remembered she had been the most beautiful woman of her generation, and the most majestic. Age had merely added a few wrinkles to her face, loosened her flesh and blurred the line of a neck once slender as that of an impala. Her younger sons tried to stop her, but she pushed them gently aside.

As she made her way to the royal palace people came out of their compounds to see her. Soon the rumor spread that Nya Kulibaly, daughter of Fale Kulibaly and widow of Dousika Traore, was going to the Mansa to demand an explanation. At once the griots who knew the genealogies of the two families began to chant the exploits of their ancestors, and the procession they formed was joined by a crowd of men, women and children torn between grief and curiosity.

The Mansa was told Tiekoro Traore's mother was coming toward the palace. What was he to do? Refuse to see her? That was impossible—she was old enough to be his own mother! Let her in? She'd start to weep and implore, and how could he hold out against her tears?

After endless discussions, the griot Makan Diabate had an idea.

"Master," he said, "have her told you're not well and get your wives to see her."

But Nya did not intend to weep and implore. She wanted to see her son. The night before, Dousika had come in a dream to warn her that Tiekoro would soon be joining him, and she wanted to clasp him one last time in her arms. Unhappy mother who has to bury her own sons! It was he who ought to have wrapped her up in the funeral mat; but the ancestors had decreed otherwise. As she went through the streets amid a din of music, recitations, exclamations of sympathy and words of comfort, Nya heard nothing. In her head she was going over the whole of Tiekoro's life, ever since he was born. How sweet is the first cry of the first child! She felt again her own pain, saw the midwife washing the ugly little creature covered in blood who was to be her pride. The woman had given him to her and they had exchanged their first look, the sealing of a pact. "You will hold many women in your arms. You will shake the hands of many men. You will go with this one and that, and be far away from me. But nothing else will matter except me. Your mother."

After the baby came the little boy, precocious and pestering her with questions.

"*Ba*, what holds the moon up in the sky?"

"*Ba*, why are those people slaves and we nobles?"

"*Ba*, why do the gods like the blood of chickens?"

Nya, troubled by all these questions, hid her ignorance behind an air of serenity.

"The ancestors have decreed it, Tiekoro," she would say. And by dint of questioning, calling things in doubt and trying to find his own explanations for everything, he had entered upon a dangerous path. But she did not dream of blaming him. She was there not to judge but to love him.

As she entered the first antechamber the king's *bara muso*, followed by two or three co-wives and a few griots, came toward her and bowed.

"Mother of sons," she said, "you are tired. Come and rest."

Nya went with them to the women's apartments. Apart from the soldiers there to guard them and the griots there to sing to them, men were not allowed in this part of the palace. It was protected by a wall with tough wooden spikes on top, pierced by a mahogany door fastened with an enormous bar. The first courtyard contained straw-thatched huts, and trees giving shade to a number of mats, rugs and cushions spread out on the ground, together with bamboo beds covered with thick cotton blankets. The *bara muso* signaled for Nya to take one of these couches, and no sooner was she seated than slaves hurried up to offer her bowls of water, to massage her feet and ankles and fan her brow. Nya accepted it all politely, but after a few moments she spoke.

"Tell me," she said, "why won't your husband see me?"

The *bara muso* lowered her eyes.

"He's ill, mother," she said. "After he ate he felt sick and vomited."

Nya realized she was lying, but not wishing to embarrass her said, "May the ancestors send him a swift recovery! Have you given him porridge made of baobab flour?"

The *bara muso* assured her six doctors were in attendance.

"Daughter," said Nya, "have you got sons?"

The other was wary of getting into this kind of conversation, and tried to change the subject. But Nya went on.

"What a terrible part we have to play, we mothers of sons! Our daughters bring us wealth, joy and grandchildren, but our sons are nothing but torment, anguish and affliction. They seek death in war, and if they don't find it there they travel the world in search of it. And one day a stranger comes and tells us they are no more. Or else they try to undo what our fathers have done and so offend the ancestors. Sometimes I wonder if they ever think of us. What is your opinion?"

The *bara muso* fought back her tears.

"Mother," she said, "I promise you that if it is in my power your son shall not be touched . . ."

Nya gave a derisive yet tolerant laugh.

"If it is in your power!" she said. "We have no power, daughter!"

Meanwhile the Mansa, his councillors and his griots were sitting in conclave. The royal fetish priests were quite categorical; no one must lay hands on the Tukulor marabout; he must be released at once, taken under escort to the frontier and told never to set foot in the kingdom again. The Mansa himself would have liked to teach the Muslims a lesson by executing this false prophet.

What had he to fear if he did so? His spies had informed him that El-Hadj Omar and Cheikou Hamadou were at odds, though they didn't know why. Macina would not react if the Tukulor was put to death. So why were they against it? Did they want to give El-Hadj Omar time to gather an army together and come back to attack Segu openly? Was that it?

Mande Diarra plucked up his courage.

"Master," he said, "all you need do is destroy the enemies within, those who are working inside Segu for the coming of Islam and your overthrow. This Tiekoro, for example—be merciless with him. As for our enemies abroad, hasn't Segu always been able to defend itself? If the Tukulor does come back, well, he'll meet the same fate as the cowherd from Fitouga!"

And so at dawn, while the inhabitants of Segu were still sleeping, detachments of *tondyons* escorted the Tukulor marabout and his suite to the Kankan frontier. The Macina lancers, who had had express orders not to confront the Bambara, mounted their horses and returned to their base. A few hours later, for good measure, *tondyons* went into the houses of Bambara who had been converted to Islam and haled them off to the palace prisons. They didn't touch the Soninke or Somono Muslims, partly because they hadn't been involved in El-Hadj Omar's visit but mostly because they paid over large sums to the Mansa in commercial taxes.

But the most spectacular operation of all was the destruction of Tiekoro's *zawiya*. Soldiers smashed its walls to pieces and knocked down the huts that served as the dormitories and refectory, together with the awnings for teaching and meditation. Then they piled dry wood on top of it all and set it on fire. They threw Tiekoro's collection of manuscripts into the flames, having first torn out some of the pages and hidden them under their tunics to serve as gris-gris.

Tiekoro followed all this through the accounts of his guards, with whom he had made friends. Prison usually unleashes the beast in a man, so that he goes around and around in circles yelling and cursing, or does the best he can to put an end to himself. But with Tiekoro it was quite different. He spent his time in prayer, telling his beads and wearing an expression that convinced the soldiers he was in communication with spirits. They asked him to obtain favors for them—one soliciting promotion, another longing for a son, another wanting his wife to come back to him: she'd taken refuge with her family after being beaten once too often.

Tiekoro laughed.

"I can only pray for you, brothers," he said. "I'm not a magician!"

Since Nya's visit he had been completely at peace. He had put his head in her lap and she had stroked his shaven head as she used to when he was a child. Basking in the smell of her, restored to the happiness of when he was in her womb, he had murmured: "See that Maryem is given to Siga. Apart from that, just act for the best."

Nya had sighed.

"Do you think Maryem will agree? Ah, Tiekoro, I foresee great troubles in the family!"

That was the only reproach she made him, and it wounded him cruelly.

Tiekoro now awaited death as a man waits for an unseen bride who is said to be very beautiful. He tried to forget El-Hadj Omar's criticisms and think only of God.

Soon he would be face to face with Him.

The men guarding his cell were called Seba and Bo: the first was the one who'd asked to have his wife back, the second the one who wanted a son. Now it so happened that when Seba went home he found his fugitive wife sitting in the courtyard, apparently repentant and dutiful. As for Bo, after ten daughters in succession he was told that at last a male child had been born to him. This was enough for the two men to start talking about miracles, and soon all Segu knew Tiekoro Traore was a magician more powerful than the greatest fetish priests. Seba and Bo never tired of describing his strange séances.

"He only uses his head," they said. "He doesn't give you anything to drink or rub on your body. It's just in his head."

For a few cowries or measures of millet they could be persuaded to pass requests on to Tiekoro, and this came to the ears of the Mansa's spies.

Since Nya's visit and the pressure put on him by his *bara muso*, the Mansa had hesitated to condemn Tiekoro to death. Sometimes he considered letting him molder in his cell for a few years and then sending him back, sadder and wiser, to his family. Sometimes he thought of putting him under house arrest in the distant region of Bagoe. But when he heard that even in prison Tiekoro went on propagating Islam, and in a spectacular manner, likely to strike the popular imagination, the Mansa came around to his advisers' way of thinking.

The date was set for Tiekoro's execution.

One thing alone had kept Nya going: her love for Tiekoro. And when she learned that he was to die her life seemed pointless. What was the use of looking at a sun he would never see again, of sitting by a fire that would warm him no more, of eating food he would taste no longer? Perhaps, if Dousika had still been alive, she might have been able to cling on with his help. But Dousika was no more, and only Diemogo was left—almost senile, and so far gone people wondered when death would make up its mind to take him.

And so Nya was brought low, like a tree eaten away from within by termites. The fetish priests who were called in knew there was nothing to be done, but hurried about in all directions to make the family think they might still bring back to her body the spiritual forces now deserting it. She lay stretched out motionless on her mat, breathing with difficulty, her head turned slightly toward the door of her hut as if she were listening to the friends of the family who had gathered there and who kept up a murmur to try to encourage her to live.

"Nya, daughter of Fale," they repeated, "your ancestors bent the world like a bow and unbent it again like a straight road. Nya, stand erect again too!"

At one point she emerged from her torpor and whispered, "I'd like to see Kosa."

Kosa was her last-born son, the child of her remarriage to Diemogo. He came toward Nya, frightened and repelled by the smell of fumigation that could not blot out the odor of imminent death. What did they want of him? He sat down reluctantly on his mother's mat.

"When you can't see me any more," she said, "I shall still be there, with you everywhere. Even nearer than if you could see me."

Everyone else was weeping, so Kosa burst into tears too.

Then Nya sent for Tiefolo.

She had no proof that he had been involved in the plot against Tiekoro, but she knew that several evenings running he had been to the royal palace to talk to the Mansa.

He came in as unwillingly as Kosa but for different reasons.

It wasn't the paraphernalia of death that terrified him but the sense of his own responsibility. He had thought he was acting for the best—getting rid of Tiekoro as one would eliminate a dangerous force or a principle of disorder. And now here he was with the prospect of blood on his hands.

"You asked for me, mother?" he murmured.

"How is your father Diemogo?" she asked.

"He won't survive the night," he said.

Nya sighed.

"So our spirits will depart together," she said.

"Don't talk like that, mother . . ."

But Nya seemed to pay no attention to the interruption. Her eyes had all their old lucidity again, scarcely darkened now by sorrow.

"Listen," she said. "We must think about the running of the family. When the council meets, make sure they choose Siga as *fa*."

"Siga!" exclaimed Tiefolo. "But he's the son of a slave!"

Nya took his hand.

"A slave who was very unjustly treated," she said. "Haven't you ever heard how she died? And Siga himself hasn't had a very happy life. So let us give him this happiness."

Tiefolo looked at the old face. What was she scheming now? Wasn't she merely avenging her favorite son? Tiefolo was neither ambitious nor proud, but he did like the rules to be kept. As the eldest son of the eldest surviving brother he had a right to the honor and responsibility of being the *fa*. But he felt so guilty toward Nya he was ready to do anything to please her.

"Depart in peace, mother," he said. "I shall propose Siga to the family council. It's true he is more worthy than I."

He couldn't keep a certain bitterness out of his voice.

Then he went away.

On reflection, Nya's suggestion suited him. People wouldn't be able to say he'd gotten rid of Tiekoro to satisfy his own ambitions. He rested his forehead against the trunk of the *dubale* tree in the courtyard, hurting himself on its roughness and taking pleasure in the slight pain. He hadn't wanted his brother to die— the gods and the ancestors knew that. He had merely hoped the Mansa would banish him to one of the provinces, or make him break off all contact with the Muslims of Macina and everywhere else. When Tiekoro reached the other world he would know very well he was innocent, and couldn't pursue him for revenge. He hadn't done anything. He'd just imagined the family being divided by Islam, the sons being brought up by Segu's enemies, allegiances shattered, ancestral values trampled underfoot.

He heard himself weeping and was surprised at the violence of his sobs. For days he had been dry-eyed, and now his tears were enough to fill the Joliba. He hadn't cried like this since Naba disappeared—Naba, whose death he had caused too in a way, by taking him on the hunt from which he never returned. His hands were soiled. Terribly soiled.

He knelt down deep in the loose earth between the huge roots. Above him he could hear the shrill cry of the bats, seeming to mock his grief and remorse. Why was life this swamp into which you were drawn in spite of yourself, to emerge defiled, your hands dripping? Left to himself he would only have been a hunter, a *karamoko*, challenging the animals in fair fight, with mutual esteem and respect. Ah, why couldn't men be as pure as beasts of prey?

Tiefolo wept for a long time.

Then he went out of the compound and made his way to Siga's house. As he approached he wondered whether this belated honor might not be the last snare to tighten around Siga's neck, a defeat in the shape of a victory. For it would mean his leaving his present home, taking Fatima and the children back to live in the compound and giving up the profession of tanner that had so annoyed the family before and would now be regarded as utterly unworthy of a *fa*. In other words, it would underline the fact that he was a failure.

Diemogo was going to die, and Siga, surviving him, seemed about to get his own back on the brother who had always overshadowed him. But his revenge would be a poor thing, tasting of dust and ashes.

CHAPTER

6

Muhammad was on his way back to the refectory when he was told his mother was waiting for him in Cheikou Hamadou's house. He had heard a few days before that his father had been publicly executed, but he hadn't shed a tear. On the contrary, his heart had filled with pride. His father had died a believer, a martyr in the true faith. Cheikou Hamadou had promised to make his exploits known, and soon his grave would be a place of pilgrimage for the Muslims. Muhammad had mingled his slight voice with those of the adults around him as they recited: "May God bless him and grant him perfect and lasting salvation until the Day of Judgment, and the same to his successors throughout his whole community!"

But when he heard Maryem was there he became a child again, impatient and spontaneous, and started to run. Alfa caught him by the arm.

"Remember," he said, "she's only the mother of your body."

So Muhammad went through the courtyards at a suitably dignified pace.

When Maryem saw her beloved son she wept. The boy was much taller, nearly the height of an adult. But he was indescribably thin: his arms and legs looked like dried silk cotton sticks, so close did the skin stick to the bone. And yet how handsome he was! A new spirituality refined his features, and his light brown eyes shone between their thick dark lashes with an almost unbearable brilliance. Unlike some of Cheikou Hamadou's disciples, who claimed to be following the Prophet, he did not shave off his hair and it grew in close curls. His graceful movements recalled those of a Fulani herdsman. He would have liked to rush up to his mother, throw himself in her arms and wipe away the tears that were running down her cheeks. But he dared not. He knew such behavior was unworthy of a man.

Cheikou Hamadou was sitting on a mat in the middle of the Grand Council room.

"Your mother has been telling us about your father's last moments," he said quietly. "It is proper that you should be present to learn from him how a man should die."

Maryem managed to stifle her sobs.

"Then they tied his arms behind his back—and he a nobleman!—and flogged him till the blood flowed. I cried out, 'Stop! Stop!' but no one would listen. Then they made him go up on a platform that had been erected outside the palace. He looked all around him quite calmly, smiling. Then the executioner, one of those brutes only the Bambara produce, with a bestial face and ferocious eyes, came up behind him and with one blow from his saber cut off his head. His body fell forward. Two great jets of blood spurted out from his neck."

There was a silence.

"Afterwards, at the request of Nya, his mother, they gave us his body. But the worst was still to come! The family were determined to have a fetishist ceremony. They . . . they . . ."

Her voice was drowned in sobs.

"Remember, daughter," said Cheikou Hamadou, "it was only his body, without his soul! So what does it matter?"

Then he stood up and improvised one of the elegies he was so good at. Muhammad wondered when he was going to be allowed to embrace his mother, but, alas, no one seemed to give it a thought. Maryem, who had been prostrate, got up after a moment and spoke again to Cheikou Hamadou.

"I am not here, father," she said, "just to talk about Tiekoro's death. The family council has met and decided I'm to be given to Siga, my dead husband's brother. I'm not criticizing the custom itself—I know it's good, excellent. But Siga's a fetishist—worse, an apostate, because he embraced Islam when he was an apprentice in Fez. Can I be forced to live with a fetishist and an apostate?"

As she said this her proud face lit up with anger. Her white veil fell back around her neck, ringed with heavy silver necklaces. Muhammad would have liked to cry out in admiration, which he believed to be shared by everyone else, but he met his teacher's eye and realized he was embarrassed. Cheikou Hamadou gazed at the members of the Grand Council as though waiting for their suggestions. Finally Bourema Khalifou spoke.

"You are certainly presenting us with a serious problem, Maryem," he said. "As you have said, it is good and right that a woman should go to her husband's younger brother. But an apostate! What do you yourself suggest?"

"Give me an escort and let me go back to my father!"

The members of the Grand Council consulted each other silently. After all, it was perfectly feasible—a good way, even, of doing the sultan of Sokoto a favor, since he wouldn't like the thought of his daughter in the arms of an apostate. But then Maryem made a mistake.

"I've brought my daughters with me," she said. "All I need now is my son."

In spite of the reserve Islam imposed on people's speech and behavior, this caused an uproar. Since when had a son belonged to his mother? Yes, but the father was dead, and the father's family were fetishists! So to whom was he to be entrusted? Perhaps for the first time, the rights of the family and those of Islam were in opposition. And however much one looked in the works of eminent scholars, from Al-Buhari's *Sahih* to Al-Ughari's *Al-fiyyat al Siyar*, there was no suggestion as to what should be done in this particular case. Cheikou Hamadou rose and clapped his hands.

"Leave us now, Maryem," he said. "We shall think it over and let you know our decision."

Maryem was already retiring, not daring to protest, when Cheikou Hamadou seemed to remember Muhammad's presence. He kindly signaled for him to go with her!

What child separated from his mother for nearly a year wouldn't be transported with joy to see her again? Muhammad covered her fine soft skin with kisses, drinking in her Hausa perfume. He sat on her lap, crumpling her veils and her skirts. Maryem laughed, almost forgetting the terrible times she had just lived through.

"Stop it!" she scolded. "You're not a baby anymore!"

Then Muhammad rushed to his sisters. How charming little Aida was—she'd been a babe in arms when he left Segu! Now she could walk, and talk a little. She was frightened of this unknown brother, and clung to her sisters' skirts.

Between kisses Muhammad asked for news of the family.

"What about mother Adam?"

"And mother Fatima?"

"And father Siga?"

"And father Tiefolo?"

At this a terrible expression came over Maryem's face.

"Don't ever mention that name again!" she said. "He was in league with your father's enemies!"

Tiekoro's death had wrought a thorough change in Maryem. Whereas before she had always doubted the depth of her husband's faith and thought she detected in his every act a strong element of narcissism, she now realized she had been living with a saint, and she belatedly began to revere him as a rare spirit.

After the midday meal they all went to M'Pene's house to see grandmother Sira. She didn't pay much attention to anything any more, but Maryem and M'Pene threw themselves into one another's arms and were soon exchanging life stories. M'Pene missed Tenenkou, where she had grown up. Hamdallay was so austere that Sheikh El-Bekkay of Timbuktu had come to complain to Cheikou Hamadou about it. But Maryem shook her head: anywhere was better than Segu.

"Fetishists!" she exclaimed. "Always busy doing someone else a bad turn or trying to find out who has injured them."

Then they got to talking about the mysterious quarrel between El-Hadj Omar and Cheikou Hamadou. A quarrel between two Muslims! Was such a thing possible? What exactly had happened? M'Pene didn't know much about it. People said it was one of those disagreements between brotherhoods—Tijaniya against Qadriya. But was it only that? There was a rumor that El-Hadj Omar had commercial and political designs on the region.

M'Pene served rice cakes cooked in shea butter and rolls made of beans and honey.

When Maryem and the children started back it was beginning to get dark. Maryem shivered in this chilly town where in every street there was a Koranic school full of ailing children. At every street corner there were visionaries calling on the name of Allah. In one square a criminal was being flogged. Such sights made her almost wish she were back in Segu. She hurried into Cheikou Hamadou's compound.

Apparently the Grand Council had found it difficult to come to a decision: it had sat all morning and met again for part of the afternoon. But at last it had delivered its verdict. Maryem was to be given presents and an escort so that she might return to Sokoto in a manner befitting her rank. Muhammad was to stay in Hamdallay: his father himself had given him into Cheikou Hamadou's charge, and might that not be regarded as the last wish of a dying man?

Muhammad nearly fainted away when he heard this. His body went hot and cold and he saw his mother and sisters through a veil, like magic islands forever out of reach. Why, why? In the name of what god? He was tempted to shout and blaspheme. But his outward behavior betrayed none of this inward tumult, and everyone agreed he was a son worthy of his father.

At the end of the rainy season he fell ill. He had probably internalized too many painful events. Whatever the reason, one morning as the other disciples were putting on their *boubous*, hurrying out to perform their ablutions and running to the mosque, Muhammad's body refused to obey him. He asked Alfa to bring him a bowl of water, but he could not keep a drop of it down. He felt as if he were being plunged into a well, then snatched out into a dull but blinding light. As all this lasted for several days, M'Pene, alerted by Alfa, sent her husband Karim and her eldest brother, Tijani, to Cheikou Hamadou, asking to be allowed to look after the boy themselves. Cheikou Hamadou agreed. This was very unusual: generally, when one of the disciples was unwell, no one tried to intervene in the struggle between life and death. Whichever was the stronger won.

Karim and Tijani put Muhammad in a hammock which they carried on a pole over their shoulders.

For several days Muhammad lay as if unconscious, though behind his closed eyes he kept seeing his father's execution. Absorbed in the joy of seeing his mother again, he had thought himself unaffected when he first heard about it.

"They made him go up on a platform that had been erected outside the palace. He looked all around him quite calmly, smiling. Then the executioner . . . came up behind him and with one blow from his saber cut off his head. . . . Two great jets of blood spurted out from his neck . . ."

Ah, that blood, that blood! It would have to be avenged. And how? By making Islam triumph in that land of fetishism. Yet Muhammad also came to identify himself with Segu, which his mother's upbringing had taught him to despise. But Segu was his. He was a Bambara. He would fix the crescents on Segu's minarets with his own hands. He tossed and turned in his agitation.

M'Pene was worried, and went to see a healer who, with a few others, lived in hiding somewhere in Hamdallay. He prescribed potions made of roots and baths made from leaves, and assured her the body of the young patient would recover.

No one helped M'Pene to nurse him more devotedly than little Ayisha, Tijani's eldest daughter. A more exquisite little maid could not be imagined! When she hurried along, taking food to her brothers minding the cows outside the town, people used to nod their heads and smile as she went by, saying, "Yes, a real Fulani girl!"

She was as fair as a Moor, with long smooth hair interwoven with colored threads and lovely feet in goatskin sandals that moved so fast they made her finely chased silver anklets tinkle. When Muhammad, still confused, opened his eyes and saw her by his mat, he said, "Who are you?"

"Don't you recognize me anymore?" she asked. "I'm your sister Ayisha."

Muhammad, his memory returning, shook his head.

"You're not my sister," he said. "You're Tijani's daughter."

Ayisha dissolved into tears and ran out of the room. Muhammad hadn't meant to hurt her: he was just instinctively defending himself against a kinship that would have had to influence their relationship in a certain direction. True, Tijani was the son of his grandmother Sira, but with Amadou Tassirou, not with his own grandfather, Dousika. He and Ayisha didn't have one drop of blood in common! He got up for the first time for a long while and followed her into the courtyard. She was leaning on the rim of the well and sobbing as if her heart would break. In her white robe she stood out against the green trelliswork around the enclosure, and a light breeze stirred the veil over her head. For the first time Muhammad realized what feminine beauty was. Until that day, the only woman who had been beautiful in his eyes was his mother. Now, suddenly, she had a rival.

His wondering gaze took in the strange perfection of a woman's body—the rounded shoulders, the curve of the back and the sinuosity of the hips; the overhang of the breasts; the delicate modeling of the belly.

He went up to Ayisha, took her in his arms, and smothered her with kisses. At first she pushed him away.

"Leave me alone!" she protested. "You've been horrid!"

As he went on kissing her, she instinctively sensed danger and disengaged herself. They stood there looking at each other. Muhammad was not entirely naive. He knew what went on at night between a man and his wives, and why the wives' bellies swelled so satisfactorily. But he hadn't yet imagined himself in such circumstances. Of course the day would come when he himself had wives, but that day was still far off, distant, on the other side of a river he didn't yet care to cross. He was suddenly seized with impatience and excitement, which bereft him of the use of his still uncertain legs. He fell down on his behind in the middle of the courtyard, frightening the chickens, which fluttered away squawking.

"You do look silly!" cried Ayisha, laughing. But she helped him up, and leaning on her he made his way back into the house and lay down on his mat. As she was covering him up with a cotton *pagne* he took her hand and pressed it to his lips.

"Don't ever say you're my sister," he told her. "Not ever!"

From then on he made rapid progress, and as his health improved his character changed too. Whereas he had always been the most accommodating kind of boy, concerned only with pleasing and serving God, he now became secretive and restless, subject to inexplicable fits of anger. Only Ayisha's company seemed to give him pleasure, and he would spend hours with his head in her lap while she told him stories.

When he went back to Cheikou Hamadou's compound he gave Ayisha a narrow silver bracelet he used to wear around his wrist.

Soon afterwards Cheikou Hamadou received a letter from Siga which he showed Muhammad. The writing and syntax were faultless, and it was plain he must have used the services of a scribe.

"Most honorable and revered Cheikou Hamadou," it began. "I might have resented your having taken in the runaway wife of my dead brother, who according to the laws of both your people and mine should have come to me, for the greater good of our family. I might have criticized you for giving her presents and an escort to go back to her father, who has written to tell me she will never return to Segu.

"In all this you have acted in accordance with what you believe to be the truth; you consider us the enemies of God. Have you never thought that each people has its own gods, just as it has its own language and its own ancestors?

"But it is not the object of this letter to persuade you of our right to reject Islam, which is not the religion of our fathers. I want to talk to you of our son Muhammad, whom you are holding in Hamdallay. Our family, to its sorrow, has seen its sons scattered all over the world. One was taken into slavery in Brazil. Another met his death in the kingdom of Dahomey. Both left sons behind them in those foreign lands. I am now the head of the family, and I shall not rest until I have brought all these children together under the same roof, that our ancestors may be consoled and satisfied. I repeat, wherever they may now be, all our children shall take the road back to Segu. Before I take any measures I may consider necessary against you, I hereby ask you to give us back our child of your own free will. He is ours. His *diamou* is Traore. His totem is the crowned crane.

"Yours respectfully and in peace . . ."

"What do you say to that?" Cheikou Hamadou asked Muhammad, guardedly.

Muhammad remembered his father Siga, an affable man with a kind word for everyone. So the family hadn't forgotten him—they cared about him, wanted him back. A wave of happiness swept through him as he repeated to himself, "Wherever they may now be, all our children shall take the road back to Segu." What a beautiful sentence, and how full of meaning! Yes, he would take the road back to Segu: it might be a barren land, but his father had fertilized it with his blood! He himself would make Islam grow there like a sturdy plant that knows neither rainy nor dry season, with roots that seek water and everything else necessary to life in the depths of the soil. He smiled at Cheikou Hamadou.

"What are you going to say to him, father?" he asked.

Cheikou Hamadou then did what many people would have considered shocking, for children were never asked what they thought.

"What do you want me to say?" he replied.

"That I love and respect him," answered Muhammad, "and that I'll come back."

The boy and the old man exchanged a look of total confidence, total comprehension. Then Cheikou Hamadou sent Muhammad away and went on telling his beads. Muhammad, back in the room set aside for teaching and meditation, took his place beside Alfa.

"What did the master want?" whispered Alfa—they weren't really allowed to talk between the recitations of the suras.

Muhammad didn't even hear him. Siga's words were still ringing in his ears: "I shall not rest until I have brought all our children together under the same roof!"

CHAPTER
7

"Eucaristus da Cunha! How can a Negro have a name like that?"

The Reverend Mr. Williams shrugged.

"He's the descendant of a freed slave from Brazil. His father took his master's name."

"But that's illegal!"

"Illegal? Why?" said Mr. Williams, casting up his eyes. "The poor devils lost their identity crossing the Atlantic. They had to be called something."

The Reverend Mr. Jenkins continued to gaze at the young man from a distance.

"How old is he?" he asked.

Mr. Williams laughed. Such questions showed how ignorant the other man was about everything to do with Africa.

"Difficult to tell that sort of thing with Negroes," he said. "I've seen a passport belonging to his mother, and according to that he must have been born in about 1810. Anyway, Jenkins, he's a treasure. He studied at Fourah Bay College in Sierra Leone, and the Reverend Mr. Kissling says he and Samuel Adjai Crowther are our best hopes in this barbarous country."

But Jenkins could neither overcome nor talk himself out of his antipathy.

"Why was Crowther chosen for the river expedition?" he asked.

"How should I know?" answered the other. "I'm not in the confidence of the Society for the Civilization of Africa. Crowther's stronger, and can speak Yoruba perfectly . . ."

"And he's not so arrogant," Jenkins interrupted. Then, "Why isn't this Eucaristus married?"

He made a swift calculation.

"He's quite old enough. Nearly thirty."

Mr. Williams chose to laugh.

"Ask him yourself," he said.

Mr. Williams had been the first Anglican missionary to set foot in Lagos, where because of the unhealthy climate people had given him less than a year to live. But now he had been there three years, and without any help he had built the first hut for the celebration of Mass in those parts. During the first year he had had fewer than ten people in his congregation, but recently there'd been an influx of "Brazilians," ex-slaves from Cuba and Brazil, and of Saros immigrants from Sierra Leone, all eager to send their children to school. These had swelled the numbers of the Europeans who despite abolition continued to deal in slaves, as well as in the lucrative trade in palm oil. So several weeks ago the London Missionary Society had sent Williams a companion in the shape of Jenkins. Unfortunately the latter, an Englishman who had never before been further than the next village, was shocked by everything here. By the lax ways of the Europeans; by the nakedness of the unconverted blacks; by the large numbers of half-castes born of illicit relations between the whites and black women. And to crown it all he had taken a dislike to Eucaristus!

And Eucaristus really was a treasure. His intelligence had struck the Anglican missionaries in Abeokuta where he'd been living with his maternal uncle, and they had gotten him a scholarship from their motherhouse and sent him to Fourah Bay College as one of its first pupils.

It was true he wasn't always easy to deal with! But the Reverend Mr. Williams, who could read him like a book, knew he wasn't arrogant, only shy and troubled. He couldn't get over the death of his parents, and was obsessed by an irrational desire to find the home of his father's family, in Segu, somewhere in the Sudan.

The Reverend Mr. Williams's one desire was to see Eucaristus become a man of God, but for some reason the Englishman couldn't understand, Eucaristus refused.

From where he sat Eucaristus could feel the eyes of the two men on him, and he knew they were talking about him. Mr. Jenkins's hostility didn't bother him in the least. On the contrary, he admired the newcomer's skill in discerning the things he did his best to hide: his weakness for women; for drink; for gambling, even. Hadn't he lost a whole month's salary one evening in a gambling den? Above all his pride, his immeasurable pride! It was because of his pride that instead of living in the Popo Agouda quarter like the other "Brazilians," he had chosen to live in the Marina among the European and half-caste traders. He thought himself better, cleverer than the rest.

He shut his hymn book and clapped his hands to indicate to the children that the lesson was over. They scattered, laughing. Once outside the mission they didn't speak a word of English, only Portuguese or Yoruba. Eucaristus himself could speak Portuguese and Yoruba, which were his mother's languages; English, the medium of instruction at Fourah Bay College; a bit of French; and the whole lot jumbled together to form pidgin, the lingua franca of the coast. This Babel-like confusion of tongues struck him as symbolic of his own identity. What was he? He could not tell!

He locked his desk and went toward the house. It was very hot and the two priests were sitting on the veranda fanning themselves with big pandanus leaves. Mr. Williams could stand the heat quite well, but the other was always bathed in sweat; his face was drawn and his eyes red-rimmed. Once again Eucaristus wondered what these two men were doing so far away from home.

After he had greeted them the Reverend Mr. Williams handed him a letter. It was from his one and only friend, Samuel Adjai Crowther, whom he had left behind in Freetown.

Although parts of Eucaristus's life were interesting, Samuel Adjai Crowther's was a regular saga. When he was thirteen he had been captured by slave merchants from his native village in Yoruba-land, taken to Lagos and put on a boat sailing to Brazil. But the British squadron patroling the coast had set him free on the high seas and landed him at Freetown, where he was baptized.

When Eucaristus met him at Fourah Bay he had just come back from school in Islington in England, where he had dazzled his teachers with his intelligence. He was as serene in character as Eucaristus was tortured, and firmly believed that it was his vocation to civilize Africa.

"My very dear friend," the letter read. "I must first tell you my wife Susan and I are in good health and cured of our fevers by a miraculous medicine from England. Our children Samuel, Abigail and Susan are well too, and if God wills we shall soon have a fourth little Christian under our roof.

"Next I must tell you of a piece of good fortune that has been bestowed on me. I've been chosen to go with a British expedition to set out in a year or so from now to explore the river Niger and set up a model farm at Lkoja at the confluence with the Benoue. The object of the expedition is commercial, but it is also concerned with the evangelization of our black brothers. The two aims go together—'the plow and the Bible' is the mission's new motto and policy. Ah, my friend, what an uplifting task ours is! Thanks to our efforts our beloved land will know the true God, and it will not be the work of foreigners . . ."

Eucaristus folded the letter up and put it away beneath his robe. Was he jealous at seeing his friend chosen for this mission? He was. But, more important, he envied the calmness and order of the other's life and the tranquillity of his faith. To civilize Africa by converting it to Christianity. But what did that mean? Didn't every people have its own civilization, subtended by its belief in its own gods? What was converting Africa to Christianity but imposing an alien civilization upon it?

Eucaristus followed the other two men into the house and joined them in saying grace. Just as he was about to dig his spoon into his yam puree, the Reverend Mr. Williams spoke.

"Do you know what Father Jenkins was just asking me? He wanted to know why you're not married!"

Eucaristus started. Did Mr. Jenkins know something? He tried to read his expression but could see nothing there but the ill-will typical of the Europeans, missionaries and laymen alike, who hated the blacks.

"I just haven't found a Christian who would suit me," he said, looking down at his plate.

Eugenia de Carvalho was certainly the prettiest half-caste in Lagos. Her father was a rich Portuguese trader who sold everything—slaves, palm oil, spices, ivory, wood. It was said he had killed a man in his own country and couldn't go back there, but that was said of every European who was wealthy and fond enough of Africa to want to be buried there. Eugenia's mother was a Yoruba who belonged to the royal family of Benin, and she often went back to the Oba's palace when she grew tired of her companion's drunkenness and cruelty.

They all lived in a *sobrado* or town house built by Brazilian masons, an enormous rectangular two-storey building with a mansard roof. In three of its walls were five arched windows and two doors, their upper panes made of red, green and blue glass which shed a dusky light on a circular gallery, leaving little nooks of shadow. Behind the house was a spacious courtyard planted with papaw, orange and guava trees and filled with the chatter of the slaves, who lived in quarters concealed behind a quickset hedge. At night lamps were hung along this hedge so that people living in the house, and any visitors, could avoid treading on the rubbish left lying about, or stepping in the puddles of smelly water.

Eucaristus had come there to give English lessons to Jaime de Carvalho the younger, the family's son and heir, a boy of about twelve with a bad complexion, already in the habit of sleeping with the family slaves. For Jaime senior, debauched as he was, was a man of education and had an inordinate admiration for the English.

"They are noblemen," he would say. "Just compare them with those Latin bastards—Portuguese, Spanish, French. Soon they'll govern all this coast and the whole of the hinterland. For the moment they're just biding their time, trading, going up the rivers, staking it out. But soon their flag will fly over the palaces of obas and alafins and sultans alike. To speak English is a supreme advantage!"

As he made his way to the Carvalhos' house for the daily English lesson, Eucaristus remembered how Malobali had compared Ouidah with Segu: "You've never seen towns like those. The towns here are the creation of the whites, born of the trade in human flesh. Nothing but vast warehouses."

How he hated Lagos and its smell of vice and mud! How glad he would be to get away! But where to? He didn't know and couldn't decide. Since he'd gotten to know Eugenia de Carvalho, however, he was less impatient to leave, for he loved the girl with a passion all the more violent since he knew it was impossible to fulfill. He might impress Africans who had never seen a book before and went about half naked, but to someone related on one side to the local royal family and on the other to a white man he was just nondescript and ridiculous. Were not the whites the new lords and masters to some? They spoke as equals to the most powerful black rulers, rebuking them, doing their utmost to prove their beliefs were wrong, and gradually getting their own way. Once again Eucaristus's heart filled with hatred—an illogical hatred, for was not he himself a creature of the whites, one of their "best hopes in this barbarous country," as Mr. Williams said? Eucaristus, his mind elsewhere, stepped into a puddle, and looked down furiously at his shoe and the bottoms of his trousers covered in mud. So he was feeling even more rattled than usual as he entered the house.

Eugenia was sitting on a stool having her hair dressed. Her hair, frizzy rather than curly, hung down her back to her thighs and gave off a smell like that of certain animals' fur—sour but pleasant. As she bent forward to let her slaves comb it, her flowered silk dressing gown fell open to show her little round almost white breasts with nipples the color of eggplants. Eucaristus trembled. She looked up and smiled.

"Oh, good morning, Mr. Eucaristus da Cunha!" she said.

She always spoke his name mockingly, as if to stress how incongruous it was for an African.

"I've already told you to call me Babatunde if you prefer. That's my Yoruba name," he said rudely.

"Babatunde da Cunha?" she said, laughing.

The slaves began to laugh too, as if they could understand this exchange. In fact Eucaristus did know his family name too; Malobali had told him what it was. But every time he tried to say it something stopped him, and this seemed to indicate the extent of his alienation. Babatunde Traore—no, never! He preferred to go away rather than argue.

"Where is young Jaime?" he asked.

"I think he's finished making love to Bolanle," she said. "You can have him all to yourself."

Deeply shocked, almost terrified, Eucaristus turned toward the end of the gallery as if expecting the girl's father to appear.

"Miss de Carvalho!" he protested.

She gave her pretty, throaty laugh again.

"And you, Mr. da Cunha?" she asked. "Do you make love too?"

This was too much for Eucaristus. He beat a retreat to the drawing room, hurried through it past a large billiard table—billiards being a passion of Jaime senior—and for once found Jaime junior waiting for him in the study.

"'And you, Mr. da Cunha? Do you make love?'"

The diabolical girl had put her finger on the wound.

Eucaristus was a product of the mission schools. They had taught him the act of love outside marriage was the most heinous of sins and purity the chief virtue. Malobali had talked to him differently, of course, but he'd been only a child then, and now Malobali was dead. How was he to accept his own body, the violent desires that made it tremble, the white shower that soiled his thighs? This hand, that sought his sex; the animal cries he uttered? And above all, those encounters in the most horrible of hovels with a whore shared with countless Portuguese and Englishmen?

"And the Eternal said to Moses," droned Jaime junior, "'Go before the people and take with you some of the elders of Israel. Take in your hand the rod with which you struck the river, and walk. I shall go before you . . .'"

The boy was surprised by his teacher's silence. Eucaristus was usually fussy and difficult, always correcting him and making him repeat whole sentences. He stole a glance at him. Eucaristus was handsome, with his high forehead, bright eyes and delicately modeled cheeks. But for the boy, used to judging people by the color of their skin, he was hideous, with his very dark complexion and fuzzy hair. Behind his back he and Eugenia split their sides laughing at Eucaristus, imitating his stiff and formal manners. How ugly blacks were when they tried to ape white men!

Eucaristus looked at his pupil.

"Very good, Jaime!" he said with surprising gentleness. "You're making excellent progress."

But both his voice and his look betrayed him. Jaime decided to strike.

"Did you know Eugenia's getting married?" he asked. "My father has finally accepted Jeronimo Medeiros. Did you know he was a quadroon? His father's a Portuguese and his mother's a mulatto."

At first Eucaristus was petrified. He knew very well Eugenia would never be his, but to hear, like this, that she was to belong to another! Then he fell on Jaime, grabbed him by the shoulders and shook him till his teeth rattled.

"It's not true!" he cried. "You're lying, you're lying!"

The boy managed to free himself and ran around the study trying to hide behind the heavy armchairs. When he was safe from further attack he started to yell: "It *is* true, it *is* true—she *is* getting married! Do you think we haven't seen how you've had your eye on her? But she isn't for you! Dirty nigger, cannibal— you stink, you eat human flesh! Dirty nigger—go back to the jungle!"

"And to think these people came from the womb of a black woman!" thought Eucaristus. "Have they forgotten?"

But however often Eucaristus reminded himself of this, it didn't do any good. Pain, anger and humiliation mingled in him with a wild desire to be comforted like a child. Romana! Why had she deserted her children to follow Malobali even to death? Where would he ever find so soft a breast? But Eucaristus could never think of his mother without a feeling of bitterness mingling with his filial piety. Has a person the right to die and leave four sons behind, defenseless in the struggle for life? Blessed be the women who are more mother than wife! Like the Blessed Virgin Mary . . .

In the absence of a woman's breast Eucaristus fell back on the nearest substitute—a drink. But after he'd had a large number of glasses his desire only increased, and he found himself, drunk and tottering, on the way to Ebute-Metta.

A disgraceful part of town: a cluster of huts where sailors just off the slave ships came to work off their frustrations with women, mostly mulattos. The previous year an epidemic of smallpox and another of influenza, intensified by a season of torrential rains, had claimed many victims. But there were already plenty of whores again; it was as if they reproduced themselves as quickly as the rats and insects that infested the place. Pedestrians had to flounder through the mud, in the midst of which women went on imperturbably selling bean fritters and slices of plantain fried in palm oil.

Eucaristus pushed open the door of the Flor do Porto, the cheapest brothel in Lagos. Often the prostitutes there would sell themselves for a red kerchief and a row of glass beads. In other words they were neither particularly beautiful nor particularly young. But Filisberta was pretty. She must certainly have had some European blood, for she was very fair. She always dressed in the Brazilian style, in full skirts of printed calico and white cotton blouses, with a checkered turban on her head. The sailors from the slave ships didn't go out of their way for her because she had an unfortunate habit of weeping after lovemaking, and what had her tears got to do with them? But Eucaristus preferred her to all the rest.

She looked at him now in amazement. Although he was a hard drinker, like all the men who came there, he seldom got drunk.

"What's the matter?" she asked.

"I've just been called a dirty nigger by a swine of a half-caste," he told her.

Filisberta shrugged, as if to say such things happened all the time. The half-castes were more arrogant than the whites, trying to make people forget that half their blood was black. As for the Saros and the Brazilians, the former tried to copy the English and despised the latter because they had once been slaves, but both groups loathed the natives and were hand in glove with the half-castes and the whites. That was the world for you. What an age to live in!

Eucaristus followed Filisberta across a line of planks that zigzagged across the mire to a sort of shanty divided into separate cells. This was where the girls entertained their clients. Everyone could hear the obscene noises that came through the thin partitions.

There are times when a man's life disgusts him, staring him in the face with its pitted skin and its bad teeth in their rotten gums. And he says to himself, "No, I can't go on. Things have got to change!" Such were Eucaristus's thoughts in the sour-smelling room just as Filisberta was slipping her blouse off over her head.

He saw himself for what he was: a teacher in a mission school, without any definite status, unable to make a place for himself in the society he admired, obliged to share the bed of a whore. He must get away. But how? What was the only possible way out? To go to a theological college in London and become a man of God. Weren't they the harbingers of the new, conquering civilization?

Yes, but what about his body? Well, he would conquer that too, would turn his lamentable fleshy form into a temple worthy of its creator. What an inspiring task, to conquer oneself! Hadn't Jesus told his disciples to enter by the gate that is strait?

Meanwhile Filisberta, lying naked on the bed, was growing impatient.

"What are you waiting for?" she asked.

Eucaristus gathered up the clothes he had already taken off and looked her in the eye.

"You're never going to see me again," he told her firmly. "I'm not coming here anymore."

CHAPTER
8

The party was at its height.

The bride was dancing with slightly more abandon than was suitable in a young woman of good family. She was wearing a dress of smooth white silk decorated with orange blossoms and with a white velvet train, and her gloved hands rested on the shoulders of a tall, rather solidly built young man with very light-colored skin, curly hair shining with pomade parted over his temples, and long side-whiskers that came down over his turned-down collar. He wore a tailcoat of light gray linen over a pair of black trousers. The other dancers kept their distance from this couple, as if in homage to their newborn happiness. The room was a riot of lace, brooches, bracelets, medallions, and bouquets of flowers almost unknown in these latitudes. Children crept in and out amid the ladies' swirling skirts, and fell upon the table, decorated with greenery, covered with candelabra and cut glass, and bearing the remains of the wedding feast. They dipped their fingers in glasses that had held Spanish wines, rum and brandy, and gnawed at slices of cold meat set in amber-colored jelly.

The waltz ended, and amid the silence that followed, soon broken by women's shrill laughter, the deeper tones of the men and the jingle of glasses, china and cutlery on silver trays carried around by servants in red livery, Jaime de Carvalho senior clapped his hands to announce that he was about to speak.

Eucaristus hated himself for being there among the crowd of

onlookers lost in admiration and envy of these fine folk. And what had they done to get so rich? Sold their fellow creatures! They were just traders in human flesh! Yet they flaunted themselves, pretending to be an aristocracy! Worse still, everyone accepted their pretensions and submitted to them. From where he stood Eucaristus could not hear Jaime. He could only see a kind of olive-skinned puppet with greasy hair and piercing eyes sharpened by the practice of every kind of cunning. Eucaristus had to admit he was suffering—in his pride, in his flesh, and in his heart also, for he desired and loved Eugenia. What had this Jeronimo Medeiros got that he hadn't? He was three-quarters white, that was all. Behind Eucaristus idlers were whispering that for his daughter's wedding Jaime de Carvalho had ordered six canteens of silver worth seven hundred pounds sterling each, together with silver plate and hundreds of fine Havana cigars. The murmur of adulation sickened Eucaristus, and he managed to tear himself away.

It was raining. It was always raining in Lagos: a heavy rain that made every kind of tree and bush spring up wherever there was a patch of soil. It was as if a forest were creeping up on you insidiously, like a reptile trying to encircle you in its toils. When it wasn't raining, a sickening mist seeped out of the air, the source of dangerous fevers. All along the coast the English sailors sang:

> Beware of the Bight of Benin,
> Oh beware. . . .
> For every man that comes back home,
> Forty are buried there.

The Marina, where Eucaristus lived, was a mixture of brick houses and trading posts fortified to discourage attack. In the daytime the lagoon, with its clear waters and fishing boats, presented quite a pleasant spectacle, but at night the place was full of sinister shapes. Eucaristus went quickly up the steps to the balcony surrounding the two rooms of his house, then stopped in surprise. There was a light burning inside and the Reverend Mr. Williams was sitting there crosslegged on a mat, reading his Bible. Eucaristus, whose conscience was far from clear, gave a start, but the priest looked up at him kindly.

"Well," he said, "was it a good wedding?"

"I suppose so," answered Eucaristus. "All the whites and quadroons and mulattos in Lagos were there."

There was a note of bitterness in his voice that did not escape Mr. Williams, but he chose not to notice it.

"I didn't come to talk about those traffickers in blood!" he said. "We've had an answer from London. The Mission Society wants you to go and talk to the Reverend Mr. Schonn, and then you can leave for England."

At a time when the Mission Society was seeking and even encouraging vocations among the Africans in the belief that they were the ones best fitted to propagate the word of God through the Dark Continent, the society's answer had been remarkably slow and unenthusiastic. Eucaristus looked at Mr. Williams in surprise.

"When I wrote to them," said the other with some embarrassment, "I had to mention Mr. Jenkins's reservations about you. He doesn't believe you have a vocation. He thinks you're arrogant, obstinate, spiritually cold."

"Isn't his objection simply that I'm black?" replied Eucaristus.

Mr. Williams didn't want to get involved in a discussion about the relationships between certain white men and the blacks. First the traders and then the white colonists had degraded the blacks by buying and selling them like beasts and making them work on their plantations. They had forced them to behave in ways quite foreign to their own people, Williams was sure of it. There was nothing in common between the Negroes of the coast—coarsened by the traffic in their fellowmen, drunkards, ready to do anything to obtain possessions like those of the Europeans—and the blacks of the interior. The latter were pure, warmhearted, full of wisdom; all they needed was to be brought into contact with the true God. And this task properly belonged to spirits like Eucaristus—the better type of African. White men like Jenkins who generalized and said, "The blacks are like this" or "The blacks are like that" exasperated Williams.

He went to the door.

"Tomorrow we'll go to the harbor," he said. "The brigantine *Thistle* is due to sail soon."

Eucaristus went to his room and undressed, folding his clothes up carefully on a stool beside his mat. All the events of the day were still going through his head. Eugenia! She would never be his! She would have children who were octoroons, and rejoice in the color of their skin! She wasn't the virtuous, modest wife a Christian ought to look for—but how wonderful her kisses must taste, how full her body must be of delights!

At that moment there was a knock at the door and Eucaristus, thinking it must be Father Williams coming back for something, ran to open it. It was Filisberta.

He hadn't seen her since his fit of conscience in the Flor do Porto, and he couldn't have been more terrified if Satan himself had suddenly appeared in front of him. She slipped swiftly into the room, and he had to restrain himself from grabbing hold of her and throwing her out.

"What are you doing here?" he asked.

She laughed.

"I hear you intend to go to England!" she said.

The speed with which news spread in Lagos! You'd think the whole population lived with their ears to one another's keyholes!

"To become a priest!" she went on.

There was a terrible irony in her voice. She continued on into the other room as if she'd been invited. Her self-assurance took Eucaristus aback. She started to take off her clothes. First her red Brazilian skirt. Then her short Yoruba *pagne*.

"What are you doing?" thundered Eucaristus.

She went on undressing, then lay down on the mat, her hands crossed under the nape of her neck.

"I'm leaving Lagos too," she said. "I can't stand it any longer. My father was some swine of a white man—Portuguese, English, Dutch . . . I never knew which, and perhaps my mother didn't either. The bastard who raped her didn't give his name. But she's from Dada, and all our family live there. So I'm going back."

Eucaristus didn't believe a word of all this.

"Go then!" he said savagely. "What the hell's it got to do with me?"

"I need a couple of pounds," she said.

He sat down beside her, frightened, foreseeing an attempt at blackmail.

"Where do you think I can get two pounds?" he asked. "What do you take me for—a slave merchant?"

"That's your problem, darling!" she laughed, saying the endearment in English.

At the same time she ran her hand, whose skill he well knew, along his thigh, bringing it close to his penis, which to his surprise was already stiff and heavy.

"Do you think your reverends would be glad if they knew the child I'm carrying is yours?" she asked.

"God be praised," he stammered, "whores like you are barren . . ."

She laughed. Her caresses grew more unequivocal still.

"So you say. . . . Two pounds, or tomorrow I go to the mission with my little story. Two pounds isn't dear for the kingdom of God, is it?"

She drew him to her, and it didn't even occur to him to protest. As he lost himself in her he was seized with a kind of rage against God, surprising in one who proposed to enter the priesthood. Why had He created sex, only to restrict it to the dreary marriage bed? Why had He given it the taint of filth and sin? Was not the deed of the flesh the most natural and perhaps the most beautiful of all acts—the origin of life?

"The best thing that could happen to our wretched continent would be for the European nations, England and France in particular, to take over its government and depose our ignorant fetishist kings!"

Eucaristus couldn't bear to listen to any more.

"Don't talk like that, Samuel!" he cried. "I don't know anything about the French, but you seem to think the English are generous idealists. Let me tell you, the only thing they think about is trade: flooding us with their drink and their shoddy goods, forcing us to grow cacao and cotton and to produce palm oil for their machines!"

But even as he spoke Eucaristus rebuked himself for losing his temper and getting drawn into an argument he knew was pointless. Because of his own peculiar circumstances Samuel Crowther was deeply devoted to England—it was father and mother to him, the great country that had rescued him from slavery.

"Weren't they the first to abolish the slave trade?" Samuel went on. "And haven't they just abolished slavery itself in their possessions in the West Indies?"

Eucaristus burst out laughing.

"My friend," he said, "I've just come from Lagos. Do you know how many slave ships were there, crammed together in the harbor?"

"Of course the British patrols can't cope with all the slaving countries in Europe—France, Spain . . ." Samuel began to reply.

Eucaristus sighed and took his friend's hand.

"Let's talk about something else, shall we?" he said.

Samuel went and got two glasses and a carafe of port and put them on the table.

"Perhaps we could talk about your vocation," he suggested. "Hasn't it all happened rather quickly? The Reverend Mr. Schonn keeps pressing me to become a priest, and I haven't made up my mind yet . . ."

Eucaristus, embarrassed, filled his glass and emptied it quickly, gazing at a fine oil painting of Samuel that was hanging on the wall.

"I'm afraid of losing my soul," he said, "if I don't put up the strongest possible barriers around it."

"You're just too fond of women, that's all!" said Samuel, looking at Eucaristus kindly. "That's the beast in you you have to fight against. So I've decided to help!"

He put on an air of mystery.

"I'm going to introduce you to a girl who's perfection itself," he said.

Eucaristus felt a foolish desire to shock him.

"What sort of perfection are you talking about?" he interrupted. "The breasts, the hips, the thighs? Do you know if she's good in bed?"

Samuel didn't seem in the least put out. He stood up, took up his hat from a chair, and signaled for Eucaristus to follow him.

Freetown was an impressive place, known as the Liverpool of Africa because of its great commercial activity. Eucaristus, after living for two years in the stifling heat of Lagos, was delighted to find himself among its green wooded hills, its sandy inlets fringed with graceful coconut palms, its profusion of shrubs and flowers—frangipani, magnolias and oleanders. Freetown had been a British crown colony since 1808 and possessed several imposing buildings, including St. George's Cathedral.

The two friends walked slowly through the town, talking. Like most African cities, Freetown was divided into ethnic districts, including one for the Akus, liberated slaves of Yoruba origin; one for the Fulani, recognizable by their ample Moslem *boubous*; one for the Ibos; and another for the Maroons,* descendants of the famous rebel slaves who had held the best-trained British troops so long at bay in Jamaica. The British had only overcome them by using mastiffs from Cuba specially trained to attack Negroes.

"Where are we going?" asked Eucaristus.

"Don't ask questions," said Samuel, smiling.

Everyone agreed that Freetown's greatest charm was the westernization of its population. Slaves set free at sea by the English patrols, others from the islands in the British West Indies, poor blacks repatriated from London—many of these had lost all memory of their mother tongue, religion and traditions and adopted with enthusiasm the ways of the white men. The only exceptions were the Maroons, who had an obstinate hatred and mistrust of the English that time did nothing to moderate. Eucaristus was therefore surprised to see Samuel going toward the district where they lived.

"Do you mix with Maroons now, then?" he asked.

"Daughters are not always like their fathers," replied Samuel. "I repeat, Emma is perfection itself. If you heard her singing in the cathedral!"

Men and women with rather fierce expressions were by now coming out of the wooden houses to inspect them.

"Oh, I nearly forgot!" said Samuel suddenly. "You remember that story you kept telling me, about a white man who was at the gates of Segu when your father was born? Well, I know who it was."

"You do?" said Eucaristus in amazement.

* From Spanish-American *cimarron*, runaway slave.—TRANS.

Samuel assumed the air of a preacher.

"Yes, and it only goes to show the morbid imagination of our people, and how sunk they are in superstition. It wasn't an evil spirit, an albino, or whatever. It was a Scot called Mungo Park."

Eucaristus caught him by the arm. So the tale Malobali had told him so often, which he had taken to be as fanciful as the story of Souroukou and Badeni, was true!

"How did you find out?" he asked.

"I just came across a book he wrote," explained Samuel. "You ought to read it!"

They had come to a huge, rather neglected house with yellow painted walls contrasting with the spinach green of the shutters. The veranda was covered with gardening tools that couldn't have been used very often, for the sweet potatoes, yams and cassava that grew in the kitchen patch were choked with weeds. A very dark and fierce-looking man, a typical Maroon, was splitting coconuts with a machete. Without returning Samuel's greeting he signaled for him to go into the house. Eucaristus, who would have liked to ask Samuel lots of questions, cursed this untimely visit. A book about that man coming to Segu! So it wasn't just some magic fable!

Inside the house a piano stood in pride of place near the window, and two grubbly little boys were playing a duet punctuated with peals of laughter. When they saw the two men they both stopped at exactly the same time and yelled out, "Mother!"

A plump little woman bounced in, apologizing profusely for the state of her house. How could anyone keep a place clean and tidy with all these children—her own, her husband's by a former marriage, those of a brother of her husband's who had just died? Was this the friend Mr. Crowther had told them was coming from Lagos? She had relatives in Abeokuta. No, she wasn't a Yoruba. One hundred percent Jamaican. Eucaristus was just wondering how he could bear this tiresome chatter any longer when he saw a small person enter the room. She was remarkably well-proportioned, with perfect hands and feet. She wore a tight lace blouse and a full blue-and-white check skirt. As she came in her head had been slightly bowed, and when she lifted it Eucaristus met the full force of an extraordinary pair of gray eyes, a feature so unexpected in that black face that he nearly cried out in sur-

prise. The eyes went with a delicate nose and a fine, openly sensual mouth, full-lipped and tinged with mauve. So much beauty
and distinction in a Maroon's daughter! Eucaristus, overwhelmed, turned to his friend and saw his expression of triumph.

"Here's the pearl I've found for you!" it said. "Christian, virtuous, and at the same time ravishingly pretty! Just the wife for
a person like you. She'll stop you from hankering after other
women, and give you fine children to bring up in the respect of
God's word."

Meanwhile the mother chattered on. Seeing Eucaristus's surprise, she explained that the Trelawnys often had gray eyes. They
came down from Nanny, the ancestress who had led the guerrilla
war against the English in the Blue Mountains of Jamaica. She
had forced the English to sign a treaty dividing the island and
guaranteeing the Maroons' freedom. Later, of course, there'd been
traitors who led the English behind their defenses, and it had all
ended in exile, first in Nova Scotia and then in Freetown.

Eucaristus scarcely listened. He was looking at young Emma
as she handed around tea in fine Wedgwood china cups. What
delicate hands, what graceful movements!

As if to remind anyone who might be tempted to forget whose
daughter she was, Father Trelawny, finished now with the coconuts, stumped across the room leaving a straight line of tracks
with his big feet, picked up a banjo from a chair and went back
the way he came, all without a word. Mrs. Trelawny, with a
martyred look at her husband's muddy footprints, explained that
it was a very musical family. All the children played the piano,
and Emmeline played the harp as well, Samuel the flute and Jer-
emy the alto violin. As for Emma, she sang, with a voice as melodious as the song of the keskedee, the Jamaican nightingale.

As she was bending over to refill his cup, Emma looked
straight at Eucaristus and the impact of those bright eyes went
straight to his heart. They were as mysterious and full of secrets
as the waves of the sea. He sensed at once that Emma was playing
a game, surrounding herself with a protective shell. But why?
That charming body contained a matchless personality which
she had chosen, for reasons known only to herself, to conceal.
She wasn't merely pretty, shapely, virtuous, a good singer, able
to delight the cathedral congregation on Sunday. She was also

something quite different, but what? Eucaristus had a vague feeling that he ought to get up and run away, to tell poor Samuel that though he thought he was acting for the best he was completely mistaken about the goods being offered. But alas, he couldn't. He was already under her spell.

The interview with the Reverend Mr. Schonn went rather badly: he was obviously prejudiced against Eucaristus, some of whose answers enraged him.

"Da Cunha? That means you're of Brazilian descent. Why aren't you a Catholic?"

"When my mother's brother took me with him to Abeokuta the only school there was run by the Anglican missionaries, so I went there."

The priest became openly aggressive.

"You're nearly thirty years old and not married. Don't you know it's not good for a man to live alone?"

This was a sore point with Eucaristus, who was always afraid lest his transgressions be found out. He was grateful to the black skin that did not allow his flush of anger to be noticed.

"I'm hoping to persuade a Christian girl to become my wife," he stammered. "Samuel Crowther introduced us."

Eucaristus used Samuel's name as a talisman, for he knew what a high opinion Mr. Schonn had of his friend. It produced the desired effect. Schonn grew milder.

"Samuel is fond of you and speaks of you very highly," he said. "I'm only afraid the qualities of your mind may be better than those of your heart."

Eucaristus seethed. What right had this man to pass judgment on him? What did he know about his heart or his mind? But he restrained himself, and the interview came to an end.

When they founded Fourah Bay College the English had really only intended to train craftsmen in European techniques of carpentry, masonry and metal work and create assistants to help in the administration of the colony. But soon their pupils' thirst for learning had overwhelmed them like a tidal wave, and they had started to train missionaries and teachers whom they sent out at first to their missions on the Gold Coast and more recently

to Lagos, Abeokuta, Badagry and Calabar in the Bight of Benin.
Fourah Bay had become a nursery of talent, a factory producing
what the English traveler Mary Kingsley called the "Negroes in
trousers" who were to spread Western civilization at the same
time as the word of God. The college was housed in a pleasant
building surrounded by spacious well-kept lawns, and the students, dressed all in black in spite of the sun, strolled up and
down the paths with their noses in their books. A few years earlier
Eucaristus had been one of them. But now he felt no pleasure
being back and was even somewhat uneasy. Was this to be the
new face of Africa? It was not very attractive. It spoke of betrayal
and scorn for the values of the ancestors.

He found himself out again in the main street.

Mr. Trelawny had a workshop for cabinetmaking and carpentry on the corner of Wilberforce Street, and everyone agreed
it turned out masterpieces of art. This unsociable, taciturn man,
who had given his two wives ten children without saying a word,
was in love with wood, and the wood, realizing this, yielded to
his will and gave of its best in return. Wardrobes, tables, chests
of drawers, chests, armchairs—all the things he made were genuine collector's pieces, fit to be in a museum. He was helped by
two of his sons, reluctant initiates into his secrets.

Emma helped by taking down orders in a big notebook, for
she wrote in a pretty round hand. She greeted Eucaristus with
the gracious impassiveness that so disconcerted him, but after a
moment asked one of her young brothers to take her place and
stood up, swirling her printed calico skirt over boots that
wouldn't have disgraced a London belle. They went out into the
backyard, at a distance from where old Trelawny and his sons
were bent over their work.

Emma sat down on a tree stump.

"Marriage is a serious matter, Eucaristus," she said. "It's important for both the people concerned to share the same point of
view about everything."

Eucaristus permitted himself a smile.

"I wouldn't say that's true of your family!" he said. "I can't
imagine two people more different than your mother and father!"

"That's true," she admitted. "All our childhood we were torn
between two contradictory models, unable to choose either be-

cause we were so fond of both . . . so I absolutely have to know what sort of person you are."

This kind of talk always terrified Eucaristus.

"But . . . but . . ." he stammered.

"For example," Emma went on, "you seem so proud of your name. But it's the name of a slave!"

Eucaristus was hurt but found the strength to protest.

"What about your own name?" he asked.

"Trelawny?" she said. "It's the name of men and women who never accepted slavery. As soon as my ancestors landed in Jamaica they ran away to the mountains, to freedom. And that's not all."

"What else?"

She looked at her pretty hands, folded over her skirt, and was clearly weighing her words.

"You're so in love with England and the English. You think the whites are our friends, and that we ought to imitate them in everything."

"You're wrong about me there, Emma," Eucaristus objected. "You're confusing me with someone like Samuel. If only you knew the questions that keep tossing and turning in my head. . . . Is the white man's civilization better than that of our ancestors?"

She listened to him with the critical attention of a master appraising a pupil.

"Then why are you so eager to go and study in England?" she asked.

What answer could he give? He decided on the truth.

"It's a sort of wager!" he explained. "I think the white man's model will impose itself on us whether we like it or not. And soon the world will belong to those who know how to make use of it."

As he finished she did something quite unexpected, a complete contrast to her previous reserve: she stroked his cheek. Then she spoke, very gently.

"I'll marry you, Eucaristus," she said. "I understood right from the start. Under all the swagger you're very lonely and troubled."

He fell at her feet, much to the amusement of two small brothers flying their kites in the yard.

"Will you marry me before I go to England?" he asked her. "If I go."

She nodded, with an expression at once mocking and tender, as if to say that in this too she understood him. He sought to bind her by an official ceremony—as if the only chains she would accept weren't those forged by her own will and determination.

CHAPTER

9

From Africa, Eucaristus had had no way of knowing what the world was like. He had vaguely supposed it to be made up of countries with governments, policies and ambitions that determined alliances and degenerated into wars. When he arrived in London at the end of the winter of 1840 he discovered the world in all its complexity. The world was Europe, and also the United States of America, Brazil, Mexico, and, further away still, India, Japan, China. He soon saw it was divided into two camps. On the one hand were the adventurous, predatory nations that fitted out fleets and armed troops to conquer treasures that did not belong to them. And on the other hand, more passive and inward-loooking nations. It was like the jungle! Two countries fascinated him. First, England. She was out there on all fronts, like a diligent workman: China, India, New Zealand, Canada. What was she seeking there across the seas? What energy, what passion! The second country that attracted him was Spain. He plunged into accounts of the exploits of the conquistadors—first Columbus, then Magellan, Pizarro, de Valdivia, Almagro and above all Cortes. Hernando Cortes. Cortes and Montezuma. The conquistador and the last Aztec emperor. The European and the Indian. Two civilizations face to face, the first inexorably destroying the second. Was that the fate awaiting Africa?

Africa! Up till now it had counted for nothing on the map of the world. It was called the "Dark Continent." Its history and its values were not supposed to exist. People could scarcely draw its outline. France and England were drawing fragments of territory out of the obscurity into which they seemed to be plunged, the French around the estuary of the Senegal River and in Gabon, the indefatigable English, after following the coasts, trying to trace the courses of the Niger, the Congo and the Zambesi and make alliances with the rulers in the interior.

Apart from that, Eucaristus suffered a good deal on account of the curiosity he aroused as soon as he went outside the seminary at Islington. In streets and coffeehouses all conversation would stop, and hundreds of pairs of unbearably bright eyes— gray, blue and green—would stare at him. People touched his skin to see if its color was painted on. They felt his hair. As soon as he opened his mouth they cried, "He can talk! And he speaks English!"

Was this the behavior of civilized people? Eucaristus recalled the courtesy with which the whites had been welcomed in the kingdom of Dahomey, where he had grown up. They had been treated like lords. So why was he regarded as a strange kind of animal? After all, blacks weren't a new thing in England. At the end of the last century there had been so many of them that Parliament had had to pass a law to send them back to Sierra Leone. But probably they had been only poor folk, just keeping body and soul together in districts where society people never ventured; whereas he shocked people by having the temerity to emerge from such places. As soon as he arrived in London he hated it—wallowing in the smell of horse manure like a whore in a dirty bed. The traffic terrified him. There were drays, carts, little omnibuses, cabs, horses, barouches and cabriolets, and occasionally carriages with a coachman perched up on a dazzling saddle cloth in front and two lackeys jolting up and down behind. Ragged sweepers collected the horse droppings; most of them were Indians with skins as dark as his own, but they were strangely distant. The dirt and overcrowding horrified Eucaristus, and caused a stench never swept away by cleansing breezes such as those of Freetown. A few yards from the Strand and its rows of luxury stores you came upon lanes and alleys strewn with filth and human excrement, and these led to hovels filled with human wrecks sleeping and copulating on heaps of straw or rags crawling with vermin. When he saw such things Eucaristus always asked himself the same question: Why did the English go spreading their religion and their way of life to the ends of the earth when there was so much to be done at home? It was because their real object was quite different—their real aim was to trade, to trade so that the rich might get richer. Eucaristus lowered his eyes when he went through the districts where prostitutes lived, streets and alleys full of women and even little girls. The gaslight made their pale skins look even more ghastly, and their straw-colored hair had the unhealthy look of mattresses never put out to air in the sun.

Of course there were the fine buildings, like St. Paul's Cathedral, Westminster Abbey and Buckingham Palace where Queen Victoria lived. But how could anyone care about constructions of stone when the finest edifice of all, the human body, the repository of the soul, was so degraded?

One day, north of St. Paul's, intrigued by the noise and the stench, he went to the entrance of an underground slaughterhouse. Surrounded by walls encrusted with blood and grease, some men—but were they really men?—were cutting sheeps' throats and disemboweling them. When he came away from this vile den, Eucaristus was overcome with nausea, and so upset he didn't hear the jests of a group of costermongers, knowing young men in linen coats and tight-fitting braided trousers who hawked fruit and vegetables stolen from Covent Garden market.

When not attending his classes at the seminary in Islington, Eucaristus, to ward off his loneliness and the now constant feelings of doubt and hatred so incompatible with the priesthood, had gotten into the habit of taking refuge in a bookshop at 20 Charles Street, Westminster. It belonged to William Sancho, one of the sons of Ignatius Sancho, the most famous black of his generation, a friend of Sterne, the author of *Tristram Shandy*, and Gainsborough's favorite model. Ignatius had come to England at the age of two and grown up in various aristocratic families, one of which was that of John, second Duke of Montagu. The duke had been dazzled by his intelligence and done all he could to enable him to set himself up as an author. He had married a West Indian girl and they had had six children. It was in this small room, drinking innumerable cups of tea, that Eucaristus read the tales of travel and discovery he came to love, as well as the novels of such authors as Laurence Sterne, Charles Dickens, Jane Austen and William Makepeace Thackeray.

Yes, one day all the children in Africa must learn to read and write, so that they might communicate across time and space with the best minds in other parts of the world. Eucaristus was utterly confused. The Europeans he hated one minute he fervently admired the next, because they had invented books, those marvelous magical objects which fix and organize thought.

Of course Eucaristus, never altogether in control of his senses, also went to Charles Street because he had his eye on William's wife. Perhaps because she too was a Jamaican it seemed to him she was like Emma, the wife so passionately desired whose body he had scarcely tasted. She had the same lively intelligence as Emma and was equally unconventional. When her husband was out of the way she whispered to Eucaristus: "Ignatius Sancho was a real idiot, you know! If you read his letters you can see he takes himself for a genuine Englishman just because a few lords patted him on the shoulder."

Every time he entered the bookshop—to tell the truth not many other people went there—Eucaristus always asked William the same question.

"Have you got my book yet?"

This was the book Samuel had mentioned: *Travels in the Interior Districts of Africa performed under the direction and patronage of the African Association in the years 1795, 1796, and 1797 by Mungo Park, Surgeon.*

But the volume had been published in 1799, and it was now impossible to find a copy.

One day as Eucaristus was finishing a meal in the refectory, a very light-skinned mulatto came up to him. Ever since his misadventures with Eugenia de Carvalho, Eucaristus had disliked mulattos, but the other greeted him with a warm smile and outstretched hand. And he was handsome, too, with his curly red whiskers!

"I've been told your wife's from Jamaica," he said. "I'm from there too—in fact, from Port Antonio in the same district as Nanny Town where the Trelawnys come from. My name's George Davis."

Though Emma had told him the story of the Trelawnys at great length, Eucaristus had attached no more importance to it than to the fanciful glorifications with which all families surround their origins. In particular that gray-eyed grandmother Nanny, who had slaughtered so many Englishmen by magic and the sword, had seemed to him as unreal as the goddess Sakpata or the god Shango. Had she really existed, then? He asked the missionary to sit down, and George did so with pleasure.

"I'm here," he said, "with a delegation of Jamaican missionaries of all denominations—Methodists, Baptists, Wesleyans, Anglicans. We've come to see Lord Howick, Under Secretary of State at the Colonial Office. Things are bad in Jamaica."

Although Eucaristus's father had died there as a slave in tragic circumstances, Eucaristus had never been much affected by what was going on in the New World, perhaps because the Agoudas had seemed to regard their years of servitude in Brazil as a visit to paradise.

"Why is that?" he inquired vaguely. "Wasn't slavery abolished there nearly ten years ago?"

George Davis shook his head sadly.

"What's the use of abolishing slavery," he said, "if you don't give the Negroes anything to live on? What's needed now is agrarian reform. Take the land away from the white planters and give it to those who work on it."

"Do you think the same sort of thing might happen one day in Africa?" Eucaristus ventured to ask. "I mean, do you think the whites might seize the lands of our ancestors?"

"I don't know Africa, my dear friend," said George, "but I'm very much afraid . . ."

Eucaristus would have liked to go on with this conversation, but George got up, promising to see him again next day.

The Jamaican was telling the truth—Eucaristus had always suspected the white men were a threat. They bought and sold from the decks of their ships, then went away. Sometimes two or three of them would install themselves in some wretched hut and talk about their God, but both the traders and the missionaries were mere harbingers, to be followed by armies, men who wanted to conquer and command. What could be done to ward off their invasion? Eucaristus felt like a fetish priest gifted with second sight but unable to change the events he sees all too plainly.

In his distress he went out. The cold bit into him like a wild beast, lurking behind the stone walls. He went past the black frontage of an asylum and followed a familiar path to the Thames. A steamboat service had just been started; it presented a strange spectacle. The boats, belching out black smoke that made the sky over the city even more murky, went up and down without either oars or sails, cleaving the river and making its waters heave. The sight usually delighted Eucaristus, but this afternoon it left him unmoved. To the aversion he felt for London was added a genuine fear. It was as if he were in Satan's den. The strength and energy of the English, admirable enough in themselves, were being directed against him and his people. How were they to defend themselves?

As he stood there, leaning his elbows on the stone parapet, he heard a voice.

"Sir!" it said.

He turned to find himself face to face with a footman in purple livery with shining brass buttons. He was holding out an unsealed note so strongly scented that for a moment it drowned the smell of manure in the street.

"Can you be at 2 Belgrave Square at eight o'clock this evening?" it said. "We desire to make your more ample acquaintance."

Eucaristus looked at the man in amazement. The other, with the decorum peculiar to his class, nodded slightly in the direction of a carriage standing on the other side of the bridge. Eucaristus, who was always terrified of having to cross the road, took his life in his hands and tried to make his way to the vehicle almost under the hooves of the horses going and coming in all directions. But just as he got there the coachman whipped up the horses and the carriage disappeared. Eucaristus was left standing, oblivious of the remarks of the passers-by.

"Hey, nigger," called one. "Are you trying to go back to the hell you came from?"

It didn't occur to Eucaristus for a moment to ignore the strange invitation, for he could tell from the scent and the writing that it was from a woman! At first he had felt a kind of repugnance for Englishwomen, with their complexions like blancmange, hair like seaweed, and eyes like those of beasts of prey wide open in the dark. But gradually curiosity had changed into desire, and he was always thinking about them. What were their nipples like? And the forest covering their pubis? William Sancho, who claimed to have known some of them, said they cried out when they made love. Soon only the thought of Emma, whom he loved and respected deeply, kept him from going to a prostitute in the Haymarket.

What should he do till eight o'clock? Go to William's bookshop? No, he wouldn't be able to contain his eagerness for his prospective adventure; he would give himself away. He went into a coffeehouse. Eucaristus's first appearances in these surroundings had caused great bewilderment. With exquisite courtesy the gentlemen pried him with questions. How did he come to speak such perfect English? Eucaristus was amazed at such ignorance in a country where the abolitionist struggle had caused such a stir. But perhaps that had involved only intellectuals and little-known politicians. In the end Eucaristus became a habitué of Will's Coffeehouse. There at least he met cultivated people, well-informed about English exploration in Africa and slave rebellions in the West Indies, as well as the difficulties of King Louis Philippe of France. There too he could enjoy a good fire, a delicious drink and above all the feeling of belonging to the better class of mankind. But that afternoon he was frankly in no mind to appreciate such pleasures.

Lady Jane, Countess of Beresford, was reaching the age when a woman's charm is at its height. Another few years and the inexorable moment would come when her flesh would begin to sag, blurring the oval of her face and the firmness of her breasts. When the luster of her teeth, set in her mouth like pearls, would dull, together with the brightness of her blue eyes fringed with their black lashes. But for the time being she was perfect! She was wearing a gown of watered silk with leg-of-mutton sleeves, and half reclining on a Louis Quinze sofa, the only furniture in the room apart from a few pieces of Chippendale.

"Do you like Canary wine?" she asked.

Eucaristus managed to murmur that he did. The room was hot. A cheerful fire was burning in the grate, and once again Eucaristus wondered if he was really awake. This was the first time he had entered the house of a member of the English nobility, and he found himself suddenly plunged into a world of luxury and beauty completely new to him. For fear of seeming naively impressed, he didn't dare look at the pictures and hangings on the walls, the patterns on the Japanese screens or the knickknacks scattered about the room.

"Tell me about yourself," said Lady Jane, inclining her head graciously. "What are you doing in London? I always thought Negroes lived among the sugarcanes in the West Indies."

Eucaristus swallowed and tried to give a spirited answer.

"Sometimes, like me, they take up theology," he said.

Lady Jane burst out laughing.

"Theology?" she exclaimed. "Come over here and explain."

As Eucaristus hesitated, she insisted, patting the sofa beside her.

"Come along!"

Eucaristus obeyed, overwhelmed with embarrassment. He hadn't been in such a situation since the first time he'd made love. The girl had been one of his uncle's slaves, who had teased him as he came out of school: "They say the priests have forbidden you to use your palm shoot!" she taunted.

So he'd fallen upon her and taken his revenge. And in spite of the difference in their ages and social status, this female here was after the same thing, Eucaristus felt it with all his masculine instincts. But was it possible?

"My story begins, of course, before I was born," he said, plucking up his courage. "It starts with the birth of my father, a Bambara nobleman . . ."

"So you have noblemen where you come from, too?" interrupted Lady Jane, laughing again.

Looking at her, Eucaristus was sure she wasn't interested in anything he might say. He took three gulps of wine.

"Why have you asked me here, madam?" he said.

Everything happened very quickly after that, with the swiftness of dreams in which events and actions rush past in confusion. Afterwards, Eucaristus couldn't remember whether he threw himself on her or she drew him toward her, or if their eager bodies met halfway. However it was, he found himself struggling with silk, muslin, lace and pearl buttons amid a heady scent of carnation. When his hand touched the warm naked flesh he drew back, thinking suddenly of Emma. Hadn't he sworn to be faithful to her? But as he disengaged himself he saw, very close, the whiteness of a skin shadowed in places by a light down, and the words of the Song of Songs came into his head: "Thy two breasts are like two young roes that are twins, which feed among the lilies."

If love was damnation, let him be damned!

William Sancho was right. They did cry out, these women, and scratched, and twisted and turned like snakes caught by the tail! Whenever Eucaristus fell back exhausted on the cushions, Lady Jane's ardent hand set him going again. He felt as if he were riding a mare across a river in a flood. Then the mare herself lost her footing, the seething waters closed over. "Mother, I'm dying," she gasped. "Mercy—I'm drowning!"

When Eucaristus came to, the luxurious boudoir was in darkness: the candles in the chandeliers had burned out. His body was still excited, grateful for all the pleasures it had enjoyed, and he tried to cover his partner's white flesh with kisses. She pushed him away.

"Go now!" she whispered. "My husband . . ."

"When shall I see you again?"

"Tomorrow at the same time!"

Out on the pavement the cold sobered him. He gazed at the lofty facade of the mansion, and wouldn't have been surprised to see it disappear, crumble away like those edifices of the imagination that cannot withstand the light of day. Suddenly he was filled with a strange kind of joy. He wasn't thinking of Emma, whom he had just injured so cruelly, but of Eugenia de Carvalho. She had taunted him, despised him, called him a "dirty nigger" through the mouth of her horrible little brother! Well, his mistress was white. Not only white, but an aristocrat, too!

He actually hopped and skipped to Leicester Square. In taverns brilliantly lit with gas, customers were drinking their grog as French musicians in red jackets played waltz tunes. Late revelers were arriving from where dancers whirled around in polkas and quadrilles; their laughter rang out, carried by the cold and the dark. The night life that had hitherto frightened Eucaristus, not because it was sinful but because he thought he had no place in it, now seemed accessible. He too could enjoy it, just as he had enjoyed the woman. Tumultuously. How quickly it had passed! How he would make up for it tomorrow, for you never really appreciated love till the second time.

The night slipped by like a dream, with Eucaristus reliving every moment of his encounter with Lady Jane. In the morning there was a knock at the door. It was George Davis.

"Goodness, you look awful!" he said. "Dress up warm—the climate's dangerous in this part of the world. Would you like to come with me? We've got an appointment with Sir Thomas Fowell Buxton. He's the one who's going to present our request to Lord Howick."

Eucaristus pretended he had an essay to finish. To hell with the abolitionists and the Negroes in the West Indies too! His mistress was white, and an aristocrat! At eight o'clock sharp that evening he presented himself in Belgrave Square. The imposing footman who had shown him in the day before opened the door to him and ushered him into the hall, but before Eucaristus had time to speak he handed him a sealed note from a Boulle chest of drawers.

"Isn't her ladyship at home?" said Eucaristus.

Without a word the mastodon led him back to the door, while two other beanpoles materialized as if by magic from between the potted plants.

Outside, Eucaristus deciphered the missive by the pallid glare of the gaslights.

"Bravo!" it said. "I give you a few marks more than Kangaroo. Farewell."

"Kangaroo? It's an animal. What more can I tell you?"

"Not with a capital K."

William Sancho scratched his head. He'd never understood Eucaristus: he always thought he was odd. But today, getting him out of bed to ask him the meaning of a word, he'd excelled himself. As Mrs. Sancho appeared in the shop, her blouse slightly awry, he asked her: "Do you know who Kangaroo is, my dear?" he asked.

Mrs. Sancho rolled her eyes. Goodness, men were stupid.

"*You* know," she said. "That Negro acrobat in the Haymarket."

Impossible to describe what Eucaristus felt.

At first he thought of going back to Belgrave Square. But no, the footmen would throw him out like a serf. Then he considered going to the Argyll Rooms where Kangaroo performed, to see with whom he was being compared. But what was the good?

And yet, thinking it over, he couldn't understand. Lady Jane must hate him, to wound and humiliate him so gratuitously. But she hadn't listened to him closely enough to know what he was like, and all he had done was give her pleasure. So was it his race she was aiming at? But why? Did people with white skins naturally hate those with black skins? What had they got against them? What harm had they done by being born?

When he didn't feel rebellious he was overwhelmed with genuine despair. He thought of the soft flesh of his mistress for a night. An island on which he would never set foot again, a land of milk and honey snatched away as soon as reached. A round bowl full of scented wine. A millstone crowned with lilies. A tower of ivory . . .

Almost sobbing, he went into the seminary. The porter, seeing him go by like a shadow, decided to tell the superior. If that black wanted to become a priest, he'd better mind his p's and q's!

On the piece of carpet outside his door Eucaristus found a letter and a parcel, both from Emma. He opened the letter.

"My poor Babatunde," it said. "When I think of you in that hellish London, I tremble and my eyes fill with tears. You, so sensitive and frail, vulnerable to every kind of temptation . . ."

How well she knew him! How he wished he could take refuge in her arms! Why had he humiliated and injured her so wantonly?

He read on.

"Your friend Samuel has left with the Reverend Schonn and one hundred and forty-five Englishmen to go up the river Niger.

You know their plan: to set up a model farm to grow cotton and
other crops, so as to encourage our people to take up farming for
profit. It seems this idea doesn't come from the missionaries
themselves; they couldn't have afforded to finance such an expedition. It originated with the politicians. Have you by any
chance met Mr. Fowell Buxton? They say he's sincerely fond of
our people . . ."

Here Eucaristus gave a sardonic laugh. No Englishman liked
the blacks. It was of crucial importance not to fall into such a
trap. The most winning smiles, the sweetest words only concealed death-dealing weapons.

Treacherous female!

"You won't believe this, but by dint of searching I've found
that book you wanted so much. It was there all the time in the
library of Fourah Bay College."

Eucaristus tore open the parcel.

*Travels in the Interior Districts of Africa performed under the
direction and patronage of the African Association in the years
1795, 1796, and 1797 by Mungo Park, Surgeon.*

There was a bookmark inserted by Emma's considerate hand at
Chapter XV:

Sego, the capital of Bambarra, at which I had now arrived, con-
sists, properly speaking, of four distinct towns; two on the
northern bank of the Niger, called Sego Korro and Sego Boo; and
two on the southern bank, called Sego Soo Korro and Sego See
Korro. They are all surrounded by high mud walls; the houses
are built of clay, of a square form, with flat roofs; some of them
have two storeys, and many of them are whitewashed.

As his eyes skimmed the page, Eucaristus could hear the voice
and words of Malobali: "One day you'll come to Segu. You've
never seen a town like it. The towns here were created by the
white men—they were born out of the trade in human flesh.
They're no more than vast warehouses. But Segu—Segu is like
a woman you can only possess by force."

Sobbing with shame, remorse and pain, Eucaristus fell on his
bed.

What was he weeping for?

For himself and his recent humiliation, yes. But also for the purity of his Segu ancestors which he had lost forever. Segu, a world closed in on itself, impregnable, refusing to admit the white man doomed to wander forever outside its walls. He would never bathe in the waters of the Joliba, and draw from it strength and vigor. He would never recover the proud self-assurance of that past.

His tears gradually dried. He sat up. In a few months he would be ordained. He knew already that his mission would bring him back to Lagos. To Christianize and civilize Africa—that was his fate.

To Christianize and civilize Africa. In other words, to pervert it?

PART FIVE

AND THE GODS TREMBLED

CHAPTER

1

For some years Siga had suffered from elephantiasis. He found it humiliating: after all the disillusionments and disappointments of his life, this struck him as the supreme betrayal because it was that of his own body. His left leg was swollen from the knee down; at the ankle it was the size of a guava trunk. The skin was cracked and swollen, covered in places by an eczema that was sometimes purulent. To drag all this weight around he had to lean on a stick carved for him by his eldest son. Once he sat down he couldn't get up again without help. When he had lain down it was much worse! He had lost so many teeth he could no longer eat kola nuts whole. The young slave girl Yassa had to grate them first and hand them to him in an earthenware bowl. Siga wondered what he had done to his body that it should let him down like this while he was still a good way from the grave. He hadn't committed any excesses— at least, no more than other men, no more than Tiefolo, who was still as straight as a palm and could walk for miles when out hunting.

The truth was that Siga had begun to be interested in lovemaking in his old age. Probably it was one way of fighting the fear that comes to every man at the end of his life. In the light of dawn he started to caress the body of Yassa, lying beside him. Her first reaction was an instinctive recoil, which he was too sensitive not to notice. Then she opened her eyes.

"What do you want, master?" she said.

"Nothing," he answered. "Nothing."

He stroked her side. She was awake now, and got up lithely. Siga lay and watched the crisscrossed branches that supported the roof. The coming day would be inexorably the same as all the others. He would wash his mouth out with warm water and then have his first bowl of gruel. Then he would listen to people's complaints. That would take him to bath time. Then he'd go and sit under the *dubale* tree, chew on a stick and listen to some more complaints.

Yassa came back with another slave girl, carrying a bowl of hot water and, more surprisingly, a sealed letter. She knelt and gave it to him.

"It came during the night, master," she said. "A Fulani from Hamdallay brought it."

Siga turned it over and over. The few rudiments of Arabic he had managed to acquire had faded away long ago. He could no longer either read or write.

"Bring Mustapha," he ordered.

Mustapha was his sixth son, the only one who made him happy to be a father. All the others were too attached to Fatima, now aging and shrewish, and always took her side. With Yassa's help Siga rose and went out into the courtyard to wait for Mustapha. It was dawn. The infernal din of the muezzins was wafted from the mosques. For there was nothing to be done—Islam was spreading like some insidious disease detected too late. It was as if Tiekoro's spectacular and tragic death had triggered off vocations even within his own family. Some people, seeing him die in that way, were full of wonder and envy and said to themselves, "What is this faith for which a man is ready to die?" And they had followed in his footsteps, as if on some treasure hunt.

Black streaks ran across the sky from east to west, and Siga wondered wearily if he would see the end of this rainy season. And the beginning and end of how many others? He rinsed his mouth, spat out the water to right and left, gave the bowl back to Yassa, waiting behind him, and cried: "Well, where's Mustapha?"

Yassa ran off and soon came back with the boy. Mustapha broke the wax seal expertly and ran his eyes over the page. Siga

called out again, not because the delay really annoyed him but
to live up to his role as a cantankerous old man.

"What are you waiting for?" he asked.

"It's from Muhammad, *fa*," answered Mustapha, "my father
Tiekoro's son."

"What does he say? Do you want me to tear your innards
out?"

Mustapha pretended to hurry.

"Father," said the letter, "my studies are over. I have learned
the Koran by heart and so obtained the title of *hãfiz kar*. If I
wanted to I could go on to study law or theology at the university,
but I'm not sure I do want to. At least for the moment. Cheikou
Hamadou, my teacher, was the only link that bound me to Hamdallay, but now that he is dead everything is different. His successor, his son Amadou Cheikou, is not at all the same. Although,
after he was installed, he said he had no intention of changing
anything, nothing is what it was. Instead of religion and thoughts
of God there is intriguing for political power and material possessions. In short, Hamdallay is no longer Hamdallay, and I no
longer have any place there. All this to tell you that by the time
you get this letter I shall be on my way to Segu.

"My greetings in peace and respect.

"Your loving son. . . ."

Mustapha was silent, looking at his father and waiting to be
dismissed. But Siga had forgotten him, torn as he was between
immense happiness and great anxiety. Tiekoro's son was coming
back to the fold, when he might have chosen to go to the kingdom
of Sokoto where his mother and sisters lived. The ways of the
ancestors were impenetrable! But Muhammad was a fervent
Muslim who had grown up in what claimed to be a holy city.
Wouldn't the religious quarrels lying dormant within the family
flare up again with his return? Siga vented his perplexity on Mustapha and Yassa, who stood there staring at him.

"Why haven't you brought me my gruel?" he yelled at one.
And at the other: "And you—clear off!"

Then, with great difficulty, he sat down on a little wooden
stool, trying to stretch his leg out in front of him. He would have
to call a family council and tell them about Muhammad's arrival.
But shouldn't he first have a talk with Tiefolo? Did Muhammad

know the part Tiefolo had played in the arrest and death of his
father? Was his heart perhaps full of desire for revenge? Once
again the fragile peace he had tried to maintain between all the
members of the family was threatened!

He was going over in his mind the little speech he would
deliver to Tiefolo when Yassa reappeared. She was not alone, and
the arrival of a visitor so early in the day vexed Siga. The stranger
wore a red and yellow silk coat over a tunic of blue silk brocade.
Around the usual Mandinke cap of green cloth he had wound a
turban of oriental silk brocaded with gold. Beyond any doubt he
was someone of considerable importance.

"*As salam aleykum,*" he said.

"*Wa aleyka salam,*" growled Siga.

These infernal Muslim greetings had been adopted even by
unbelievers! Then his natural courtesy got the better of him. He
invited the stranger to be seated, and offered him the kola nut
that Yassa had run to fetch.

"I am Sheikh Hamidou Magassa," said the stranger after a
moment. "I come from Bakel. I'm not a Tijani . . ."

With a wave of the hand Siga conveyed that he knew nothing
of these quarrels between brotherhoods. The other went on.

"I have come to tell you that the grave of your brother Oumar
belongs to us, and ought to be venerated as a place of pilgrimage.
Now we know that in accordance with your traditions Oumar
is buried in your compound. So we humbly pray you to allow us
access to his grave. You can't refuse. For us, Modibo Oumar Traore is a martyr to the true faith."

His suggestion was so farfetched that at first Siga almost burst
out laughing. Then he grew really exasperated. So Tiekoro, even
when he was dead, went on sowing dissension and above all mo-
nopolizing attention. To think that Tiekoro should be regarded
as a saint and a martyr! At the same time Siga felt vaguely flattered. This man had traveled for days and nights in order to
present his petition! The Traore compound would soon be regarded as a holy place! The prestige of the family, which had
vanished, would be restored. At this point Siga began to indulge
in his favorite pastime, self-criticism. It was his fault if the prestige of the family had declined! True, the lands of the Traore were
still extensive and fertile, tended by hundreds of slaves. Their

storehouses were full of grain, their paddocks too small for all their sheep, goats, chickens and shining horses. But was there anyone in Segu who could forget that their *fa* once lived like the *garanke*, cutting out boots and sandals? When Siga started to summon up the dreams of his youth he could no longer understand them.

He looked at the visitor's face. It was a grave countenance, reflecting maturity and experience. He and his countrymen were convinced that Tiekoro was a saint. What was a saint, then? Perhaps just an ordinary mortal, made up of faults and virtues, but with a ruling idea to which he subjected all other considerations.

"With us," said Siga slowly, "everything is decided collectively. I shall tell the members of our family of your request. But you know we are not of your faith?"

Sheikh Hamidou Magassa gave a benevolent smile.

"Everything is changing, Traore," he said. "Didn't you know? Don't you pay any attention to what's going on around you? Soon Segu will be doing all it can to show it has been converted to Islam."

"Segu will be doing all it can to show it has been converted to Islam." What did that mean?

The phrase haunted Siga still as he came out of his bath hut, where he had scrubbed himself at length in the secret hope of halting the corruption that was eating up his body. With two serious problems to deal with, he thought he had better take advice from superior intellects before facing the family. It was true that the world was changing. In the past all a man needed was a bit of willpower to keep wives, children, and younger brothers in order. Life was a straight line drawn from the womb of a woman to the womb of the earth. If you fought behind a ruler, it was simply to get more wives, more slaves or more gold. But now the menace of new ideas and values lurked everywhere. In his confusion Siga decided to go and see the Moor, Awlad Mbarak, head of the Koranic school to which Fatima sent the children.

Because of his elephantiasis Siga had to go slowly, taking very small steps. But he didn't mind that. He was like someone forced to look closely at landscapes he would otherwise have passed through unseeing. Segu was changing all the time. There were new houses with their flat roofs and turrets with triangular loopholes. Not many straw roofs now. Everywhere, children imprisoned in the cages of Koranic schools. Seeing them, Siga felt an illogical pang of regret: why hadn't he studied more when he was in Fez? But in those days learning had repelled him because it was associated with Islam.

Awlad Mbarak was swathed in yards of crumpled indigo cotton and wore light yellow heel-less slippers just like those Siga had once dreamed of producing. Like a true Moor he was drinking mint tea, and between each cup he put a silver tube full of snuff into his mouth. He had seen all Siga's six children pass through his courtyard, eaten couscous with Fatima on all the feast days, and regarded himself as almost one of the family.

"How's the leg?" he asked Siga.

"Let's not talk about it!" answered Siga with a sigh.

"I believe the whites have marvelous powders and ointments for that kind of thing."

"The whites?"

"They make other things besides brandy and guns, you know!" said Awlad Mbarak. "I went to see a kinsman of mine who's gone to live in Saint-Louis on the Senegal River, and while I was there I saw what the French are doing. Marvelous things! They're growing plants you can't even imagine. They've got medicines for everything—stomachache, headache, sores, fevers . . ."

Siga listened openmouthed. He'd seen Spaniards when he was in Fez but had never set eyes on a Frenchman.

"What are they like, the French?" he asked.

Awlad Mbarak shrugged.

"One white man looks just like another to me," he said.

Siga got down to the object of his visit.

"Awlad," he said, "my father lived longer than I, but it seems to me I'm older than he was and that I don't understand anything. This morning a man from Bakel came to see me. He thinks my brother Tiekoro was a saint . . ."

"So he was!"

Siga ignored the interruption.

". . . and he wants to turn his grave into a place of pilgrimage. But the main thing he said was, 'Soon Segu will be doing all it can to show it has been converted to Islam.' What does that mean, eh?"

Awlad stirred up the fire of his stove and poured out two more cups of tea. He started to sip at his own. Siga didn't like to hurry him.

"For a long time," said Awlad, "you people in Segu regarded Cheikou Hamadou of Macina as your fiercest enemy, and you took up arms against him, fought him unflaggingly. But now there's a much more formidable enemy emerging—the Tukulor marabout who once stayed with your family."

"El-Hadj Omar?"

Awlad nodded.

"It's too long a story to go into, and I don't know all the ins and outs. But what I do know is that he's very powerful now, and he wants Segu, and Segu ought to make an alliance with Macina to defend itself."

Siga was dumbfounded.

"You mean Muslims would ally themselves with non-Muslims against other Muslims?" he said.

"Yes," answered Awlad. "Don't ask me why—it's too complicated."

These surprising tidings were marked by a cloudburst, and the two men had to take refuge inside Awlad's hut. A ladder made of two crooked pieces of wood, with sticks tied on with strips of raw leather for rungs, led up to the roof in the dry season. The main room was furnished with divans made of millet canes, upon which Siga and Awlad now stretched themselves. Siga hated the rainy season, like most old men. It wasn't just that his body was full of aches and pains, with every joint creaking like those of a canoe badly handled on the Joliba, but also because the incessant murmur of water sounded to him like the loom of a weaver making a shroud. And yet he wanted to die. He feared death, and he desired it. What did it look like? What sort of smile would it have on its face when it bent over his mat?

He took the third cup of tea that Awlad was offering.

"Do you understand the attraction of Islam?" he asked. "Can you see why so many of our people are rubbing their foreheads in the dust?"

Awlad laughed.

"You're talking to a believer, remember!" he said. "What do you expect me to say? For me the attraction of Islam is simply the attraction of the true God."

Yes, of course, it was a silly question. Religion wasn't a thing you could discuss. With great difficulty Siga got up. Awlad's answers to his questions hadn't shed any light on his problems; on the contrary, they had deepened the mystery. Would Macina, to justify making an alliance with Segu against the Tukulor, demand that Segu show it had been converted to Islam?

The rain hadn't emptied the streets entirely. Children in loincloths or completely naked were playing in the puddles under the bamboo gutters. As Siga dragged his elephantiasis past them they stopped and stared after him, almost frightened.

As he entered the compound Siga saw Fatima hurrying out of the women's courtyard as fast as her bulk would allow. If age had been cruel to Siga, leaving him none of his former good looks, it hadn't been kind to Fatima either. What remained of the girl who had boldly written, "Are you blind? Can't you see I love you?" not knowing that this word "love" condemned her to everlasting exile far away from her own people?

A pair of fine eyes in a fat, puffy face. Silky hair, unfortunately always hidden under carelessly tied kerchiefs. Ten living children and three dead in infancy had distended her belly and transformed her breasts into the likeness of empty leather bottles. And yet, although Siga had feared the worst, once she was raised to the rank of *bara muso* to the head of the family she had seemed to come to terms with Segu and accept the Bambara people as her own. She was present at every name-giving ceremony, wedding and death, and had no rival for regaling the gathering with a big dish of couscous and a sheep roasted whole on the spit and stuffed with aromatic herbs. Because she could read and write Arabic a little she enjoyed great prestige among the women in the compound and in the neighborhood, and they all consulted her about everything.

She was furious.

"So!" she began. "It appears Tiekoro's son is coming back, and of course I'm the last to know!"

Before Siga could try to explain, she went on: "Where's he going to sleep? Have you thought of that?"

Siga went into the doorway of his house and pulled a stool toward him.

"What do *you* think?" he asked.

Fatima loved to be asked her opinion. She calmed down.

"As he was brought up in Hamdallay he'll be a real Muslim," she said self-importantly. "He won't be able to stand living among fetishists."

"Fetishists, fetishists!" growled Siga.

But he was only protesting as a matter of form: he knew she was much better than he at resolving delicate situations. How old age managed to bring people together and at the same time relax the tension between them! No more desire. No more emotion. But also no more need to dominate, humiliate, hurt. Instead, a strong sense of solidarity. Siga hadn't had physical relations with Fatima for years. When she spent the night in his hut they chatted together as they had never done in their youth. They talked of the old days in Fez. They talked of Tiekoro, as if Fatima's brief love for him was a secret that brought them closer together. They talked of Islam: Fatima tried to overcome her husband's unshakable opposition to Allah. All their discussions on this subject ended with Fatima shrugging her shoulders and saying, "Anyway, Islam will win."

And Siga envied the calm faith of such believers.

After a moment Fatima went on: "Have our house replastered—the rats and mice have been running riot. And give him a few slaves to look after him."

Siga nearly asked whether Muhammad wouldn't feel left out of things, but he refrained: didn't Islam carry its own exclusion with it? When Fatima had gone he went to the door of his hut, gazed at the *dubale* tree, and spoke to Tiekoro.

"Help me," he said. "What ought I to do? Come to me in a dream tonight and tell me what you want."

Tiekoro had been with his brother ever since his death; Siga was like a newborn infant inhabited by the spirit of someone dead. He never made any decision without asking himself, "What would he have done in my place?" He never put any food in his mouth without setting a morsel down on the ground for him. He never enjoyed anything without wishing to share the pleasure with him.

He was so deep in thought he didn't hear Yassa approach, didn't notice she was there until she was holding out his bowl of kola nut. Yassa wasn't a house slave. She was from the kingdom of Beledougou, with which Segu had quarreled yet again, and had come with a string of other captives, half naked, with tears streaming down her face. Tiefolo, wanting to offer some presents to his fifth wife, had bought her among a batch of others.

For some reason or other when Siga met her a few days later in the compound, his old body was stirred. His withered penis, grown useless, had stiffened, and stretched the soft linen of his loose drawers. Rather shamefacedly he had approached Tiefolo to arrange to buy the girl from him.

As he rolled the little ball of bitter but soothing pulp around on his tongue, Yassa came up and whispered something.

"Master," she said, "I'm pregnant."

Siga was filled with joy and pride. So, old and decrepit as he was, he was still capable of giving life! But he hid his feelings as decorum required, and said nonchalantly, "Good. May the ancestors grant that it's a boy!"

Yassa was still prostrated before him. He could see the pretty coils of her braids.

"Master," she went on, very quietly. "What will happen to me and my child when you're gone?"

Siga was taken aback. Since when did a slave interrogate her master? But before he could give vent to his anger Yassa spoke again.

"You have ten children by our mother Fatima, and as many again by your two concubines. What will be left for my child? Think of that, master—think of that . . ."

Whereupon, as if frightened by her own boldness, she withdrew. It was just as well she did, for Siga was reaching for his stick. Impudent, insolent creature! Who did she think she was? Was it just because she had shared his bed? What right did that give her?

But Siga was also thinking of his own mother—she who had thrown herself down the well. Why had she done it? Wasn't it because she had been disposed of as if she didn't count? And hadn't he himself been marked for life because of it? Women! What could you do with them? What did they want? What lay behind their beauty and docility, those traps to imprison men?

It had all started with Sira, going off back to Macina one fine day and breaking Dousika's heart. Then came Maryem, gathering her children together and leaving, refusing the husband tradition ordained for her. And now here was Yassa, claiming rights for her child. It was as if they'd conspired to rebel, each in her own way. Rebel? But against what? Wasn't it enough for them to know that no man is grown-up to the woman who bore him? That, apart from the shared game of appearances, no man is strong against the woman he loves and desires?

It was growing dark, and Siga yelled for light. Had everyone forgotten about him? Was he dead already? Was he no longer master? A young slave hurried in to light the shea butter lamp, and Siga grabbed him by the arm to relieve his feelings. But just as he was going to strike him he saw the boy's face, resigned, almost pitying his senile fury. And Siga was ashamed of himself and let him go.

All the events of the day kept going through his head. The news of Muhammad's return. Sheikh Hamidou Magassa's surprising request. What Awlad Mbarak had said. And finally Yassa's pregnancy. All those responsibilities! All those decisions to be made!

But the most important thing was to give a proper welcome to Tiekoro's son. He seemed to hear his brother's voice just before he was arrested: "Above all take care of Muhammad. I can tell he's like me—he'll never be happy."

Who was happy on this earth?

But, yes, he would do his best, and protect Muhammad against those still antagonized by his father's memory. It wouldn't always be easy. Was Fatima's idea a good one? Should he arrange for Muhammad to stay outside the family compound?

Siga sighed, took a pinch of kola from the bowl and rose painfully to go and see Tiefolo. As he dragged his outstretched leg upright, scraping the sandy floor and leaning heavily on his cane, a stabbing pain shot through his side and everything went dark. He just had time to see Tiekoro's smiling face bending over his own before he fell back. His spirit began to go around and around like an imprisoned beast. Was this death?

Not yet, not yet! He still had so many things to settle!

CHAPTER
2

Muhammad's horse went at a walk, its ears cocked, starting at the slightest noise, sensing in the shadows the smell of the herds of buffalo and antelope disturbed at their grazing and fleeing to the shelter of the thickets.

Muhammad himself, jolting about slightly as he followed the movements of his mount, ceaselessly told his prayer beads, not because he was afraid and wanted to ward off the evil spirits that lurked in the darkness, but simply because prayer was the natural state of his being.

A few months earlier it would have been dangerous to take this route from Hamdally to Segu via the ford at Thio. The Tuareg Meharists, riding two on one dromedary, used to attack the Fulani villages under cover of night, seeking revenge for their domination over Timbuktu. The Bambara from the left bank of the Joliba, hoping to take advantage of these squabbles between the "red monkeys," would gallop to Tenenkou to raid the Fulani cattle and kill their owners. The Fulani, under attack on two fronts, would hurl their spears at anything that moved.

But recently peace and unity had prevailed, as Tuareg, Fulani and Bambara all licked their wounds and prepared to band together against El-Hadj Omar, who was raising conscript armies of converts and captives for purposes as yet unknown but already feared.

This reversal of alliances, brought about by politicians and holy men, left the people confused. For generations they had been taught to hate and despise each other, and now they were being asked to learn to live together and recognize a new enemy in the Tukulor people. Muhammad had heard of a letter from Sheikh El-Bekkay of Timbuktu, formerly the deadly enemy of Macina, to Cheikou Hamadou's successor.

"Do not allow Segu to fall into the hands of El-Hadj Omar," it said. "What would you do if he took possession of the city and seized all its power—horses, men, gold, cowries? You don't think he would leave you alone even if you didn't threaten him. And undoubtedly what would happen then is that your people would go over to his side."

All this bargaining sickened Muhammad. He could see that Islam was a secondary consideration—what it was all really about was the struggle for power and territory.

Suddenly his horse stumbled over a root. The beast was tired and must be allowed to rest. They would stop in the next village.

Muhammad was twenty, and a nobleman. Yet his heart was racked with pain. Tijani's words yesterday had been as searing as an executioner's scimitar on the neck of a man condemned to death.

"Say no more about it," Tijani had ordered. "It's impossible. You can never marry Ayisha."

Muhammad had guessed that this would be his answer, yet as he heard it he felt as if he were being buried under shovelfuls of earth.

"But, master," he had stammered, "there is no common blood between us."

The other had risen in a fury.

"Say no more about it," he repeated.

Muhammad was prepared to admit he had not waited to observe the usual procedures. He ought to have gone back to Segu, informed his family, and then approached Tijani through griots laden with presents. But might not his impatience be forgiven when he was setting out on so dangerous a journey? He didn't want to admit to himself that he had wanted to force the hand of Ayisha herself, to make her declare herself, reveal her true feelings. After his interview with Tijani he had gone to see her where she sat under the awning mixing curds with honey.

"My father has spoken, Muhammad," was all she said.

Did that mean she didn't love him? In that case he might as well die. Take off his burnous and the rest of his clothes and fling himself into the dark waters of the Joliba. Let himself be swept away by the current, for his body to be found by Somono fishermen.

Muhammad could see the dark shapes of village huts and patted his horse's side to urge it on. It was a Sarakole village, identifiable by the shape of the houses, which together with their adjoining storehouses were perched on slender wooden piles and grouped around a fine mosque built of clay. Muhammad went into the first courtyard he came to and clapped his hands, and after a moment a figure emerged on the veranda. The person was lighting his way with a shea butter lamp. The floor of the veranda was made of beaten cow dung.

"*As salam aleykum!*" cried Muhammad. "I'm a Muslim like you. Can you put me up for the night?"

"Are you a *bimi*?" came the answer.

Muhammad laughed and moved nearer. He could make out the man's face now. He was young, suspicious, with bushy eyebrows and hair.

"Half *bimi* and half *n'ko*,"* he said. "A good mixture, don't you think?"

The man was clearly undecided, torn between the traditions of hospitality and the memory of all the persecution and exactions to which the peasants had been subjected. How many times had warriors of every race, Fulani as well as Sarakole, used the Koran as a pretext for seizing their harvests and their women and threatening the men with their weapons? Muhammad jestingly held up his hands.

"Look!" he said. "All I've got are prayer beads!"

The man finally signaled to him to approach.

"Tie your horse up by the chicken house," he said. "I hope it won't frighten them."

Muhammad obeyed and then followed his host. His wife had already gotten up, and without waiting to be told came out on the veranda to warm up some millet couscous. At every step the

* Fulani nickname for Bambaras.

rows of beads around her hips, hidden beneath her loose night *pagne*, jangled together, and their sweet sound reminded Muhammad of the music made by Ayisha's anklets of twisted silver. Yes, if Ayisha didn't love him he might as well die right away. But how could she not love him? Could his own love fail to reach her and flood right through her from her heart to her lips, obliterating all other thoughts? Yet he had never been able to see anything more in her eyes than the affection she might feel for a brother.

His host's wife brought him a gourd full of water, and Muhammad emerged from his reverie and thanked her with a smile. To judge by the furnishings of the hut the peasant was well-to-do. The bed, made of two low earthen walls with thick mats of palm-leaf fiber laid across them, was covered with a European blanket. Besides a couple of baskets for keeping clothes in there were two small rugs on the floor. And, luxury of luxuries, there were candles in metal candlesticks, though they were not lit. This mixture of traditional articles and imports from the coast—from Freetown, the rival of Saint-Louis in Senegal—was fascinating; but Muhammad was too obsessed to pay any attention.

Once he was back in Segu he would urge his father Siga to ask Tijani formally for Ayisha's hand in marriage, and Tijani would be bound to give in in the end. If not . . . if not . . . ? Muhammad didn't dare think any further.

"It seems Mansa Demba of Segu is going to be converted to Islam," said the man.

"Or perhaps just pretend," said Muhammad, smiling. "That's all Amadou Cheikou asks."

All that could be heard for a moment was the sound of Muhammad eating. Then: "Doesn't it all disgust you?" asked the man. "They'll do anything to keep their empires—change their religions; fight one another and then exchange presents; do their best to slit each other's throats; and then call themselves brothers."

Muhammad washed his hands of it.

"What do you expect?" he answered. "That's the world of the powers that be. The beasts in the jungle are peaceful and quiet in comparison."

Muhammad resumed his journey before sunrise. He was in

a hurry to get to Segu. If night belongs to spirits and makes men
and animals seek refuge, the latter have their revenge at dawn.
Wild guinea fowl and partridges scurried under the horse's
hooves. Dog-faced baboons with their lionlike manes perched on
the rocks and barked furiously as this rash human being went
by. Swarms of bees buzzed overhead. Here and there could be
seen the tracks of hyenas, now drowsing under some bush. At
one point the brush suddenly caught fire, and by the light of the
flames, brighter as yet than that of the sun, Muhammad saw
gazelle, wild boar and buffalo taking flight. The wind was not
strong enough to disperse the thick clouds of smoke, as black as
the rain clouds now fortunately building up in time to put out
the fire.

The peasant's wife had given him a basket containing some
white hens, eggs and a little bag of beans, gifts of peace and friendship, as well as something to eat on the way. He had slept in the
hut kept for visitors passing through, and hardly had he stretched
out on the bed than a young slave girl had entered, for the peasant
and his wife meant to do him honor.

She had scarcely reached the age of puberty. Her braids were
ornamented with glass and carnelian beads, and she wore a shiny
little metal ring in her nose. You could tell she had been awakened in haste and told to bathe and scent herself before presenting
herself for the stranger's pleasure.

"What's your name?" Muhammad asked her.

"Assa," she answered, almost inaudibly.

He went over to her.

"Go away, Assa," he said. "I shan't defile you."

Bewildered, torn between the fear of her master's anger and
joy at not having to surrender her body, she obeyed. In the morning the peasant observed Muhammad furtively, dying to ask questions. But Muhammad was chaste: his love for Ayisha forbade
him to look at any other woman.

The horse began to trot, suddenly joyful because of the sunrise. The great red globe was beginning to roll through the sky,
struggling as best it could against the rising mist. Muhammad
rode through Sansanding without stopping. It was a sizable city
in which Muslims and non-Muslims mingled freely. The Muslims had built some of the finest mosques in the region, thanks

to gifts from traders. They didn't seem to mind the fetish huts of the non-Muslims which were often built close to the markets and where one street crossed another. As Muhammad knew, El-Hadj Omar abhorred this tolerance, this Islam ready to coexist with the heathen. Was he in the right? Muhammad had no definite opinion in the great controversy. The generosity of his heart told him all men were brothers whatever the name of their god. But was that heretical? Was it not tantamount to forgiving the men who had murdered his father?

After leaving Sansanding Muhammad directed his horse toward the shell-strewn bank of a river, then sought a dry corner near a spinney of grasses and thorn bushes. In the distance a boat was veering about, its raffia sail filled by the wind and held more or less in place by ropes. He prayed at length. When he stood up again he saw that some women had appeared, carrying bowls of washing on their heads.

Muhammad had learned to fear the effect he produced on women. As long as he had been just a boy, begging in Hamdallay, they'd only wanted to pamper him, piling his bowl with rice and scraps of chicken and other dainties. But as he grew up their eyes shone with other desires, and this filled Muhammad with horror. It was as if he'd seen Maryem, his far-off beloved mother, or Ayisha, the forbidden princess, looking at a man in this way. Should a woman feel desire? No, she should accept that of the man, purified by his love for her.

The women unfolded their linen, steeped it in the water and began to rub it with senna soap. But their eyes, bright and made larger with kohl, were still fixed on their prey. They were not Muslims and their religion did not require them to behave in a reserved manner toward men. On the contrary, they were used to mocking them and exchanging jokes full of sexual innuendo. Muhammad, brought up in Hamdallay, wasn't used to all this.

What should he do? Collect his things and go? He was already thinking of leaving when the women started to sing a little song, at once ironic and tender:

> The wind blew and the wind threatened.
> The *bimi* sat under a tree.
> Poor *bimi*!

He has no mother to bring him milk,
No wife to grind his grain.
Poor *bimi!*

Muhammad plucked up his courage and went over to them.

"To start with," he said, "I'm not a *bimi*. I'm a *n'ko* like you, and I'm going back to my family. So this evening I shall have someone to bring me milk and grind my grain."

One of the women was particularly pretty, with breasts like mangoes and a curved belly hung with several rows of beads.

"Are you married?" she asked him boldly.

Muhammad crouched down on his heels.

"No," he answered. "The one I love cannot be mine!"

The women broke into peals of mirth. They clearly couldn't understand. Was not a man strength, virility, brutality even? Shouldn't he seize the woman he wants? But Muhammad could feel nothing inside himself but weakness and gentleness. He had no thoughts of fame or conquest. All he wanted was to be loved.

"Why do you talk like a *bimi* if you're a *n'ko*?" asked another of the women.

Muhammad smiled.

"Don't you know there soon won't be *bimis* and *n'kos* any more?" he answered. "All will be united against the Tukulor."

Then he went back to his horse, which was halfheartedly munching a few blades of grass on the riverbank. He entered Segu before dark that evening.

The hubbub he met with there almost frightened him after his eight years in the austere quiet of Hamdallay, where the only noise was the call of the muezzins. When he was a child Segu had consisted for him of the Traore compound, his father's *zawiya* and the Mansa's palace, where he admired the guards and their guns. He suddenly understood why, like the Fulani before them, the Tukulor now dreamed of getting their hands on Segu. They were attracted by all this wealth, this prosperity overflowing into the markets and stalls, reflected in the frontages of solid houses with their turrets reaching up to the lower branches of the mahogany trees. A crowd of men and women in clothes made of wide strips of cotton, worn beneath silk burnouses or *boubous*, were coming and going, stopping to listen to musicians or watch the antics of the acrobats. *Tondyons* in yellow uniforms with guns over their shoulders were on their way to the taverns, full of *dolo* drinkers talking and laughing. Muhammad was surprised to see mosques everywhere! Before, the only mosques had been in the Somono or Moorish quarters, but now the crescent decorated countless minarets, rearing up like herdsmen's crooks.

Muhammad was the object of many glances. What family did he belong to? People stopped to see which way his horse would go. Good gracious, was he going past the cattle market, where young Fulani were rounding up their herds before taking them out of the city? Was he going toward the Somonos' promontory? No, he was still riding along the streets, his horse's hooves thudding against the soft earth.

Suddenly Muhammad felt a pang, for at the spot where his father's *zawiya* used to be there was only an empty patch of mud. Women had planted *nosiku* there, a plant that asked the ancestors to pardon sin. As for the compound itself, it struck him as even more imposing than before. He dismounted, tethered his horse to a ring in a wall, entered the first courtyard and clapped his hands.

Everything was in turmoil. Slaves were running to and fro in all directions. Fetish priests were burning herbs or examining cowrie shells. Children were left to do as they liked. No one took any notice of Muhammad. He went on into the second courtyard and spoke to a young man scarcely older than himself.

"I'm a son of the house," he said. "My name's Muhammad."

The young man took him in his arms.

"Muhammad!" he cried, "I'm your brother Olubunmi. We were afraid you'd arrive too late. Father Siga is at death's door."

The idea of being reunited with someone when he had embarked upon the inexorable journey of death! When his spirit was already departed, his eyes dim, his words inaudible.

The hut was full of smoke from fumigations, and Muhammad would have liked to send all the fetish priests away. Only prayer is appropriate for a man's last moments. At the same time a refrain kept running through his head: "Make him look at me! Make him know I'm here!"

It seemed to him he couldn't be received back peacefully into the family unless Siga recognized him. As if his only stay was the old man on his deathbed.

Olubunmi touched him on the shoulder.

"Our father Tiefolo is asking for you," he said.

Muhammad put his prayer beads away in the pocket of his burnous.

While the years had destroyed Siga, they had respected Tiefolo's fine figure, solid torso and shapely legs. Only his hair, which he wore long and braided, had yielded and gone gray. He was torn between fatherly feeling toward Muhammad and the memory of the role Tiekoro had played in the family. So his behavior was full of contradictions.

When Muhammad first appeared Tiefolo's heart was touched to see him so young and vulnerable. He clasped the young man in his arms.

"What a sad return our gods have prepared for you," he said. "A house in tears."

In spite of himself he couldn't help saying "our gods" aggressively, as if to underline the fact that they weren't those of Muhammad himself.

"Father," replied Muhammad, "only an unbeliever weeps for the dead. For he forgets the joy of the soul, the lamp of the body, at last reunited with the divine."

The word "unbeliever" was unfortunate, but Muhammad was too upset to be diplomatic; he was preoccupied with the circumstances of his return, and his confrontation with the "father" who, according to his mother Maryem, had played a part in Tiefolo's death. He irritated Tiefolo by reminding him of the superior tone and sententiousness of his dead brother.

"Would you be prepared to stay with 'unbelievers,' as you call us?" Tiefolo asked roughly.

Muhammad did his best to repair his blunder.

"Is not blood stronger than all?" he replied.

In reality it wouldn't have taken much for Tiefolo and Muhammad to love one another despite the past, for they had many things in common: shyness, sensitivity, lack of self-confidence and above all the sense of family. But they were unaware of all this. Tiefolo thought Muhammad was prejudiced against him by

rumors and gossip exaggerating the role he had played in Tiekoro's arrest. Muhammad thought himself unwanted.

Suddenly there was an outburst of women's lamenting, followed by singing and clapping of hands:

> *Mother, I shall go to the marsh!*
> *A bird of ill omen has sung to me!*
> *Mothers, I shall go to the marsh!*
> *A bird of ill omen has sung to me!*
> *The women lament*
> *For their great farmer has lain himself down!*

Tiefolo started up, and Muhammad followed. As they went
toward Siga's hut they saw a young girl leaning against a wall,
shaken with sobs, tears streaming down her face. Hers were
clearly not ritual tears, but the reflection of a crushing, personal,
solitary despair. To Muhammad's unspoken question Tiefolo replied: "That's Yassa, your father Siga's latest concubine."

Muhammad went away with a vision of a young face infinitely forlorn, infinitely disturbing.

CHAPTER

3

Death that comes by stealth is cruel. Of course, death never does beat a drum. But it does leave some men time to dispose of their wives and property and give instructions to their successors. But in Siga's case none of this was possible, and when the funeral was over Tiefolo, now head of the family, found himself faced with a multitude of problems. They had hitherto been concealed by the consensus of pity and affection that had grown up around the departed, but now they became suddenly urgent.

One thing that had to be done was give a reply to Sheikh Hamidou Magassa, waiting patiently in a rest hut. Another was to see that the non-Muslims and the ever-increasing number of Muslims in the compound lived together in peace. Yet another was to make the widows sheltering behind religious pretexts accept the husbands chosen for them by the family. Above all there was the problem of receiving Muhammad in such a way as to prevent his becoming a special kind of heir, a flame of Islam bringing together converts and rebels. To tell the truth he was a charming boy, easy to get on with, respectful, courteous to the point of self-effacement. But in these very virtues Tiefolo sensed a possible danger: too much idealism, too much magnanimity, a kind rejection of everything that was supposed to make a man. Thus every time Muhammad was in his presence Tiefolo was torn between the desire to comfort him like a nervous child and an impulse to bully him.

"Why didn't you go and study in one of your own universities?" he asked.

Muhammad stood hanging his head, and once again Tiefolo was struck and almost repelled by the perfection of his features. This feminine beauty was another danger. Muhammad seemed to pluck up courage.

"Father," he stammered, "I must tell you what I have on my mind. I know a dutiful son takes the wife the family gives him. But I . . . I love a girl . . . and if I don't have her . . . I shall die."

Tiefolo looked at him in amazement, almost in terror. Die for a woman? Was that what Islam taught? Not surprising in a religion that banned alcohol and castrated men, turning them into so many sheep grazing side by side. Was it because of this girl that Muhammad slept alone every night when there were plenty of slaves to satisfy him?

"A Fulani of Macina?" he asked, restraining himself.

Muhammad at once began to talk about Ayisha, but Tiefolo frowned and cut him short.

"Your grandmother Sira's granddaughter, you say? So she's your sister?"

Muhammad embarked on the speech that had failed to persuade Tijani.

"Father," he said, "my grandmother Sira was married again, to a Fulani of Macina. What kinship is there between her descendants there and our family?"

Tiefolo went on pondering, evidently deep in the maze of genealogy. Finally he declared, with a shocked expression: "It cannot be, Muhammad. She's your sister."

And as Muhammad was preparing to urge his case, Tiefolo indicated with his usual firmness that the interview was at an end. Muhammad went away, sick at heart. What a foolish and ridiculous idea of the geography of the blood! Must he give in and renounce Ayisha? Never! Never! For the thousandth time he repeated to himself his infallible argument, the only drawback of which was that it didn't convince anyone.

Muhammad, who had never disobeyed before, would gladly

have given up everything else and ridden off to abduct Ayisha. But would she let herself be abducted?

"My father has spoken, Muhammad!" she'd said. Were those the words of a woman in love?

Muhammad reached his hut, not far from the enclosure containing the family graves. Tiekoro's was set a little apart as if to symbolize the singularity of his fate. Muhammad, in his despair, went and sat by it. If only his father had lived! He would have been able to understand and overcome the ridiculous prejudices of both the families. But no, he was alone, his mother far away and all who might have been able to help him dead and buried. Then he was ashamed of his despair. And yet how could he overrule his heart? If he didn't have Ayisha there was nothing else he wanted from life.

While he was sitting there Olubunmi came up to him. As the only living offspring of a long-lost son, Olubunmi had been coddled like a sort of wonder child. But this hadn't managed to spoil him, and even those on the lookout for a likeness to Malobali agreed that the son was very different from the father. Muhammad had conceived a great affection for the brother who had been there like a symbol to welcome him on the day of his return. But he despaired of making a Muslim of him. Olubunmi met all his attempts at conversion with a skeptical smile.

"All gods are equal," he would say. "So why try to put one above the others?"

He sat down near Muhammad, taking care to keep his distance from the grave.

"A messenger from the Mansa has just come to see our father Tiefolo," he said. "Apparently it concerns you."

"How so?"

Olubunmi couldn't resist the pleasure of sounding important.

"It seems the Mansa's sending a delegation to Macina and wants you to act as interpreter."

"Me?" cried Muhammad.

It was certainly a strange idea to include in a royal delegation a boy hardly twenty who'd never done anything to distinguish himself! Olubunmi put on a knowing air, though he was only repeating what he'd heard.

"Obviously Islam's time has come in Segu, and, believe me, they'll make good use of our father Tiekoro's blood . . ."

Once again Muhammad was revolted. Yes, Islam was fading like a washed-out garment. Cheikou Hamadou's death had been swiftly followed by temporal preoccupations that corrupted the faith. Had not the saint revered by all broken the rules to ensure that he was succeeded by his son, Amadou Cheikou? And was not this same Amadou Cheikou already preparing for the accession of his son, to the detriment of his brothers? Who could divine the motives that governed a man's heart?

What Muhammad did not know was that beneath his apparent calm Olubunmi was full of dreams of travel and adventure. Those who thought him a son unworthy of Malobali were wrong, for the same impatience, the same desire for action, seethed in his veins too. He was one of those who gathered near the markets to listen to the increasing number who had lived on the coast, seen the whites, spoken their languages and handled their weapons. Old Samba, who had spent many years there, had described Freetown to him with its ports and its boats full of timber sailing for Europe. It was from him he had learned that the whites had a different sort of writing from the Arabs, and that they hated Islam just as much as the fetishists did. He had learned to put together the letters of his own name, Samba. How did one write Olubunmi? Old Samba didn't know.

As they went by Tiefolo's hut they saw him sitting in the entrance deep in conversation with the Mansa's messenger and Sheikh Hamidou Magassa. Important decisions were evidently going to be made. But what decisions?

Muhammad didn't know what to think. Was he perhaps going back to Hamdallay? True, he'd sworn not to return except to obtain Ayisha's hand, but at least he'd be able to see her for a few days, and above all find out what she really felt about him. "My father has spoken, Muhammad!" Were those the words of a woman in love?

It was after the evening meal that Tiefolo told the men of the family about the decisions he had had to make under pressure from the Mansa. Muslims were to be allowed to come on pilgrimage to Tiekoro's grave. Muhammad was to be part of a delegation leaving shortly for Macina to bring about a reconciliation.

It was with a shrug of the shoulders that the good folk of Segu learned that Mansa Demba and the ruler of Macina were preparing to make friends. They gathered by the gates to watch the procession set out for Hamdallay—the nobles, preceded by their griots, riding magnificent horses and followed by slaves bowed down under the weight of gifts. They had been told that the machinations of the Tukulor had made this reconciliation necessary, and they were not unduly surprised. The name of El-Hadj Omar had become synonymous with wickedness, and what had happened when he visited Segu had been vastly exaggerated. There was talk of rain and blood and ashes falling from the sky, of an earthquake that engulfed the Mansa's palace and then a terrible drought which had turned the banks of the Joliba into a stony waste. The well informed knew that El-Hadj Omar now lived in Dinguirye in Futa Jallon, where they had never set foot, not far from the Joliba but much further south. Travelers said the place had been turned into an impregnable fortress and a place of even more fervent prayer than Hamdallay. There were mosques on every street. In the middle stood a fort with walls thirty feet high in which El-Hadj Omar lived with his wife, children and advisers. Travelers also said his followers made everyone pronounce the famous phrase "There is no god but God," and if they refused, cut off their heads.

To those who compared them to the Fulani of Cheikou Hamadou some years before, the travelers declared that the people of Macina were mild and tolerant beside the hordes of El-Hadj Omar.

When the dust from the horses' feet had settled, Olubunmi went sadly back to the compound. Muhammad had gone off surrounded by adults who treated him as an equal because of his knowledge of Islam and of life in Hamdallay. What adventures awaited him? Perhaps he would have a chance to make his name? In any case he was escaping from the routine of Segu, and that was already something to be envied!

Olubunmi had done several years of Koranic study, and also been initiated into the secret societies. So he wore gris-gris around his waist intermingled with squares of parchment bearing verses from the Koran, of which he could also recite a few suras. He dressed like a Muslim but wore his hair long and braided. In short, he epitomized the transitional period through which Segu was passing. But he couldn't forget the foreign blood in his veins. Who else in Segu could boast of having an Agouda mother from Benin? Or a father who had traveled as far as the coast, when most Bambara had never even crossed the Joliba?

Olubunmi had very conflicting feelings about his father. He admired and envied him because he had made the sort of journeys he dreamed of himself. On the other hand, having died far away and not been buried among his own people, he had probably become one of those unfriendly spirits that despair of being reincarnated and wander in the invisible world. Sometimes at night he thought he could hear his wails in the sound of the wind, the patter of the rain or the splutter of the lamp. He faithfully remembered to offer up sacrifices to his memory, even though Muhammad kept reminding him of the words of the Prophet: "Neither their flesh nor their blood shall be of any use. Only your piety will succeed."

He went into Samba's hut and found him sitting on his bamboo bed.

"So your brother's gone," said Samba, with a grimace.

Olubunmi shrugged, rather glum still at the thought of Muhammad galloping along on his fine steed.

"Yes," he replied, "the blackener of tablets has gone . . . Samba, tell me about your travels."

Old Samba was coy.

"I've told you about them dozens of times," he said. "What more do you want to hear?"

But then he filled his pipe—which put the finishing touch to Olubunmi's admiration, for it was made of Scotch briar and came from a white man's country—and began.

"You people who've never seen it can't imagine what the sea is like. You are astonished by Lake Debo, and yet you can see its banks, its surface is dotted with islands and your boats maneuver between its reeds. But the sea is like a vast continually changing sky. It doesn't get on with the wind, and when it blows it gets angry and arches its back like a furious panther, and heaven help the boats on its surface. I was a ship's boy for three years. When I was little some Moors stole me from my parents and took me to Cayor, and there I met some Frenchmen . . ."

"What are they like—the French?"

Old Samba didn't like being interrupted and pretended not to hear Olubunmi's question.

"I worked for Monsieur Richard. He sent for all sorts of plants from his own country and experimented with them here. And he invented others too. If you only knew what his hand managed to coax out of the ground! Cotton, indigo, Gambian onion, banana trees, guavas, soump, senna, peanuts . . . he used to say our countries are gardens! Then one day I'd had enough of bending over the earth and I took off. And that's how I got to Freetown. But don't forget the English are a different kind of white man . . ."

"Tell me about Freetown, Samba!"

But again Samba ignored the question.

"I myself never worked with the English," he went on, "because I knew French and so went on the Frenchmen's boats. I sailed down as far as Cape Coast . . ."

"My father went there too!"

Old Samba spat out black tobacco juice.

"Maybe," he said, "but he wasn't a ship's boy!"

Olubunmi had to admit this, but he pressed Samba again to tell him about Freetown.

"But what can I tell you? You've never seen the sea; you don't know what a brig is, or a schooner, or a brigantine, or a felucca. All you know is a Somono canoe."

Olubunmi hung his head.

"They say," the old man went on, "that the whites make their boats run on steam now . . ."

"Steam!"

To avoid having to answer questions on this topic, which he knew nothing about, Samba changed the subject.

"You can also be a soldier with the whites. A double-barreled gun, a pair of red trousers with braid down the sides, and there you are!"

"What do you do if you're a soldier?"

"Fight, of course!"

"But against whom?"

Neither the old man nor the young could answer that question. The whites had no need to fight to obtain slaves because slaves were brought down to them voluntarily on the coast. So what were they aiming at with their guns? Olubunmi didn't like to think the old man was wrong, but what he said about soldiers seemed very improbable. Perhaps they went to the land of the white men to fight against their enemies there?

Olubunmi went back to the compound perplexed. To think Muhammad was riding along in his fine sky-blue *boubou* while he, Olubunmi, was here, bored to death and dragging his feet through the loose earth! There was a large crowd outside the compound. The courtyards were deathly quiet. Even the children seemed to have stopped playing and shouting. They stood there with the adults as if rooted to the spot.

"What's wrong?" whispered Olubunmi.

"It's Yassa," he was told. "She's swallowed *fa* Tiefolo's poisons."

This brief news had such horrible implications that Olubunmi was speechless. To swallow hunting poisons! Although Tiefolo went out hunting more rarely now, he was still one of Segu's great *karamokos* and attended all the *foutoutegues*, the anniversaries in honor of a hunter's death. He kept his quivers of arrows in a little hut where he also prepared poisons, mixtures of kombe and matter from decaying corpses. The year before some sheep had broken loose and tasted these brews out of curiosity, and they had all fallen down dead, foaming at the mouth.

"Is she dead?" stammered Olubunmi.

"They're giving her potions of tiliba."

Olubunmi had never taken much notice of Yassa. She was only a slave, though he knew she was attached to his father Siga. But the sudden rashness of her act turned her into an individual. Why had she done such a thing? He looked at Yassa's hut, where she perhaps lay dying, as if it were some temple where mysterious forces were at work. To kill oneself! What a terrible deed! How could anyone dare defy the ancestors like that?

A woman came out into the courtyard and chased away the children and grown-ups who stood there gaping. Another followed, carrying a bowl, covered with a cloth, that gave off a fetid odor.

Meanwhile, inside the hut, death had decided not to take Yassa yet. After sniffing at her and playing with her like a wild beast with its prey, it had let her go. But as a result of that terrible confrontation Yassa's body had opened and brought forth its fruit before its time. A child had been born, a bundle of membranes and mucus.

Moussokoro, the midwife who'd been sent for in haste, took the little body over to the door of the hut to get a better look at it. Was it stillborn, a being which had lost its spiritual elements, so that its soul must be tracked to its refuge before the body could be buried? Moussokoro's fingers felt a feeble flutter. No, it was alive! She told a woman to bring some millet beer diluted with water, to purify the child after its dreadful journey. Then she made out a frail little excrescence like the shoot of a plant. Her heart filled with joy. She turned to one of her helpers.

"Go and tell Tiefolo," she said, "that the family has another *bilakoro*!"

Fatima, Siga's widow, hearing that mother and child were both alive, had meanwhile hurried in. She had never hated Yassa; she had looked on her rather as the last pleasure allowed to a man who had had very few. She knelt down by Yassa, who still lay inert, with her eyes closed.

"May Allah forgive your sin!" she whispered, but not unkindly.

Then she went and looked at the child, which Moussokoro was now bathing in the millet beer before anointing it with shea butter. It was so small, scarcely bigger than a handful of chicks, that you couldn't yet make out its features. But Fatima thought she recognized Siga's high forehead and the curve of his chin. She was moved.

"Welcome, Fanko!" she said, in her heart. She knew that, since he had been born after his father's death, that would be his name.

Tiefolo and Soumaworo the fetish priest now entered. A birth meant a celebration. Soumaworo bent and slit the throat of a red cock, then daubed the child's penis and brow with its blood. As he did so he scrutinized the baby's face. Of whom was he the reincarnation? They put the child into Yassa's arms. It was so weak, so fragile, it eyelids like tiny shells, its nose no wider than a millet stalk, its mouth like a tiny tomato, round and slightly wrinkled. Yassa looked at this marvel. Who had created it? Her own body, which had begrudged Siga his pleasure, repelled by his smell of sickness and death? The body of the old man who had panted as he penetrated her? No, the gods must have coupled to produce such a prodigy. And the gods must be thanked.

She hugged the new little creature. With a greed astonishing in such a ridiculously small body, it licked its lips as if to savor the last drops of the goat's milk with which they had been moistened. The movement reflected the life-force which inhabited it, and which she had almost deprived it of forever. Oh, her whole life would not be enough to expiate, with love, care and affection, the crime she had tried to commit!

"Welcome, Fanko," she whispered into the baby's ear, "to the world of the living, which is now your home. And mine . . ."

C H A P T E R

4

Alhadji Guidado, one of the seven marabouts in charge of policing Hamdallay, was also a member of the Grand Council without which no decision was taken in Macina, so he was one of the most influential men in the kingdom.

The Grand Council consisted of forty members, all doctors of law and theology. Thirty-eight of them now sat in the Hall of Seven Doors which opened onto the grave of Cheikou Hamadou, a place of pilgrimage for the Muslims in the region. Alhadji Guidado was one of those who opposed any kind of alliance with Segu, reminding the others that Islam allied to polytheism was no longer Islam at all. Alas, for the first time his advice had gone unheeded, and he and his supporters were in a minority. He restrained his anger and chagrin. All he said was, "Allah grant we do not regret the decisions we have made today. But I repeat, to prepare to muster troops to help unbelievers against Muslims, and to regard fighting against Muslims as something permissible, is incompatible with the faith."

All eyes turned to Amadou Cheikou, sitting where his father once sat. But for nearly three months Amadou Cheikou had been undermined by an illness against which doctors and prayers were equally powerless. As a result he allowed himself to be completely manipulated by Sheikh El-Bekkay from Timbuktu, who was convinced of the necessity for an alliance with the Mansa

of Segu. The present relationship between the two men was all
the more surprising because in the past Sheikh El-Bekkay had
not concealed his hostility toward Macina, which had made Timbuktu its vassal and imposed its own order upon it. But it was a
sign of the times! The friends of yesterday became the enemies
of today, and vice versa.

Amadou Cheikou said nothing, exposing for all to see his
waxen face and eyes already absent, distant, conversing with the
invisible. Alhadji Guidado slipped his feet into the babouches he
had left by the door.

"Allow me to withdraw," he said. "As you know, today my
third son, Alfa, is being married."

There was a murmur of ritual blessings from the assembly.

"And whom have you chosen for him?" asked Amadou Cheikou kindly, still not taking the marabout's opposition seriously.

"Ayisha," was the reply, "the daughter of Tijani Barri, whose
father, Modibo Amadou Tassirou, lived in Tenenkou."

Amadou Cheikou nodded to show that this genealogy was
satisfactory.

"I'll come later on," he said, "and join in the young couple's
prayers."

This was mere politeness. Everyone knew he never went out
now. As Alhadji left the Hall of Seven Doors he went by the
master's grave. His heart filled with pain. If the saint had lived
he would never have yielded to these political considerations!
He had spent his whole life fighting the infidels of Segu! Fortunately sons don't always take after their fathers, and who could
say whether Amadou Cheikou's decisions might not be undone
in their turn by his son Amadou Amadou? Alhadji was filled with
a faint hope, but he tried not to think of anything but his son's
marriage. To tell the truth, he didn't like it. True, Ayisha was
pretty, perfect in fact, but her family was made up of lukewarm
Muslims who could just about recite a few suras but had never
read a religious text. Alhadji even suspected them of wearing gris-
gris under their clothes and offering up sacrifices to idols from
time to time. But Alfa was apparently infatuated with the girl,
and young people nowadays prided themselves on falling in love
instead of abiding by their parents' choice. Alhadji had let himself
be persuaded because he had been rather worried about Alfa. He

was an excellent son and had just finished the first part of his religious education, praised by all his teachers for the profundity of his intelligence. That was the trouble. If something wasn't done he was in danger of being ruined by a taste for monasticism.

He was always repeating the sura that said the future life was better than life in this world. Please Allah, this marriage would bring him down to earth. For it is not good for a man to become a eunuch, unable to burn for the body of a woman.

Alhadji Guidado's compound was opposite the mosque. While many of the Fulani in Macina, like the Bambara and the people of Jenne, built themselves big mud houses with flat roofs, Alhadji had made it a point of honor to preserve the customs of his own people. His compound was made up of round huts with walls of woven straw, and in the middle of the courtyard stood a sort of shed supported on pillars made from tree trunks. It was here that the crowd of guests were gathered around the couple about to be married. Some silky-fleeced sheep from Armagha were being held by the horns by little boys until it was time for them to be sacrificed. The women were handing around bowls of curds mixed with dates and mint leaves. A delicious smell of *tatiri masina* came from the kitchens.

How beautiful Ayisha looked! She was wearing a dress made from a single length of silk from Timbuktu. But what really attracted attention was her hair—a tall, beautifully arranged crest in the middle, and on either side, big braids interwoven with gold and silver thread. Her mother and the other women in the family had decked her out for the occasion in earrings of twisted gold a good three inches in diameter but so light they swung in the slightest breeze. You couldn't count her rings and necklaces or the bangles around her wrists and ankles. Alfa was dressed with his usual simplicity in a *boubou* of fine linen. But at a time when he should have been transported to the very heights of happiness and pride, he looked at Ayisha quite coolly. If he had followed his own inclinations he would never have married at all, but Ayisha loved him so much she had won him over. It was as if he had unexpectedly been exposed to a fire and been hypnotized by its brightness. Alfa wished Muhammad were there. How his friend would have made fun of him!

"So you've succumbed to feminine attractions too, have you?" he'd have said.

As a matter of fact, even in his absence Muhammad had played a part in the marriage. Wasn't Ayisha his sister, and didn't marrying her bring Alfa even closer to him than before? Yet each time he tried to talk to his future wife about this she had shown a strange aversion to the subject.

Tongues wagged as everyone awaited the arrival of the imam, who was also Alhadji Guidado's brother. The universal topic was Segu. The lookouts had announced that the delegation had passed through Sansanding and already entered Diafarabe.

Some people accepted the reconciliation with Segu and merely asked that Amadou Cheikou send trustworthy observers to see what was going on there regarding religion. If the Bambara were sincere, let them knock down their fetish huts and build plenty of mosques.

Others absolutely opposed the reconciliation and wanted Macina to go back to the rule of collateral succession they had departed from after Cheikou Hamadou died. Then Ba Lobbo, his brother and supreme head of the army, would come to the throne. He was the most intransigent of Muslims, and people would soon see which side he'd be on!

Others again didn't care to admit that they were tempted by the Tijani approach. They had read *Ar-Rimah* (*The Lances*), El-Hadj Omar's masterwork, and were attracted by this strict form of Islam, recalling the old days in Hamdallay and to a certain extent reviving the virtues of earlier brotherhoods. They recited the *Jawharatul-Kamal*, *The Pearl of Perfection*, a dozen times:

> O God, shed your grace and your peace
> On the fount of divine mercy, sparkling
> Like a diamond, sure in its truth, embracing
> The center of intellects and meanings . . .

All the chatter ceased when the imam appeared. A white veil was thrown over Ayisha's head and the wedding ceremony began.

At the same moment the delegation from Segu entered Hamdallay. In accordance with a kind of pomp now banished from this Muslim city, the procession was headed by the griots and the full sound of the *dounoumba* alternated with that of the *tamani*, stopping every so often to let the flutes and violins be heard. The horsemen in their yellow uniforms fired their guns, and there was a smell of powder that Hamdallay had long forgotten. The citizens hurried out of their compounds and stood along the streets to watch, torn between admiration of the fine spectacle and scorn for the fetishists.

Muhammad came along slowly at the end of the delegation, just in front of the slaves carrying the Mansa's presents to the king. For several nights he had been tortured by the same dream, always the same: he went into Ayisha's compound to find her lying on her mat with her eyes shut, her head to the south and her feet to the north. The family stood around her in tears, and as he went up to the body, aghast and not believing his own eyes, a voice whispered, "You see, she wasn't meant for you, and now she is lost forever." Then he would wake up bathed in sweat and shivering as if he had *souma*, malaria.

The delegation from Segu reached the mosque; Amadou Cheikou's compound was opposite. The *talibes* had abandoned their studies and swarmed out to look at the Bambara, and were surprised to see that they were tall and handsome with noble features. They had been told they were fiends with reeking breath and teeth black from tobacco, which was forbidden in Hamdallay. The crowd that had gathered outside Alhadji Guidado's compound to see Alfa and Ayisha's wedding came running now to see the Bambara. Some recognized Muhammad, who had spent so many years among them, and met him with laughter, greetings and blessings.

"You've chosen the right moment," cried one merrily. "Just in time for your friend's wedding!"

"Alfa Guidado?"

Muhammad said no more. He was overwhelmed by a terrible intuition that soon changed into certainty. If Alfa Guidado had yielded at last to the charms of a woman, the woman could only be the one he himself loved. Was not Alfa his other self? Muhammad dismounted and went into the compound with such an expression on his face that all sound ceased as he advanced, succeeded by a stupefied silence. For nights Ayisha had had the same dream, too: the imam had just pronounced the ritual blessings,

Alfa was holding her hand, the poet Amadou Sandji had thrown back his head and begun to recite one of his finest compositions, when Muhammad appeared, brandishing a Tuareg *tilak* over his head.

And so when Muhammad now tottered in among the terrified musicians, she thought her dream was coming true and made an instinctive movement to protect herself.

She had forgotten that Muhammad was not a violent person. If he was coming toward her it was not to threaten or injure her. It was just to embrace her and fall at her feet in tears.

"Why didn't you ever say you wanted to marry her?"

Muhammad looked around. How could he explain? It was simply that he had been ashamed: Alfa was so pure-minded. He went about with his head full of thoughts of God, not seeing the earth or human beings. For him a woman's beauty didn't exist. So how was he to talk to Alfa about the agonies of the heart and the hunger of the body? How was he to describe his desire to be united with Ayisha? Alfa would be sure to exclaim, "A creature should only want to be united with his creator!"

Alfa looked at Muhammad.

"Did she know you loved her?" he asked.

Muhammad was incapable of lying.

Alfa sprang up in anger. "Cunning, unchaste female!" he cried.

Despite his weakness Muhammad protested. "Don't insult her!" he said. "How can you know what love makes other people do? You can think only of God."

"Only" of God? The blasphemy was so enormous that Alfa wondered if Satan had taken possession of his friend's mind.

After the scene at the wedding Muhammad had been carried half conscious to a rest hut. Everyone tactfully pretended his behavior was due to fatigue after a long journey in the sun. But nobody was taken in, and Ayisha would always be known as the girl whose marriage was tarnished by a guilty love. Alfa went to the door of the hut. The celebrations were still going on. He could hear Amadou Sandji, accompanied by the warbling of the flute, singing:

I rejoice in my peace, the wombs are full.
O my many wives, my many sons!
Many are my camps
And many my villages of slaves!

Alfa could not stay longer with his friend without being discourteous to his relatives and guests. He must act naturally, go on as if nothing had happened. Fortunately custom decreed that three days must pass before he was alone with Ayisha, for it would not be decent for their marriage to be consummated too soon. So he would have time to decide how to act toward her. For the moment he was unable to look her in the face, so he went past her and joined his father, in conversation with the imam from the mosque who had just celebrated the marriage.

The two old men were talking about El-Hadj Omar, who had left his capital Dinguirye and was marching on Kaarta. Alhadji reiterated his position: no alliance with Segu, no agreement with the fetishists! According to him Amadou Cheikou ought to have sent the Tukulor reinforcements to help him in his great task! Had not the Prophet said, "The fires of the believer and the unbeliever do not meet"?

Alfa listened, his thoughts elsewhere. He was suffering, not so much on account of Ayisha's betrayal—was not woman born to cause trouble all around her?—but because of his friend's behavior. Muhammad, to whom he'd thought he was so close, with whom he'd shared everything, had hidden something from him. He'd believed their souls were made of the same substance, that their breasts rose and fell to the same rhythm. But alas, all his friend had in him was the desire to fornicate!

As for Ayisha, she hid her face under her white veil. The day she had looked forward to with such happiness was ending in shame and grief. She knew Alfa would never forgive her for having hurt his friend. But was she guilty? If so, of what? Of being beautiful? Of inspiring feelings she did not share? Guilty, guilty—the woman is always guilty. When had she started to love Alfa Guidado? It seemed to her he had always been there in her heart. In the morning she used to listen for his voice, more fervent than that of his companions, when he came begging for food at the doors of the compounds. Every evening she saved up scraps of food for him and ran to put them in his bowl. Compared with him the other *talibes*, Muhammad himself, seemed vulgar, made of the heavier clay that came from certain fields. Love cannot be confused with any other feeling. Muhammad was a very dear brother. Alfa was the master she had chosen for herself.

Amadou Sandji was singing a traditional bride's song:

> *He is right, the king, to beat us.*
> *He beats the royal drum for us to hear,*
> *He wraps up wives for us with light skins*
> *And sends them into the marriage chamber.*
> *He buys kola nuts for us to eat,*
> *He buys horses for us to ride . . .*

And the women took up the refrain:

> *He is right, the king, to beat us.*

Suddenly a *talibe* ran into the courtyard, rushed up to Alhadji Guidado and whispered something in his ear. The marabout at once clapped his slender hands. The news was important. Amadou Cheikou had been taken ill and ordered everyone to come to him.

This development, which might otherwise have spoiled the party, acted as a diversion from the general malaise. The marabouts went off to pray aloud. The imam left to direct a public recitation of the Koran. Others hurried away to hang around the king's compound. Hamdallay was clearly about to go through days of intrigues and bargaining. Who would succeed Amadou Cheikou? Who would have his cap, his turban, his sword and his prayer beads, the symbols of sovereignty? His son Amadou Amadou? His younger brother? Or one of his father's younger brothers? It was said Amadou Cheikou had appointed Amadou Amadou his successor several months ago.

So the party ended sooner than expected, and the women were left with their bowls half full of *tatiri masina*, their dishes half full of fresh dates, and their jugs half full of curds mixed with millet flour.

Alfa went back to the rest hut where he had left Muhammad.

It was empty. He questioned the slaves and the women anxiously. No one knew what had become of him.

Muhammad came to the pool at Amba. At this time of year the water was high, its center hollowed out by the impatient swirl of the waves. Flights of *dyi kono*, winter birds, skimmed the surface, dipping their beaks in search of fish or stems of juicy *bourgou* grass. Muhammad dismounted and clapped his hands to drive his horse away; he didn't want it standing and staring at him. But it whinnied and refused to go.

Muhammad had galloped from Hamdallay without stopping. His one idea was to end it all. No, there was no use living! There was no use letting his pain grow dull and turn into a vague discomfort like a wife you no longer love but to whom you are bound by innumerable ties. He didn't want to become like all those men who lived without either real desire or real happiness because they hadn't the courage to break free from the common run. He wanted to die at twenty, to reject life with anyone else but Ayisha. Methodically he took off his clothes—first his white silk caftan with its neck edged with Hausa embroidery. Then his half-length tunic. Then his sleeveless cotton shirt. And lastly his little close-fitting skullcap. He was left in nothing but his loose drawers, shivering in the cool air, standing on the soft, sodden ground. He decided to walk forward.

Just as he had nearly reached the bank and its fringe of water lilies, a Fulani herdsman appeared on his left. He was wearing a black woolen blanket and a conical hat and standing motionless on one leg like a heron, the other leg drawn up at the knee. This apparition surprised Muhammad, for when he arrived at the pool it had seemed deserted. And what was the herdsman doing here without a herd, and at nightfall? He nearly beat a retreat, but then was ashamed of this impulse of fear, unworthy of a believer. But he did get his prayer beads out of his pocket and start to tell them. And what was he to do now? Jump in the water in front of a witness? He was standing there half naked, shivering, when the wind suddenly came up. The water in the pool started to lap furiously, and a crowd of transparent crabs swarmed out of their hiding places. A big black-and-white snake appeared on a water lily pad and began to sway its flat head and amber-colored eyes to and fro. These things were not natural. Muhammad was just turning around when he heard someone calling his name. It was the voice of Tiekoro, his father, a voice he hadn't heard for years and that turned him into a little boy again, trembling and trying awkwardly to form letters on his writing tablet. He fell on his knees.

"Father, where are you?" he asked.

The Fulani herdsman threw off his hat, revealing a face full of grief. Tears were pouring down his cheeks.

"Why are you weeping, father?" stammered Muhammad.

But didn't he know the answer? His father was weeping because he was condemning himself to eternal fire, deliberately destroying the temple of his body. And for what? For the love of a woman. All the horror of what he had planned to do rose up before him. He must live. Live. Live purified of trivial desires and emotions. How glad he was Ayisha hadn't shared his feelings, for if she had he would have spent his life chained to her body, whereas now he was alone, alone with God.

"Father, forgive me," he said.

As he hastened toward the motionless figure to embrace it and show his repentance, the Fulani herdsman vanished. It happened so suddenly that Muhammad thought he'd been the victim of an illusion. But that was impossible! He could still hear the echo of his name, still feel on his face the other's burning look. Then he realized that for his sake Tiekoro had left for a moment the fabled Janna, refuge of those who have been able to keep their hearts free of passion. He was filled with a new strength. Yes, he would live. Fight. From now on he would be a soldier of Allah. He dressed quickly and caught up the bridle of his horse, which was standing motionless, as if petrified by the apparition.

"Come along, my beauty!" he said soothingly. "We're going home now!"

He was stopped by the lancers as he reached the Damal Fakal gate at the south of the city. Amadou Cheikou was dead. Lamentations were rising up from every corner of Hamdallay:

> *He is dead, Amadou, father of the poor and their support.*
> *He is dead, Amadou, who always was obedient to Allah*

And who so often
Was merciful when he might have been severe.
He is dead, Amadou, who lifted the name of the Fulani
so high . . .

There were crowds at every street corner even though it was dark. Veiled women concealed themselves among their brothers and husbands. People were uneasy, repeating Sheikh El-Bekkay's prediction: "Amadou Cheikou's death will cause a storm. Before the country has counted up years equal to the fingers on a man's two hands, a cataclysm from the west will fall on Hamdallay and we shall gnash our teeth."

For years the Fulani had laid down the law in the region. Even the Bambara had come to fear them and to avoid open confrontation. Was this peace and security now to be threatened anew? Were those days to return when the people's cattle were raided, when they had to send their wives and children abroad and the men themselves were put to death? Muhammad joined the Bambara in the big one-storey house where they were being put up. People were beginning to worry about his disappearance: Alfa Guidado had come to ask where he was, while they had been thinking he was at the wedding! Mande Diarra, the head of the delegation, was afraid lest the king's death force them to prolong their stay in a town he already hated. Others were wondering whether the future ruler of Macina would adopt the same attitude as Amadou Cheikou, or whether instead of seeking an alliance with Segu he might decide to join with the Tukulor and fight against it.

Muhammad took his place in the circle of men sitting on thick rugs decorated with Moroccan flower patterns. Up till now, the rest had expected him to be silent except when asked to read or translate some document. But now he spoke.

"What's the use of bewailing something before it happens?" he said. "It's as if a mourner started lamenting while the soul was still in the body."

They all looked at each other in surprise. What had come over Tiekoro Traore's son?

CHAPTER

5

Mande Diarra had been right. Because of Amadou Cheikou's sudden death the Segu delegation was obliged to stay on in Hamdallay for nearly three months.

First there was the period of official mourning, during which no Grand Council meeting could be held. Then Amadou Cheikou's body in its seven pieces of clothing—trousers, cap, turban with one end over the face, and blankets forming a hood—was buried beside that of his father inside the compound where they had both lived.

After the burial, attended only by relatives and influential figures, letters were dispatched throughout Macina and to friendly countries abroad, inviting the recipients to attend the enthronement of the new king, Amadou Amadou.

He was still very young, and having been coddled and spoiled by his mother and grandmother was incapable of making decisions. He was therefore clay in the hands of Sheikh El-Bekkay, who had no difficulty at all in making him adopt the same policy as his father. Soon Sheikh El-Bekkay had made him sign a declaration consisting of ten points, the first reiterating the need for an alliance with Segu against El-Hadj Omar.

The Bambara were growing impatient. In their eyes Hamdallay was a horrible place, shut away behind its walls like a prudish woman in her hut. The days there were monotonous, punctuated only by the eternal calls of the muezzins, after which the men crowded together like sheep bleating toward the east. The evenings were even more of an ordeal, without any gatherings around the fire, without any storytelling or dancing. Sometimes there would be the piping voice of a *dimadio* or Fulani slave singing, accompanied by the sound of an instrument no less ridiculous. They were deeply shocked by Amadou Cheikou's funeral. Did they call that a royal burial? Where were the offerings? Where were the sacrifices, the singing, the music, the recitation of genealogies and of the exploits of the dead man's family? They compared this hasty, unimpressive ceremony with those attending the death of a mansa in Segu.

One morning Amadou Amadou sent for them. He was a real *bimi*! He had very light skin and hair as curly as a Moor's, and he was dressed extremely simply in a white caftan without any embroidery: but at the same time he gave an impression of subtle arrogance. He was surrounded by the whole of the Grand Council. Even those who lived far away in Fakala or on the shores of Lake Debo were there, together with the *amirabe* or generals from the various regions.

The session began with prayers—prayers that exasperated the Bambara.

"O God, bless our lord Muhammad, who opened that which was closed, completed that which had gone before, and sustains truth with truth . . ."

At last they could all sit down.

Amadou Amadou spoke.

"Kaarta is in the hands of El-Hadj Omar," he announced soberly. "Mansa Mamadi Kandian has agreed to be converted to Islam. This letter from the Tukulor confirms it."

Kaarta! The Bambara kingdom of Kaarta, founded by N'golo Kulybali while his brother installed himself in Segu! Admittedly there had been plenty of quarrels between the two Bambara kingdoms, but at this news they were forgotten, leaving room only for grief and the desire for revenge. Amadou Amadou held out to Muhammad, the only member of the delegation who could read, a parchment whose authenticity was proved by a circular seal. It bore the writing of El-Hadj Omar. Muhammad scanned it before telling his companions what it said.

"The infidels of Kaarta have been vanquished," it began. "The country is wiped off the map. Such is the will of God. I wish merely to reform things as much as lies in my power. My only help is in God. Let us form a single front against His enemies, our own, and those of our fathers—the polytheists! The only feelings that should exist between us are love and affection, respect and consideration . . ."

There was a silence. The Bambara were terrified. If Kaarta was defeated and Mamadi Kandian had been converted, anything could happen.

Amadou Amadou spoke again.

"I shall not conceal from you that I haven't the unanimous support of the Grand Council. I even admit I have had to force the hand of men wiser and more experienced than myself. Nevertheless, this is my decision: a group of our people, led by Alhadji Guidado and Hambarke Samtata, will go back with you to Segu, to knock down your fetish huts and take note of the conversion of your mansa."

Even Muhammad was dumbfounded. He no longer shared the religion of his ancestors, but that was a far cry from knocking down the fetish huts. The people of Segu would never allow it! Every compound would rebel! The whole kingdom would be shaken to its foundations!

"If you agree," Amadou Amadou continued, "I shall write to El-Hadj Omar, telling him that Segu has entered into my allegiance. Then he will no longer be able to attack you and peace will be preserved."

"Segu has entered into my allegiance"—The words were utterly unacceptable! Beside himself with fury, Mande Diarra rose, clearly intending to box this Fulani's ears. He had to be held back, and the Bambara delegation withdrew in the utmost disorder.

Going out of the Hall of Seven Doors where the council met, Muhammad ran into Alfa Guidado. Instead of taking advantage of the period of seclusion after marriage, during which the bride devotes herself entirely to her husband, Alfa went out every night to see his friend and stayed with him until late into the night. The two young men never spoke of Ayisha. At first Muhammad had been tempted to ask Alfa how he was acting toward his wife, whether he had forgiven her, even whether he had consummated the marriage. But he had restrained himself. Since he was trying

not to think of the woman who had almost made him commit
the gravest of sins, what was the point of inquiring about her?
So Alfa and Muhammad went on endlessly discussing the hadith,
the future of Macina and Segu, and above all the supernatural
appearance of Tiekoro. This last event hadn't surprised Alfa.

"When a man has the true light of religion within him," he
said, "he can do anything. Your father was a saint. He was able
to come to you, and I shouldn't be surprised if he appears at all
the great turning points in your life."

He linked arms with Muhammad.

"*Gore*,"* he said, "I'll come with you when you go back to
Segu. I've got my father's permission to be one of the Macina
delegation."

Muhammad disengaged himself with a violence that surprised even himself.

"Don't be so sure of yourself!" he cried. "We haven't decided
yet to accept your proposals!"

Alfa looked at him sadly.

"You have no choice," he said. There was pity in his voice.

The two youths were at odds, for Muhammad was seeing
himself for the first time as a Bambara and not as a Muslim.

He had never forgotten what his father said to him before he
left for Hamdallay: "Believers are brothers even when separated
by kinship or space, because, through religion, they share the
same origin in faith." Moreover he had grown up with Alfa Guidado, forming his intellect and sensibility at the foot of the same
masters. And now suddenly he found himself cut off from him,
ready to accept a heritage of which his knowledge was incomplete
and which he had learned to despise. Segu was in him, and he
identified himself with it. Segu, with its fetish huts, its bloody
sacrifices, its dark and mysterious practices.

Hamdallay, usually so quiet, was in turmoil. The death of
Amadou Cheikou, the succession of the new king, the news of
the fall of Kaarta which meant that El-Hadj Omar had entered a
region where Macina alone had thought itself free to make converts—all these events had overcome the reserve the people derived both from Islam and from their Fulani upbringing. Even

* Fulani for friend or brother.

women were to be seen gathering at street corners to hear news come from none knew where. The masters deserted the Koranic schools; the children reverted to happy laughter and noise. Great oxen, unattended, munched the millet stalks in the fences surrounding the houses. Alfa and Muhammad parted outside the place where the Bambara were staying. For the first time they didn't feel as if they wanted to be together.

And yet Alfa was right. Segu couldn't refuse Amadou Amadou's proposals; they had to accept the alliance. El-Hadji was too strong, his armies inspired by too formidable a force.

In Guemou-Banka he had had all the menfolk slain.

In Baroumba he had put the whole population to the sword.

In Sirimana he had had six hundred men executed, and carried off thousands of prisoners into captivity.

At Nioro, in Kaarta, he had been particularly bloodthirsty. At first he had spared the Mansa, who said he wanted to be converted to Islam. Then he changed his mind and had the Mansa decapitated in the presence of his wives and children, after which the children were executed one by one. Then he allowed his followers to massacre the rest of the population, first with swords and then with guns. The dead were too many to be counted.

People ended up by wondering if El-Hadj was really a man born of woman. Wasn't he rather the instrument of some terrible anger on the part of the gods and the ancestors? But what crime could have made them so angry? On thinking it over, Mande Diarra prudently decided to go back to Segu with the Macina delegation and submit its proposals to the Mansa.

How painful it is to find an enemy in one you have loved like another self! Muhammad discovered this as he and Alfa rode along together.

Outwardly nothing had changed between them, and yet nothing was the same. Alfa was a Fulani from Macina, which might soon be imposing its will on Segu.

So they journeyed without talking to each other through landscapes that the rains made as somber as their mood. They avoided the Joliba, which was in flood, and went via Tayawal, crossing the Bani River some days' march away from Jenne. There was

no one to be seen. The peasants were hiding in their hastily fortified villages. Herds of buffalo came up and looked at the horses.
The singing of the Bambara griots traveling with their masters
frightened off the gazelle, who stood like buff spots under the
shea trees.

The men spent the night in a camp put up by Fulani slaves,
accustomed by ancient nomad tradition to protecting themselves
against nature wherever they happened to be. They cut young
branches from shea trees, stuck them in the ground and wrapped
long mats of straw from the doum palm around them, held in
place by millet stems.

They arrived in Segu before midday.

Muhammad had never asked himself whether he liked Segu.
When he went back there after his studies he had been very glad
to get back. It was where he had been a child, spoiled by his
mother and sisters, a place of personal memories. But now he
suddenly saw it through new eyes.

Its mud walls still rose up over the gray waters of the Joliba,
but instead of the usual bustle of women, children and fishermen
there was nothing but a jumble of straw huts and hide tents,
pathetic rudimentary shelters.

They belonged to Bambara who had escaped the sack of Nioro
and come to the kingdom of Segu in the hope of finding protection
there. Their cheeks were hollow, their bodies gaunt. Men had
seen their wives and daughters raped, wives had seen their husbands disemboweled. Children had lost both father and mother
and were only alive because of the strong solidarity between the
women: each mother suckled two babes and carried two children
on her back. A griot was standing on a mound, singing. The followers of El-Hadj Omar had murdered his three sons and shared
the wives of the family who had the misfortune to be beautiful.
And all he could do was sing:

> War is good because it makes our kings rich.
> Wives, slaves, cattle—it brings them all these.
> War is holy because it makes us Muslims.
> War is holy and good,
> So may it set our skies aflame
> From Dinguirye to Timbuktu,
> From Guemou to Jenne . . .

When he heard this, Muhammad could not hold back his tears. It was true that El-Hadj Omar made war in the name of Allah, the only true God! It was a holy war! But these were his people, their wounds were his own, and he found himself hating a God who manifested Himself through fire and sword! He stopped his horse beside the griot, a human scarecrow with his leather miter starred with broken cowrie shells, his almost naked body scarcely covered by a goatskin, his open sores.

"What is your name?" asked Muhammad.

The man looked at him with eyes darkened by the suffering of the world.

"Faraman Kouyate, master!" he said.

"Come with me!"

The man followed him, limping on injured feet wrapped in baobab leaves. He went on singing:

> *Oh yes, war is holy and good.*
> *Let it set our skies aflame . . .*

The Macina delegation, accompanied by Bambara dignitaries, entered the Mansa's palace, where the visitors were to stay. Muhammad set out for the family compound, slowing his horse so as not to leave Faraman too far behind. He was glad to be away from Alfa. In other days he would have had him stay and share a hut with him, and introduce him to his family, especially Olubunmi. But now he would have felt like a traitor if he'd done that.

Wasn't he, Muhammad, just a bad Muslim, though? The love of a woman had already distracted him from the love of God, and now attachment to the gods of his people was outweighing for him the brotherhood of Islam. He thought of his father, who had received El-Hadj Omar as a guest, founded a *zawiya*, stood out against a king. He was overwhelmed with a sense of unworthiness. He would never be able to live up to his father's example.

Olubunmi had heard of the delegation's arrival and was waiting at the entrance to the compound with Mustapha, little Kosa and others among their brothers. The two young men threw themselves into one another's arms.

"So the *bimi*'s back!" joked Olubunmi.

The *bimi*? It was true that he had Fulani blood, through his mother. Muhammad realized he had forgotten it. He took Olubunmi's arm and went into the compound, happy to recognize the solid row of huts, the *dubale* tree in the middle, the smell of the burning *makalanikama* which promoted family unity.

Olubunmi chattered ceaselessly, he was so happy to have his favorite companion back.

"Did you know Yassa has had a son?" he asked. "He's been called Fanko, the same as me, and I take great care of him. Everyone laughs at me and asks if I've turned into a woman."

Muhammad suddenly noticed that Faraman was still silently following, and was slightly ashamed of his thoughtlessness. He took the griot's hand and led him to the courtyard where Tiefolo's *bara muso* lived, for her to give him food and clothing.

Mansa Demba accepted the proposals brought by the Macina delegation from Amadou Amadou.

Small groups of *tondyons*, supervised by Fulani, entered every house in Segu, going through the series of courtyards to the huts containing the *pembele* and the *boli*. They took them out into the daylight, then brought them to the palace square and the bonfire presided over by Alhadji Guidado, Hambarke Samatata and the royal marabouts. Fur, bark, roots, bits of wood, tails of animals—all were consumed by the crackling flames. The *tondyons* brought a harvest of sacred objects from all over town, smashing the red stones that represented the ancestors and couldn't be burned. Then they tackled the fetish priests' quarter by the city wall, not far from the Mougou Sousou gate. Tools belonging to distant ancestors and kept hidden in holes in the ground, a reminder of the ancient underground dwellings of the smiths at Gwonna, were taken from their shrines. Since the iron of the hoes, picks and axes would not burn, they wrenched off the wooden handles. Then they dragged the holy men to the square and stripped them of their necklaces of horns, teeth, leaves and feathers, and their belts hung with magic charms. Then they were forced to kneel so that a barber might shave their venerable heads. As each lock fell, the crowd that had gathered outside the palace let out a groan of grief and anger. One overzealous *tondyon* tore the fiber garment of a high priest of Komo, and the old man stood there dumbfounded, his aged, gnarled old body exposed for all to see.

What was the Mansa thinking of? People couldn't make it out. How could he hope to keep his power, turning his back on the gods of Segu and insulting the ancestors who had protected him? What blindness, what folly! After such crimes the name of Segu would disappear off the face of the earth. Or else become the name of some miserable little hole dozing on the banks of its river, unheard of. "Segu—where's that?" people would say.

Men were in a quandary. Should they rush to the defense of the fetishists? But careful, the *tondyons* had guns, and the swine wouldn't hesitate to use them. But if they just stood there with their arms folded, wouldn't that make them accomplices and bring down upon them part of the penalty of the crime?

While this auto-da-fé was going on, other *tondyons* and other Fulani were going through the town noting where the mosques were. They didn't count those of the Somono or the Moors because these were traditionally Islamic communities. They were only satisfied when the imam, the muezzin and the worshippers were all Bambara. So in a supreme hoax the Mansa had sent out people in long robes with shaven heads who sang out in chorus, "*Al hamdu lillahi!* God be praised! *La ilaha ill'Allah!* There is no god but God!" and other obscene mockeries.

The Koranic schools were also counted, their masters questioned about the number of pupils and the level of their studies. Sometimes the soldiers tried to trap them with trick questions. But the pseudoschoolmasters, duly primed, gave perfect answers.

Who had organized this masquerade?—that was what Muhammad wanted to know. The Fulani from Macina were well aware they weren't dealing with genuine Muslims and that the great royal fetishes were safe in the altar huts in the palace, together with some albinos who might be offered up to Faro if necessary. They knew these ostentatious conversions meant nothing and had no effect on the population as a whole, who would immediately ask the priests to make new *boli* and *pembele* and make twice the usual number of sacrifices in order to appease the gods. So what shameful alliance was being hatched, and why? Contempt and anger vied with each other in his heart.

Muhammad was in the palace square, followed by Faraman Kouyate, who almost never left him, when a man came up to him.

"Aren't you a Traore?" he said. "Tiekoro's son and Dousika's grandson?"

Muhammad said he was.

"Hurry up then!" said the other. "Misfortune has struck your family!"

Muhammad ran home as fast as his legs would carry him.

CHAPTER

6

When Alhadji Guidado left the palace square on the way to the Traore compound he was bound on an important mission. As everyone knew, what El-Hadj Omar hated most was tolerance on the part of Islam toward fetishism and the mingling together of Islam and fetishist rites. So there was one good way of proving to him that Macina now adopted the same attitude as he and did not take such things lightly. Tiekoro Traore had been a saint, a martyr to the true faith. At present his grave was in the middle of a compound of unbelievers, a stone's throw from huts full of altars reeking with blood amid the noxious vapors of magical plants. It was said that a Muslim who came from Bakkel to ask for the grave to be turned into a place of pilgrimage had been kept waiting more than six months and then given an ambiguous answer. Well, all that was going to change! There would be a great deployment of forces, the altar huts would be knocked down and Tiekoro Traore's grave would be raised to the preeminence it should always have enjoyed. If all the huts around it had to be destroyed that it might stand forth like a lily in a bed of nettles, the *tondyons* would see to it.

But Alhadji hated his errand. What hypocrisy! Here was the Macina of Amadou Amadou practicing *muwalat* with the kingdom of Mansa Demba so as to get its hands on his wealth, when the Most High particularly condemned such dealings: "You who believe, take not as your partner a people with whom Allah is wroth."

O Amadou Amadou, unworthy son of his father Amadou Cheikou, enemy of unbelievers, friend and fearer of Allah!

Alhadji Guidado found himself outside the Traore compound and was impressed in spite of himself by the facade with its carved ribs enhanced by alternate patterns of red and white. These people certainly knew how to build!

He went into the first courtyard, followed by his son, a few Fulani dignitaries and a number of *tondyons*, and found himself face to face with a handsome old man who introduced himself firmly: "I am Tiefolo Traore, *fa* of this dwelling!"

Tiefolo was wearing a short shirt made of two strips of cotton dyed red and tied at the sides with three strings, together with a leather cord around his waist decorated with cowries. He also wore a tall headdress made of skins stretched over a frame and covered with cowries and gris-gris of every kind. Most striking of all were the animals' tails hung around his neck, waist and arms. A bow and a huge quiver full of arrows were slung over his left shoulder. Alhadji Guidado looked at it all in disgust. He knew Tiefolo wasn't dressed like this by chance, and that this display of gris-gris was not fortuitous.

"I am sent by Allah," he said curtly. "Permit me to do my duty."

"Who is Allah?" came the reply.

It was true that Alhadji had no taste for his mission, but he was a strict and convinced Muslim and he wasn't going to let the name of God be taken in vain, especially in front of all the men, women and children who had come out from the inner courtyards to watch his confrontation with the *fa*. The latter's quiet impertinence in pretending not to know the name of Allah drove him into a fury, and he advanced upon him, crying: "Blasphemer, bow down before the only true God!"

It is not clear what happened next. The Traore maintained that Alhadji Guidado accompanied his words with a shove. Tiefolo, insulted, reached for his quiver. Then the *tondyons* threw themselves on him and knocked him down.

The Fulani declared that Tiefolo spat in Alhadji's face and the latter, unable to endure the insult, ordered the *tondyons* to seize his adversary, who fell resisting them. Whatever the explanation, Tiefolo lay on the ground for a few moments, his efforts to rise rendered more and more ineffective by anger. At last he managed to kneel, clutching onto the skirts of Alhadji's white silk caftan. His lips parted as if he were about to speak, but no sound came forth and he fell back on the ground, lifeless.

For a few moments there was complete silence. Neither the Traore family, nor the Fulani from Macina, nor the royal marabouts and the *tondyons* with them dared to move. Then Tiefolo's *bara muso* went up to her husband. He had fallen on his side, his face in the mud. She turned him over, revealing his drawn face with a fleck of foam on lips as red as if they had been dyed with *ngalama*.

"Allah has killed my husband!" shrieked the *bara muso*.

Her cry galvanized all the men in the family. Even those who had secretly converted to Islam, or planned to do so in order to win the women's admiration for being able to write, seized whatever weapon came to hand—cudgels, stones, arrows. But what could they do against *tondyons* armed with guns? In no time at all they were lined up against the walls of the huts, the round black mouths of the Fulani's guns turned upon them. Without a glance at Tiefolo's body Alhadji Guidado and a handful of Fulani dignitaries walked through to the last courtyard, where, as they now knew, the altar huts were. There they broke the *boli* to pieces, overturned the *pembele*, scattered the red stones, and smashed the pots which held the breath of the family dead waiting to be reincarnated. Then they turned loose the white fowls kept to be sacrificed to the god Faro.

Alfa Guidado stayed slumped beside Tiefolo's corpse. A moment earlier he had never doubted his own religion. He had lived only through and for Allah. He could go for two days without food or drink. The sexual act, to which he was condemned as a married man, he regarded as a defilement. He started to pray every morning as soon as he opened his eyes. But that cry—"Allah has killed my husband!"—echoed and reechoed in his mind. He suddenly understood there was no universal god; every man had the right to worship whomsoever he pleased; and to take away a man's religion, the keystone of his life, was to condemn him to

death. Why was Allah better than Faro or Pemba? Who had decreed it?

Tears streamed down his face. He leaned his forehead on Tiefolo's chest as if he too had lost a father, like the orphans in the
compound now beginning to realize their misfortune. Olubunmi,
who for once had not gone with Muhammad to the palace square,
came and knelt by Alfa. Then, weeping, they lifted up the body
between them and carried it to Tiefolo's hut.

Tiefolo lay like a tree that has fallen when it is still full of
sap, its leaves still bright and its branches stretching out proudly.
But gradually the peace of death spread over his face. There was
just a fleck of white on his lips that would soon be washed away
with warm water scented with basil when the women prepared
the body for burial. As Tiefolo had been one of the great hunters
of his generation, slaves hastened to the four corners of Segu to
announce his death to all the hunting brotherhoods. *Karamoko*
and their pupils, hearing the news and above all the circumstances of his death, arrived in haste, relieving their feelings by
firing off their guns until it was time to turn them against the
Fulani, the cause of all the trouble. All the women of the family
and the neighborhood, Tiefolo's wives excepted, had begun their
lamentation! The din of death could already be heard.

Muhammad rushed into the compound like a madman just
as Olubunmi and Alfa were coming out of Tiefolo's hut. The three
young men embraced each other without a word. Muhammad
and Alfa came together again, hugging each other like a pair of
lovers who have just missed losing each other forever. In a very
short time they had discovered all the horror of religious fanaticism, and of the scheming for power that so often lay behind it.
Alfa felt he would never forget the sight of his father profaning
the altars of the Traore. God is love. God is respect for everyone.
No, Alhadji Guidado was not the servant of God; he was merely
the unwitting tool of Amadou Amadou's earthly ambition.

Meanwhile the family council was meeting. It was too soon
actually to appoint Tiefolo's successor to the responsibility of *fa*,
even though it was known that the office would go to his younger
brother. But it was important his death should be avenged, and
claims presented to the Mansa. Reparations must be exacted from
the Fulani who had entered the compound as if they were con-

querors. Some hesitated. Should they wait until Tiefolo had been buried? Was it disrespectful to do other things during the time that should be devoted to funeral ceremonies? But others said immediate action was needed, and they prevailed. So a procession left, made up of Tiefolo's brothers, his older sons and the master huntsmen who had been his friends. Muhammad, Olubunmi and Alfa brought up the rear. They had had some difficulty in being allowed to come: the others thought them too young.

But when they reached the palace square, where smoke was still rising from the last of the *boli*, they heard the sound of the great royal *tabala*. Mansa Demba was dead.

Usually, when the Mansa died, the kingdom was orphaned. Nothing could be heard but funeral chants, lamentations and tears. In addition to the great public ceremonies, every household killed a goat and then went to file past the body, lying in state in the first vestibule in the palace. All was desolation.

But Demba's death was an exception to the rule, and the occasion of what might almost be called popular rejoicing. All the Segukaw took it as a sign that the gods had responded swiftly and strongly to the insult offered them, and that Allah had been defeated. It was said that Demba, until then perfectly hale and hearty, had been suddenly seized with mysterious pains as he was talking to the Fulani from Macina. The conversation had been interrupted by a stream of blood gushing from his lips. Then his body, and in particular his face, became covered with pustules, and a few minutes later he was dead. His corpse had at once given off a terrible stench.

Such joy, such happiness! People didn't dare show their feelings openly for fear of the *tondyons*, so they danced inside the walls of their own compounds, from which now and then bursts of laughter could be heard. A song went the rounds:

> *Pemba, you are the builder of things.*
> *Faro, all the things in the universe*
> *Are in your power.*
> *But he who sits on the oxhide**
> *Forgot!*

---

* The Mansa.

The song was soon banned, but how can a song be stopped from passing from one to another, popping up where it is least expected? A song is as elusive as air. And the women hummed in chorus as they plied their pestles:

> He who sits on the oxhide
> Forgot!

Despite their recent bereavement the Traore rejoiced most of all. What need was there to seek individual reparation when vengeance, divine vengeance had been wrought? The family proceeded to share out Tiefolo's wives and appoint a new *fa*. This, as expected, was Ben, Tiefolo's younger brother, a peaceful farmer who didn't mind lending his slaves a hand with the hoe and who had a more conciliatory attitude toward Islam than his brother. He had sent three of his sons to the Koranic school run by the Moors.

While the Fulani from Macina were obliged to stay on at the palace for the official mourning and the appointment of the new Mansa, Alfa Guidado had left his father and the other dignitaries and gone to share the hut of Muhammad and Olubunmi. He hadn't known what to do about his marriage, but now he had the feeling that God had acted for the best. For weeks he had been far away from Ayisha, living in Segu, where he had been reunited with one friend and made another. He was as captivated by Olubunmi as Muhammad had been—by his desire to see what the world was like beyond the Joliba, the Bagoe and the deserts outside Timbuktu. Olubunmi had taken the other two to see old Samba, who told them the usual tales about ships and white men.

"Didn't you know the Toubabs, the whites themselves, are afraid of El-Hadj Omar?" he said. "They have built a fort on the Senegal River, and El-Hadj Omar wants to drive them out."

This gave rise to endless discussion. Why had the Toubabs built a fort on the river? Wasn't El-Hadj Omar right to want to dislodge them? The two young men didn't share old Samba's admiration for the whites, their guns and their medicines. These intruders with skins like albinos had no business to be here. They were real infidels—drinkers of alcohol, eaters of unclean flesh, speakers of a formless jargon no one could understand.

There were only two things about which Muhammad and Alfa disagreed with Olubunmi, and these were alcohol and women. Olubunmi was always ready to go into a tavern and fill his belly with *dolo*. And there was scarcely a night when he didn't sleep with some slave from the compound. He made fun of his friends, especially Muhammad, who had never made love to a woman.

"If you don't watch out your penises will rot between your thighs," he would say.

And so it was that Muhammad and Alfa at last came to talk about Ayisha. They were alone in their hut at nightfall, savoring the peace of the hour and of this interlude in time, knowing how fragile it was and how the threat of El-Hadj Omar still rumbled in the distance. Yassa had just gone by with her son at her breast, and it was wonderful to see how this little creature had restored his mother to happiness. So the desire for the body of a woman stirred in them, together with the more remote but no less disturbing desire for fatherhood, both fanned by the memory of Olubunmi's lyrical descriptions.

Muhammad spoke first.

"So you've never been in love," he said, "and yet you've possessed Ayisha. Isn't it a sin to possess a woman without loving her?"

At first Alfa remained silent. It seemed to Muhammad he was growing more and more handsome. Perhaps because he imposed fewer religious mortifications upon himself now, and let the mothers in the compound pamper him, like the others, with their ready offers of food. He turned to his companion.

"I didn't want to take her for that very reason," he said. "And also because she'd hurt you. But then she cried."

"For love? Of you?"

And in spite of himself, in spite of his attempts at self-discipline, Muhammad was consumed with jealousy. Why did women love one man rather than another? He had been ready to die for Ayisha, and all she'd ever given him were smiles and looks of harmless affection.

Alfa went on. You could tell this conversation was torture to him, but that he had made up his mind to go through with it.

"She was crying," he said. "She snuggled up against me. She was half naked. I don't know myself what came over me."

Muhammad came closer.

"Was it nice?" he asked feverishly. "Even like that . . . ?"

Again Alfa was silent. Then he answered, in a troubled voice:

"Nice? The fabled land of Janna can't contain more delights than a woman's body."

Muhammad was astounded.

"Even if you don't love her?"

"I think if I'd stayed in Hamdallay," said Alfa, "I'd . . . I'd have come to love her. That's why I asked to go with my father. To get away from her."

For a while they said nothing. After such a confession, what could be said? Muhammad was tortured by jealousy and curiosity at the same time. Jealousy when he imagined Ayisha and his friend in one another's arms, the caresses they lavished on one another, the sighs they heaved, the pleasure they shared. Curiosity when he wondered when he himself would at last experience such sensations. Soon the family would start to think of arranging a marriage for him. What complicated matters slightly was that as he was Tiekoro's son, brought up in Hamdallay, they would have to find him a wife who was a Muslim. Or a girl willing to be converted. But alas, would she be as beautiful as Ayisha, and would he, like Alfa, find himself loving her in spite of himself, after having merely desired her?

From the next courtyard came the sound of singing, laughter, and the merry chatter of children putting off the hour for bed. How warm and friendly life was in this compound! Alfa and Muhammad remembered their strict upbringing in Hamdallay—hungry, cold, beaten by their teacher. And all in the name of Allah! They got up and went to join the family circle.

Faraman Kouyate was sitting under the *dubale* tree delighting his audience with his song. Strange to say it had spread all around Segu, as if it symbolized the people's mocking yet fatalistic attitude to the decisions of the great.

> *War is good because it makes our kings rich.*
> *Wives, slaves, cattle—it brings them all these.*
> *War is holy because it makes us Muslims.*
> *War is holy and good.*

may it set our skies aflame
From Dinguirye to Timbuktu,
From Guemou to Jenne . . .

Since he had been living in the compound the griot had been transformed. The women had fed him and tended his wounds. He would have died for the Traore, and he revered Muhammad like a god.

CHAPTER

7

Segu received two terrible pieces of news in one day. Almost as soon as he was enthroned the new Mansa, Oitala Ali, took over his elder brother's alliance with Macina, and to give it substance sent soldiers to support the Fulani battalions who were to try to halt El-Hadj Omar in Beledougou.

Everyone was astonished. Don't kings ever learn? Think how Demba had died, and here was Oitala Ali bent on making the same mistake! Did he want to meet the same end?

Some voices, however, were raised in support of the Mansa. What was he expected to do? Fold his arms and wait for El-Hadj Omar to arrive at the gates of Segu? Face him alone? Couldn't people see this was impossible?

Those in a hurry to talk about the victory of the ancestral gods would do well to think again. Victory? What victory, when the scourge of Allah was destroying all in its path? Demba was dead. But why? For having laid hands on the fetishes of the people of Segu, or for having secretly refused to destroy his own, hoping to get away with it by trickery? There is no deceiving God.

The point of view of the Muslims of Segu began to prevail and people were worried. The fetish priests, who had recovered their former prestige after the Mansa's death, were rapidly beginning to lose it again. Muslim marabouts in long burnouses went through the streets crying, "Be converted! Be converted!

Segu is a woman with smallpox. The spots haven't yet appeared on her face, but death is at work within her."

One fanatic had installed himself in the palace square beside a barber, and exhorted passersby:

"Start anew! Cut off your braids! Come to God!"

But people hung back. They didn't like these public conversions. Once again the Segukaw found the ostentatiousness of Islam incomprehensible. Shouldn't religion be something private? But what completed the confusion was the Mansa's decision to raise troops, as if the *tondyons* weren't enough. Even slaves were being recruited! They were asking for men not older than twenty-two dry seasons, and giving them an axe, a lance or a bow and arrows, occasionally a gun. Then, in groups under the command of a leader wearing a curved saber slung over his shoulder, they were sent to join the Fulani lancers waiting over the ford at Thio.

The danger from El-Hadj Omar produced strange reactions, and there was no shortage of volunteers. Soon every family in Segu had contributed half a dozen of them to the crowd camping in the courtyard of the royal palace, waiting for the day of departure. Their mothers didn't know whether to weep or be proud. Their fathers were secretly sorry they were too old to go too. They'd have enjoyed getting their teeth into a few Tukulor!

Of course this wasn't the first time Segu had gone to war. Ever since its earliest days it had lived on war, raids, the capture of booty and prisoners, the taxes imposed on vassal peoples. But not on this scale! It was as if the very existence of the kingdom were threatened. As if every soldier that went knew he must win or die.

Olubunmi went back into the compound. All morning he had been wandering around in Segu, excited by the smell of gunpowder, the sound of trumpets, the beating of drums. Most insistent of these was the *tabala*, its oxhide renewed since the Mansa's death, held horizontal by two men while a half-naked third beat upon it, a thin stream of sweat running down between his shoulder blades. The youthful voices of the new soldiers rose above the sound of the drum, chorusing the motto of the Diarra: "Lion, breaker of big bones . . . you have bent the world like a sickle, and straightened it out like a path. You cannot resuscitate a great corpse, but you can raise many new souls."

Olubunmi's mind was fired with violent images of fame and adventure. He wanted to break away from the authority of his elders, go off like his father Malobali before him! For Olubunmi, going to war was only a prelude to other departures. Religious quarrels didn't interest him.

Muhammad and Alfa were reclining on a mat under the *dubale* tree, drinking tea brought them by a slave girl and analyzing a hadith. Perhaps for the first time Olubunmi felt exasperated by his two friends, dearly as he loved them. Were they going to spend their whole lives discussing Allah, groveling in the dust when they weren't crouching over a mat? Would their days go by without either their minds or their senses aspiring to some earthly satisfaction? He squatted down beside them.

"I've just enlisted," he said.

"What!"

"Yes, I'm off to the war, too!"

Olubunmi was really talking like this out of bravado, to jolt Muhammad and Alfa out of their inertia; he didn't expect to be believed. Alfa looked at him with his fervent eyes and said: "Do you know what I dreamed? I was going to be circumcised again, and I protested, and hid my penis so as not to feel the knife a second time. I said I was already a man, and suddenly someone whose face I didn't see burst out laughing and said, 'You! You can't even protect your mother's compound!'"

"What do you think it means?"

Alfa grew more serious still.

"My mother!" he said. "That could mean the one who gave me birth. But mightn't it also be the land where I was born—my country?"

He was silent, looking at his companions, who gazed back at him not understanding yet what he was driving at.

"My country," he said. "The Tukulor may well end by destroying Macina! They say he's written a very violent letter to Amadou!"

This was the last reaction Olubunmi had expected from Alfa, whom he had regarded as even more timid than Muhammad. He stammered, taken by surprise.

"What did you say?"

Alfa lowered his eyes.

"Ready to protect my mother's compound!" he said.

Muhammad was speechless, and looked at the other two as if they had suddenly gone mad. He had no desire to go to war! What for? El-Hadj Omar was a Muslim, and if he sowed death around him it was in the name of Allah! It would be a crime to bear a sword against him. Yet he wondered what would become of him if his two friends went away and he was left alone in the compound with the fathers of families and the women and children, alone in a Segu drained of the sap of its youth.

Olubunmi guessed what was going on in his mind and finally said, with a sardonic smile: "What are you afraid of leaving behind? You haven't even got the woman you love!"

The long column of ten thousand soldiers was going through the village of Ouossebougou. It was raining. The men were up to their knees in mud, and this was demoralizing the young recruits and adding greatly to the *keletigui*'s anxiety.

The rainy season is not a good season for war: it exacts too heavy a toll. It exhausts beasts and men, slows down their progress, floods rivers and cuts off roads.

Only the Macina lancers in their thick padded coats were oblivious of the elements. Apart from them in uniforms, everyone had dressed as best he could. Some had thick Muslim burnouses, some wore woolen blankets, others hunting tunics or cotton shirts. The fetishists displayed their gris-gris, the Muslims their verses from the Koran. All had, hidden in their clothes, the talismans their mothers had given them before they set off. Besides the volunteers and the lancers there were also two detachments of *sofas*, horsemen from the Mansa's personal guard, in their loose red drawers: they had inspired terror on every battlefield in the region.

But it wasn't the presence of the *sofas*, their compatriots, that reassured the young recruits, but that of the Fulani lancers, brandishing their famous white cotton flag. They were said to be invincible, with their horses specially trained to break down walls surrounding villages. As well as lances with flat, heart-

shaped heads they each had a saber, a knife, a long stick curved
like a sickle and an iron ball and chain. Strangely enough, the
Fulani *amirabe* got on perfectly with the Bambara *keletigui*, as
if for the time being they had buried their religious and racial
differences. They had agreed on the number of scouts to be sent
out to clear, widen or level their route. Behind the scouts came
the main body of troops, protected by the lancers, with sentries
bringing up the rear. Spies on swift little horses rode up at regular
intervals to report their findings. Griots ran in and out among
the troops, singing, playing musical instruments, whipping up
the soldiers' courage.

They had been on the march for two days, but still there was
no sign of El-Hadj Omar; it was as if he had gone underground
or existed only in people's imaginations and fears. As most of
those present had never seen a Tukulor they thought of them as
short, squat, animal-like; but those with some knowledge of geography pointed out that they were related to the Fulani, and so
must be tall and light skinned.

Faraman Kouyate walked level with the unit, the *bolo*, in
which Muhammad was marching, together with his two friends.
It was to give Muhammad courage that he sang:

> War is good because it makes our kings rich.
> Wives, slaves, cattle—it brings them all these. . . .

For he knew Muhammad would have gone back to Segu if he
could. He hadn't had an easy childhood, but his sufferings then
had had some meaning: they were designed to make him as perfect as possible, as like to the divine model. But what were they
suffering for now? For Islam? Which brand of Islam, that of the
Fulani of Macina, or that of El-Hadj Omar? No, men were fighting
merely to satisfy the interests and flatter the pride of kings. Faraman wanted to stand up and shout aloud. But his voice would
be drowned by the war drums. That was what the war drums
were for—to drown men's cries of revolt!

As it was still raining and would soon be dark, the army halted
on a plain as bare as the palm of your hand except for the blue
stones shining in the wet. The column broke up, and the *sofas*,
with some difficulty, kindled fires on which they cooked sweet

corn and quarters of mutton. The main body of the army got only watery millet gruel, while the lancers, without dismounting, drank curds from leather bottles.

Muhammad asked himself yet again why he had let himself in for this escapade; why he hadn't dissuaded Alfa and then joined him in bringing pressure to bear on Olubunmi. Poor Olubunmi! What had he been hoping for? Not this muddy adventure! His heady dreams wouldn't survive one campaign.

Thanks to the skill of the Fulani, shelters were rigged up and everyone lay down, wrapped in their clothes as protection against the mud. Muhammad went straight to bed and shut his eyes. Ever since he had started out, Ayisha had taken complete possession of him again. How wrong he'd been to think he could banish her from his thoughts! She was there day and night—perhaps because that image of beauty helped him fight the ugliness all around him. Whatever the reason, she came and went behind his closed eyes, arranging her long hair, rubbing her skin with Hausa perfume or shea butter, fixing golden rings in her delicate ears. How did she fill in the time with her husband away? Was she eagerly awaiting his return? Perhaps he had planted a son in her before he left her, and she was watching the gourd of her belly swell. Oh no, Allah wouldn't allow that! That Ayisha should be pregnant by someone other than himself! At this point Alfa came into the shelter and began to say his prayers. Muhammad realized he had forgotten his, and was ashamed.

The men had been asleep for only three or four hours when they were awakened. The sentries suspected El-Hadj Omar was somewhere in the area. The ruins of some villages were still smoking, and fragments of horribly mutilated corpses had been found. The column set off again, and at dawn reached a totally deserted village. Where were its inhabitants? Were they hiding in the nearby thickets?

The rain had stopped but the humid heat was overpowering. By common consent the *keletigui* and the *amirabe* gave the signal to halt. There was general relief, and as the ground was in the form of a hollow circle, straw shelters were put up at the foot of the slope, not far from a little creek. Its edges had been trodden down by elephants and hippopotamuses, whose enormous prints were filled in with murky water. Faraman set about massaging

Muhammad's feet, which were sore because his leather sandals were worn to shreds. Olubunmi, always up and around, went off with some other young recruits to look for wild fruit. You could hear the sound of their laughter. Laughter? How could people laugh when they were at war? Muhammad, rebuking himself for these negative thoughts, curled up on his side. Near him Alfa, apparently indifferent to dirt and lack of privacy, and immune from hunger, was reading his Koran. Did he ever think of his young wife, whose body he had admitted he loved? Did he desire her? Muhammad looked up at the sky between the weave of the mats. It was as dark as an anvil, low as a lid. He shut his eyes again.

He fell asleep and had a dream. The war was over. He was going home, and could see the walls of Segu from the other side of the Joliba. Faraman was at his heels, singing. They both got into a boat, but just as it was approaching the other bank the wall between the Tintibolada and the Dembaka gates collapsed, and files of blood-colored termites streamed out and started to swarm over the Somono boats. The dream was so striking it woke Muhammad up. His exhausted companions were asleep all around him. Alfa, his face already grown thin, his cheeks dark with stubble, was fast asleep on a pillow made from his turban. Muhammad felt his heart swell with affection. He also felt a twinge of remorse: he hadn't been a very pleasant companion since they'd left Segu, acting as if he held the whole world responsible for his being a soldier. Well, since he'd gone to war he'd better get on with it! He might even get to like it.

It was then that he heard shouts, ferocious howls. In a flash, everyone was up. The recruits ran to the doors of the shelters. The slopes down to the creek were black with a solid flood of men rushing down toward them. They wore big conical hats with a tuft of straw on top, over caps of dirty yellow. Their *boubous* were rust colored and over their heads they waved an enormous red flag. Blue-turbaned horsemen were spurring on their mounts.

A cry went up: "It's the Tukulor!"

Trumpets and drums all burst forth together, soon to be drowned by the griots, their voices seeming amplified by the imminence of battle. While the *keletigui* tried to organize the already terrified recruits, the Macina lancers attacked.

"*La ilaha ill'Allah . . .*"

Who was it who shouted that? Probably those who thought they were fighting in the name of God. Muhammad found himself swept along with other bodies in an acrid smell of sweat, gunpowder and horse dung. Soon he heard the rattle of arms, sword against sword, lance against lance and the occasional gunshot. For a moment he wanted to run away, turn his back on this battle he didn't understand. Alfa and Olubunmi stationed themselves on either side of him as if they divined his weakness.

Faraman Kouyate, behind him, began to sing:

> *War is good because it makes our kings rich.*
> *Wives, slaves, cattle—it brings them all these.*
> *War is holy because it makes us Muslims.*
> *War is holy and good.*
> *So may it set our skies aflame . . .*

Muhammad thought of his mother Maryem, whom he hadn't seen for so many years. He thought of Ayisha. Then he set his teeth and didn't think of anything except staying alive.

N O T E S

*Page 3:*The Bambara live mainly in present-day Mali and form the largest part of its population. From the seventeenth to the nineteenth centuries the Bambara had two powerful kingdoms, one with its center in Segu and the other in the region known as Kaarta, between Bamako and Nioro.

*Page 3:*As soon as a child gets his teeth, the upper and lower incisors are shaped to a point by a fetish priest. Filing the teeth is supposed to give speech its true power.

*Page 7:*Mansa Monzon ruled from 1787 to 1808. He came to the throne of Segu following a long period of anarchy, after which his father Ngolo Diarra usurped power.

*Page 84:*Bambara women's lower lips are tattooed by means of thorns tipped with a mixture of shea butter and charcoal. The tattooing is done by a woman belonging to the shoemakers' caste. According to a proverb, a woman is not mistress of her words: tattooing is supposed to remedy this defect.

*Page 91:*The Ashantis, who live in present-day Ghana, formed a very powerful federation around the eighteenth century and inflicted a series of defeats on the English, who were trying to establish themselves in the region, attracted in particular by gold. The Fanti speak the same language, but living along the coast, they became protégés of the English and fought many bloody battles against the Ashanti.

*Page 124:*The Yoruba live in present-day Nigeria, in the forest region of the southwest. They are one of the most dynamic and creative peoples of Africa, and founded many kingdoms, of which perhaps Oyo was the most powerful.

Page 131:Da Monzon succeeded his father Monzon. He ruled from 1808 to 1827, and had the difficult task of defending the empire against the Fulani, Amadou Hamadou Boubou of the Barri clan, commonly called Cheikou Amadou of Macina.

Page 257:From 1835 on there was a large return movement to the African ports including Ouidah, Porto Novo and Lagos, involving thousands of freed Africans from Brazil. All were known as Agoudas. They all spoke Brazilian except those from Cuba, who spoke Spanish.

Page 304:Dahomey was one of the most powerful kingdoms in Africa in the eighteenth and nineteenth centuries.

Page 339:The Tukulor came late to Mali, in the second half of the nineteenth century. They came from the banks of the Senegal and spoke the same language as the Fulani.

Page 339:El-Hadj Omar Saidou Tall came from Futa Toro. He was born about 1797, the son of a famous marabout. He was a schoolmaster for twelve years, before setting out in 1825 on the pilgrimage to Mecca. He then visited all the Islamic states in west Africa. Back home, he gradually became master of all the region of upper Senegal. In 1854 he launched a jihad, more deadly than that of the Fulani of Macina before him. He came up against the French, who were beginning to establish themselves in the region, then defeated the Fulani and entered Segu as a conqueror on March 9, 1861. He met with a mysterious death in 1864.

Page 357:Sheikh El-Bekkay belonged to the great Kounta family, and fought against the hegemony of the Tukulor.

Page 383:Samuel Adjai Crowther was a Yoruba captured and sold into slavery in about 1821, but saved by an English ship and brought to Sierra Leone. He was the first student at Fourah Bay College. He was a member of the Niger expedition in 1841 and later ordained as a priest in Islington, England, in 1842. In 1864 he became bishop of Nigeria, the first African to occupy such a position.

Page 401:Nanny of the Maroons was a half-legendary figure from the past of Jamaica. Her supposed tomb can be seen in More Town in the province of Portland, Jamaica.

Page 423:Amadou Cheikou, also called Amadou II, and Amadou Amadou, also called Amadou III, were the son and grandson of Cheikou Hamadou. The first reigned untroubled from 1844 to 1852. The reign of the second was interrupted by the arrival of El-Hadj Omar, and he met with a mysterious death in 1862.

Page 473:Albinos were supposed to have been conceived as the result of the breaking of a taboo; i.e., sexual relationships in the daytime, hence their color. They were believed to possess formidable powers, and were favorite victims when the Bambara practiced human sacrifice.

Page 483:Oitala Ali was the last Bambara Mansa before the coming of El-Hadj Omar, who reigned in Segu from 1856 to 1861.

About the Author

A native of Guadeloupe and herself a descendant of the Bambara, Maryse Condé lived for many years in Paris, where she taught West Indian literature at the Sorbonne. The author of several novels that have been well received in France (both *Segu* and its sequel were bestsellers), she has lectured widely in the United States and now lives with her husband in Guadeloupe.